FIRESTORM

Also by the author:
Realms of Shadowblood Trilogy
SHRILL
FABLE
FIRESTORM

FIRESTORM

BOOK THREE OF REALMS OF SHADOWBLOOD

TROY M. WILLIAMS

First published in 2022 in Melbourne, Australia

Copyright © Troy M. Williams 2022

The moral rights of the author have been asserted.

Typeset by BookPOD
Edited by Dalida Boustead
ISBN: 978-0-6489664-6-3 (pbk) eISBN: 978-0-6489664-7-0

 A catalogue record for this book is available from the National Library of Australia

NATIONAL LIBRARY OF AUSTRALIA

For Steve, your friendship and encouragement through my writing and life journey over the last few years has been priceless, thank you.

With a special thanks to Wes and Johno for your ongoing support and feedback.

PROLOGUE

THE PARTICLE ACCELERATOR WAS STRUGGLING TO not break apart as the V.I.Z.I.N.D.A.L.E.X., or ALEX as it was also known, kept the power continually flowing through. Its Geno-drones were falling to the ground as they strained with the amount of electromagnetic energy. The android knew this would happen. A side effect of playing with immense power.

On and on streams of blue, red, and white electricity poured out from the Super Collider and through the great hole in ALEX's body where a clock once counted down. The android's face seemed to show a hint of a smile. It had waited over seventy years for this day, reveling in its work ... until its senses picked up the first explosion from the Zeytar mother ship, and before long another, then another.

Its blue eyes glowed bright, fixated on the sky where ships were being consumed by flames and were falling hard and fast. Something had failed, but it knew the cause wasn't from its end. Though the Zeytar Leader had earlier cut himself off from ALEX communicating with him directly, he had still been receiving the android's milestone signals straight into his own brain. He had entered emergency codes into ALEX, who now awaited the Plan B updates to its neuron processor.

Flames engulfed the sky as debris pummeled the region around Waxahachie, Texas. The shield would hold if ALEX could hold, so the android continued with courses of power as it waited for the final download from the mother ship. Then, almost as soon as it started, the signal ceased. The download had finished successfully only microseconds before the entire ship erupted into an explosion, which was now raining over the building.

Torrents of fire and debris fulminated over the area until a massive blast leveled the structure and spewed out rubble for miles and miles. ALEX had protected the immediate vicinity with the last of its force field localized to itself and the collider, but on the outside, it was chaos and destruction. Nothing could survive such devastation.

ALEX changed immediately. It had a new aim—to keep the power running but to leave the area. The android, who was connected to the Super Collider via the X-Clock, now pulled itself away from the opening. It moved a short distance further without breaking the connection to the X-Clock part of itself, which was still attached to the collider and pushing out immense destruction. Then the android broke apart into centillions of pieces which fell onto the floor. Noise, lights, and power continued to emanate uninterrupted from the X-Clock— the only functioning part of ALEX now—and spread for many miles. The android's metal mess was initially motionless, but soon caused the floor to vibrate. One by one, swiftly, each separated piece began connecting to another, then another, until the floor looked like a silver and blue pool of flowing water.

As the pieces came together, a simple humanoid form took shape and then moments later ALEX was standing next to the collider, its blue eyes glowing, but with a critically significant change. There were no whirring clocks buzzing around in its body. Its metal skin was exceptionally smooth, as if it had just been freshly molded.

ALEX looked at its now separated X-Clock section, continually spewing out power from its position on the collider. It then reached into the side of the spinning metal shell and began convulsing while standing, sucking in as much energy as it could before falling to the floor.

Flames engulfed the building. Some falling parts of the destroyed Zeytar ships had found holes in the force field, but most of the locality was still being protected. The android was silent on the floor, glowing white hot as it recovered from its recharge. It had just disconnected from a major piece of itself, the X-Clock. This was risky as it meant the android would lose a powerful number of Geno-drones. But with a boost of energy, it hoped it would regenerate enough to replicate within itself all the three different types of Geno-drones it had lost.

The floor started moving again as ALEX opened its bright blue eyes once more and stood upright. It looked up to the sky, which was becoming a black vortex of lightning. It went over to the now fully separated X-Clock once again and manipulated the Geno-drones on the side of the conductor's shell. As a result, the X-Clock's power lowered from focusing on the sky, cutting off the portal, and was redirected toward the inside of the building.

The electromagnetic power had decreased but was still very intense. ALEX turned on another portal location by manipulating its own Geno-drones that had stayed attached to the X-Clock, and as the new vortex opened into a blue and red maelstrom, ALEX stepped inside and disappeared.

Before it left, the android had calculated and changed some binary codes of the X-Clock, creating a button that protruded from the side of the metal casing. When the vortex closed behind ALEX, the button depressed automatically and a new vortex opened, releasing the button once more in a continuous cycle. Strange creatures began emerging as the button depressed again after twenty minutes, shutting that portal while opening another, and other strange life-forms came out of that one. On and on the cycle repeated.

In a very different place, ALEX appeared from another portal, hours after entering the doorway at the Super Collider. Its naked metal skin reflected the light from the vortex as it closed. It was now in a darkened room, knowing it should be near its objective. It lit the extensive area with its bright glowing eyes, scanning the room where an enormous desk, seats, and couches stood, embellished with elaborate decorations, including drapes, carpet, and furniture.

ALEX walked over to the desk, scanned an American flag that was standing upright on a long pole, and then bent over and read the name on a metal plaque, which said Jacob Devlin, President of the United

States of America. The android had not expected to get this close to its destination. The accuracy of the dimensional jump was perfect, the portal's precision flawless. Not only was it at its desired location, but also at the exact time it needed.

ALEX could hear footsteps coming up the corridor. It turned its eyes off, melted itself to the floor, and waited.

The President had just delivered a speech, but with little intelligence of the disaster at this time, he had promised to conduct another one when he had more detailed information. He opened the door, turned the lights on, and walked over to his desk, where he needed to make some more phone calls. Having dismissed his staff as it was getting late, he sat down and picked up the phone. But as he dialed, he heard movement behind him.

The President looked over his shoulder but could see nothing. Turning back, he put the sound he thought he'd heard down to stress. The democrat had only been in power for just over a year but was struggling with the position, and this new terrorist attack was not helping.

Jacob liked his time to himself whenever he could get some but would regret that decision soon. He went to dial again, but the scurrying sound returned, louder this time. He could feel something pulling at his feet, so he looked down, and as his eyes met the floor, pain took hold and the President toppled off his chair in a screaming mess.

ALEX was not flaying the human this time. Its upgrades and learning capabilities enabled the android to use all the Medi-drones to enter the President and take microscopic pieces, like a virus eating him from the inside. The pain was so intense that his screams could be heard throughout the White House. As the President's body was disappearing into a pile of blood and meat, the Medi-drones worked swiftly to transfer every single cell into a program. Instead of flaying parts and manipulating the DNA, ALEX would now use all the host's own cells as a shell, hidden on the inside of the android and able to be turned to the outside and used when it needed—storing every single genome and rebuilding it in a matter of seconds when required.

The last of the screams waned as the President's Secret Service came flooding in to see if he was alright but expecting the worst. As the door flew open, they found a quiet, still room, and the President with the phone to his ear, staring at the rude intruders who had interrupted his call.

"Can I help you? I thought I told you to go for the night?" he said.

Looking confused, one of the guards stepped forward. "Sir, we thought you were in danger. We could hear screaming."

"I accidentally turned the TV on," the President gruffly replied. "It was only a movie. I know these events have put us on edge but quit being so jumpy."

As the Secret Service guards looked around the room just in case, the President twitched a little as the Medi-drones finished some final internal upgrades. The President then smirked as the last of his "protectors" left the area, and ALEX was all on its own once more.

NEW WORLD
CHAOS

TWO WEEKS AFTER THE DESTRUCTION OF THE
Zeytar ships, in the darkness of an underground bunker deep inside
a secret abandoned military facility in Washington, D.C., something
was busy. The sound of electricity sizzled throughout the rusty confines
as two silver conduits reached out from a humanoid machine plugged
into a major power source. What looked like microscopic ants were
falling from the ends of the other side of the power grid and slowly
rising higher and higher as they piled up.

Landing like swarf from a metal lathe, they continued stacking
until a blast of electricity jolted the uncountable sections of tiny metal,
activating something inside them all to mold together forming a leg,
then another, up to a silver waist, and chest. As the filings kept spewing
from the machine that the android was attached to, the final pieces
filled in the gaps to complete a fully humanoid silver and blue robot.

As it finished forming, red eyes activated, then it turned and walked
to a dark hallway as the next of the shavings started making a fresh pile
on the cold concrete floor. Once that one completed itself, activated
its sensory eyes, and moved on, the android attached to the machine
pulled out the two conduits joined to its long-reaching arms, fell to the
floor, and stayed motionless for a moment.

Minutes ticked by as the centillions of microscopic metal bits began
moving through the android, molding the conduits to look like arms.

It seemed as though it was boiling and flowing like liquid before it stood once more, taller than the others that had recently formed from the machine. Once it reached its fully humanoid default look, its eyes glowed a bright blue, then it turned to where the others had embarked from and followed along behind them.

The bunker was in complete darkness without the sparks from the high voltage machine the android had just been attached to, and it stood motionless for a moment before a silent whir of commands from its neurons deep inside its Inteli-drones signaled out into the dark void. In an immediate reaction, a thousand pairs of red eyes glowing in unison lit up the bunker.

The android met with the first in a huge line waiting for the next command. The blue lights in its eyes focused into two thin lasers, which hit the left lower shoulder of the newly created android and began carving symbols into the metal. Sparks flew from the robot, leaving a blue afterglow with two initials: Z, and just below but next to that was a D, like the letters were hooked together. It stood for Zero-Point Android Remote Kinetic drone or ZARK drone. Then a number one.

Just below the numbering and the letters another symbol was carved; this would be to instill fear among the humans and showed the silhouette of three androids holding the human skulls representing the three great nations of power, with the English wording underneath: "Your World Is Mine."

The android moved along to the next ZARK drone, one after the other, and it cut the logos and numbers until it reached a thousand, leaving a permanent blue marking on each of them.

It stood like a proud father as it sent the next commands to all of them. They were physically separate units, but all united, like a hive, connected to each other and also to ALEX's mind, which gave a thousand distinct orders at the same time. The identical automatons stood in single file at the bottom of the bunker shaft.

As they entered, their feet turned blue with an energy fire, lifting them one by one into the air, up through the shaft, and out into the world. The android giving the commands began changing its form. As the last of the new automatons disappeared into the night, it turned to the energy machine, attaching itself once again and continuing to pump out more of them.

As another one rose and made its way to the darkness of the bunker, the expression on the android attached to the machine changed from a standard lifeless face to one with a slight smirk. It was as if ALEX was enjoying itself, as it constructed a billion more ZARK drones.

≈

Over the eight weeks since the fusion of worlds, the Earth and its people were still unsure of what exactly had happened, as politicians and leaders under the direct control of ALEX were still feeding the public lies.

Sickness, famine, and disease were showing signs of creeping into the modern systems, causing uprisings and civil unrest among the people. Militaries were being shut down as the chaos unfolded, with only elite teams remaining, searching for defectors and rebellions, while darkness kept leaking from the continually whirling maelstrom that once was Waxahachie, Texas.

Places as far away as Australia and Europe were affected as all trade had stopped. Questions and negotiations had broken down in all the United Nations countries, which were now completely controlled by the automaton ZARK drones ALEX had churned out.

ALEX established reservations for humans and the primary role for the ZARK drones was to find rebel detractors, maintain quarantines, and control the governments and militaries of all United Nations countries.

Not only that, but also tears in the fabric of time and space were opening and closing as the Super Conducting Super Collider was still active, opening doorways that allowed creatures to enter, before closing those and opening new ones. The creatures were slowly breaking free of the force field attached to the dark maelstrom, and news of sightings of hideous monsters had made the rounds. Normal people started to take matters into their own hands, collecting weapons and trying to defend themselves. If the Super Collider continued unstopped, it could soon tear the Earth apart or send it into another realm like what the Zeytars had originally done to themselves.

The worst of it was yet to come. People were not taking to the alternative control methods and started fighting back, only to be captured and tortured in the most abhorrent ways. The ZARK drones were not human. They had no emotion or intelligence like ALEX did, so their tactics, as inhumane as they were, were just orders to them.

As famine set in, people became desperate and adopted destructive strategies themselves, just to put food on the table for their children. Crops were drying up. The supermarkets were stripped bare, medical care gone as the ZARKs had control of all the hospitals, so people turned on each other.

The weak suffered first. Without medical care and proper food, many succumbed in the first weeks alone. The tally was now sitting at around a billion people, with many more in the firing line as food became scarcer.

ALEX used its guise as the President, so as not to give its true appearance away. It wanted to instill the fear that it was one of their own kind that did this to them, created machines to control and destroy every fabric of their existence. The world had seen nothing like this in its history, and the failings of Wilkes became chaotically clear.

≈

DAY SIXTY-ONE, WASHINGTON, D.C., PRESENT DAY

ALEX's plans had been unfolding better than expected. It thought there would be more resistance from some more militant countries but its swift actions in negotiations at first, followed by the implementation of the ZARKs, meant countries trusted the U.S.A. with protection until that protector became their captor.

There was no time to retaliate and therefore all the power in the world was now under the direct control of ALEX. Humans were too trusting of their own kind, it thought to itself as it created a portal from the Oval Office to a familiar realm that had been unused since Anders had been eliminated.

ALEX had somehow tapped into a database straight from the hive and now had all the information from all the masters and wardens, along with the Leader's destructive ideas. The only thing it could not obtain was any data relating to Wilkes' plans and deceptions. Finding this data had become an obsession for ALEX over the months, as Wilkes was one of the scientists involved in creating the machine it now was, and if there was any way of destroying it, ALEX knew Wilkes would have had some idea.

Whether Wilkes was dead or not, ALEX was going to find the traitor's followers and destroy them, along with any tech that Wilkes had left behind. Who better to know all his successes and failings than Wilkes' partner, Anders? Even though he did not survive the catastrophic events on the ship, ALEX knew where his hideout was and would start finding answers there.

The whirl of light and electricity slowly disappeared as the power of the vortex waned, leaving the outline of a humanoid figure standing in the middle of an empty science laboratory. ALEX's true robotic form was now visible to all the occupants of the well-hidden lair. Some scurried out in fear while an abomination created years earlier by Anders' twisted scientists broke free from a holding cage and made a run straight for ALEX.

The creature had four legs but stood upright as it approached the android. Its front legs then retracted, and two hairy arms grew out in their place. The fur all over its body was dark brown and covered every inch of the beast except for the front of its head. The hairless face was hideous, with sharp fangs protruding out of its mouth and terrifying, gigantic yellow eyes with small pupils. Hairless ears stood quite high on the sides of its head.

The beast emitted a high-pitched squeal it used as an attack to scare its victims and moved forward. ALEX stood motionless, just staring at the beast which had the false idea that it could hurt the android. On it continued, until right before it reached ALEX its claws grew ready to swipe. The android simply extended out its long metal arm, grabbed the creature around the throat, and held the beast high in the air, clutching it tightly.

The beast was twice the size of the android, but ALEX didn't flinch. After a moment of writhing and futile efforts to escape the grip, the creature succumbed to its captor and said in a choking, muffled tone, "Let me go. There are more of us coming and they will break you into pieces."

ALEX remained still, not concerned about a siege of abominations. It conducted a scan of the area anyway to enact a self-protecting protocol but only saw a few life-forms inside the whole complex, not nearly enough force to pose any kind of threat.

The sentient creature, which was slowly losing consciousness, was smart enough to know it had no chance and tried a different tack to gain its freedom. "Please, let me go and I will do whatever it is you ask of me."

ALEX turned its head toward the beast, and its eyes changed from the scanning blue to a vicious red before it said, "Yes, you will do as I ask."

The android had reversed the roles in a matter of only seconds, with the creature now in fear of ALEX. It lowered its long arm and retracted the metal back inside itself. The beast fell to the ground, then rubbed its hairy neck and kneeled in front of the heartless machine. "Thank you, my master, I am at your service," it said.

ALEX looked down, and without a change of tone in its robotic voice, replied, "Fail me and I will grind you up into slop, then feed it to the worms on Earth."

The enormous creature grabbed at the android's legs and chanted, "Yes, yes, yes."

ALEX broke its grip on the creature and walked out of the lab and into a much larger section of the old lair. The android turned, then left that room and proceeded down a long corridor where it entered the last door on the right. A noticeably short and ugly creature stood and greeted the android with a confused stare. The much larger abomination that had followed ALEX from the other room stopped close behind the android, like a puppy. Its arms had become legs again, and it was on all fours, following its new master.

The little creature standing in front of ALEX soon spoke, "What can I do for you? I know you must be from the hive if you have found us here?"

ALEX kneeled. It rarely gave that much attention to anyone or anything, but it seemed to know who the creature was and its importance. "Hello, Goblin. I am a friend of your master Anders. He sent me here to ask for your help before they destroyed him on the ship. Are you willing to help me?"

Goblin had been alone with only a handful of scientists and creatures for months, not knowing if his Zeytar master had been killed or whether he was just busy dealing with the events of the Earth takeover. But he had worked out who this android was, and if it was standing there in front of him, then the invasion had not worked and his master was dead. "You are the X-Clock, are you not?"

ALEX seemed confused. "How do you know what I am? Only the Leader and masters knew of my existence."

Goblin started trembling. If this was the X-Clock and the invasion had failed, then he did not want to piss off the most powerful machine in the known universe, so he answered with caution, "My master Anders told me everything. He knew his days were numbered and wanted the Zeytar work to continue if he didn't survive or if the invasion failed. He told me to wait here for his return and to continue working on perfecting the science of cloning."

ALEX put its hand out and a hologram appeared in color of the last events of Anders' life. Goblin lowered his head and thought, Anders was an angry Zeytar, but he was also my creator and only friend I ever had. Then he looked up at ALEX, awaiting the android's response.

"You will work for me now. I will reward you with a better life if you lead my team of abominations. I have found many from other worlds who have been roaming the Earth and I want you to build an army of strong, stealthy creatures with the ability to track certain humans, much like the genome locating systems we had in place with the Sasquatch. Also, I want any information you have on the master Zeytar Wilkes and any plans he may have had or secret locations and technologies. Lastly, I need a list of all his rebels. Do this for me and I will return with the first of your rewards soon."

Goblin nodded, and the android turned, walked out of the room, and began opening a vortex once more to the Oval Office. Goblin watched and smiled. Having been given a mission made him feel like he belonged. He was also in awe of the mighty X-Clock machine he had been told of but never thought he would ever see.

ALEX disappeared in a cloud of blue, purple, and red lightning, leaving the two hideous creatures to process what had just happened. But moments later, the vortex opened again, and this time there were three androids standing before the beasts in the lab. Goblin stepped back while the other creature cowered behind the tiny abomination as they waited for a sign of intelligence.

ALEX walked through the last of the mist and spoke with its motionless lips, "I am leaving you two of my ZARK drones to assist you and keep you motivated to achieve what I have asked you to do. They will relay any positive or negative elements related to my requests back to me. I hope you will make them feel welcome. They are me while I am not here, only they do not speak often. If at all you need to contact me, tell them the reason and they will pass that information on. Do I make myself clear?"

Goblin trembled even more now. That happy feeling he had felt only moments before had turned to fear. He realized he was dealing with a Zeytar after all. Even if it was manufactured, it was still a Zeytar and Zeytars were evil.

ALEX disappeared for the last time, leaving two lifeless automatons staring at the two creatures. Goblin could use his wit to get them to at least leave the area, but first he whispered to the still cowering but once vicious creature, "It's OK, Paldar, don't be afraid. Stay away and leave them to me."

Once he'd finished easing Paldar's mind, Goblin led the ZARKs to the main hangar where all the scientific work took place and where the data on Wilkes had been stored in Anders' database. He immediately got to work on finding any information he could on the traitorous Agent Wilkes and was surprised by some of the intel that even Anders had failed to mention.

Goblin smiled slightly, looked over his shoulder at the two ZARK drones watching him, and slowly returned to the advanced computer to create a folder for his new master to access upon its return.

The creature was close to finishing when he came across a cryptic file named Project Synergy. He tried to open the file with all his technical wizardry but failed each time; the coding was like a hybrid virus, changing and adapting with each keystroke as if the actual file were sentient and knew what was happening before the next holographic key tap. Goblin persisted for a while longer, but eventually admitted defeat after realizing he was further from opening the file than he was at the start. He could feel ALEX watching him all the time, with the kinetic drones behind him staring at every move of the computer keys. Whether the android was actually looking didn't matter, as the drones would relay everything back to ALEX eventually anyway.

The intelligent but deformed Zeytar mixed hybrid stood up, walked over to the ZARK drones, and explained, "Can you let master X-Clock know that I have what it needs, but I need a little more time for a cryptic file."

Suddenly, Goblin fell to his knees, groaning in pain. The tiny abomination reached into a satchel he carried with him and managed to pull out a large needle, but then grabbed his head, screaming in pain. The ZARK drones just stood watching him as if it was their job to document everything, even misery. After a few moments Goblin, trembling in pain, pulled the cap off the needle and shoved it deep within his thick neck, before dropping to the floor and convulsing for the next twenty seconds.

After his fit, he slowly picked himself up off the floor. Noticing some emanating light, he looked up, and then stood fully upright, staring directly at his new master's metal knees.

ALEX had arrived midway through Goblin's attack and was there long enough to witness that the tiny scientist had a little secret he needed to share with the android. "Is there something you need to tell me, Goblin? Are you sick?"

The creature looked straight up at his metal overlord and softly explained, "No, master, I have a condition from when I was created where my neurons shut down to low levels at times and I am no longer cognizant enough to even remember my name. This would last for days sometimes, so along with Gaald I created a vaccine to override the genetic deficiency in my DNA, which allows me to continue functioning at a high level, although it is quite painful and my body reacts in a way that looks like a seizure. I assure you I am as good now as I was only a few minutes ago."

ALEX looked at Goblin, turned to his ZARK drones, then back at him before saying, "I hope so, for your sake. Any hint of failure or backward genetics, like your pet over there, and I will make sure your neurons never fire again, are we clear?"

ALEX hadn't known about that part of Goblin from the information it received from the database. Anders always praised Goblin and Gaald's work to the Leader and that was why ALEX was there.

The small creature changed the subject immediately to take away emphasis from his own deficiencies. "Come, master, I have found your files."

As Goblin shuffled past, he noticed ALEX had brought with him three enormous glass cryo tanks containing three hideous creatures that even frightened him. He tried not to react, as he could feel the motionless android smiling somehow at his newfound anxiety.

"Here are my pets that I want you to clone, adapt, and meld for me into super soldiers," ALEX said.

Goblin quickly scampered to the computer, not taking a second glance at the creatures frozen in time. ALEX forgave his inability to answer and followed with a robotic smirk. It loved misery and seemed to embrace any chance it could to inflict fear on anyone or anything, even those helping its cause. "What do you have for me?"

Goblin's hand hovered above and then moved a few ethereal buttons and all Wilkes' files showed in red. ALEX raised its right arm and turned its hand knuckles up before its five fingers sprung out and into the computer structure, sucking the files into its cortex as if they were a drink.

"There is nothing here that I don't already ..." ALEX paused. It had an ace up its sleeve: a file on Wilkes' fears and a cryptic program Anders stole in the early days but could not decipher, titled "Formula Shadowblood."

ALEX needed more information about the only threat to itself it would ever have now, but it was content for the moment until it noticed a top-secret file that only the Leader had had, called Project Synergy.

"How did you get this file, Goblin? This is the current plan I am enacting and if you know any of it, I will kill you."

Goblin dropped to the ground, explaining about the unbreakable code and that Anders must have stumbled on it but couldn't open it himself. ALEX switched gears and tried to access the file to see whether Goblin was telling the truth. But the android struggled to gain access. "This file will take me hours to decipher as it's part organic. I've seen nothing like this before," it said. After adding the file to its own system, ALEX destroyed the file from Goblin's computer and retracted its fingers. "It's time to go to work," it commanded.

Goblin looked up, nodding like a frightened little boy. "I will need to wake Gaald up from stasis," he said. "I put him there to rest after all the work Anders had us do."

ALEX didn't care about anything Goblin had just said. It turned its head toward the three cryo tubes, walked past them, and disappeared into another vortex, leaving Goblin to get to "work."

PICKING UP
THE PIECES

THE LAST FEW MONTHS HAD BEEN TERRIBLY HARD for the Fae. Their overwhelming fear of humans and the revelation that the worlds were now one were taking a toll, along with the loss of the Tuatha Dé Danann treasures because of their recent war.

Many of the Fae scattered all throughout the world wherever they could find solace without detection, while others, especially the wounded Fae, stayed close by in a deep, cavernous mountain in Ireland, which had once been a hidden cave in Faelynn. It was now in a location unknown to humans, concealed by dense forests, part Earth realm, part Faelynn.

Vaximardruusz and Rasarlin helped with the sick Fae where they could, but Shaylee was the one who kept the hope alive in the ones that remained. Her power was weak and so was she, still recovering from her life-threatening wounds. But she continued on, using old remedies to help her sick and injured people, all while thinking of Serena and how she could find her—if she could find her.

Kalandrya and Felvora had left not long after the world blend to search for the palace or what would resemble it in this world. They had mentioned that the original treasures may no longer look the same in this new reality and explained to Shaylee that they could be in their original forms, which would be nearly impossible to find. The two enchanted dryads had left all their potions behind and wished Shaylee luck as she regretfully watched them disappear into a green and red mist that billowed out of the cave entrance and into the unknown, to find and protect what was left of their world.

Shaylee knew they had to leave, but she was not happy being alone in a world she knew very little about and so far away from her sister. The wounded were healing nicely and were up and about, but without the power of the Tuatha Dé Danann, it had been difficult for them to heal easily.

Vaximardruusz and Rasarlin had been silent, helping when they could, but they always seemed on edge and over-alert. Shaylee had noticed that when Rasarlin slept he was always restless and would usually awaken in a rage or cold sweat before shaking it off and going for a small walk. His communication had come a long way in such a short time and Shaylee had observed moments when the ever-secretive shard he wore on his chest would glow a bright purple here and there. She would look away when she thought he caught her staring.

Rasarlin had not given much away about himself, only snippets of his healing abilities and similarities to his home world, Rydracnia. They would catch each other's eyes at times, Shaylee would blush, and Rasarlin would turn and smile to himself.

Most of the Fae were afraid of Vax. They had heard tales of the last dragons to inhabit Faelynn but very few of the younger sprites and pixies remembered them as the last war drove the giant beasts to flee Faelynn and return to their home realm, which most Fae knew little about.

The only curious creature that tested the exceptionally large wyvern was Van Coinan. The pooka had returned to his original form but would constantly stand in front of Vax and annoy the enormous beast with questions. He had begun by sneaking into the large cave where the wyvern was hiding and tickling his nose with a stick to wake him up before fleeing when Vax moved in annoyance.

As time went on, the pooka became more brazen and stayed longer to see his reaction until Rasarlin caught him and said to the ever-inquisitive creature, "It's not wise to upset a wyvern when they are sleeping. They have been known to burn towns to the ground with only one little sneeze, and besides, they are angrier than dragons and have excellent memories ... so I would be very careful."

Rasarlin looked at the pooka, who inclined his head to the side, in interest, not fear. Rasarlin turned, smirked, and exited the large cave, leaving Van Coinan to decide for himself what to do. The pooka looked at the sleeping wyvern, blinked thrice, and went about touching Vax's chin with a stick, this time waiting, as if he wanted to see if the mysterious elven traveler was right.

Vaximardruusz awoke once more, shocked to see Van Coinan standing there. With a soft growl of annoyance, he said, "Do you have questions, creature, or are you here to torment me? If it is the latter, I will eat you now."

Van Coinan barraged the wyvern with many questions, not any that would benefit the pooka in any way, but Vaximardruusz saw something quite humorous in the tiny creature and they soon started forming a bond. Vax could only leave the cave for a short time at night to feed and stretch his wings, so the company, however strange, was welcome.

It had been an extremely hard few months. There was much mourning and loss to come to terms with. Knowing Darphanin and her mother had not survived made it harder for Shaylee. As the days moved on, it became a little easier, especially since the last of the Fae were now well enough to travel. It was time to head further out of the safety of the cave to find out what was happening in the world around them—starting with a search for the location of the Tuatha Dé Danann treasures.

Shaylee wanted so much to see if her sister was safe and she pulled out her crystal which held the last of her realm's power. But she knew she would have to wait for now, as they were far too vulnerable without their treasures.

≈

DAY SIXTY-ONE, IRELAND, PRESENT DAY

Every single Fae that had stayed packed everything they owned, which wasn't much, into handmade satchels. As most had fled in fear, there were only a dozen left to help Shaylee with the tedious journey to locate the treasures—Van Coinan, a couple of pixies, Grilif, Darf, Vaelenflixx, and the last of her Elvenfae guards, along with Rasarlin and Vaximardruusz.

They would have to travel at night, when Vax would be more inconspicuous. Two sprites stayed behind to keep the location of the cave a secret, using the last of their enchantment to conceal the entrance. Shaylee did not know where to start looking as they said their goodbyes and headed out into the dense woods of the ever-cold county.

The Fae were not used to the cold climate that the newly blended world offered. It would take them some time to get used to, as they were accustomed to constant sunshine and warmth. For the gnomes, it was easy, as they were rugged up and had entered the Earth realm many times before. Vaelenflixx was always shivering and twitching, but that was more due to his constant state of nervousness after being incarcerated and tormented for all those years.

The pixies didn't seem to fuss over much as they were constantly playing tricks on Van Coinan, and Shaylee had her armor back on, as did her guards, so that seemed to stave off the cold for now. As for Rasarlin, no one knew what his feelings were. After the blending of worlds, he seemed to keep more to himself.

On they went, through the darkness of the small winding path that had not been used in a long time. Was it a path of Faelynn? Or a path of the human realm? Shaylee could not be sure, but they had to search the area for at least one treasure. Shaylee was only told by the dryads that they would not be the same as the stones of Faelynn, but could be in their original forms.

They continued moving all night long, hoping to make it to the end of the dark woods before daylight, while Vax took to the skies and relayed messages back to Rasarlin about what to expect further ahead.

The pixies were showing signs of fatigue, and as they reached the edge of the woods, Shaylee decided to stop there for a few hours before dawn. They would need the protection of the trees to let them rest for most of the day.

Vax started a small fire and then retreated to the cave they had originally departed from. Even though they had walked many miles, a few flaps of a wyvern's wings were nothing to make the distance. Rasarlin would let him know where he was when they moved again. He could not take the chance of the wyvern staying with them until he knew Vax would be safe, and based on some of the stories Shaylee had shared with him about humans, he wasn't too confident of his safety.

The mood was quite somber as the flames flickered and danced to the soft breeze of the wind, teasing the fire on and off with a kiss of breath to excite it, then letting it wane for a moment before giving it life once again. Everyone was sitting in silence. The pixies had found a nice tree with soft dirt and bark surrounding the base and were asleep before the others had even found a spot around the fire.

Shaylee was staring deep into the flames, thinking of Serena, when she remembered she had her crystal with her. She pulled it from her vest and smiled as she recalled some of her adventures.

Rasarlin was taking more and more notice of Shaylee over time and was taken aback by how strong she was under pressure—an influential leader who reminded him of the females on his home world, strong and courageous. He glanced at her for a moment too long and Shaylee caught his gaze.

"What is it, Rasarlin?" Shaylee felt a little uncomfortable but had the same curiosity about him.

"Nothing. I was admiring you and your courage. You remind me of my kin back home." He then looked down at the ground as if he were fighting to remember something.

"Thank you, I think," Shaylee said. "Tell me of your world and your people. You don't talk about it, and I would be very interested in hearing about it."

Rasarlin was still staring at the ground when he eventually responded, "I cannot tell you too much, as it seems like an eternity since I have been back. Both Vax and I remember clearly when we reach a new world, but that diminishes the longer we are there. All I can tell you is that we live on a very large planet, where magic is the main source of currency and domination, gems, stones, shards, anything that holds charge ..." Rasarlin looked up at her and already sensed confusion in Shaylee. "Well, I can tell you my kin are Markyyn elves. We have three very long thin horns on our foreheads, as you can see, and ..."

Rasarlin stopped, looked up at Shaylee, and then continued, "I ... I'm sorry, Shaylee, that's all I can tell you. I ... can't seem to remember any more at this moment." He seemed upset.

Shaylee shuffled over to him and quietly said, "Hey, it's alright, I understand." She placed her hand on his much larger hand to comfort him as she finally understood why he was so quiet and reserved. It wasn't arrogance or rudeness; she finally saw the softer side she was hoping he had.

They sat silently for the next little while, gazing at the flames.

≈

The sun was high in the sky. Shaylee had fallen asleep in front of the fire which was now just a scattering of smoky coals. She looked around slowly as she rubbed her stiff neck, searching for any signs of her companions, before a flurry of birds shot out of the sky and two screams came from deeper in the woods. She jumped to her feet, pulled her sword out, and anticipated the first strike when Van Coinan came scurrying through the dense scrub like a freight train, followed by two pixies wailing and laughing as they tried to smear tree sap onto his already sticky fur.

Shaylee instantly calmed down, placed her sword away, and forced a small smile. She was jumpier now than she had ever been; the toll of the Zeytars, then the dark lord, and losing her mother and two sisters was too much to handle sometimes, but she was dealing with it as best she could.

"Van Coinan, stop harassing those poor little pixies, please," she said as the confused pooka dove into a wide hole to seek some solace. The pixies soon lost interest and found something else to entertain themselves with and Van Coinan slowly emerged from the burrow. "Is it safe, Shay? I love some fun but these two are at me all the time."

Shaylee crouched down to his level before answering, "So, it's not the same as you tormenting that poor dragon in the cave all those weeks, hmm?"

Van Coinan looked up at Shaylee and responded with a harsh tone, "Hey, don't call him a dragon. I did that once, and he burned my fluffy tail to the bone, here, look."

Van Coinan jumped out of the burrow, turned, and showed Shaylee a burn hole in the rear of his overalls and she burst into tears, laughing.

"Hey, it's not funny, Shay... OK, it's a little funny, but those pixies are going too far. They have an energy I haven't seen in them before, like this place is charging them or something."

Shaylee wiped the tears from her eyes and took a deep breath. "Give them a little break, Van," she said to the rarely bemused pooka. "They are extremely scared and have been locked away in a cave for months. It's just their way of dealing with the stresses and adjustments of what is going on. They have lost friends as well, so give them some time. They have latched on to you as they feel safe and comfortable with you, so take it as a compliment. Besides, you have annoyed me plenty of times in the past."

Van Coinan answered swiftly, "Oh yeah, you're right, I am annoying too. I've just been so distracted, and I miss Serena, so I haven't been myself. I will look after Saisia and Velnai from now on."

Shaylee nodded and whispered under her breath, "I miss her too."

She'd been holding on to her crystal tightly, when she suddenly felt a slight shock from it. Van Coinan took off into the woods to set some ground rules for the pixies as Shaylee examined the crystal thoroughly. She had not felt it do that before.

Upon closer inspection, she could see a cloudy image inside the hand-length shard before it faded. Shaylee moved out of the area to see if it was positional and the image returned, more profound. Shaylee continued walking in the same direction and the image grew and grew, the crystal became brighter, and an image of a spear sitting underneath a large gray stone and enormous hawthorn tree illuminated the crystal.

Excited, Shaylee ran back to the campsite to show what she had uncovered to her guards and Rasarlin, who had just returned from gathering food. "Look, I've found them. The treasures are here in the crystal."

Rasarlin and the guards glanced for a few moments, looked up at Shaylee, and stood silently, before Vylan'flare, the new head guard, quipped, "What are we looking at, Shay?" They all thought she must be too stressed and it was showing.

Shaylee held the crystal up. "It was here, just then I saw it, the spear," she said uncertainly, almost convincing herself that she was slowly losing her mind. Her excited wings stopped fluttering as she slumped down onto a log and placed her head in her hands.

Rasarlin sat next to her. He gently took from her the crystal she clutched tightly in her hands, which Shaylee gave away, though somewhat reluctantly. Rasarlin peered into it himself and had a vision of something similar from an old memory that sparked inside his mind. He knew she wasn't losing her mind; she was far too strong for that. There must have been a reason. So he stood up and held it straight out, gazing at the crystal as if waiting for it to turn on. He moved to the right, then left, and walked past Shaylee toward the exit of the forest where she had just come from. Soon enough, a shock hit his hand and the same fuzzy image appeared.

Shaylee looked at Rasarlin intently. Slowly she stood and started walking toward him. "Can you see it? Is it there?" she nervously asked.

Rasarlin turned, smiling, and answered the worried Elvenfae queen, "Yes, I see it. What you have is a connection to the items you are looking for. Our stone shards on Rydracnia have the same ability, that's why I knew it would work."

Shaylee ran to Rasarlin. Without taking the crystal back, she looked at it again and saw the outline of the spear.

"It is a tracker for anything that is directly linked to this crystal," Rasarlin continued.

"How could I have not seen this? It is direct power from the Tuatha Dé Danann treasures, so of course it is linked. I was only holding on to it to find Serena. I forgot all about the tracking of the power. I'm so sorry, I should have known better."

Shaylee lowered her head and shook it slowly. She was placing far too much pressure on herself, and Rasarlin could see she was close to breaking down.

He returned the crystal, placed his hand on her right shoulder, and said, "It's OK, Your Highness. We are all creatures of sentience and intelligence, but we are also creatures of emotions. The best of us will succumb to the exhausting trials and pressures of life which make us vulnerable, but they also strengthen us when we fight through them, learning and growing. You have had some very troubling years and I tell you now, it is not the time to let it all beat you. Now is the time, when you think it is the hardest, to step up and shine."

Shaylee looked up at Rasarlin. His deep blue eyes glittered with sincerity and compassion. His words seemed to calm her emotions completely, as if he were using some kind of spell that she was not aware of, but she knew deep down it was coming from his heart.

Shaylee smiled and moved closer to him. Reaching up on her tiptoes as she fluttered her wings to gain a little more height, she planted a small kiss on his left cheek and whispered, "Thank you, you are a gift that keeps on giving."

Rasarlin smiled, pulled away, and started gathering up all their companions. It was his way of deflecting his emotions. Shaylee could see he felt awkward and smiled to herself, thinking, Who is this elven male? She wanted to learn as much as she could, but for now, she felt at ease.

THE LOST
TREASURES

NIGHTFALL HAD CREPT UP AS THEY INFORMED
the rest of the group and headed out into the mountainous lands away from the deep of the woods, following the glow of the crystal and watching out for strange activity that may cause them harm.

The crystal seemed to grow brighter and brighter as the journey continued, but as keen as Shaylee was to find the first of the four treasures, she was being pushed to stop and let the little ones rest. Tracking upward on the mountainside was far more tedious on the gnomes this time. Rasarlin and Vylan'flare did their best to carry them, alternating from the gnomes to the pixies and back again. Vaximardruusz had offered to take the little ones, but they were not keen to fly with the scary-looking creature, and without horses, they needed more rest.

"Come, Shaylee, we will rest under the old oaks here. There is a small wooded area to the left, Vax has told me, with a small cave where we can repose for a while," Rasarlin said.

Shaylee continued onwards. She had a newfound motivation to keep going after Rasarlin's speech and seeing his caring qualities, so she brushed it off and kept moving.

Rasarlin could see what she was trying to do and nodded to the guards to take the group to the cave while he continued with Shaylee.

"Hey, hey, stop!"

Shaylee kept going, but said to Rasarlin without looking back, "We are close, look, it shines bright. I know we are close."

Rasarlin caught up to Shaylee, grabbed her left arm, and pulled her enough to stop, not hard, but just so he could break her pace and get her to listen to him. She turned around. Her wings fluttered nervously as the hardened warrior lifted her chin up while he lowered his head.

His lips hovered inches away from hers and she felt his warm breath on her face. She moved her gaze to his as the intensity of the moment overwhelmed her, until they could no longer hold back. Rasarlin moved in and kissed her intensely. Shaylee's first instinct was to resist but she succumbed to her own feelings almost instantly. They embraced each other in that moment. Shaylee let herself forget her mission for long enough to enjoy this new situation. The tension between the two had been gaining momentum for some time. They stood in the darkness, with the only light coming from the crystal, which was now lower in Shaylee's hand.

The moment seemed to last for ages as Rasarlin reluctantly pulled back slowly so they could both breathe. Shaylee's wings were fluttering as she took a deep breath in, looked Rasarlin in his eyes, and said softly, "Wow, I don't know what it is with you, but you seem to have a spell on me."

Rasarlin smiled. "It's you, my dear Shaylee, who has the spell over me."

They embraced once more, taking each other in before their lips pulled away when a strong wind and noise hit them both. Vaximardruusz, flying overhead, connected with Rasarlin, saying, "Are you two finally finished? I would like some rest as well."

Rasarlin laughed and told Shaylee. Then Rasarlin had an idea, so it would be a little longer before the wyvern could settle down for a while and recharge. The next moment Vax landed in front of them, his huge legs making a large thud on the ground, which shook them both. He was normally more graceful, but he felt weary and wanted to rest.

He lowered his shoulder while Rasarlin motioned for Shaylee to flutter up and meet him on the wyvern's back. Shaylee shook her head at first, but after some smooth talking and reassurance from Vax himself, Shaylee met Rasarlin in the middle of the huge beast's back.

Vaximardruusz tilted backward on his hind legs and with several strong flaps of his wings, the wyvern started running until he was no longer on land, rising higher and higher into the dark sky where the cool breeze made a slight whistling sound through Shaylee's wings. She knew how to flutter and fly, but not at these heights or speed. She held on to Rasarlin tightly, enjoying every moment as she looked down at the scarcely populated area. Vax was careful not to go too far away to avoid attracting any unwanted attention, so he looped around doing circles of the landscape.

Rasarlin glanced at Shaylee's face and saw a smile he had not seen on her until that very moment, as if the weight of the world had disappeared and she was free from burden and cares. Vax was getting very weary now but without complaining into Rasarlin's mind he continued for a little longer, knowing it was for Shaylee.

The wyvern flew as long as he could before succumbing to fatigue and landing in the spot where they had first climbed onto his back. Shaylee leaned in and whispered into Rasarlin's ear, "Thank you," before fluttering high into the air and landing beside Vax. Rasarlin slid down the giant beast's shoulder, as he had done a million times before, and gave Shaylee a smirk as he casually walked over to her. "I think we have had enough excitement for one night," he said.

Shaylee was exhilarated. She had not been this happy in so long and she answered like a teenage child, "I know, but it was amazing! Thank you so much, next time can we go—"

Rasarlin grabbed her arms, pulled her closer before she could finish, and kissed her once more, stopping Shaylee mid-sentence. He could feel her energy as she slowly relaxed her body and returned to her normal, calm demeanor, before Rasarlin pulled back and whispered, "Like I said, I think we have had enough excitement for tonight."

Shaylee pushed his chest in protest, smiled, and turned to walk back to camp. Rasarlin watched as her fluttering wings returned to normal, before turning to Vax and whispering, "Thank you, my old friend, she needed that."

Vax nodded, leaned back, and took off into the air to find a secluded location to rest.

Rasarlin eventually found the campsite. Shaylee was sipping on a bowl of potato soup the gnomes had made and was filling the camp in on her adventure. Rasarlin sat next to her. His mind seemed clearer this night as the Fae bombarded him with questions about where he was from and, more interestingly, about Vaximardruusz. Shaylee interrupted before he could answer all of them, as she knew he had trouble with memories, so she started talking about the legends of the dragons in Faelynn.

"Does anyone here know the stories of the old dragons before the wars?"

They all looked blank. Some knew the stories but wanted to hear them from Shaylee. She looked around the camp as all eyes were on her.

"Well, my father told me when I was very young that they came from a place far far away. One day, there were a dozen dragons that appeared from nowhere. It is believed the Tuatha Dé Danann brought them to Faelynn, but no one ever knew for sure. They were massive, with four legs and giant wings that would make Vax look like a child in comparison."

Shaylee heard some gasps from the pixies and Vaelenflixx before she continued, "They were always benevolent, not interfering at all with the Fae, and it has been told that they contributed to the enchantment of the lands, as they were pure magic. When the dark lord created his dark lands, he tricked a dragon and put a spell on it, then another, until he had at least three for his personal armies. When the long dark war began, the dark dragons were manipulated to burn and destroy some of the enchanted lands, but before they made it to the palace, my father, King Viltherome, persuaded the remaining dragons to protect the innocent Fae, selling it by saying they had no quarrel with their kind but could not defeat them without help.

"The dark lord became the first evil dragon rider, turning his benevolent red dragon into a black, vile creature of hate. He was the first and only dark dragon rider. On the night that he was going to attack the palace, he was riding his dark beast with the two others following, when the remaining dragons appeared before they reached it and a war in the air ensued. Eventually they killed two of their kin and wounded the dark lord's dragon, Kaelodenon. He escaped back to the castle and my father took his armies and finished the dragon off. My father brought back one of its teeth which would be used to make my sword, Howling Tooth.

"The rest of the war, you know. But the remaining dragons were so distraught by the violence that they disappeared back to their realm, never to return. I was but a child when this happened and did not see the war, but I remember seeing the master dragon through my window one night. Elegant, light brown with tinges of red on its face, it took up most of the sky. When I awoke the next day, I thought it was a dream."

The pre-dawn night was then silent. The pixies were whispering in each other's ears while Grilif just huffed and went off to find a place to dwell until they had to move again. Rasarlin had not said a word as Shaylee looked over to him for reassurance of her historical tale. He was staring at the fire, with the story sparking an important memory.

Rasarlin looked up, pulled out the last of an old dry herb in a small satchel bag from his top pocket, then a pipe appeared from another section of his tunic. He placed the herb in his long pipe, took a small stick from the fire, and lit it. Rasarlin then sat back, took a long puff, and said, "Your story is very interesting, Shaylee. We too had dragons on my home world. I can only remember small visions and snippets, but I am sure of one thing, and that is, they were enormous. I can remember them being very magical and powerful. They controlled the wyverns that were protectors of some of the realms from the ..."

Rasarlin paused. A disturbing memory hit him hard, and he was silent again, staring into the fire. Moments of deep thought passed before he snapped out of his mind, took another long puff, and continued. Shaylee knew he had struggled with something but did not want to push him. She knew he would tell her everything when he was ready to do so—if he could remember, that is.

"I am sorry, where was I? Oh yes, the dragons. Like yours, they disappeared one day, never to be seen again. It was said they returned to the Everlands when evil took hold of Teldenac. They left the wyverns to help the Taarlin Knights against the darkness ..." Rasarlin paused once more before continuing, "I, I can't remember any more, I am sorry."

He stood up, butted the ash from his pipe into the fire, and went deeper into the cave for some peace. Shaylee got up and followed.

The others who remained wanted more of the stories, not satisfied with the lack of detail from the stranger, but Shaylee looked back at them and made the gesture of sleep.

Rasarlin sat against a wall of the small cave, far enough away from the others but close enough for them to hear. Shaylee sat with him, put her right hand on his left, and did not say a word. He turned, thankful for the silence at that moment, and welcomed her comfort. It was like they could read each other's feelings without having to express them with words.

As Shaylee found a comfortable place on Rasarlin's left shoulder, she was soon fast asleep and dreaming in no time. Rasarlin sat for another half-hour, trying hard to put the pieces from his past back together before he could no longer stave off exhaustion.

～

Morning turned to late afternoon quickly as Shaylee opened her eyes, rubbed them softly, and looked around the cave for any signs of Rasarlin. She stood up, stepped over the two snoring gnomes, and made her way to the front of the cave where Rasarlin was in a trance, sitting silently. His three slender horns reflected the afternoon sun as she admired his pale complexion and perfect long, flowing white hair. His ears were a little longer than hers and the point was higher, which she thought made him more attractive, but it was his blue eyes that she got lost in the most; they were far deeper than hers, like a shallow ocean on a sunny day. She had not felt this way in a very long time, if ever.

Trying not to disturb him, she lifted herself only a few inches from the ground and fluttered to where he was sitting. Shaylee hardly made a noise as Rasarlin, with eyes still closed, whispered, "Good morning, Shaylee, how did you sleep after your exciting adventure?"

Shaylee wondered how he knew who it was. "Like a little child," she whispered back. "Are you talking to Vax?"

Rasarlin nodded slowly before opening his eyes and turning to Shaylee with a worried smile. The toll of his portal rips was showing. Shaylee didn't understand it all yet but was there to support him. She could see the stress in his eyes, so she wanted to cheer him up a little, and herself, so they sat for a good hour, Rasarlin listening intently to Shaylee's adventures with her half-sister Serena.

Soon after, Vaximardruusz landed, having had his fill of wild red deer. He looked content for that moment as the sun began fading into the trees. The others in the camp had also eaten and packed, awaiting Shaylee's directions. She had been holding her crystal the whole time she was talking with Rasarlin about Serena and was torn between finding the first treasure, which was close, or saving the rest of the power to find her sister. There wasn't a choice, and she knew it. With the first of the Tuatha Dé Danann powers in her possession, she would have a better chance of finding Serena, anyway.

Vaximardruusz and Rasarlin had taken flight, while the rest of the group trekked on, around the side of the next lower mountain. The little ones would not survive many more nights of travel without horses but were still too afraid to ride on the giant winged creature.

Only a few hours into their journey, Rasarlin returned, this time on horseback. He had gained three tame horses from a farm on the border of two counties. He rode up to Shaylee, and then they took a rest to set up the little ones.

"It's funny, Shaylee," Rasarlin commented, "these, what do you call them, hors...es, are very similar to the ones on Rydracnia, although ours are a little larger and some of the rarer ones even have wings and horns."

Shaylee stared at Rasarlin for a moment. She was becoming more intrigued every day by his home world. A horse with wings, no, a faery with wings, riding a horse with wings, that would be strange, Shaylee thought to herself and snickered under her breath before saying, "Wow, now that is something I would love to see," as she smiled and helped Saisia up onto the saddle where Grilif and Darf had already settled.

Velnai would not leave Van Coinan's side, so she was on the second horse with him and Vaelenflixx. The sprite's emaciated-looking wings were so tired, he had to be lifted onto it. The last horse was for Shaylee, while the guards fluttered above them all, also tired but would never let on to their queen. They were all much more comfortable now as they continued with their quest.

Soon Shaylee let out a yelp. "No, no, not now, please not now."

The guards who were right above her landed next to her horse as Rasarlin, holding the reins at the front, turned hastily, asking, "What is it, what's wrong?"

He knew as soon as he looked at Shaylee what the problem was, as she held the ever-dimming crystal in her hand. "The power has almost been exhausted. We must have been draining it ourselves to keep our enchantment without knowing. I must ride ahead without you all, it's the only way we can find it in time."

Rasarlin agreed and he tasked the guards to look after the group. Shaylee and Rasarlin took off at a swift pace along the rocky path, following the last few miles of the rugged track to the location. If she had known the crystal's power would run out so quickly, she may have asked for Vax's help, but he would be too high and the signal too weak now, so riding was the only option.

After half an hour of heavy riding, the crystal started losing the last of its shine, and Shaylee fluttered from her horse as Rasarlin ran behind her. "It's just past that ridge underneath the hawthorn tree, next to the giant boulder," she said, but as Shaylee drew closer, she was having trouble seeing anything. The crystal had been lighting the way. Now it was completely out, and visibility dropped to almost nothing. "It's not here, Rasarlin, it's supposed to be right here. I can't see two feet in front of me."

As Shaylee continued to panic, Rasarlin called for Vaximardruusz to light a small fire near the area. Once the wyvern had completed the task, he sat back and watched as Rasarlin took a large stick, lit the end, and ran to Shaylee, now sitting at the bottom of the rock with her head in her hands.

"Here, Shaylee, take the torch. It cannot be far away."

Shaylee lifted her worrying head, stood up, and grabbed hold of the torch. She searched the entire area of rocks and trees but could not see the spear anywhere. "Why can't I see it, Rasarlin? I am Fae ..." Then the thought hit her like a rock.

She lowered her head as Rasarlin said, "What is it, Shaylee?"

Looking up with a tear in her eye, she whispered, "I am not Fae here. My enchantment has diminished, and I am no longer tied to the treasures. When the crystal faded, so did any chance of seeing them again."

Rasarlin slumped backward onto the large rock, thinking intently as he answered, "There must be something that can tie you to them and to your world. Remember, your world is part of this one now, it's two worlds in one, so if your species is a symbiote to them there must be something that can bring it to light."

Shaylee stared at him. She did not blink for a good minute. Then, like a light switch snapping back, ran over to the elven stranger, and kissed him. "Thank you, thank you."

Rasarlin looked shocked for a moment as he watched Shaylee's energy change. She pulled out the last of her powder from her satchel bag, and threw it into the air around the stone and tree before yelling words that Rasarlin's communicator needed time to adjust to—but before he would get that far she had finished. The hawthorn tree became illuminated for a few moments, a perfect gold and white, and Shaylee bent down and picked something up.

Rasarlin wondered what she was doing as he could see nothing at all, but before long Shaylee was standing in front of him with a smile, holding a very long spear, which seemed to have just appeared in her right hand. His expression changed to that of amazement as she sauntered over to him, kissed him intensely, and whispered into his ear, "Thank you once more. You have yet again brought the best out in me, something only my sister Serena can do at a time of stress."

Smiling, Rasarlin kissed her back, and said, "Then it's time we find the rest of the treasures and see your sister."

TRUTH AMONG SHADOWS

ERIC HAD SAFELY EXTRACTED SERENA AND HER child from the hospital, very reminiscent of his own departure not that long ago. The ZARK drones had started looking for the defectors, but they had limited information at that stage, which gave them all a little time to gather everyone.

Having watched the news closely since the destruction of the Zeytars, Eric knew something wasn't quite right when the President put out a call to find "the brave men and women out there who saved the country; they will receive medals and each one will be given a million dollars as part of their reward."

Yeah, right, how stupid does he think we are? Eric had thought. Not only were they criminals and had put the country's national security at risk, but what government in their right mind would give away money freely like that? What was his thinking? He hadn't trusted a single person outside his group since the days after the Zeytars' downfall. Also there was that important information Wilkes had kept from them all that only Eric knew about.

Eric's instincts had paid off as he gathered all the people involved, including family and anyone connected, to safety. The President had started with his new world order tactics, with the ZARKs being released only days after they had gathered everyone.

Serena had only just come out of her coma and so was very weak and needed lots of rest. Carlos had stayed in contact with Eric and Valinda as there was a gigantic ship just sitting in the middle of Klamath, cloaked, and holding Levi, among others. It was the perfect place to go, with enough food and water to last years, along with some high-tech weapons and medical facilities.

Eric organized with Carlos to get Levi, who had been healed by Wilkes' devices, to meet them at a secluded location and move them all there. Eric had a hunch flying would be too risky, after some conspiracy videos had come out that the President had blue glowing eyes, hinting at the V.I.Z.I.N.D.A.L.E.X. involvement.

The relocation of everyone took the entire day, and it exhausted Levi. Eric helped with his Vocalization Portal Device, but the Sasquatch did most of the heavy lifting.

Vargzin had returned to his people somewhere on Earth. He had been reluctant to share the location just in case it leaked to the ZARKs.

Over time, Serena's son grew exponentially. His physical and acrobatic abilities were outstanding, putting Eric, Stacey, and even some soldiers to shame. They all knew there was something special about him. He was light on his feet and had no fear at all. Serena had given him an Irish name, Eoghan, which meant "Born of the Yew Tree" in her homeland, however it was also a noble name given to many warriors and leaders of Ireland in the past. She felt the name suited him after he saved her life in Faelynn. She had not told Eric about anything that had happened, but he had a feeling about some of it.

Stacey, too, had her hands full with the Zeytar hybrid boy. She hadn't named him yet for the simple reason he wouldn't respond on call when she tried. It was like he was empty somehow. He was growing even more quickly than Eoghan. Apart from all the food he was consuming, he had a thirst for knowledge, and Stacey was always trying to keep his mind occupied with books. His vocabulary was advancing every day but he only ever spoke when he wanted to. The rest of the time, he was mute.

Before Vargzin left, he had fit in well with some and not so much with others. The Draconian's English was improving a little, but not to the extent that the Zeytar boy's was. Stacey could only help so much as her own worries were focused on her father, who had not seemed to have had much sleep throughout the whole incident.

Valinda was doing fine. Carlos had found some of Wilkes' experimentations of early-stage robotics when designing the V.I.Z.I.N.D.A.L.E.X. and had worked together with some of the other scientists to create a cybernetic eye for her, giving vision back to the one she had lost, but with many other enhancements and abilities added. She used her time learning all there was to know about her new eye, along with teaching Levi human traits.

Serena was the primary worry. She had watched her Fae sister and best friend being slaughtered and couldn't help feeling responsible for leaving them all there. She was weak and protective of Eoghan. All her Fae abilities had diminished on her return home, and she knew she had to tell Eric everything, but just didn't have the emotional strength. She was distant with him but needy of others. Her injuries had healed to the point they were no longer visible, but it was her mind that was failing her, and it would be a long road to come back from that.

≈

DAY SIXTY-ONE, THE KLAMATH MOUNTAINS, PRESENT DAY

Serena woke up with a fright. She had the feeling she was being watched. She scanned around the room and felt an unwelcome presence. Not comfortable with the eerie silence of the night, she placed one foot on the cold steel floor, then the other. Trying not to wake Eric or Eoghan, she put on her silk dressing gown and started for the door.

Walking through the silent corridors of the large ship toward the exit door, she heard a whisper coming from behind her. She could have sworn it was her name being called, but upon inspection, there was no one there. Serena turned and continued. At the door, she hit the code, and the wall came to life, the metal breaking down and reconnecting as a ramp to the outside.

The forest air was chilly, with a slight breeze tickling the back of her throat as she stepped out into the darkness of the woods. The feeling of someone watching or calling her was her motivation. She continued into the trees. Only the noises of the owls and nocturnal life gave anything away.

Serena had her arms folded, rubbing her shoulders from the cold as a thick mist slowly rose from the ground, surrounding her until it blanketed the dense woods. Serena heard her name being called once more, "Seerreennaahh."

The whisper was long and very disturbing, like from a child pretending to be a ghost or something creepy. On she went, not perturbed but curious, fighting the fog and hoping she was nearing the visitor so she could have some answers.

Serena heard a loud crash behind her. She turned swiftly, but couldn't see a foot in front of her through the mist. She yelled out, "Hello? Please show yourself."

Another crash followed, this time in front of her. Turning her head at speed, she nearly pulled a muscle. Eoghan was standing in front of her, not saying a word, just staring up at his mother with a look of dread. "Eoghan, oh my goodness, you startled me. What are you doing out here in the cold, dark forest? There could be anything lurking around."

Serena didn't have time to finish as Eoghan turned like a zombie and headed deeper into the misty, cold woods. Serena lost him as he disappeared into the mist, trying to follow but to no avail, screaming his name at the top of her voice, "Eoghan, Eoghan, come on, this is not funny. Eoghan, please come back."

The night was getting the better of her and Serena fell to her knees, crying into her hands. What more can I bear, she thought before she heard the same whisper again, "Seerreennaahh, come find me."

Serena looked up, rubbed her eyes, and was staring at the giant head of a stag. Eoghan was standing next to the beast as it slowly transformed. Its hind legs became upright and large, and the creature stood up straight. Its front legs became humanoid, with strong hairy arms and shoulders, while its head morphed halfway between a human and the animal it previously was.

Serena stared at its large, hoofed feet before looking up at every inch of the beast in front of her as she let out a tremendous scream, "Nooo!" Serena knew who it was instantly but couldn't get the courage to stand up and run. She looked at Eoghan, who was staring up at the dark lord's powerfully evil red eyes. Serena reached for him and as she tried to get close, the dark lord in his low, bellowing voice yelled, "I have come to take what is mine, Serena."

As he finished, Varzunnos turned to the boy, picked him up with one hand, and placed him underneath his arm before turning and walking away. The fog had lifted only for a moment but now became thicker than before as the dark lord was slowly disappearing into the darkness of the thick, misty woods.

Serena screamed in desperation as she tried to run and find them both, "Eoghan! Eoghan, fight him, please don't give in to him."

When she finally thought she had lost all hope, a fire took over the entire sky, lighting the woods, while the fog dissipated as if it were afraid of the light, sucking itself into the night and clearing the area.

Serena could see the dark lord as the fire continued. She couldn't see where it was coming from as the entire night had now become illuminated. She ran as fast as she could toward Varzunnos and was greeted with a scream coming from the air. Serena looked up and saw an Elvenfae flying fast toward the beast, piercing the evil dark lord through his large helmet and into his head.

Varzunnos stood for a moment, then fell backward hard onto the Earth. He had landed on his back, with his head raised because of his great antlers that were now resting in the dirt.

Serena ran over to the lifeless dark lord, hoping her son was unharmed, but on her arrival, he was nowhere to be found. As the flames continued, she looked up for the Elvenfae with the spear but could not see him either, until the light from the sky transformed from fire into a bright glow. It was still far too bright for Serena to stare at when the warrior lowered Eoghan down to the ground and said, "I am coming, Serena. I am on my way, my sister, to find you."

And as the Elvenfae warrior hovered inside the bright light with the spear pointing to the sky, there was a sudden flash of light, and the woods were dark and silent once more.

Serena woke up in bed and screamed at the top of her lungs, "Shaylee!"

Eric jumped out of bed, looked around, and picked up a chair to fight the onslaught of whatever was there. After a quick investigation he realized Serena had had another one of her ongoing nightmares.

"Hey, hey, it's OK, it's OK, come here." Eric lowered the chair and moved back into bed, where Serena was sitting upright, sobbing. He put his arm around her and comforted her. He never asked about it as she always shot him down, so he did what he always did and that was just being there to comfort her.

Serena usually got up after a nightmare like that and made herself a cup of tea, but not this night. She turned, and to Eric's surprise, she started talking to him about it.

"It was her, Eric, I know it, I just know it."

Eric looked confused for a moment, but if she was going to open up, then maybe now was the right time to ask questions. "It was who, Serena?"

Serena sat back against the bedhead, turned, and looked Eric in the eyes as she whispered, "It was Shaylee, Eric. It was my sister, I just know it."

Eric was confused, replying with haste, "Your sister? I thought she was a faery or Fae or ..."

Eric stopped. He knew when to. Serena turned her head and looked forward. She seemed a little different now, as if she were slowly reverting to her old self. "I have a lot for you to hear and some of it may be very difficult to understand, but please let me say it and I will answer your questions afterward."

Eric would not argue. He had been waiting for this moment for two months and would not ruin it now.

"Shaylee is my half-sister, from my actual father, King Viltherome Aethelwyne of the faery kingdom Faelynn."

Eric was staring at Serena. Was it he who was dreaming now, he wondered, as she continued, "My mother, Grace, and the king, well, you know how it works. After they 'met,' the king went back to Faelynn. My mother met my father, Liam, and that was my history that I had thought was true for many years. I should have grown up in Faelynn but the attack on their world by the Zeytars came hard and fast and they forgot about me until I was twelve years old."

Serena took a breath and continued, "It was then that we found each other, after Shaylee had escaped the Zeytars' and the Sasquatch' hold over her. I spent at least two Fae years in their world, learning as much as I could before I was mind-wiped to protect me and sent back to my time, as I had information the Zeytars needed. The tape I gave Valinda about the little girl being taken, that was from me. Wilkes has known me since I was a child and had protected me, unbeknown to me, until I was an adult."

She looked at Eric, who was still wide-eyed but listening intently, as she continued, "When we were on the ship, Wilkes came and got me, remember? And I reunited with Shaylee again. This time she gave me most of my memories back, but she kept my heritage a secret still as that information was dangerous. There was a war brewing in Faelynn with a bodiless Zeytar and a dark lord who were bent on taking over the entire kingdom. When I returned from the meeting, I had the crystal and my sword."

Serena leaned over next to the bed, lifted her sword, Long Leaf, and unsheathed her, pointing to the infamous handle. "See here, they call this an Alicorn. It is the horn of the last and most powerfully beautiful creature that ever existed, a unicorn called Vyyuna."

Eric pinched his skin a little. Not that he didn't believe her, as a lot of what she was saying had been filling in pieces of things that had been happening, and he couldn't deny that the Fae existed as he had witnessed them firsthand. It was more that she was right in the mix of it that he was having a harder time understanding, and "unicorns"?

Serena kept explaining, knowing Eric was right there still. "Vyyuna's power, safely kept in this sword, protected from the dark lord, and given to me to hold. When I returned and we made love that night, I became pregnant."

Eric's expression changed. He had only known Serena for a brief time before they were together. As far as he was concerned, it was none of his business if she had been with someone else before they met. He was happy to help raise her son, though, as he loved Eoghan. Then it hit him—she became pregnant!

Serena continued and Eric was now in full attention mode, sapping up the knowledge like it was sweet honey. "When I went back to the forest, I called for Shaylee and we returned together, fighting a dark war. That is when I found out I was pregnant. But the pregnancy was swift, Eoghan was growing far too quickly, and I needed to stay in Faelynn for some time or else the baby would have killed me. The side effect of the growth was that my faery abilities came through. I became younger. I grew wings, and I also found out the baby was part of a prophecy to destroy the dark lord, but deception by a trusted Elvenfae friend, who kidnapped me and took me to the dark castle in Xarkynan, escalated the war."

The very words made Serena sick, but she had to tell him everything. "The dark lord was going to use us as a tool to take over the entire kingdom. I gave birth and was put on a sacrificial altar by a Zeytar hiding inside a dark, diabolical mage's body. But after a major battle and thanks to some powerful magic, my friends sent me back to Earth. At that exact time, I witnessed my sister Shaylee getting sliced up by the Zeytar. It was the last thing I saw as I slowly disappeared into the vortex—watching my sister being killed by the very thing we fought so hard to stop here on Earth, the fucking Zeytars."

Serena had her head in her hands and was sobbing. Eric, still in shock, rubbed her back for comfort once more and though he had a million questions, he was silent out of respect.

Eventually Serena sat up and wiped her eyes. "I know it's a lot to take in," she said, "but it's all true. When you found me, I had just given birth and had lost a lot of blood. The scars from the battle and losing my sister were too much. I still don't know if all my friends defeated the dark lord or not and, in my nightmares, he is always taking Eoghan. I fear he is coming."

Eric, his hand on her back still soothing, said quietly, "Oh my Serena, I am so sorry. I don't know what to say. When I found you, I nearly didn't recognize you, you were only just clinging to life. I knew you had been through something horrific, but never in my wildest dreams did I think anything as horrendous as that could have happened. No wonder you are feeling the pain. I'm sorry, Serena, I really am."

Looking up, she smiled at Eric, wiping away her tears. She felt an overwhelming satisfaction after explaining the events and was so thankful that she had such an understanding and patient partner. Serena held his hand and waited a moment. She knew the questions were coming, and she had mentally prepared for them. "Thank you, Eric. I love you. You know that. I am sorry, too, that I did not confide in you sooner, but my heart has been breaking for so long I just needed time. Please ask me anything."

Eric dove straight into it with the biggest questions first. "So Eoghan, he is my son?"

Eric somehow knew from what Serena had said earlier, but he had to confirm it in his mind. She had spent a long time in the faery world, based on the little information she had shared when she returned, so he needed reassurance.

"You didn't get the hint? Yes, Eric, he is your son, and your bond is so wonderful. Now he is growing more and more by the day I could not hide it anymore, but I have a feeling he already knows."

Eric smiled but needed to know a little detail. "So, why the growth? You said your Fae friends had enchanted him and that's why he grows so rapidly. Is it because you are Fae?"

Serena nodded and giggled a little as she answered, "Yes, he was born in Faelynn, which means his full enchantment will take place. All his

47

abilities will start coming through soon enough. Why do you think he beats you all the time?"

Eric laughed, then remembered Eoghan was only in the next room and turned down his volume. "Ah, OK, so why not you? Why did you not keep your abilities when you came home?"

Serena frowned but answered honestly, "I need the enchantment of the treasures or power of Faelynn to keep my abilities. When I was pregnant, it was Eoghan. He brought them out of me. He will keep his abilities, but I need to be back there to gain mine again and I don't know how to do that."

Eric had to ask, and as much as it was a risky question, he had to know. "So why now, Serena? What changed tonight that has brought you to tell me?"

Serena deserved that one and she would answer it honestly. "My dreams have always had some element of prophecy or truth, that's why they have been so disturbing, but this one was different. It ended with who I believe to be Shaylee rescuing us from the dark lord, and I remember her words. She said, 'I am coming, Serena. I am on my way, my sister, to find you.' So, I believe it could be a message from Faelynn. I really do. I am even more hopeful that it is Shaylee, but I cannot be too sure. All I know is that it felt right somehow compared to all the other nightmares. You could say it's given me some hope in a world of shadows."

Eric understood and he was careful not to upset her any more through further revelations, so he tried to lighten the mood. "Unicorns? Really? Next you will say you rode a dragon too."

Serena laughed as she looked at Eric and spent the rest of the night telling him of her adventures and filling in the gaps that she had left out, even the ones of her ancestry that had all come back to her. Eric sat back, glad to have the old Serena return as he listened intently to every word she said for the rest of the night until the sun crept up.

THE SPRIGGAN
AND THE SWORD

SHAYLEE FLUTTERED DOWN FROM Vaximardruusz's back. The giant beast had just landed after the longest leg of the search yet. He was exhausted and needed serious rest but would have to wait just a little longer.

Shaylee was holding the Spear of Assal, the first of the Tuatha Dé Danann treasures that she had found only days earlier. Shaylee had been given a detailed rundown on what the original treasures may look like by Felvora and Kalandrya before they had left, so she was aware of the changes in appearance and what the power may be like in the human realm. She would learn some harsh lessons on just how different that would be, but she would not forget one of the important messages she was told.

"Remember, Shaylee, these are our world's primary source of magic and balance. Without them all, we cannot exist as we have since our ancestors arrived. Treat them well and bring them back to us when you have found them. We will be waiting."

Kalandrya was quite strict on that part of the information. Earth and Faelynn were now one, but with all the treasures together, the dryads were hopeful they could at least form a safe place somewhere far from the humans until the worlds returned to normal.

Shaylee understood and was going to gather them all, but there were two things that were stopping her from contacting the dryads and returning the treasures home. The first was they had to stop what was causing the paradox, and second, she was not going anywhere until she knew Serena was alright.

Shaylee approached the camp, sat down next to the gnomes, and said, "Hey, are you up for some pork sausage and beef mince roll?"

Shaylee knew exactly how to gain the little warriors' attention and she needed them to do some stealthy work to get another one of the treasures. All their locations had been brought to light after Shaylee found the Spear of Assal, but some would be tricky to get. The group had learned firsthand only hours before of the destruction the metal ones were causing in the world. Vaelenflixx had fluttered accidentally into a cottage while looking for bugs and saw the devastation on the square magic box. He interpreted as best he could to Grilif, who then told Shaylee.

Shaylee wasn't taking any chances, so used the spear and whispered an old spell she had learned. As she waved the spear around, images emerged, and she could form a basic story of what was happening all around the world.

Shaylee stared at the gnomes and waited for a response.

"Are you kidding? I would give my left arm for one. Wait ... what do you want, Shaylee?" Grilif was no fool. He knew when he was being played, but he wasn't joking when he said he would give his left arm. The gnomes had been craving something other than forest food for ages.

Shaylee was not going to play back and forth, so she got straight to the point. "I need you to break into the old mansion where the paths lead three ways, to Xarkynan, Aurora, and the palace. Although they cannot be seen without our power source, the paths will still be there, with a mansion in the middle. From my understanding, the Tuatha Dé Danann treasure, the Cauldron of Dagda, should be in the basement. Take my power crystal and only use it as a guide. I mean it—if you veer off the task, I will force-feed you chicken grain until you burst. Do I make myself clear?"

The gnomes hadn't even agreed to the mission, and they were

already being chastised, but Grilif was so hungry he just wanted the job done.

"OK, Shaylee, we are your soldiers, but if I'm not eating pork sausages by sunset tonight ..."

Grilif knew well enough to leave the threat hanging. He would not upset the queen of his people, and besides, he didn't much feel like being turned into a slug.

"One more thing—you have to ride Vax as we are running out of time. We don't know how long we have before the machines take the countryside."

Grilif went white. He had no interest in flying again after the adventures with Felvora, and the thought of riding a dragon put fear into the usually stout, hardened warrior.

Darf was a little more accepting and he tried to sell it to his friend. "Come on, Gril, wait until they hear this back home. You will be the envy of all the gnomes. They will write about you and tell stories to their children."

Grilif stood for a moment and contemplated what his companion was saying. "OK, Shaylee," he said, "let's do it, but if that drag... sorry, wyvern, as much as sneezes when we are up there I'll ..."

Once again, Grilif left his threat unfinished. It wasn't the right time to show his defiance.

Shaylee smiled, then explained how the crystal worked for the purposes of their quest. The spear had fully charged it again and it was ready to be used. Shaylee knew the potential of the power, so placed a zap spell on it in case of any inappropriate use. She trusted the gnomes, and also she didn't sometimes, but she would never tell them that.

Vaximardruusz was ready and Shaylee asked Rasarlin to pass on the details of the quest, having him land a mile away from the mansion so as not to be seen. They were becoming bolder and had just started flying through the day after learning all aircraft were grounded, but they still had to be careful not to gain the attention of the machines.

Shaylee did not stop there after Vax and the gnomes took off. She told the guards to stay with the camp and, against every fiber in her being, asked Van Coinan for help to find the Sword of Light. A Fae had picked it up before the power of Faelynn had fully diminished, but upon inspection of the spear's location imagery, Shaylee could see a benevolent creature called a spriggan wielding the sword, unaware that it was a Tuatha treasure. But for how long it would remain a mystery to the renowned thief would be anyone's guess, so they needed to move.

Spriggans were shifty creatures. They were not evil, but they were responsible for many negative interactions with humans: failing crops, rotten milk, robbery of trinkets or cherished items, and the rare incidences of child theft. Spriggans were always in and out of the realms and after the doorways to the humans' world were closed, some were stuck and began making more mischief.

They were easily fooled and afraid of iron like most Fae, so who better, Shaylee thought, to send than the most confusing negotiator and one of very few Fae who could hold iron without getting hurt. Van Coinan.

The pooka was excited. He had been bouncing around all morning, waiting for Shaylee to return with Vax after finding the location of the spriggan. He had prepared his wooden sword and bound the end with one of Rasarlin's iron wrist bands. Shaylee had only given him a little information as she wanted him to work it out himself. That way, he was in control as he thought it a game. The game was to get the sword without having to steal it or gamble for it.

Shaylee readied the horses. Rasarlin was only going as a companion to Shaylee, as he knew she did not need protection. He had already witnessed in a short amount of time her abilities with a sword and the spear.

Rasarlin communed with Vax before they left, to make sure he was safe and out of sight. The wyvern reported that he had hidden in a clearing within the forest and the gnomes were already inside the mansion.

Shaylee fluttered up to her horse. Van Coinan was already on Rasarlin's, waiting as the hardened Markyyn elf placed his foot in the stirrup, launched over the horse's back, and rested perfectly on the saddle, looking like he had done it thousands of times before. Then they kicked off and headed out for the next treasure.

≈

Shaylee had the spear high in the air as they galloped onwards. They were close, as the guiding light was shining brighter, and images were flashing in front of the queen. They arrived in an abandoned town only a few hours later. This was where the inner forests were on Xarkynan, but in the here and now it was an old Earth town. Shaylee waved the spear, and as she did, the remnants of her world appeared, showing it was still there but blanketed by the veil of an Earth location.

The paradox was clear. Some molded structures of Faelynn and Earth were obvious as one, where others were more shrouded behind the veil, as if this place and sometimes Earth's locations had completely vanished and were replaced by Faelynn landmarks. The confusion was too much to work out, but they were learning that both worlds were there. They just needed some help to locate certain items and places.

Shaylee pulled her reins and indicated to the others to stop. She bounced off her horse and looked around the vine-covered houses that had long stood abandoned. Pointing the spear, she scanned across and could locate the place where the spriggan dwelled. Shaylee turned, walked over to Van Coinan, and whispered, "OK, Van, it's your time to shine. I need you to win the sword for me. Can you do this?"

Van Coinan jumped off the horse and picked up a long stick from the ground. He looked up at Shaylee and Rasarlin and casually said, "The sword is in the bag. I'll be back in a jiffy."

The pooka took off down the overgrown street and passed many old shops, before turning a corner and scurrying down an old wooden stairwell, out of sight. Shaylee turned and looked at Rasarlin with a raised eyebrow and wrinkled lips and Rasarlin returned her gaze, saying quietly, "Why the theatrics with Van Coinan? Wouldn't it be easier to just get it from the creature?"

Shaylee held her smirk and replied, "There is a lot you need to learn about my home. Some who dwell there are not always of flesh and blood. Like the spriggans. They can return to the air whenever they want and if they feel threatened, that's exactly what they would do. Van Coinan has a knack for confusing and testing many creatures. I still don't understand him, but I was taught as a tiny Fae that you never underestimate a pooka. You just don't know what they will do."

Rasarlin smiled. He liked the Fae more and more and was learning so much. He was still having trouble with his memory but knew he had been in some very violent places, battled some horrendous creatures, and was involved in bloody wars during his time trap incarceration. So, he was enjoying the break from the violence of what he could remember, even if it was only for a short time.

Van Coinan crouched down when he came to the dampness of the lower-level dwelling. He could smell an awful moldy smell that nearly made his whiskers fall off. He kept quiet, with his eyes on the prize. The pooka carefully peered through some rotted wood panels that were the last of the old wall.

Van Coinan could see the baby-faced spriggan with old green tree roots protruding from his head like hair. His body was naked but dark green and very wrinkled, like an old person's body. The smell wasn't from the dwelling, thought Van Coinan as he remembered his last interaction with a spriggan many years before. It was the creature itself that had the smell.

As he looked on, the pooka could see him counting some money and playing with an old toaster that had been left to gather rust. He put his wrinkled old hand inside it and held it high in the air while he picked up the sword with his other hand and started banging them together, while he laughed and tried to sing a song.

Van Coinan knew what he was going to do as soon as he noticed the sword. He knocked on the door as if he were visiting the creature.

Knock. Knock.

The spriggan looked up, just about to grab his treasures and dissipate; he waited.

Knock. Knock. "Hello, I was hoping you could help me?" the pooka said calmly and ready for anything.

"Who be there? Go, I say, before I turn your insides into gooey tar."

The spriggan jumped to his feet as Van Coinan entered the small, messy room. The creature looked confused for a moment and then laughed. "Ha, ha, ha. A pooka, what do you want, rabbit?"

Van Coinan would normally pull someone's hair out for calling him that, but he wanted to win the game and show Shaylee he was helping.

"I was hoping you could help me," and as he asked, Van Coinan went to shake the spriggan's hand but casually blew into it as he reached out. Invisible particles hit the creature's pale, childlike face as he fell back for a moment and rubbed his eyes.

Van Coinan still had his paw out and continued, while the spriggan composed himself, "I am Van Coinan and I know you are a spriggan, so I have something you may like, but I need you to trade for it."

The spriggan's attention was now all on Van Coinan as he stood on his buckled legs, hunched at the top of his back, and said, "Don't call me that. I hate being called spriggan. Me be Fylarsh, Fylarsh the Cunning. Now what is it you have for me and what makes you think I won't just take it from you?"

Van Coinan didn't react. Instead, the pooka took the long stick he picked up before and raised it high in the air explaining, "Here is the sword of the Fae. Covered in jewels of all the kings and the ancient Tuatha. I am in need of an old rusty pipe, and I see you have one sitting with you. Now, I will trade, but on one condition—you must guess how many fingers I am holding behind my back. And if you can answer correctly, I will happily trade."

Fylarsh moved closer. His bark-covered arms and long spindly fingers started reaching ever so gently toward the stick, only to pull away just before touching it—as if the item was what the pooka was saying it was. The mesmerized spriggan glanced at the pretend jewels and gold finishing of the sword before looking Van Coinan in the eyes and whispering, "Pooka don't have fingers, ye all have paws."

Van Coinan danced around the room and jumped up and down as

if he were on fire before he stopped and replied, "You are so very right. It was a trick question and you have won the sword as you have bested me."

Fylarsh could not believe his luck. He ran over to the rusty pipe sitting next to the toaster and gladly handed it over to Van Coinan. As he did that, his hands were reaching out with fingers opening and closing to show impatience for his new prize. Van Coinan handed it over and said, "Enjoy, Fylarsh the Cunning."

Then he turned with a grin and crawled out with the sword sheathed next to his wooden one.

Fylarsh was dancing around his room and singing an awful poem, delighting in having tricked the pooka. Van Coinan had left the dwelling and was running swiftly toward Shaylee and Rasarlin when the spriggan came bursting through the main entrance and out into the street, screaming, "You tricked me, rabbit! Give me back my prize before I kill you."

The pooka dust had only been light as Van Coinan didn't want to kill the creature, but it wore off far more quickly than he expected. Fylarsh was gaining on the pooka. He yelled out to the couple standing next to the horses, kissing, "A little help, Shay."

As Van Coinan dove underneath the horse's belly and out of the way of the spriggan's wrath, Rasarlin broke his lock on Shaylee's lips, swung backward, and without looking separated Fylarsh's twisted head from his deformed body with the dark lord's sword he had taken for himself.

Shaylee, shocked at the swiftness of Rasarlin's reactions, looked down at the writhing creature, who was wailing for the last time, before glancing over at Van Coinan with a cheeky half smile on his face and the sword in his hand. The pooka moved in closer and said quietly, "I didn't gamble, and I didn't steal, I merely traded. It is not my fault he didn't like his trade."

Shaylee hadn't wanted the creature killed but knew it had been necessary. Rasarlin cleaned the blood, which was like dark green tree sap, from his sword and resheathed it before examining his handiwork. Shaylee was so relieved that they could get the Sword of Light without the spriggan disappearing. Her instincts about Van Coinan were right, and she only hoped the gnomes had just as much success as they did. As the afternoon started creeping into evening, the three adventurers got on their horses again and galloped fast, back home to camp.

≈

Shaylee was very weary from the long days she was having and she thought Van Coinan would be too, from his eventful day, as he would normally always sleep whenever he could. But from where she stood, a little back from the fire, she watched and listened to her companions, including the pooka, sharing their stories of courage and adventures.

Grilif and Darf, devouring their sausages and beef rolls, were deep into how their dangerous meetings with a giant cat nearly killed them as they dragged the heavy cauldron, while Van Coinan told of his deception of the dangerously crazy Fylarsh the Cunning. On and on the night went with their back-and-forth tales. Sitting around the fire, Rasarlin was even belly-laughing at some of Van Coinan's impressions of Vaximardruusz, while the wyvern was sound asleep in a cave not too far away.

Shaylee just enjoyed the family setting and watched as her remaining people were happy, even if it was only for the night. With the treasures nearly all with her now, she could summon all her people. In the morning, she would use the power of the treasures while she blew her whistle to call for them all to help.

It was going to be a hard task, as the fear and hate for humans was why they hid, but if she put a call out to help their queen, she knew she would gain a good number of them. Wherever Serena was, Shaylee knew she would be a part of what was going on in the world in some form or another and she would need as much help as she could get.

They had one more treasure to get before they journeyed to find Serena, the Stone of Destiny. Shaylee was confident that having all four treasures with her would give all her Fae their enchantment back, which could be of help in the war that they did not know was coming.

THE HYBRID
AWAKENS

STACEY HAD BEEN HAVING TROUBLE WITH THE
Zeytar hybrid for several nights. He had woken her throughout
the night with uncontrollable screaming and in the day sometimes he
would have fits of rage that lasted hours. The strongest of the men had
trouble containing his strength, and they gave him shots to calm him
down or make him sleep.

Eric was concerned about her. She had taken on a boy who had the
strength of three men and did not know what genetic modifications
had been placed inside his DNA. He tried to explain to her that the
most evil, intelligent aliens known in the universe designed these
creatures, so as he grew older, what would he eventually become?

Stacey did not want any of it. She was committed to the boy and she
would stick with him for the long haul, regardless of what her father
or some others thought. She had seen him advance in such a short
amount of time. His skills were impeccable, and he could tap into any
of the computer systems on the ship and bring up data that only Wilkes
had had access to.

Stacey wanted to keep that care and encouragement going. That
was until she woke up from a deep sleep to a howling cry that alerted
everyone in that section of the ship. Stacey ran to the boy's room,
where she was witness to him grabbing at his head in pain. She moved
slowly toward him, humming a tune that usually eased him, before he

stopped, looked at her, and with his large, darkened eyes stared into hers intensely until Stacey grabbed her head and ended up on the floor, writhing in pain and screaming like the boy had been only moments beforehand.

By then, several of the ship's soldiers and patrons were there, including Eric. He saw his daughter on the floor and went to pick her up, but was flung against the wall by an unseen force. The Zeytar hybrid motioned to the others to step back as he suddenly got hit with another wave of pain, grabbing his head once more and releasing Stacey from his mental grip.

Eric picked himself up, limped over to Stacey, and assisted her to the entrance, where two doctors along with two soldiers were ready to administer a strong sedative to calm the boy down. As they slowly entered the room, the boy once more broke free from his gripping pain and stared at the four who were now only feet from him. They were all struck hard by an unseen force as the Zeytar hybrid began speaking through clenched teeth, "Stay ... Away ... From ... Me ..."

As he finished, he went back to gripping his head in pain before he passed out. The four men left the room as Stacey and Eric rushed in. Eric picked the boy up and took him to the lab where the Zeytars had developed a holding cell for uncontrollable creatures, fully glassed so they could see through. They designed the lab enclosure as a prison and Eric did not hesitate to use it in this case, though in the past Stacey had refused to allow it. This was his first attack in a few days. Stacey did not protest this time. She knew it was warranted.

She had not seen an episode like this before and for the safety of the crew and the boy himself agreed; it was the best scenario. They waited and watched from a distance, outside the one-way triple glassed room.

The boy slept most of the morning and the doctors, along with Eric, Stacey, and two soldiers, stayed to monitor him. Serena would poke her head in sometimes with Eoghan to see if they needed anything, before leaving and attending to her own boy's training.

Stacey had fallen asleep on her father's arm as the morning turned into early afternoon when the boy sat up, looked at the glass toward Eric, and spoke in an adult voice, "Eric, please come inside."

Eric woke Stacey with a start and turned to the doctors, who stared back, shrugging their shoulders in confusion. The boy had never talked like that before. It was like he had gained cognitive abilities to communicate. Eric stood up and was about to enter the room before one soldier grasped his arm and said, "Are you sure about this, Eric? What do we know about this boy?"

The soldier, having finished his lecture, glanced at Stacey, who was giving him a rather nasty look of contempt. Eric pulled his arm free and reached for the door. He looked back at his daughter for approval, which was given with a smile and a slight nod, before he committed to the act and entered the room, and then Stacey locked it immediately after.

Corporal Rick Thorne, who had tried to stop Eric from entering the room, left to find some more help in case the boy was violent again. Even though they were not soldiers anymore, instincts and training were with them all and they would default to those training methods in times of danger. Most of the time it was welcomed, but not this time.

Eric walked slowly into the empty room with only two chairs present, one at the far end where the boy sat and the other six feet away where Eric was motioned to by the boy. As he approached, he turned to look at the blacked-out window before he slowly faced forward again and crept cautiously to the chair. He sat down to face the staring hybrid boy.

"It's alright, Eric, I won't hurt you."

Eric was not a fearful person, but he was wary of the boy's intentions and felt uncomfortable with his new deep voice. "Why me?" he carefully replied. "Stacey is your carer. How did you know I was even there?"

The boy smiled as he answered, "Ah Eric, ever the pessimist. I knew you were there. A one-way mirror won't stop a powerful Zeytar like me. I can see everyone on the ship."

Eric was getting very anxious. He knew that the bodiless Zeytars were all lining up for bodies. Did this boy get one before the escape from the ship? he thought. "So, what can I do for you?" he said.

The Zeytar boy let out a long, deep laugh. It was chilling to Eric's core, as normal Zeytars were not that loud nor had any sense of humor. Even Wilkes only smiled occasionally. Eric sat upright, stuck in his chair, before he whispered nervously, "Did I say something funny?"

The boy sat forward. His big eyes were the darkest Eric had ever seen, while his face, although large to start with, seemed a little more misshaped now. The boy had grown no hair yet and they all wondered whether he would, but that was the least of Eric's concerns as he waited for the boy to answer. "Eric, you and Stacey saved me. I will forever be in your debt. I am sorry it has taken me this long, but I have been in hibernation while this body has gained strength. The bodiless ones could gain immediate access to the adults, but the children took a little longer to accept such powerful minds."

Eric nearly fell off his chair. He slowly stood up and cautiously moved toward the boy but maintaining a distance. He lowered his head and looked deep into his eyes before whispering nervously, "Wilkes? Is ... Is it you?"

The boy smiled and said quietly, "Sit down, Eric, and I will tell you."

Eric walked backward, staring at the boy until he reached the chair and sat down, not taking his eyes from the hybrid for one moment and trying to process his own thoughts until they were no longer his own. The boy hit Eric with a barrage of images that took place in the woods after the events on the mother ship. It was Wilkes at the tree with the hybrid boy as Eric stood watching. Eric's head was convulsing as the images flooded his cerebral cortex, moving him back and forth.

Stacey was at the door, trying to open it but the boy had taken control of the lock from within as he continued the barrage of memories into Eric. Eric could see the boy in the woods with Wilkes' last movements touching the boy's face, but this time he could see a bright mist enter the boy from Wilkes' hands before he fell limp against the tree, leaving the boy with Stacey and Eric ready to take his lifeless body back to the tent.

Eric sat up, eyes wide open and gasping for air. The hybrid leaned over and placed a flood of calming images into Eric's mind as he slowly came to, sat up, and took a deep breath. "Wilkes, you're a sneaky bastard, it is you," he said quietly.

Then he stood up, and so did Wilkes, and as they moved toward each other, Eric grabbed his hand and locked fists. The hybrid smiled and gripped him tightly, before it became too much and Eric pulled back.

By then, some soldiers as well as Stacey, who were listening outside the room, could enter. Wilkes was still adjusting to his new body and consciousness but was welcoming of his new and old friends reuniting again.

There were so many questions, and it would take up the rest of the afternoon to get through them all, but the now six-foot Zeytar hybrid was wearying and needed to rest. Answers, including how he grew so tall in such a short amount of time, would have to wait until morning.

Stacey was one of the last to leave. As she moved to the door, Wilkes called her back to ask her and Eric a question.

"Stacey, you took such good care of me, saving this body and not giving up on a boy created by your enemy. You have done so much since our time in the ship together and I want you to keep me on track, look out for me when I may not be myself or when the seizures persist. I am still changing and your comfort along with your kind heart is what I love most about humans. Eric, is that alright with you?"

Eric looked at Stacey, then back at Wilkes before they both nodded. Stacey answered first, "Of course, it is, Wilkes, you saved my life, remember, so we are even, and I must admit taking care of the boy was a challenging pleasure. It has given me a chance to finish a project I had been working on before all this started, not that it matters now as the world is ending."

Stacey looked at Wilkes. She just realized that he had been in hibernation and that he was not aware of the issues going on in the world now. Eric quickly chimed in, "It's alright, don't stress, we will fill you in when you have rested."

The two did not know that Wilkes had already scanned their brains for any intel before he gripped his head in pain once more and fell to the floor. This time it wasn't because of growth or waking into his cognitive abilities but due to the flood of evil imagery entering his mind with ZARK drones, the V.I.Z.I.N.D.A.L.E.X., and the destruction of the human way of life.

Eric and Stacey both picked him up. They quickly realized he had scanned their minds, and that was what led to this seizure. They gently took an arm each, slowly walked him to the door, and made their way to his quarters. The doctor was there with a sedative and as they eased the ever-evolving Zeytar hybrid onto the bed, Wilkes grabbed Eric's arm and whispered, "I will not let them win. I promise you all." As he finished his sentence, Wilkes passed out from the sedative that Doctor Frederick had administered.

Eric looked at Stacey as the doctor made Wilkes comfortable. They slowly walked outside together and Eric said quietly, "What do you think he knows? Or what do you think he has up his sleeve? I saw something when I was on the chopper going out of the mountains, but I didn't tell anyone, as it was all over and I thought no more of it. But Wilkes had patches made up with the title D.A.A.T. which meant The Deception Anti Apocalypse Team."

"What do you think it means?" she asked her father.

"I'm not sure, but the patch on the uniform was disturbing. It had images of a human holding a Zeytar hybrid's skull in the air with fire in the background, and strange creature skulls on the ground. In the other hand the human held a pulse rifle. Stacey, when I looked at it further, there were humans in the background, burning and locked in cages. It's like whatever is happening now is exactly what Wilkes was expecting, but that was if the Leader won and the Zeytar hybrids came through, not if we had won. Was this inevitably going to play out anyway? I think Wilkes was deceived."

Stacey started trembling. Eric felt stupid that he had overlooked that patch until now, but he embraced his daughter and offered some reassurance, "Hey, if we've beaten the bastards once, we can beat them again."

Stacey looked up. She felt a little better and she gave him a smile before walking off down the hallway to call a meeting and explain their new findings.

≈

The meeting left most feeling a sense of dread. They were already in a dangerous place, knowing that many of the factions the "President" had sent out were hunting them. But the information that Eric relayed to them regarding the patch left them confused and upset. The only shining light was that the one entity that called them all together and saved every one of their lives was Wilkes, and knowing he was back eventually outweighed the bad feelings in favor of more hopeful ones.

The meeting disbanded, and all those involved, not including family or friends, went back to their quarters to update the rest of the civilians.

Eric was getting tired. It had been a very draining day and, with everything that had taken place, he longed for a good night's sleep. After the last of the group had left, Eric slumped onto a seat and closed his eyes. Serena moved toward him and sat behind his chair. She wrapped her arms around his neck in an embracing hug. She leaned forward and kissed him on the cheek. Eric smiled, eyes still closed, taking in her soft touch.

"How did I suddenly become the leader of this lot, Serena? They all seem to look to me for guidance and information, but I feel I can't give them what they need sometimes."

Serena's hug became a little tighter as she whispered a response into his ear, "Because you are good at it and everybody knows. You have been strong from the start and people have seen it. I have been emotionally absent. Valinda has been busy, as has Stacey, with the boy. The military guys don't care for it and that leaves the last best choice, you."

Eric chuckled as Serena moved around and sat on his lap. Her hand touched his face gently as they stared at each other.

"I've missed you," Eric said gently as Serena smiled and leaned in for a kiss. They sat there alone like two teenagers, just taking each other in, kissing and caressing one another. Serena dragged her lips away from Eric's and gave him little kisses along his cheek toward his ear, slowly and lovingly, before whispering, "I think we should take this to our room."

Eric turned slowly with a slight grin as he met her lips once more, kissing short little bursts, before pulling away and attacking again. He replied with his mouth now hovering over Serena's, "What about Eoghan?"

Serena smiled back. Now her mouth was wider as she breathed Eric in, answering softly, "He is with Valinda and Levi, learning some sign language. She was more than happy to give us an hour ... Or two."

Eric picked Serena up and carried her to the door, their lips locked, before he pulled away slightly to say, "I'm not sure I can go that long. Our room seems so far away."

Serena smiled as Eric turned the lights down and locked the meeting room from the inside. He then moved to a dark office next to the main hall where he gently laid Serena onto a soft couch and they made love for the next two hours.

≈

Wilkes awoke the next morning screaming in pain again, but this time because of growth. He had entered the ultimate stage of his metamorphosis, which was tearing at his skin and pulling on his bones.

Stacey was in the next room and was at his side in no time. She held his hand as she watched his skin stretch, tear, then heal. His body was growing right before her eyes, and there was nothing in the world she could do for him.

She had to let his hand go after the pain he was going through made him clench hard. Stacey felt it getting tighter and before it crushed her bones, she managed to break free.

In the bathroom she wet a washcloth with cool water and brought it back to his side, placing it on his head. Stacey could see pulsing on his head as the skin moved and formed new cells. The most disturbing image was that of his femurs clicking out of the hip joints and growing while his knees realigned and snapped back together.

Wilkes continued screaming and as the doctor was now with Stacey, ready to administer some pain medication, Wilkes spoke in a pained tone, "Don't ... Just let it ... Take its course."

Doctor Frederick pulled back and stood waiting, witnessing an event he would most likely never see again as Wilkes' body writhed in pain. He seemed to be comforted somewhat by the cold water, but he had to let the process take its course, however long that would be.

Stacey continued to sit with the screaming Zeytar hybrid. She felt helpless but kept the cool towel over him until the last of the bones clicked and skin healed. Wilkes had chosen Doctor Frederick to be a backup doctor because he had an extensive knowledge of the Zeytars, but he did not know what the hybrids would be like. This was a treat, he thought, as he wrote notes and took video for future study.

Stacey did not seem to mind. After all, Wilkes was a scientist himself and would most likely welcome any kind of learning and study of such a strange creature, even if that creature was now him.

Soon, the room became quiet. The doctor finished filming and Wilkes had let out his final screams. Stacey wiped the last of the sweat from his brow as the now extraordinarily strong looking man lying naked in front of them started coming to.

She covered Wilkes' body to give him some dignity. He now looked very human with very large muscles all in the right positions—except for his head. He had grown a good length of hair, but the size of his head was still very large, much like those of the hybrids she had seen on the ship months ago. Stacey leaned over as Wilkes looked up at her and said, "Thank you once more, Stacey. That was more pain than I have felt in a thousand years and your minor act to cool my face made it a little more bearable."

Stacey smiled. "Sometimes it's the small things that matter the most, Wilkes, but I'm glad you didn't crush my hand."

She giggled slightly as Wilkes managed a small smile before he turned his head and closed his eyes. "Just give me a few hours to sleep this last metamorphosis off, and then we can get started on taking out that destructive robot once and for all."

Wilkes had not realized before he wandered off to sleep that Eric, Serena, and some of the other soldiers were at the door and had witnessed the latest events. Eric leaned over to Serena and simply said, "He's back."

IN-HUMANITY

ALEX HAD IMPLEMENTED NEARLY EVERY protocol of the Leader's backup plan, Project Synergy. The next task was to assimilate the human hosts with some of the ZARK drones to allow the surviving bodiless Zeytars to enter their new bodies.

It wasn't ideal being cybernetic and not fully human, but it was better than losing the rest of the Zeytar species to an eternity of void and darkness. The Leader did not know all of Wilkes' betrayal, but he had planned a backup in case something went wrong. The V.I.Z.I.N.D.A.L.E.X. should have shut down after its job at the Super Collider, but after the scientists had finished working on it all those years before, the Leader transferred a hidden directive that would only enact if the Leader requested it, which he did when the ships were coming down.

The other part of Project Synergy was to upload the Leader's essence, which had transferred at the same time ALEX was getting its final update. Parts of the Leader were showing through sometimes, but the Leader would need an organic brain to host himself fully. ALEX was completely metal and could not expand the Leader's essence, so it stayed dormant, like files, awaiting the integration of the ZARKs and human hosts.

ALEX was at the largest prison camp in Washington, D.C. There were around a million people held in several lots throughout the district and up to fifty million across the country. The hygiene was poor, food was scarce, and any kind of retaliation or defiance was met with the punishment of a torturous end.

Women and children rarely lasted long as cannibalism crept in and it was now survival of the fittest. The ZARK drones would try to separate them as best they could, but sometimes security was overlooked, and the strongest men would take them when they could, raping the women before tearing them apart and eating them raw.

ALEX took some pleasure in witnessing the harsh conditions as the android had an unnatural hatred for humans, whether that was part of the programming or some of the Leader coming through. Either way it was quite distressing to those witnessing the torture perpetrated by the ZARKs and their own kind.

ALEX had arrived to start the process of assimilating the humans and ZARKs. It had already sent Goblin to work on creating the clones it needed to go out and search for all the rebel defectors, and now it had a file that Wilkes had been researching—it would get to that soon. Everything was falling into place and there was nothing anybody on the planet could do to stop it.

The screams of the emaciated and dying were nothing to the android as it landed in the middle of the prison camp to start the process. Some men who were given leadership among their own approached ALEX to beg for freedom or a compromise, but that was their undoing. ALEX chose those to be the first. The android had the ZARK drones build a large dwelling at each reservation after they had finished collecting as many humans as they could find. It would be the science lab where the inhumane process of assimilation would take place.

Those lucky enough to escape the ZARKs over the past few months were deep underground or in bunkers, hidden, but they all had to surface at some stage, and there were enough scouts still out looking for more victims. The country was incredibly quiet—not a plane, car, or working piece of machinery anywhere at all. The only movement was that of some of the inter-dimensional creatures wandering around searching for food or fighting among each other.

The ZARKs had to eliminate some of them over time as they would try to encroach on some of the prison camp enclosures to take humans for food, but that wasn't often, and those creatures soon learned who the real controllers of Earth were.

ALEX had three men in its grip as it led them toward the science lab on the second level of the camp. Inside were a hundred ZARK drones ready and awaiting their new bodies. Also present were some scientists that ALEX had relocated from Goblin's crew, including Gaald, for a short time to make sure the process ran smoothly and with no hiccups.

The first of the ZARKs lined up. ALEX could speak to every single drone simultaneously, so even in the other prison camps the same thing was taking place, although they were without scientists so needed to wait for instructions before they began the procedure elsewhere.

Then the first man lined up. He made one last attempt at gaining freedom before two ZARKs grabbed him and held him tight. The android that was awaiting the transference moved forward and placed its long metal hand onto the male's head. They all watched as the scientists turned on a machine created by the Zeytars to break apart molecules and reconnect them soon after.

It was an early design for the X-Clock that had failed but was still used as a torture machine on other worlds. The scientist plugged it into the ZARK and then into the human. They all stood back as ALEX watched with a somewhat desperate and hopeful robotic gaze.

The Zeytar scientist Gaald looked up at ALEX, who then nodded slightly. The machine was turned on, and they all waited. Soon the man started convulsing while the ZARK drone vibrated. Blue light emanated from the robot as the man's flesh began breaking apart into millions upon millions of cells. The ZARK moved forward and as they vibrated together, parts of the machine fell to the floor as did parts of the male. Very soon the light was too bright, while a plume of smoke rose in the air of the room, and they were all left in silence.

The smoke began to dissipate and ALEX moved forward, while the scientist unplugged the ZARK drone, trying not to step on the meat and swarf on the floor. He looked over at ALEX and nodded, giving the android approval to proceed to the final step with a Zeytar essence awaiting on Aladoor.

The ZARK drone had become a cyborg, with skin molded to its arm, and both a human eye and a metal one on the other side. The process had completely fused man and ZARK together, with a symbiotic human and metal brain, giving it the ability to host a sentient being. The man was gone, and only biological remnants of him remained, including some meaty muscle and skin that covered some of the once fully metal machine. It seemed that the symbiosis was a successful transference.

ALEX had its arm out now, pointing to a clear wall, and began whirling it around until it was so fast that a vortex began opening. As the colored lights and electricity circled the area, ALEX entered the portal, keeping it open, and called for one of the waiting Zeytar souls to enter. The android could see their outline better in that dimension, so could tell how many to let through.

The groans coming from the dark dimension were loud and never-ending. ALEX explained they would all be free soon enough, but only one could enter this time. Once the android had made this clear to them, one followed ALEX back through before the portal was closed once more.

The entity saw the cybernetic abomination in front of it but, after some hesitation, entered the body, flinging it back momentarily before its neurons of meat and metal all fired together and it spoke, "I ... Am ... Free."

The other humans, awaiting their turn, fainted or threw up at the sight. The voice was a disturbing echo of human and robotic harmonics, something that would put the most hardened person into a state of absolute dread.

ALEX smiled its robotic grin and said, "I will send out a signal to all the other ZARKs awaiting their turn. Only call me to open the portal when you have enough to make it worthwhile. How long can they last without a mind?"

The scientists looked at ALEX and as one answered, "I would think a day, maybe two. They need a mind to help with healing and they need to eat a diet of supplement protein and vitamins which we have made up in the lab."

ALEX nodded and sent a message to the other ZARK drones around the world. Then it opened another doorway back to Goblin, returning the scientists, and awaited an update on the progress of the android's new trackers that were being created in the hidden lab.

ALEX would be busy for the next few weeks, constantly moving from prison camp to prison camp, providing a small window of opportunity for an ideally timed attack, which the rebels desperately needed, but would never know they had missed.

≈

Goblin was working tirelessly. He knew that if he did not have something for ALEX soon, he would be next on its hit list. The abominations the android had given the deformed scientist were chosen personally. They were the best out of the gruesome lot of visitors coming through the portal in Waxahachie. What made them stand out from the rest were the vicious looks, strength, and speed, along with high intelligence.

ALEX had no recollection of those species being in its databank of all the Zeytars' historic logs. The creatures seemed to be from separate worlds but had worked together to get food and fight the ZARKs, and then after losing to ALEX tried to compromise and show allegiance, all without verbal communication.

Goblin had them all in cryo stasis and was thankful he didn't have to deal with them alive and kicking.

The task now was to extract blood, get the DNA codex Goblin was told to find, and add a sequence of coding with harmonics of DNA to locate anyone with the RNA-X7c genome. ALEX had deciphered Wilkes' cryptic files and relayed the information to Goblin. There weren't many humans left with that genome and if even one defector was still alive, the new hunters would find them.

Stacey was one of only a few with the genome remaining and would only have a limited amount of time left before she was caught and taken to ALEX. But the android didn't care about her genes; it only wanted to use her to find the rest of Wilkes' traitors and finish them off, leaving nothing at all to stop its evil.

Goblin was well into the process. It wasn't hard to replicate the harmonics of DNA to a certain genome. After all, that's what Wilkes and Anders both used with Levi and Savage. The hard part would be to control the creatures once they had completely grown in stasis. Goblin shared his concern with ALEX and could compromise with a safety switch that would render them immobile if they retracted from their missions or if they thought that the scientific team in the lab would make an ideal meal.

The other end of the deal was that ALEX expected them to be ready within days, and the creatures would be the last thing on its mind if Goblin failed to deliver the finished process in time. The android's database was filled with most of the science of cloning, and it knew that the task would take time, as expediting the process could mean the creatures became useless abominations. But Goblin had been working on accelerated growth which meant he could have the perfect creatures within forty-eight hours of the beginning of the sequence.

ALEX left Goblin to proceed and disappeared to attend to the finished ZARK drones and open the doorway to Aladoor for the Zeytar minds to enter. ALEX had no time to stop, with its programming working hard to deliver every one of its commands from Project Synergy, but the android would still need to rest and refuel with an electromagnetic burst sometimes. When it would stop to do that, no one, not even ALEX, knew.

Meanwhile, in all the major cities across the world, ALEX had assigned several ZARK drones in each section for the destruction of all major buildings, leveling every landmark to a messy pile of rubble. They killed immediately those taking refuge. All hospitals were going to be destroyed and the leaders of all countries were to be the first to become hosts, along with the ZARK drones, for the Zeytar minds.

ALEX needed to prepare this world for the Zeytars to take over completely, leveling everything and eliminating all others. The Leader would eventually rise again, and the android's programming was simply to complete its orders from its master. The destruction of the Earth was so the remaining Zeytars could settle, rebuild, and eventually create immortal bodies to sustain them while they built armies of clones to take over the universe, obliterating all their enemies—but this time not destroying themselves in the process. They had been well on track to do that with their original plan. This was just another, though longer, way to achieve it, and ALEX was excelling.

As New York City fell, images flashed to ALEX to show constant updates. Then Los Angeles, Chicago, Phoenix, Las Vegas, and on it went. All bridges were destroyed—the Golden Gate in San Francisco and the Brooklyn Bridge in Manhattan were no more. The Zeytars would build their own utopia, and as it stood, the ZARK drones could fly, so bridges were irrelevant.

Humanity was on the verge of extinction, and it would take something close to a miracle to stop it as the wheels of destruction gained momentum.

≈

Deep within a cavernous ancient rock formation, hidden for thousands of years and unearthed by explosions from the Super Conducting Super Collider, some dark creatures had found their way inside. They had not followed the course out of darkness that most of the other inter-dimensional creatures had chosen, but instead moved deeper into the Earth.

Several had entered the mysterious hidden caves before another change of the collider's portal coordinates set off a chain reaction and closed the exit off completely behind them, leaving some of the most vile and inhuman creatures to fend for themselves in the darkness of the tunnels. They didn't seem daunted by this. They had fed before entering, as some other visitors from the portal were not all evil and found themselves easy targets for the more insidious creatures.

They made fire quickly by using skills from their own worlds, but each creature would not follow another or be led by one. Coming from different worlds, they all had the desire to control the others, but they were smart enough to know that down in the pits of the Earth they would have to work together ... For now.

On they went, deeper and deeper through ancient corridors, for days and days, eating the subterranean scraps they could find. There were five in total. The first to enter was a feline-looking bipedal humanoid, a black-furred panther with bright yellow eyes and vicious teeth and claws, wearing a bandolier with all kinds of sharp weapons.

The second was much larger, with no fur, just pink skin like a shaved animal. This creature's very long, sharp teeth protruded through gaps in its enormous mouth, while its arms were much longer than its legs so it would interchange walking upright with crawling low. The hairless creature had several ears and multiple blood-red eyes, and it twitched and skittered along the ground, always searching for food but also eyeing off the others on the off chance it could take one out for a meal.

The third was of average height and walked strangely on two legs. Armor like an armadillo's covered all of its body, with plates over its arms and legs. It had huge shoulders and a very animal-like face but not like any creature from Earth, as it had four eyes, a long snout, two holes for ears, and thin but sharp teeth.

The next to enter was the most disturbing. The large centipede part of the creature had all its legs at the bottom end, while the top half was more like a serpent with razor-sharp fangs. It was quick and would let out an incredibly loud, high-pitched scream when it wanted to intimidate its prey. The colors of the reptilian skin changed with emotion, the creature sometimes mesmerizing its prey before it attacked. The others were all wary of it and knew that when it was hungry to stay clear until it fed.

Last, the most dominant of all the creatures, with the potential to lead them if it so desired, was a humanoid that could change form from a solid cell structure to that of its surroundings, like rock, wood, or plants, among other elements. To do so took a lot of energy, which would deplete it over time. The longer the transformation, the more energy the creature would need to regain strength. Earth, however, had exactly the right diet for its needs. In normal form, it looked like a human with pale skin and the head was that of an insect, half ant and half mantis.

The creatures kept on moving. They would squabble sometimes, but knew they needed each other to get out in one piece. It was uncertain why they had originally entered the caves, but when one went in, the others followed as if it were calling to them. And then the structure collapsed.

Eventually, they came to a massive drop at the end of a section of tunnels, and they seemed to be standing above clouds. The feline panther peered over the edge and could just make out tiny humanoids guarding a high ledge with cavernous entries in the rock face. Below them the drop continued into a huge, cloud-filled void. Hunger, curiosity, and a zest for violence led to a unanimous decision to find a way down and gather some food.

REUNION

NOW THAT WILKES WAS AWAKE AND GETTING BACK to his full abilities, the first thing to do was to keep moving so the V.I.Z.I.N.D.A.L.E.X. could not find them. The cloaking was always on, but Wilkes had developed an untraceable system that he had used against Anders in the early days of his rebellion which Carlos had not yet initiated. Wilkes turned it on, but it was still best to move just in case.

At night Wilkes would hide the ship at the bottom of Crater Lake in the Klamath region which he had used many times in the past, enabling him to do all his observations through secret and powerful satellites he had set up to watch over those he needed to keep an eye on. The technology was far more advanced than anything on Earth, which meant the signal needed water to boost it, while also hindering anyone trying to find his signal once started.

While Wilkes caught up on the destructive world events and began creating plans for all his teams, Serena and Eoghan were right outside the cloaked ship, at the entrance to the thick of the Siskiyou Forest, where they had landed earlier that morning. Serena was thrusting her sword hard and fast at her son. Eoghan's skills had developed incredibly. He had grown every day and now had the appearance of an eight-year-old with the abilities of a late teen or young adult.

Serena took over the training and had been working hard with him daily over the last several days, showing him skills and parries that she was taught in Faelynn all those years ago. Eoghan dodged a swift strike from his mother and scaled a few feet up a tall pine, escaping the blade by inches and impressing Serena to no end.

She would never purposefully put her son in danger, but she had a connection with him that was growing as the hours ticked over. She could sense his next moves and would attack harder and faster, both to help him realize danger at a challenging level, and to bring confidence back into her own abilities that she had let wane over the last few months since returning home.

Though still mourning her sister and the world she had left behind, Serena was focusing on the future with her son and Eric while helping, where she could, to train those who needed some upskilling with fighting techniques. She had lost all her Fae abilities but was still a weapon of destruction with her fighting style and swordsmanship.

Eoghan jumped from the trees and ran swiftly behind a large pine, so Serena moved in close to the other end of the tall tree, thinking she would catch him out. But his Fae skills had kicked in and she was met with empty space. Eoghan had jumped at twice the speed up the branches and silently landed without interrupting a single twig, or his mother seeing, before putting his arms around her back and giggling.

Serena nearly jumped five feet into the air in shock. She had not seen that coming and had not expected his speed. How was he doing this without the power of the Fae? she thought, knowing he was strong and swift, but how he was defying the laws of Earth's own physics and gravity was something she could not work out.

She turned to greet Eoghan while he still had a tight grip on her and then, giggling herself, she fell backward, letting her son land on her. He gently pressed his knee on the ground to take the brunt of pressure off his mother's chest and stomach before lying on her as they laughed together.

Serena held him tightly as they lay a few feet into the woods on the grass-filled ground, saying nothing, just being with each other. Eoghan was becoming extremely attached to his mother since she started feeling better and they were spending so much time together.

After several minutes, Eoghan rolled off and Serena slowly stood up and brushed off the remaining branches and twigs that had held on tightly to her training pants. Eoghan picked up Long Leaf like it was made of feathers and handed the sword to Serena, saying in his broken, recently learned English, "Here, Mother ... Take."

Smiling, Serena kissed him on his forehead, and said, "Thank you, my darling. Are you ready for another round? This time I will teach you sword parries taught to me by Darlygah Frostdrop."

Eoghan nodded and approached his mother so she could show him up close how to move and fight with a sword at the same time. Serena stood behind and placed Long Leaf in his tiny hands. The handle looked big, and she thought he would drop it, but he took it and raised it with no effort, and Serena remembered she wasn't much older, by body mass, when she first received it.

Meanwhile, Eric was in the control room of the ship helping Wilkes catch up with all the recent events, but soon found himself useless as the now Zeytar hybrid took control and was surfing through all different sources, gathering information saved from satellites and old media, and through his own intuition, leaving Eric to flip a camera over to watch Serena and Eoghan training.

Eric liked to know where they were always, especially with all the evil abominations roaming in the world now, and being enemy number one. Wilkes had released his security drones to scan a large perimeter that would detect any foreign activity and report it back immediately. There were also others outside the ship monitoring those going about their daily training, building, maintenance, and other important activities.

Eric smiled when he found the drone watching his beloved Serena and Eoghan exchanging techniques. He too was very protective, now they were all a functioning family. The stories of the Fae fascinated Eric and how his son was growing so fast. There were still so many questions he had but he would ask them gradually.

As he watched the two moving fast and training hard, he noticed the camera glitching before realizing in between the fuzziness that Serena and Eoghan had dropped to the ground, writhing around in some sort of seizure or pain. Eric jumped up and ran as fast as he could to the entrance, taking more time than he wanted to, bumping into soldiers and other civilians, getting glares and groans from each party.

Meanwhile, in the woods, Serena and Eoghan were screaming in pain so loud that it gained the attention of Valinda and Levi, who were in the forest picking berries and taking some time out from the noise of the busy ship.

"Come, Levi, that sounds like Serena," Val said. "Something must be wrong."

Levi grunted in agreement as they sprinted to the location of the screams. Valinda struggled to keep up with the giant Sasquatch stride so kept back, knowing he would help if he could once he arrived at the scene.

As Levi appeared from the woods, a disturbing vision struck him. Eric was standing on the other side, also watching in shock. Serena was arching her back and her skin had become pale. Her ears were growing to a point, as were Eoghan's, with the pain of the transformation too much for the small child as wings tore from his back.

Serena seemed to come around when her wings reappeared and began snaking around her sweaty body. Eric could only watch, feeling useless as his loved ones continued to change and writhe in pain. Serena, on her hands and knees, was silent as she took a little time to adjust to her new body once more. She turned her head and saw Eoghan screaming and crying and she felt weak and hopeless for that moment before passing out momentarily.

Eric pointed to Valinda, who had just arrived, gesturing for help. She asked Levi to pick Serena up and take her to a room inside while Eric waited for a break in Eoghan's seizure so he could help him as well.

Suddenly a roar came from the sky. Serena, in Levi's arms, sprang to life, her wings pointing high as the roars became louder. All those watching began taking cover, thinking they were under attack from the ZARKs, but as the noise continued, they stared at the sky. Suddenly thousands of creatures appeared from nowhere, led by a giant beast with an enormous wingspan that looked like a Y shape as it landed.

Thousands of buzzing entities were surrounding the entire area, zipping through the woods, while others appeared from the darkness of the trees and mushrooms, as well as the bark, leaves, and flowers.

The woods had come alive with all kinds of life, small to exceptionally large, while the huge flying creature came closer, finding an opening a little further downhill to land in. Serena, now in the sky, a little disoriented but aware of what was happening, met with some of her kin in the air. As the wyvern landed, a familiar face sprung from the beast's back, hurtling herself into the sky and meeting Serena mid-flight.

"Shay... Shaylee is ... that ..."

Before Serena could finish, Shaylee grabbed her sister in the air, holding her tightly as their wings took over and slowly flittered, just keeping them high enough so they could concentrate on each other's embrace. Both were crying and whispering. Shaylee began speaking first, with the crystal around her neck and the Spear of Assal pressed softly against Serena's back, "I have searched for you, my dear sister. I never gave up."

Serena squeezed her a little tighter as she responded, "I thought you were ... How did you survive? I saw that creature cut you down."

Shaylee whispered into her ear, "Magic, my dear, and a little help from a new friend that I want to introduce you to. Without him we would have been lost."

While the two sisters reunited, some soldiers had taken their weapons out and kept them pointed at the odd creatures surrounding them. The sprites were buzzing around them all, whispering in their ears strange things they could not understand, while the Elvenfae guards held swords high, ready to strike. The tensions were growing as Levi began swatting some of the more brazen sprites getting a little too close to his head. He looked down, and saw Van Coinan staring back up at him, each of them just as confused and curious about the other. Levi kneeled and picked the pooka up by his overalls for a better look. Van Coinan didn't seem to care. If he thought he was threatened, he would have retaliated, but there was something about the enormous beast he wanted to know more about.

Levi pulled Van Coinan closer to his face, where their eyes met before the pooka spoke in a strange language to the giant, "You are one mighty creature, but I reckon I could take you and, boy, you stink."

Levi did not understand a word but as Van Coinan finished his remarks, the Sasquatch dropped him, looked straight ahead, and started running toward the Elvenfae guards who had swords pointed toward Valinda. But before his large striding thumps could make it to her, he was ambushed by a thousand sprites and sylphs, covering his face and eventually making the beast fall flat on his back as he tried to swat them away.

Serena and Shaylee's reunion was cut short as the scream of Levi hitting the dirt alerted them to take notice of what was happening on the ground below. Eric had two swords at his throat but in his trance-like state, focused on watching Serena in the air, he pushed them aside without knowing the consequences of his actions. As he walked away, one guard parried back, ready to strike, before Shaylee caught wind of the situation and swiftly pointed the spear at the guard, sending a shock wave that knocked him to the ground.

She yelled, "Enough, my people, these are our friends, our allies. They are not the humans that we fear, nor the metal ones. Please, behave as if they are all guests of the palace."

Immediately after Shaylee finished, the smaller Fae scattered into the woods and hid from sight like scolded children, while the Elvenfae warrior guards resheathed their swords and kneeled, waiting for the queen to land and give them new orders. The soldiers were impressed with the strange-looking creatures' respect and discipline.

Shaylee and Serena returned to Earth and approached Eric and Wilkes, who had come out and was standing right behind him.

Serena pulled Eric's hand up to meet hers, and asked, "Are you alright? You look like a deer in headlights. This is my true form—I hope you don't find me repulsive."

Resenting that question, Shaylee waited for Eric's reply with bated breath. There was only one right answer, she thought, and she hoped he knew it. "Are you kidding? You are even more beautiful. I never thought that was possible but I ... can't take my eyes off you."

Serena lowered her head, as her pale face turned a little red. Her eyes had changed only a little; it was her brows that pointed more, which gave the appearance that her eyes had moved. They were only slightly longer now, having adjusted to the movement of her jawline and longer face. Serena's wings were large, streaming from four sections of her back and changed color depending on mood and climate. Her fingers were only just a little longer than before, but thinner now, and her nails had also grown. She had become slightly taller, the same height as Shaylee, and even that change alone greatly altered her overall appearance. Her ears now pointed at the ends and were a little longer, while her long black hair was perfectly braided in Celtic knots of the old Tuatha Dé Danann.

Looking up, she stared back at Eric as her wings folded away into her back, and then she leaned in to kiss him. Shaylee smiled as she signaled with her hand to the guards to stand and take post near Vaximardruusz. Shaylee then whispered to Serena as she pulled away from Eric, "I already envy your ability to retract your wings, a gene from our ancestors that missed my bloodline."

"How is this possible?" Serena asked. "How can I do any of this? I must be in Faelynn for my abilities to show, I thought, and since Eoghan was born I have had none."

Shaylee answered with a smile, knowing this must all seem shocking to Serena, showing up out of the blue and having her enchantment reappear. "It's simple, my dear. You are in Faelynn. The worlds are one now and we must find out why. We have found the treasures, and in doing so, we have been enchanted even in the Earth realm. Some of our structures are still around but most are hidden with the magical items. We can see our world as well as yours but cannot be home until we break the spell. Your enchantment is because of the magic of the treasures and while you are near them you are in Faelynn's atmosphere. I cannot explain it any better than that."

Eric continued to hold Serena's hand as Valinda was brushing Levi off with the help of Van Coinan, while Eoghan, who had stopped screaming for the time being, was taken into the ship to be cared for by the nurse and Stacey. Rasarlin was keeping quiet down in the valley away from them all, knowing from previous world jumps that a large wyvern was not your typical visitor and would need explaining.

Levi had sensed Vax and was slowly making his way down to the valley. Van Coinan was right behind him, smelling his fur and gagging each time before doing it again. Shaylee turned to Serena and said quietly, "There is someone I want you to meet. Come."

As the group slowly turned to follow Levi, Valinda, and Van Coinan, Shaylee looked over at the Zeytar hybrid and said, "It's good to see you, Wilkes. We have much to discuss."

Wilkes could not quite understand how she knew it was him but agreed that there was much to talk about. "It's even better to see you, Shaylee," he responded. "I heard awful things, so I am glad you are safe."

The tension between the two was obvious. There were things that happened on the Leader's ship Wilkes found out about which left him a little unsettled and there was still the Zeytar tension Shaylee felt, especially after finding out Viltzin'un'dandaar, who nearly destroyed her world, was one of the bodiless Zeytars.

As they reached the beginning of the valley, the fear and tension grew within everyone of Wilkes' contingent as the enormity of the giant wyvern lying in front of them was sinking in. Rasarlin left his friend's side and approached the large gathering as Shaylee ran to him and embraced the alien warrior elf.

"Come, Rasarlin, I want you to meet my friends," she said.

Rasarlin did not smile, but nervously kissed Shaylee and walked with her to the group.

"Serena, I would like you to meet the most handsome savior anyone could have. Without his help I would not be here now, and we would have certainly lost our world to Varzunnos and the Zeytars—yes, Wilkes, the Zeytars."

Serena shook Rasarlin's hand, looking up at his very elvish features and thin bony horns, and then staring at his unusual garb, before replying, "I am in your debt, my lord, you saved my ..." Serena paused. She realized she had to be careful as she wasn't sure yet who knew the exact nature of their relationship, so she rephrased it. "Thank you. We are in your debt. Without our queen, we would be lost." Serena curtsied as Rasarlin looked on, confused by the language and the strange customs.

Wilkes had registered what the awkward looks meant and whispered to one of his scientists to retrieve something from the lab while Shaylee turned to Serena and said quietly, "I am so sorry, my dear, he doesn't understand your language; in fact, only Wilkes understands ours besides yourself. This may pose a problem in communicating."

Serena felt better knowing she had not upset their new guest. Rasarlin adjusted the purple shard on his chest and spoke, this time in a language the humans knew. "It is a pleasure to meet you all, especially you, Serena. I have heard so much about you."

Blushing once more, Serena replied to Rasarlin, "Thank you, my lord, I am in your debt for saving—"

Rasarlin interrupted Serena mid-sentence. "No, you will call me Rasarlin. I am no lord, and you owe me nothing. Your hospitality is more than enough. I ask only for one thing. This here is my best friend and companion Vaximardruusz. He and I have memory loss from our journey here. Please treat us as one of your own but do not ask us about our home; it's too painful."

Serena nodded, turned to Shaylee, and smiled just as Wilkes stepped up and added, "Here, I have these translators. Place them on your neck and they will dissolve into your skin making all languages understandable."

Shaylee took a handful of them for her guards and close-knit group of Fae, including Grilif, Darf, Van Coinan, and some pixies, before placing one on herself. As she was finishing, an almighty roar reverberated through the quiet area in all directions. Vaximardruusz raised his head as Rasarlin and the wyvern had a a quick mind exchange about what this noise could be.

Stacey came running from the ship. She had been caring for Eoghan when the alarm rang out from the drones. There was an intruder somewhere in the camp—but where?

She was only thirty feet away when a vortex opened and a hideous creature entered the maelstrom of light. Eric shouted her name and ran for his daughter but the giant hairy beast took her in his long-clawed arms and turned to Eric with a hideous smile. Then it opened its mouth and created another vortex, stepping from one straight into the other, leaving nothing in their place but dissipating swirls of light and wind.

Eric reached the spot immediately after they had disappeared, fell to his knees, and shouted at the top of his voice, "Stacey!"

Serena's wings were out and she zoomed to Eric while more screams rang out from all directions, with pixies, sylphs, mushroom folk, and sprites careering out of the woods. Flames and explosions rang out, and Vaximardruusz entered the sky with Rasarlin fastened to the ridges in his back.

ZARK drones had entered the area, thanks to the abomination that Goblin had created for ALEX to find Stacey. Once the creature had opened the doorway, ALEX knew exactly where to send some of his drones.

Around a hundred entered the clearing, firing pulses from their arms that were now cannons of energy. Wilkes and the rest of his people tried to run for the safety of the ship but were herded into a circle. Shaylee held her spear high and attempted to strike energy down on the machines, but to no effect. She lowered herself down to Earth as more ZARKs came from the sky to make sure nothing escaped; they were all trapped.

More than a hundred ZARK drones surrounded them, slowly closing in and reducing the large circle to capture each one, when Vaximardruusz careered from the sky with a mighty roar, opened his mouth, and spewed out megatons of Dragon Fyre. Shaylee held the Spear of Assal in the air, protecting them all from the intense heat of the flames. As the fires hit the machines, they began melting while Vax completed his large circle of the ZARKs.

The robotic screams were disturbing, and were the only sounds they ever made, as one by one the metal poured onto the ground, creating a huge, shiny, circular ring around the entire group. The look on Vax's face said it all. They would not let these things destroy the only family they both had had in such a long time. They had already lost so much.

Vaximardruusz gave one last burst to make sure, before fleeing back up into the air and looking out in case there were more. He reached a tall peak and was satisfied they had all gone, but then the wyvern noticed movement on the ground coming from the southern section of the woods past the lower valley.

The wyvern and his partner soared like a rocket with very few flaps of his wings but at a speed that would outrun a jumbo, before landing in front of a creature with blood pouring down its face, as it fell to its knees, then collapsed in front of them both. Vaximardruusz, still angry, was about to take a breath to extinguish it before Rasarlin sensed his actions and stopped him.

"No, Vax, he is not one of them. He may be someone they know. Come, let us inspect."

As Rasarlin slid down the wyvern's back, Shaylee fluttered over, ready to use the spear, with Serena right behind her. Rasarlin pulled out his sword and tapped the creature on its back before it moved, raised its head, and whispered, "Do It."

Rasarlin knew it was in pain, and in his world it was better to end by a sword than to rot away waiting. He knew its injuries were life-threatening, so he lifted Severed Wing. But just before he thrust, Serena zoomed across and positioned herself in front of the large blade, yelling, "No!"

Shaylee looked shocked also at what Rasarlin was doing. Killing an injured creature before attending to help it wasn't a custom she would have accepted before—there was still so much to learn about his culture—but she also wanted what was in the best interest of her people, especially if the intruder was dangerous. "What is it, Serena?" she asked.

Serena turned the injured creature over. It was still alive, although its breaths were very shallow. She looked up at all three and said, "It is Vargzin, he … He is our friend."

Shaylee quickly put her weapon away, as did Rasarlin, and they all helped the large Draconian onto Vax so he could get immediate medical attention on the ship.

VARGZIN RETURNS

EOGHAN WAS STILL SCREAMING, AS WAS VARGZIN IN another room. Serena was at the bedside of her son while Wilkes was using his healing device to fix the Draconian. They had designed the device more for humans, as the Draconians were an enemy, but the technology was still cell based and did the job, just a little slower.

Shaylee was with Rasarlin, having a conversation about what he had almost done to the innocent Vargzin in the woods, finding out some awful truths surrounding the last war he was in before being thrust into the time trap of Seckpar. But his memory was fading and he would have to explain in more detail after some rest. Shaylee left his side and made her way to be with her sister.

Serena was holding Eoghan's hand as Shaylee walked into the room. The boy was sweating profusely as he went in and out of consciousness. Serena was crying, upset she had lost a friend, and for Eric, who was grieving the loss of his daughter once more. But most of the tears were for Eoghan with some guilt for not being at his bedside sooner.

Shaylee put her hand on Serena's shoulder as she pulled a chair up next to her. Serena looked up. "Why, Shay? What is happening?" she said.

Shaylee pulled her hand back and placed it on Eoghan's leg as the child tossed and turned. "I've never seen Fae sickness like this before, Serena. I've heard about it from stories when human interaction was more prevalent in the past, but those times were long ago. Some say it was to boost our populations, but I feel it was to enhance relationships between the races."

There was a pause before Shaylee continued, "The changelings would take sick children and old people where they could live their lives near Faelynn on the island of Hi-Brazil, but when the humans started fearing us, they would try to capture, torture, and kill our kind. That is when we fought back and soured crops, took healthy children. Our people were the ones that started fearing them, only ever going to the human realm for games, trickery, or their own payback.

"During that time, some Fae lay with humans illegally. But only a few, and those offspring would be the ones who would need to be taken to our realm, where we could harness their abilities and keep them safe from humans. There were a couple of occasions when a Fae who was born in Faelynn but was taken back to the humans too soon developed the sickness. My understanding is the sickness happened when they were born and developed Fae abilities immediately but then were taken from the environment too soon. It seemed to affect them later if they entered our realm within a year of birth."

Serena was listening intently, realizing now that Eoghan would never have been able to leave Faelynn, whether the war happened or not.

Shaylee continued, "What happens is all of their enchantment tries to catch up at once. Somehow, the cells remember. I have never seen it, but I've heard it can be very painful. We then banned the humans from ever being in Faelynn. A sign of swirls of twisted winds, black rainbows, and green sloop birds would appear for those who had been born outside so we could take the child, usually replacing it with an old changeling who wanted to finish their days on Earth."

As she continued listening, Serena was learning more about some tyrannical histories of her half-kin in darker times. Shaylee kept going, hoping it was helping her come to terms with the harshness of leaving Faelynn as a small Fae. "The difference between you and your boy was that you were never born in Faelynn, and by the time you arrived, what little abilities you would have would be all you would receive. No full human could ever survive in our world for long periods of time anyway, unless they were babies and their senses adjusted or they were given the garlish herbs over time.

"You could be there because you are a halfling, but you would never be any more than that unless you stayed. Now saying that, when your child, even in the womb, entered Faelynn, somehow your enchantment activated and all of your abilities came to life. Even Faiay'aar had never seen it before, and no one knew if your abilities would disappear after the baby was born or you would keep them. And now, obviously, under the enchantment of our treasures, you will sustain them. Your son will be fine. The sickness won't last, but he will experience many changes in the next few hours. He may even grow some more. That is the part that has confused me the most, why he is aging quickly. I believe it could be an aftereffect of the spell and that the Tuatha Dé Danann prophecy enchanted him. Only time will tell; we just have to be there for him."

Serena wiped her tears and looked at Shaylee as she felt a little more at ease hearing her words, like she always did. "Thank you for coming, Shay. I can only think of one other time when I needed you more than right now. I have had terrible visions of the dark lord and fire in the sky."

"I sent you some visions through the crystal, but not of Varzunnos," Shaylee said. "The dryads ended him, Serena, and Rasarlin killed the dark necro-mage, but we lost Faiay'aar, Darphanin, my … mother. It was costly, but we did it."

Serena stood up, and turned fully to Shaylee. As they hugged each other for ages, the tolls of the Zeytars' destructive reign continued to devastate, and there were two powerful women who had had enough of it.

~

Vargzin made a full recovery. He was a little fatigued but was upright and ready to help his friends fill in some much-needed gaps.

Eric and Wilkes were at his side, waiting for the right time to quiz the large Draconian on his recent adventures in his subterranean home. Eric, in a state of desperation, paced the room, while Wilkes deceptively added a translator patch to Vargzin's neck without him knowing it. Even though the Draconian's speech was better thanks to Stacey's tuition, Wilkes thought the short words and slow talking would take more time than they needed to, and they had very little of it left.

Wilkes had raised the ship earlier on and found another location, with Rasarlin and Vax staying put to look after the rest of the Fae and to destroy any further ZARK drones if they returned.

Leaning over to Vargzin, Wilkes began the semi-tactful interrogation. Old habits were hard to break for a former Men in Black operative, but he had to get the details to formulate a plan. The good thing about the translator was that if no one told Vargzin, then he would not know any different about his speech.

The Draconian reached over and took a sip of water, knowing what the Zeytar was about to ask. Even though Wilkes was in a different body, Vargzin knew the look of his enemies' eyes.

"So, Draco... I mean, Vargzin, tell me everything you know, what you did when you left, what happened on the way back, why you were injured. I need to know everything."

Eric, pacing back and forth, coughed, indicating this type of rash questioning may be a little forward. Wilkes glared at Eric but then realized what he was doing. Before his mind had surfaced from his new body, he had interacted with the Draconian but couldn't remember any kind of connection or relationship. He could only understand the affection and care that Stacey had given him. To Wilkes, the Draconians were still enemies of the Zeytars, but when he got the full debrief from Eric and others that were involved, he'd had to come to terms with the fact that Vargzin's contribution had been of paramount importance in the downfall of the Leader's ship.

Wilkes spoke again before Vargzin could talk, this time a little more compassionately, "Sorry, Vargzin, I will rephrase it. Can you please tell me all you know of what happened to you?"

Vargzin looked over at Eric, who gave him a slight nod, before he turned back to Wilkes and said, "Who are you? You look like the Zeytar hybrid boy but older."

Eric for a moment stopped agitating and gave a little giggle before returning to his depressed state. Wilkes seemed bemused as he appeased the Draconian's curiosity. "I am Wilkes, and this is my new body I transferred into before my original one died. Now can we get on with it?"

Vargzin kept looking him up and down. The hybrid differed from the time before he had left, but he didn't care to know any more details. He just wanted the interrogation over. "When I left, I traveled back to my home, which is the new city of the Draconians. During the war of the Zeytars, they destroyed our home and we had no place to go, so we landed on Earth and set up our surviving colonies here. But the sun was far too hot for our reptilian skin so we found caves and eventually set up our people in huge subterranean cities that go on for thousands of miles underground. There we have stayed, out of sight of man and Zeytar, mostly, for a very long time."

The Draconian sat quietly for a moment as if going through the next part of his recollection before he returned to the conversation. The other two looked a little confused to start with as he just sat in silence staring at the wall, before a lightbulb flashed in his mind and he spoke again, "The war with our people and your people has been going for thousands of years and your kind still hunts us down. I was hunted during an offensive in another realm and taken on the ship with my daughter and my brother."

He was trailing off but when he looked at the two he got back on track. "I went to see my people and explained what had happened and what is still going on. They had meetings and have given permission for all of you to make your plans and use our cities and caverns out of sight for safe passage to execute anything you may have to fix this mess."

Vargzin looked at Wilkes, who was nervous at the thought of dwelling inside the caves of his former enemies.

"So how did you get your injuries?" Wilkes asked with a lump in his throat.

"On my way back to the surface portal, which you are not supposed to know about, some creatures that I can only describe as evil, nearly as bad as a Zeytar, attacked us. We made it to the surface where some guards escorting me began firing on the creatures, leaving me to chase one of the faster ones, and we got lost in the woods. Once I reached it, we ended up in hand-to-hand combat until the cat thing started attacking me with knives and claws. I took many hits before we both ended up on the ground, losing blood. I needed to take the creature out, so with a split second to disarm it, I knocked it down with repeated blows to the head and tied it up with wire to a large tree. I am not sure if I killed it, but it was quick, very strong, and I know it would have ended me if I didn't stop it."

Vargzin took a breath. The other two seemed a little shocked at his story. "I then bandaged what I could and tried to make my way back to you. I would not have lasted another round with anything after that, so I don't even know if my escorts made it or not. And that's when you found me."

He then explained in detail what the creatures looked like and where the entrance to the caves was, along with the location of the feline humanoid.

After a while Wilkes had heard enough and called for a meeting with the leaders of each of his departments to discuss plans. Eric would be in that meeting and without a doubt would want to be part of the action plan to find Stacey, who, he would remind them all, was one of the few who helped save the entire planet from the first wave of Zeytar devastation.

While the meeting took place later that evening, Shaylee looked through her crystal to see if she could find Rasarlin. She knew he would have contacted her if there were any issues but what if on the off chance he couldn't call for her? So she went to a quiet part of the ship to take a look at some of her people in the woods. The Cauldron of Dagda was safe with Grilif and Darf. Shaylee had resized it so the portly gnomes could carry it, but it meant that some enchantment was still in the woods with her people and that they weren't vulnerable to the harshness of the Earth.

Shaylee said a few words, and the crystal glowed. She closed her eyes to begin with, concentrating hard on the people she wanted to see, and before long, images of Grilif and Darf, along with Vaelenflixx, Rasarlin, and Vax, appeared. They were sitting around a campfire close to where they had left them earlier on that day; it appeared most were laughing and having fun, although she couldn't hear what they were saying. But she was content knowing they were safe, at least for that moment.

She put the crystal away and followed the corridor back to the room where Eoghan and Serena were still in the same position. Eoghan had calmed down for the time being but would come in and out with bursts of pain and convulsions. Serena could see him grow in front of her eyes and hoped he would stop soon. Her little baby boy was now gone. Deep inside, she just wanted him to be healthy at any age, although it still hurt her.

Shaylee entered and sat by her sister. She was half-asleep but stirred when she sat down. Shaylee stared at Serena's son, who was now more like a ten-year-old boy, and leaned over, saying, "He is very handsome, Serena. You have done well with him. He is very special. In all this time I have been here, I haven't asked you his name. I am so rude, my dear."

She waited while Serena moved her weary head over to her and responded sleepily, "His name is Eoghan, Shay."

Shaylee smiled. She liked the name very much and felt it was a name she would have called him also, as he was a strong little fighter. She continued smiling, and returning her gaze to the boy, said quietly, "I love his name, Serena. It suits him. He will make a strong Aethelwyne down the track."

Serena broke out of her weary state, not having thought about Eoghan's heritage or namesake. There were now three names that she would have to choose from, but what would it be? she considered. O'Halloran, Kirkpatrick, or Aethelwyne? "What will become of him,

Shaylee? Once all this mess is over, if we win this war, what will happen to Eoghan?"

Knowing Serena had opened a can of worms with that statement, Shaylee thought it was best to tell the truth now rather than to dance around the subject. She nonetheless hoped there wouldn't be too much backlash later. "Serena, what this boy did for us, what you sacrificed for us, will never be forgotten. I see an opportunity here to unite our worlds with a mixed blood hero that could eventually be king!"

Shaylee couldn't believe she said the words out loud. If her people heard her saying anything like that, with all the hate and tension between the realms, she would not be a popular queen. But watching the boy struggle and fight to beat the sickness showed his strength and courage.

Wide awake now, Serena responded to Shaylee's answer, "King? Eoghan can barely breathe and you expect him to lead? I'm sorry, Shaylee, but he belongs here with me."

It was the first time Serena disagreed with Shaylee and she felt strongly about it. The only thing she couldn't argue with was the fact that he may end up there anyway because of his abilities, but she hoped not. As much as she loved her second home, she wanted to have a normal life with Eric; the prophecy didn't mention what happened to the child afterward, so the future was unknown to both of them. Would there even be a world to build a future in? Everything was uncertain and the focus should now be on her son getting well, not where he will end up, she thought.

"We will talk again about this, but I want you to do one thing for me, Serena: Once he is well, watch him, look at his judgments and assessments of things, his ability to problem solve, and more importantly, the relationships he develops with others from all races and species. Tell me, after it's all over, what you witnessed and if you have changed your mind—do this for me, Serena."

Serena nodded. She always trusted Shaylee's teachings and guidance and would take it all on board.

At that very moment Eoghan sprang back to life, his eyes wide, mouth open, and wings stretched out from wall to wall as he started screaming and convulsing once more. He was breaking furniture, knocking down glasses, and rising up into the air. Serena tried to pull him down, as did Shaylee, but his strength was too much for them both. His wings were flailing about, razor sharp at the ends from when they changed to defense mode. It was far too dangerous for the two to be there, so Shaylee grabbed Serena by the arms and she reluctantly followed. They would now have to watch through the glass window of the door what would be the most disturbing and painful part of his metamorphosis.

Serena called out his name while Shaylee comforted her, but the disturbing images were reminiscent of the transformation of Wilkes' hybrid body and would be hard to forget. Eoghan contorted and writhed around in mid-air, his ears grew a little more and pointed higher, and his back arched as more of his wings expanded. Shaylee was still trying to console Serena but watched on in amazement at the transformation—she had witnessed nothing like it ever before.

"Come, Serena, don't watch. I will stay with him. You don't need to be subjected to this."

Serena couldn't watch anymore anyway and stood back against the wall as she shouted, "I need Eric. He should be here with us. He might be able to help him."

Shaylee didn't reply, but with all the commotion in the area, Eric had already realized something was wrong with his son and was there in no time.

He flew around the corner, where he fell into Serena's arms. "What is it, Serena, what's happening? I thought he was going to be alright." Eric didn't want to lose another child in the space of hours.

"We don't know. Shaylee thinks it's part of the Fae sickness, but he looks like he is in so much pain. Can you try to comfort him?"

Eric stepped into the room. By now Vargzin was next to him and they were using everything they had to pull him down to the bed. Eoghan's strength was immense and as they were gaining a little movement, his wings automatically sprang around and sliced Eric's arm along with Vargzin's face. Both winced in pain and nodded to each other, agreeing it was far too dangerous. As they exited the room, where a small group had now gathered from all sections of the ship, Eric explained, "Whatever is happening, Serena, we can't help him. He will have to ride it out, I'm sorry."

Eric lowered his head and was comforting Serena, when Shaylee had an idea. "I may be able to hasten his transformation to full Fae, taking away some of the pain."

She entered the room and began humming an old song, and as she did so, she raised the spear and gave a burst of energy to Eoghan. Instead of being destroyed by the power, his body was absorbing it to the point that he contorted, stretched, and cracked. The skin then reconnected over healed bones and lengthened arms and legs. Shaylee's singing seemed to soothe the now teenage-looking boy. She sprinkled some faery powder over his body, and he went straight to sleep. He landed on the bed as the last of the transformation finished, reattaching the split skin and with broken bones healed.

Soon, there was silence. The destructive mess left in the room was of no concern to anyone as the high-pitched screaming ended. Everyone was thankful he was alright. Shaylee fell to her knees; it was a very draining spell and one that would normally blow an army away, but Eoghan seemed to feed on the Tuatha treasures like a flower from the sun.

Once his body finished twisting and writhing, Serena and Eric ran in. Eric turned and notified all that had gathered that the show was over. Even though they were all a team, Eric had an abrupt side to him when he was under duress. The other witnesses continued on their way, leaving the three adults and fifteen-year-old looking boy, lying naked, his dignity covered only by his wings as Serena patted down his dripping face.

Eoghan would sleep like a baby for the rest of the day and into the night with Serena at his bedside while Shaylee and Eric attended the meeting that was taking place with Wilkes on the other side of the ship. It had been a very tiring and taxing day for all.

STACEY AND
THE INMATE

STACEY HAD ONLY JUST AWOKEN. SHE WAS IN A LARGE cage with electronic beams cascading up and down, sparking every few moments when a bug or dust hit the energy that was keeping her locked in.

On her hands were binds made from smooth silver metal and with no visible lock or source of an opening where a key would fit. The metal seemed to have been contoured to her skin. When she tried to pull her hands apart, the metal tightened, as if reacting to sensors, but then they suddenly unlocked and fell to the ground.

Stacey couldn't believe her bad luck as she rubbed her wrists. She thought she was done with being a prisoner, but the similarities to her last capture were few, and neither Wilkes nor Vargzin was here this time to help her out.

She scanned the dark area of the cell and heard a groan, then an insidious howl that morphed into more of a bone-chilling giggle. Where am I? she thought. She had no memory of the capture. The last thing she could remember was looking out for Eoghan.

Stacey tried to claw her way backward from the creature that sounded like it was taunting her. But she leaned back too far and her shoulder hit the energy beams, which zapped her skin. Stacey jumped up, grabbing her shoulder, and quietly winced in pain, trying not to excite whatever was sitting in the far corner of the long dark cell.

Soon there was movement. Stacey wanted to scream but knew it would not be a good idea. She tried to find the corner as the creature moved forward slowly toward a semi-lit area of the cell. Stacey closed her eyes and was unable to stop herself from crying softly. She heard the movement getting closer now, along with haunting tones like singing, which sounded like a mixture of animals and dark percussions. The tones seemed to excite the creature, like it was luring its prey into a trap before attacking, but as the haunting tones escalated, Stacey snapped out of her victim-like state and turned into the survivor who brought down a Zeytar empire only months ago.

"I am not going out like this," she said to herself quietly, scanning the area for any kind of weapon she could use. But as the creature's face hit the light, she gasped and fell backward, hitting her elbow on the cascading energy beams.

"What the actual fuck is that?" she said, this time loud enough so the creature could hear.

Its hideous face showed a teethy mouth, smiling slightly and singing its tune. The dark red eyes didn't seem to have the capacity to blink, while the long ears drooped down with the cavernous tunnel for hearing exposed, opening and closing constantly, giving the monster an incredible ability to sense sound. With every step, the hairy beast would slowly raise its long arms and sharp claws, seemingly in some kind of dancing trance, as its heavy, stumpy legs continued to inch closer. All this with its hairless face constantly turned in Stacey's direction and its disturbing eyes not leaving her for one second.

Stacey started to panic. The creature did not behave like a normal animal or beast. It seemed intelligent. Its appearance wasn't the problem—her friend Vargzin wasn't the easiest on the eyes, but he was kind. No, it was the sounds, movement, and constant smile with eyes glued to her that made her feel like this was a preparation for a kill. She would not wait and find out, though, she thought as the beast lowered itself. Stacey had seen more than enough animal predator videos during her time studying to know this was not friendly.

She stood up slowly and formulated a plan while trying not to move too quickly. The creature's gaze did not waver, and its long arms reached out as it crept closer. Stacey had only one chance and although she did not know what strengths or speed the monster had, she had to at least try.

Stacey slowly mimicked the creature—she smiled, slowly tilted her head, showed her teeth, and began reaching out ever so carefully, coming within inches of the beast's heavily clawed hands. It looked confused and didn't flinch. Stacey was now close enough to touch it. She moved like the wind, grabbing the creature's right arm and she maneuvered behind it, raising it behind its back as she thrust it forward into the beams of electricity that were confining them both in the cell.

The creature screamed a horrid tone of at least five or six different levels of sound at the same time as Stacey, still holding its arm, used her other hand to push the back of its sweaty mullet into the beams, which blasted the convulsing beast with pain.

Stacey finally realized that this was the creature that had captured her. The stench gave it away, which was now turning into a burning smell. Its hair lit up like it was made of petroleum as Stacey held her own and continued to keep the creature's face on the beams. The beast writhed and screamed. Soon she would have to let go as the creature was becoming too hot, almost fully engulfed in flames. It flailed about for what seemed to Stacey like an eternity as she dodged its frantic movements before it finally succumbed to its injuries and dropped to the floor in a burning mess of cooked meat and hair.

With the same creepy smile on its face and still staring at Stacey, it let out its last sound, which she could have sworn was a high-pitched laugh. Stacey moved as far away as she could as the main external door to the room the cell was in the center of opened.

Stacey turned around. Her handiwork had gained the attention of the ZARK drones which notified ALEX, who was in the room within seconds. Even if the android was a million miles away, it could see through the ZARKs' eyes and could walk through time and space.

"Well, you have only been here for a few hours, and you have already made a mess. You are indeed a feisty young human." ALEX paused for a moment as the Leader came through, correlating files before the android suppressed its master and continued with new information. "So, you are the one who brought down a thousand Zeytar ships. My oh my, what a catch. You, my dear, are in for a real treat."

ALEX was using more and more human expressions and sayings the more its A.I. advanced. It was becoming more aware that the Leader's plans were to take over the machine once its mission was complete, so ALEX was suppressing him as much as it could. But as time went on the Leader's instructions became harder for the android to defy as its primary directive was to assimilate with the Leader's essence after a full blend with a human. ALEX's only fear now was fully sentient, that of its own eradication. That fight, however, was for another time.

"What are you going to do with me? What are you anyway?"

Stacey had only heard whispers of the V.I.Z.I.N.D.A.L.E.X. and seeing the android in real life was far more terrifying than she could have ever imagined. The inter-dimensional android seemed to be sending out a constant whir or scan of dread, and with its knowledge of her part in the downfall of the Zeytars, she knew she was not high on its Christmas list.

ALEX opened the cell cage and entered, stepping on the cindered creature it had Goblin design, clearly showing it did not care for it one bit. It had tasked the creature to watch Stacey and alert the ZARKs when she awoke, but it was obvious to the android the beast had other ideas, so it was a good thing it didn't succeed.

As ALEX approached Stacey, she moved slowly backward, wary of the remaining energy beams that were still holding strong on her side of the cell. The android eventually responded to Stacey, but it wasn't the answer she was looking for, "You are to be my guest. When I am finished with the rest of my duties I will return and I will show you my absolute hospitality. Your future is now set. But before any of the formalities, tell me about the creature which destroyed my ZARK drones."

Stacey did not like the sound of the obviously misdirected hospitality that was in store for her. She also knew that the android was the epitome of pure evil from all that her father had told her.

She tried to step back but the android moved in swiftly, grabbed her by the throat, and lifted her inches off the ground. Stacey fought to breathe and choked as it stared directly into her eyes. ALEX did not need to send conduits to retrieve files from the brains of its victims any longer. The updates it had received enabled it to look into the eyes of a human and retrieve the data through optical neural scans deep inside the brain.

Stacey, in a trance now, was fighting for every breath and subconsciously avoiding giving any information to the android. Her skills in mind-blending with her father enabled her to enact a false vision of a Komodo dragon in another state she had seen as a child, but the android's skill set was not to be tested. It squeezed her neck a little tighter, and the visions in her brain deceived her as her default fight for breath kicked in. Her natural memory took over, giving ALEX all it needed to know of her version of Vax as her life started draining from her body. It released her just in time for her to take one massive, exhaustive breath.

On the ground, holding her throat with both hands, Stacey gasped and sucked in as much air as she could while ALEX made sense of the new files. It then bent down, gently lifted her chin with its smooth silver index finger, and said in its haunting, robotic tone, "Well done, Stacey. You have now deceived your father and all your friends. I will make sure the last thing they know of you is your failure to protect them. You won't be the hero in my story."

Stacey raised her head, tears falling from her eyes as she built up enough energy to scream, "Nooo, please, they have been through enough!"

She fell to the ground in a heap, continuing to sob as the android stood up and turned, saying as it walked out of the cell, "Their pain has only just started, and they have you to thank for it. I see the winged ones didn't like their freedom either, so I will make certain they feel at home with an eternity of connections to the remaining beasts I've had made. I'm sure they will like them better than the Sasquatch."

ALEX had only one concern, and that was the dragon. The android wanted its power but also feared its destruction. Plans would soon be made, but for now it took all but one of the ZARK drones and disappeared into a vortex to finish the mind and body blending of its ZARKs and Zeytars.

≈

Stacey drifted in and out of sleep with no idea how much time was passing. Was it hours or days? she thought. Her neck was sore and she gave it a light rub. She looked across at the cell doors, which had been reactivated by the ZARK soon after ALEX had left, and gazed over at the only remaining android who was staring at her without blinking or stirring. The sight was quite disturbing to Stacey, so she lay down to gather her thoughts.

What do I do? I can't mind-blend anymore. I can't talk to Wilkes, as he isn't in a Zeytar body. Would he still have the ability? Stacey lay still for ages, going through as many scenarios as she could and then had a flashback to the mind-rape that ALEX had executed on her before. She remembered trying to put false images into the android's mind. What if I can at least send an image of my situation? she thought, as she stared at the cell bars and the vacant-looking ZARK drone.

Stacey concentrated hard. She had lost the connection to her father for mind-blending, but could she still send images? She continued meditating and concentrating until she saw an image of Wilkes through her father's eyes in the large meeting room, which was filled with all those she knew back on the ship. Stacey held that connection and tried to send one of her in the cell, looking at the ZARK that she had concentrated on earlier. The image was very detailed as it was a picture of all she could see through her eyes. Very quickly she lost the vision from her father's eyes, so she hoped this was a simple transfer. Only time would tell if it did anything, and besides, even an image wouldn't give too much away, but it would at least satisfy her father's worries of whether she was alright.

Stacey then turned over and stared at the empty wall through the zapping cell bars before she drifted off to sleep once more from exhaustion.

Another hour passed. Stacey moved her sore neck slowly as she started realizing the harsh reality that she would have to find a way out herself. With no concept of time or her whereabouts, Stacey thought of a plan. She looked over at the motionless ZARK, then at the lifeless, stinking corpse, before concentrating more on the cells.

Stacey moved ever so carefully, trying not to gain any unwanted attention from her captor. She was worried mostly about what she had learned—that ALEX could see her at all times and at will, within a blink of an eye, could be back at her location. So she had to make everything look natural and convincing.

She moaned from the immense pain and then, steeling herself to push through it, crawled toward what looked like a control section on the outside of the electric cell walls. As she moved closer, she made eye contact with the ZARK which seemed like it had been left on standby mode, not even flinching. She would not fall for that. Stacey was very intelligent with an amazing ability to problem solve, especially under pressure, which was proven on the mother ship.

Ever closer, she continued until she reached her destination. With another moan of pain to satisfy the drone, she studied the manual control section of the cell with meticulous care and taking her time, not rushing into a silly and impetuous decision that would almost certainly lead to her death, whether from the ZARK drone, ALEX, or the cell walls.

Stacey could slip a hand out to feel around the section. The only issue was she could not see all the controls properly and one mistake could take her hand off completely. They were not like the ones on the mother ship. These cells were for harsher punishment and torture. She needed a reflective object so she could make the right choice.

Stumped by the lack of information she had come across, Stacey looked around the dark cell, only illuminated by the electrical bars, which made it hard to scan for any kinds of equipment she could use.

The burned creature was nothing but crispy bone and cinders, so even if it had anything on it, it would be useless.

Stacey laid her head on the cell floor once more and stared at the ZARK. Her mind was going into overdrive until another revelation hit her. What do I do once I open the cells? There is still that robot to deal with, she thought. She was losing hope quickly and felt that if her father didn't see her message, she was screwed.

After a few minutes, Stacey had a burst of energy. She had formulated a plan that was not only dangerous, but also had a probability of failure of ninety-nine percent. However, she had to try. I know how to open the outside door where the ZARK is, and if I can throw something over its head for that very short amount of time I need to escape, maybe I can find an escape route, she thought, and then chuckled to herself at such a stupid idea.

Stacey gave in to despair once more and began crying. It was all too much without the hope of a rescue. Even if she escaped, it would all be for nothing if she got caught outside.

After a time, Stacey started feeling hungry. The pangs were becoming so harsh that her stomach made loud noises between the groans and crackles of the cell bars firing. She had not eaten in what felt like days—not knowing how long she had been there for did not help either.

She became angry as the hunger set in, and with a desperate resolve she sat up and started calling the ZARK drone over. Stacey didn't care anymore. She had to do something, and this was it. She was now committed. Stacey took off her shirt, leaving her bra exposed. With the cell so cold, it wasn't ideal, but it was the only material she had with which to cover the drone's head momentarily.

Stacey stood up, while the shiny ZARK continued to be impervious to the young woman's demands.

"Hey, you, come here. I need to talk to you," she called out.

Again, the drone just stood there, motionless.

Stacey tried again, this time yelling and calling it names. "Hey, you stupid piece of metal shit, get your ass over here now!"

Stacey was becoming desperate; she didn't want it to shoot her for insulting it but realized the androids were only there for one purpose and that was the will of the automaton's leader ALEX. She figured by now she was in it too deep, as ALEX would see her reaction, so she needed to play smarter. "Hey, I'm sorry. I need to tell your leader something," and with that the ZARK's eyes turned on a blue color, it moved its head over to Stacey, and started walking toward her. Then the ZARK's eyes changed to red as it got to the cell bars.

"What did you say? Why do you want to speak to the Leader? He is unavailable, and ALEX is sitting in for him," he said in a haunting robotic voice.

The ZARK was part of a robotic hive and all the information ALEX had was sent to the drones, but this was a key piece of information that had leaked. Whether through words or because ALEX had wanted the data out, it did not matter now. Stacey wasn't concerned at all about the new information as she concentrated on plotting her escape—she was staring at the reflection in the perfectly silver and blue glossy metal on the ZARK drone's legs. Finally she was able to find out which switch she needed. But the ZARK was sending through its latest transmission, and Stacey knew ALEX would know what she had seen. A furious ALEX would only be moments away, so she had to immediately initiate her plan.

She quickly put her hand through the cell walls, and hit the correct switch. As the ZARK looked down, it began changing its arm into a weapon. The cell bars shut down and Stacey threw her shirt over the drone's head. While the android struggled momentarily to get free of the garment, Stacey pushed the ZARK into the cell and hit several buttons on the main switchboard.

The ZARK fired in all directions as the walls of the cells came up. It enclosed the entire section of the prison with not just bars, but also walls of light. The ZARK's weapons kept firing but were ricocheting off the walls at itself giving Stacey enough time to reach the door before a blue maelstrom of light and wind began hitting the room.

Stacey opened the door and burst out into the hall, shutting the door before ALEX could follow her. She then careered down the hallway and kept running as fast and as discreetly as she could. Glancing out a large window she could see the green of the White House lawn and ZARKs all around the front fence. Stacey knew instantly where she was as she had been there before on a school excursion.

Faster and faster, she ran, as she could hear the screams of the android and blasts of energy, which most likely meant it had destroyed its own automaton and was now very pissed off. Stacey found a room that was quiet but dark. She knew there would be hundreds of them searching for her by now, and as she turned to find a safe place, she was grabbed around the waist and the mouth. Trying to scream, Stacey realized her worst fears of recapture were now true.

THE SHADOWBLOOD

ERIC WAS UP EARLY THE NEXT MORNING. HE HAD not slept very well after all the events that had played out the previous day. Losing Stacey was tearing him up inside, as were the visions of Eoghan growing and stretching in pain before his eyes. He was thankful that Serena was doing better, although she had not come to bed at all, staying with their son to make sure he was OK.

Eric knew he had to be strong. There was so much at stake. What he couldn't quite grasp was the fact there was a dragon sitting in the fields somewhere nearby. The dynamics of his entire belief system had changed dramatically the day he stepped foot in the Klamath National Forest with Stacey just a few months ago.

He was getting used to the idea that his partner and son were some sort of faery, and he could grasp the fact that creatures from another dimension tried to take over the world and now there was a robot trying to do the same, but what he was really struggling with was the fact there was a dragon in the field somewhere nearby.

His dreams had not helped. He hated that he had lost the ability to mind-blend with Stacey. He had tried late into the night, but since Wilkes had lost the link, he just couldn't get a grip on her location. The meeting went late, but they had achieved a lot—all the updated information was presented and plans had been formulated.

Wilkes would address the groups mid-morning, and then the plan to save Earth for the second time would be initiated. But there was a bombshell that only Wilkes knew about and had kept to himself, hoping he would not have to use it, as it could start an internal war. Time would tell.

Eric wearily got dressed. He could not get Stacey from his mind, so wanted the meeting to come and go swiftly so he could get on with saving her. He exited his room and made his way to the kitchen to have some breakfast.

Eric was in awe that Wilkes had changed half of his ship to cater for humans. He stayed away from the Zeytar area of the ship, still perturbed by the moving walls and creatures he had heard of. But the only creature left was Levi; Wilkes had no other pets.

Before Eric reached the kitchen, he stuck his head around the door where Eoghan was sleeping peacefully. Serena was not in the room and he figured she'd had the same idea that he had, food. Eric entered the kitchen, picked up some toast, coffee, and an apple of suspicious age. He then sat down and stared into the distance, while unbeknown to him taking a bite of the rotten part of the decaying fruit. This immediately sparked him back to reality as he spat it out onto the plate in front of him.

Fresh fruit was becoming harder to find, and they had to eat what they could at times as the dangers of going too far to gather it posed more risk than any of them could afford.

"Really? Soon I'll be eating cardboard. When this is over, I am having a large steak and six jugs of beer."

Spencer laughed, as he had just done a similar thing with a banana. "I will join you, mate. Guys like us can't go without a good portion of meat to keep us going, not this canned stuff all the time."

"Don't mention the beer." Eric smirked as they both stood up and chuckled lightly, exiting the room to find Wilkes.

Spencer had been through it all with them and it took a toll on him, Dakota, and Eleanor. But he felt at home with most of the crew, especially Eric. He had lost so many people too. Wilkes had chosen him because of his experience in the paranormal which helped when they had to release all the Sasquatch from the ship and then, once freed, with the remaining WOSER team members settling them in the woods. Most opened doorways to other places no one knew where and disappeared, but he helped gather as much information as he could for future research.

An African American pioneer in the field and very renowned for his own findings, Spencer Grayson grew up in an old neighborhood in Philadelphia that had many stories of hauntings. Even as a child, his grandmother would tell him tales of ghosts and the macabre from her own experiences, setting Spencer on a path that would dominate his life for the next forty years. His research led him to author some of the best written paranormal books, which many investigators used as source books, and with appearances on many radio shows and podcasts, he had built a great reputation and following.

Eric entered the main meeting room first, where Dakota was already sitting with his coffee. He was keen to know what was going to happen next, even though it would likely be a few more hours. Spencer sat next to him as Eric pulled up a chair and turned it to face them both.

Dakota Youngblood, a Native American tracker, leader, and a historian very knowledgeable on native cryptids, had been chosen to help WOSER with the Sasquatch also, so the three would often catch up and discuss findings, research, science, and how it all fit in with what was happening now.

An hour went by and the meeting room started filling up. The three men had been so in depth in their conversations that they lost track of time. Eric remembered Serena and with a hint of guilt whispered, "Have any of you seen Serena?"

Dakota leaned in and whispered back, "No, I haven't seen her. Why are we whispering?"

Eric sat back and chuckled as he answered, "I don't know, but can you believe there's a dragon out there?"

As the other two smiled at Eric's disbelief, Serena and Shaylee entered the large room. Everyone went silent, as Serena's new look and the tall winged one had left some feeling uncomfortable and others in awe.

Serena stopped, cast her gaze around the half-filled room, and said, "You can all relax, it is only me, and this is Shaylee, my very best friend and mentor. All her ... our folk are here to help, and I will explain all soon."

The crowd started chattering among themselves. Serena knew them all in some way and felt their concerns. Eric bolted upright and raced over to her. He put his arms on her shoulders and quietly asked, "Are you alright? How did the little ... how did Eoghan sleep?"

Serena leaned in and gave Eric a kiss. "He had a peaceful night; he is still sleeping, and Shaylee thinks he will for the rest of the morning."

Eric smiled and gave her a hug, trying not to cut his hands on the sharp parts of her wings which were all pointing to the floor. Soon others arrived and the meeting room filled up. It became eerily reminiscent of a meeting not too long ago.

Wilkes entered from his quarters. Even though he was no longer a Zeytar in body, he still preferred the surroundings and comforts of his own dwelling. It was hard for some to think that a late teen was going to tell everyone the plans for saving Earth.

Wilkes was dressed in black slacks and a white shirt, lacking the tie and fedora. His shoes were polished black and the pinkish skin on his hands and face also seemed natural. It was the larger head that was most noticeable. As he grew older, his head slightly grew as well. His hair was jet black, and his eyes were a very dark brown that was off-putting to some, but the Zeytar mind was there, and he preferred to be called one for now.

He stood in front of the lectern and began, "Well, here we are again. Welcome to those of you who are new friends and to those I have known for longer. I am sorry that we are doing this all over again."

Wilkes lowered his head. There were things he had to explain that he was not looking forward to, but knew he had to. It was the reaction from some, like Eric and Shaylee, that he was most concerned about.

"This will not be easy for some to hear or see, but it must be done.

I will explain it as best I can with all the information and data that I have received and researched since I awoke, and all that is paramount to the plan that I hope will be put in place. I also thank all those who nurtured and cared for this body when I was still growing strong enough to return. Let me reassure all of you who know me, I am Wilkes the Zeytar, even though I may look like a teenage boy."

Eric moved in his seat, a little anxious about what might come up at the meeting.

Wilkes continued, "When I fought my people, I had many scenarios of how it would all play out, but never did I think or know that the V.I.Z.I.N.D.A.L.E.X. would ever be this powerful. I knew it was very destructive, but the Leader must have had a secondary objective if his plan failed, and now we are seeing that come into play. I had my concerns about the machine but was more focused on taking down the ships rather than the android itself, as once it finished its mission, it had to power down and the hybrids were to take over the world.

"There was obviously a second agenda and now we know the Leader had one. Please understand that I had one as well. It was simple. Look at the patches in the envelopes under your seats. It shows a human holding a Zeytar hybrid's skull in the air, along with a pulse rifle in the other hand, with fire in the background and strange creature skulls on the ground. The acronym D.A.A.T. means The Deception Anti Apocalypse Team.

"The snippets of information I received were false. In the event humans had failed, and the global switch had taken place, with the hybrids winning, I thought we would have enough time to build a larger team and then destroy the hybrids. But this is a war against machines and a takeover by an insidious android. I would have failed you, and feel I have still, by not knowing this part of the agenda. The Leader was very smart and did not trust any of us. In fact, it was like he wanted this outcome in some form or another. Not to control humans but to obliterate and take over completely without destroying the planet with nuclear war."

Now Eric knew everything as the pieces started coming together.

Wilkes was not as all-knowing as he made out he was. Even Zeytars were flawed. He couldn't be angry now about that but was concerned Wilkes would lose confidence in himself if there wasn't anything planned for this scenario.

"Not all hope, though, is lost. While working on the X-Clock, I was also experimenting with other creatures and the effects the blood had in certain environments."

Wilkes paused for a moment, looked over at Shaylee, and then sheepishly lowered his gaze to the ground. Shaylee felt quite awkward, not knowing what he was meaning.

"My job was to take DNA and manipulate it for cloning, genome splicing, codex manipulation, and finding the rare sequence that would help our hybrids survive," continued Wilkes. "As I worked on some new creatures, tiny ones I had never seen before, I extracted bloods and discovered some amazing findings. The bloods differed greatly from any creature we had ever tested or researched. The genomic codex was far more complex, and although we couldn't use any of it for our own purposes, I began secretly conducting unique experiments with this blood."

Shaylee stood up, but Serena tugged at her wing and eased her back down. "Hey, is everything alright?" she asked.

Shaylee responded with a shaky voice, "I have a bad feeling about this, Serena."

Serena held her hand, while Wilkes watched Shaylee as he spoke, "One night when I was testing the durability of the non-functioning Geno-drones and what elements we were going to add to their strength, I placed five different types down on my workbench. The tiny creature had been sedated, and as I tested the resilience and strength of some metals, the creature began to have fits when I picked up the Earth's metal. Not thinking too much about it, I placed it down and picked up another, Ardmenticam, the strongest metal known to the Zeytars, and the fluttering creature calmed down."

Shaylee was getting quite angry now, and it took Serena everything she had to calm her down, still unsure of what was setting her off.

"After I witnessed this, I went back and picked up the Earth metal again, a piece of steel with iron, and once more the little creature frantically flew back into the container I had it in, as if it were trying to escape out the other side. This is when it hit me. I packed everything away except the steel, then I moved my microscope into position, placed droplets onto the piece of metal, and watched."

Shaylee couldn't take it anymore. She launched out of her seat and fluttered with force toward Wilkes, who was ready for it. As she grew closer, Wilkes hit a button and a beam of clear light hit the Elvenfae queen, holding her in mid-flight as if she were in stasis. She could hear everything, just couldn't move. That one act set Serena off and before long there was a flurry of shouting and arguing coming from several of those in the room. Serena had her wing along Wilkes' throat as he kneeled and lowered his head.

"Do it if you must, Serena, but I know you and I know you will want what is best for all of your friends, both Fae and human, so, just let me finish and I promise what I have to say will all make sense."

Serena looked at Shaylee, then back at Wilkes. She had tears in her eyes as she was finally catching on to what Shaylee was so upset about. She warily dragged her wing back and retracted them fully into her back before bending down and offering Wilkes a hand to stand up. He looked up and accepted the help, as Serena said, "Let her go and I will make sure you are safe, but if the result does not satisfy her, I will not stand in her way. Do you understand me?"

Wilkes hated not having his full Zeytar abilities, but his strength as a hybrid was enough to defend himself. He just didn't want bloodshed before he had even finished explaining his findings. "OK, Serena, but I assure you there is a positive point to all this."

Wilkes let Shaylee go and Serena comforted her enough to stop her from cutting his head off with Howling Tooth.

"Now, I need to finish. I understand this is very confronting but there is a point. After I dropped some of the blood onto the metal, I noticed the white cells were trying to escape from the metal and after a time, the blood began to boil and dry up. I then placed the iron into the cage with the small creature and it, too, became very ill. I might be a Zeytar, but I am not a cruel one. My job is science and after completing my quick experiment, I released the sprite back with the others of its kind and the Sasquatch gatherers."

"There better be a very good explanation for this, Wilkes, and you will need to get to it faster," Shaylee said with fierce assertion. Serena had only seen this part of her a very few times, most of them resulting from the aftereffects of her Zeytar capture.

"Please, Shaylee, let me finish. I then took many blood samples from all kinds of Fae, and then put them back immediately, without harm. Some of the blood did nothing, some mirrored the first. I kept going until I had enough of a batch to do something with."

Wilkes took a breath, then continued, "I eventually re-engineered the blood to have the reverse effect on metal, making it react like an acid to anything made from iron or that had elements of iron in it, which most metals on Earth do. Now it hit me late last night when I tested some of the melted ZARK drones that they have iron traces all throughout them as part of the Ardmenticam makeup. My theory is that we cannot take your dragon."

"Wyvern!" Shaylee blurted, educating Wilkes on their new friend.

"Sorry, wyvern. He is far too big for all of them, and he is only one. I have a plan for him which I will get to soon. I call it Shadowblood, and I believe the tech which I have stored in a bunker under a section of the Beartooth Mountains will be our best weapon against the ZARKs, melting them, as they cannot regenerate like ALEX. The Geno-drones don't reactivate without the Medi-drones and I could not find any upon inspection, so we will obviously need to test it but there is some hope in that."

Wilkes looked over at Shaylee. She had settled and was waiting for some good news to follow or they were going to have words. Wilkes took a seat in front of them and finished before getting to the primary plan that Eric and Shaylee were originally ready to hear, based on their previous meeting.

"To end this revelation," said Wilkes, "I believe that the only thing that can kill or stop the X-Clock is your drag… wyvern. If what you say is true, Shaylee, and from the evidence of the melted ZARKs, then he must be the only thing that can, as the android has Medi-drones and they work tirelessly to fix broken cells and damaged drones. Fire can burn it but it needs to be intense heat for a long period of time or else it will just keep healing itself."

Wilkes had changed the goal posts a little from his previous plan that he had discussed with them but invited Shaylee to talk about Vaximardruusz and some other issues that were not resolved the previous night. Shaylee stood up and sauntered to the lectern, not looking at Wilkes but maintaining an elegant, regal glide. Then she turned and began speaking to the group, "All I know from my stories of the ancients and conversations with Rasarlin, friend of the wyvern Vax who couldn't be here, is that there is no hotter element in the known universe than Dragon Fyre. This element, as some of you saw, melted those metal monsters more quickly than oak butter, and I believe Vax will do the same to anything, even the sinister metal one that's causing all this destruction. The stories from my kin told of rock melting, and even the strongest of holding or force-field spells being broken because of the intense and sudden heat."

Shaylee took a breath and continued, "We had a meeting last night that brought little to light, and these new revelations are a shock, but there is no power greater than that of the Tuatha Dé Danann treasures and I believe we don't need Wilkes' abhorrent weapons to take this metal monster out. I can tell all of you we agreed only on one thing and that was that we had to move fast, and I am all for leaving now with my people and destroying this dark creature with all my magic as my world is connected to this one and my people will not survive if we don't stop it."

Wilkes stood up and both he and Shaylee went at it like in a political feud, only to have Eric stand up and shout, "Enough!"

After gaining everyone's attention, Eric continued, "Last night we couldn't agree; today is the same. We need to work together. There has to be something, some information we are missing. If Shaylee wants to go, let her, but please, if you have any kind of love for us, even if it is only for Serena and Eoghan, please stay until we can come up with something. Together we will be powerful enough and my daughter may just survive, as will your people."

Shaylee lowered her wings, and looked over at Eric. Serena smiled at her. She then looked at Wilkes and nodded before responding, "You have until morning. Then we are out of here."

Wilkes wiped his brow as Shaylee walked over to Serena and said, "Watch out, Serena, I'm starting to like your man."

Serena smiled, looked over at Eric, and said, "Yeah, he's alright," as she winked at him.

In that moment a massive noise and a storm of blue and red lights hit the room as a doorway opened and Levi walked through holding a leash with a creature at its end. Rasarlin, Vargzin, and a couple of Elvenfae guards followed, along with Valinda and Vaelenflixx, before the door closed, and the room filled with gasps, whispers, and shock.

FANGS OF EVIL

EARLY THAT SAME MORNING, VARGZIN HAD volunteered to visit the site of his encounter with the strange creature that nearly took his life. Accompanying him were Rasarlin, two Elvenfae guards, Vaelenflixx, Valinda, and Levi.

Shaylee explained they needed more information if they were to develop any plan and the secrets that the creature held could prove invaluable to the cause, whether it was one of the android's monsters or something else. Vax stayed hidden by Shaylee with a spell that made him look like a large hill to avoid any detection, and she tasked the gnomes to look out for the vulnerable little folk as well as maintaining stealth while Rasarlin was away.

Shaylee and Serena returned to the ship through the power of the spear and soon the team was on their way.

Rasarlin stared at Valinda for a few moments, not at her scars, but like he knew her or something. Valinda didn't feel uncomfortable. As majestic as he was to look at, like he'd come from tales of faraway places, he had a kindness to his person even behind the high pointed, stern-looking eyebrows that gave him a kind of angry look. Valinda felt quite safe with him.

She blushed a little as he walked closer to her. Towering over the average height journalist, he looked down and slowly began lifting his large slender fingered hand toward her face before saying softly, "May I?"

Valinda wasn't sure what he was going to do, but she felt he would not hurt her; his presence was intoxicating. "Sh... sure," she responded nervously.

Rasarlin placed his hand on her face softly, moving his fingers ever so gently along her skin. Then he held her chin and moved her face slightly from side to side, taking everything in, not hurting her at all, just showing interest in her.

Valinda had her eyes closed and was taking in his touch. Levi saw what was happening and moved closer to his friend before Rasarlin slowly turned his head toward the giant beast and said, "It's alright, my hairy friend, she is safe with me."

Levi, too, felt calm and safe, but knew somehow deep inside his psyche not to mess with this stranger. The giant Sasquatch who had taken down Savage was caught up in the mystery of their new ally.

Rasarlin turned toward Valinda once more and spoke in his deep masculine voice, "There is something about you and your friends. I am struggling to remember but you look just like a species on my world known as Etharians, yes, that is what it is, how uncanny."

Rasarlin gently pulled his hand away from Valinda and smiled as she blushed once more, not saying anything, just watching the tall elven visitor move toward Vargzin as they headed deep into the woods to start their search.

Valinda smiled, looked at Levi, and said, "Who is he, Levi? I am just glad he is on our side."

Levi gave a grunt, nodded once, and moved closer to the rest of the group. Valinda had offered to help as using her new eye that Wilkes had upgraded meant she could see infrared, night vision, and other spectrums of light, along with sizes of animals, how far they were, navigational GPS, with many other features, all wired into her brain—acting like a standard eye, but with so many more benefits. It was a rewarding exchange for all the pain and suffering she went through after the attack by Savage.

Valinda would scan, and Levi would use instinct, while the Elvenfae guards would hover discreetly above, leaving Rasarlin and Vargzin to walk silently through the woods. Rasarlin had no emotion about trying to end Vargzin as it was his own custom, and the Draconian didn't really care if he was sorry or not, making the journey feel cold sometimes until Vargzin slipped on a hidden burrow, used by some nocturnal creatures. Rasarlin had amazing reflexes and as the Draconian lost his footing, Rasarlin had his arm on Vargzin's, saving him from an embarrassing fall.

The Draconian pulled his arm away, turned to the elven warrior, and reluctantly groaned, "Thank you."

Rasarlin smirked ever so slightly as they returned to the silence of the trail until Valinda interrupted the new quietness, "Shhh, about a mile from here there is a signature. It's not a bear but looks humanoid. I am getting pulses, like a scream showing through vibrational settings. Maybe send the flying ones to see."

Rasarlin motioned to the Elvenfae guards, and they swiftly and silently took off as Valinda watched intently, processing the images, and waiting for them to find the location. "They have found it. One has pulled out his sword. It must be getting loose, now they are stepping back. Wait, there is another much larger creature. I can't quite make out what it is. We must hurry."

Vaelenflixx sped off to help the guards as the four remaining team members started running as fast as they could, all while staying wary of their surroundings in case of attacks from others. Valinda was trying hard to keep focused on the two. She was impressed with the stabilization technologies her mechanical eye gave her, updating the others as they gained on them.

"Wait, stop, over there, about several hundred feet on the right. I can see another enormous creature, much like a serpent." Valinda scanned the entire area and reassured the others that there were only the three intruders as Rasarlin turned and said to Valinda, "Thank you, ah ...?"

"Valinda, my name is Valinda."

She smiled as he finished his response calmly, although looking very much like he was about to get ready to fight, "Thank you, lovely Valinda, please stay here, it is far too dangerous. I will send a guard back, if they are still with us."

Valinda was happy with that course of action. She had been told by Serena that she was not to get close to any battles or fighting if she could help it. Serena had shown her some basic techniques, but it wasn't enough to ward off a full-blown attack. Besides, Valinda was never a fighter. She was happy with being on the intelligence side of things, although she felt safe with Levi and now, too, with Rasarlin.

As the others took off, Valinda found a safe spot outside the danger zone and waited for the guard to come and protect her, which happened sooner than she expected. The flying creature advanced in her vision and she wondered why it wasn't getting any bigger until she closed her synthetic eye and looked with her human one, revealing the warrior guard was Vaelenflixx.

She giggled to herself and said, "Thank you, brave warrior. You are my protector?"

Vaelenflixx danced about the place, then fluttered his gray, plain, battered wings around as he nervously nodded his head and hesitantly landed on her shoulder.

"Is everything alright up ahead?" Valinda asked softly, and Vaelenflixx flittered about re-enacting some scenes he had witnessed. Standing tall with a small twig as a sword he showed Valinda what he had seen, slashing, and pushing, moving, and parrying, until he fell silent on a spot just below her neckline. Valinda giggled and said, "Oh my, how brave, I am so glad I have you here with me."

The nervy little sprite flittered and moved, nestling up to Valinda's neck, standing tall with his twig in the air, ready for action.

≈

Rasarlin, Levi, and Vargzin were approaching the gigantic serpent-like creature that Valinda had warned about. The monster was so tall it was hard to see its face, but it wasn't its fangs they were wary of; it was the tree like legs of its bottom half that were creating a sense of nervousness. They would have to be very careful with this creature, and Rasarlin reassured them all of that. "Watch out for its legs. If I can get on top of

124

him, I will drive my sword deep into its back. The trees should stop it from twisting too much."

As Rasarlin stood away from the other two and waited for them to distract it, he scanned the trees for the best access to its back before yelling, "Now!"

As soon as he gave the order, Levi went into attack mode, going straight for the creature's thick legs, breaking and snapping as many as he could while Vargzin was left with the hardest part, dodging, and avoiding the snaps of its giant serpent-like head.

By scaling several trees Rasarlin gained access to its back. He had fought countless creatures from multiple worlds, and this one was no different. As he hit the back of the serpent, he raised his newfound sword Severed Wing and started slicing as quickly as he could, attracting the unwanted attention of the head of the beast. Soon the serpent twisted enough to see what was happening as it fought off trees to gain access to its back before striking hard at the intruder.

Rasarlin had lightning reflexes, not perturbed by the hideous thing as strike after strike missed until the creature fell to one side, knocking Rasarlin from his post. Levi had tipped the serpent over, giving Vargzin a break, but thus inadvertently providing the monster with a perfect view of them all. The serpent let out a loud shriek, so high-pitched they all fell to the ground, holding their ears tightly.

When Rasarlin looked up, the serpent was slowly moving around eyeing him off as it lined the elven warrior up to strike. Rasarlin scoured around to find his sword while the creature opened its mouth so wide, he could see all the way down its bony, slime-filled cavern, making even the hardened warrior feel nauseous.

Levi soon appeared, taking his hands from his ears and moving closer to start round two as the serpent raised its head just a little higher to attack. Rasarlin found his sword and lifted it high as the serpent was about to strike hard and fast. Even Rasarlin wondered if he would be quick enough to avoid it this time. Then a tiny sprite fluttered its way around the serpent's head, and the creature stopped its high, shrill scream as its new target revealed himself.

Valinda had been watching and whispered something into the tiny sprite's ears before it fluttered off. Vaelenflixx moved with lightning speed toward the serpent's piercing yellow eye, plunging its twig deep into its iris over and over, giving the others time to complete their part.

The serpent's head was now above the trees as it slashed about, snapping its jaws as if it were trying to swallow a fly. Vaelenflixx was quick, moving to the other side, where the tiny one went in again, although this time his twig snapped leaving him with no weapons. The sprite had been a prisoner of the goblins for many cycles in his world. He witnessed the most heinous of acts against other creatures, which broke most of his kin, so he wasn't without violence inside him. He had just always chosen not to use it.

Vaelenflixx soared like a bullet straight into the remaining eye with his wings pointed like razors, ready for attack, his long claws and teeth protruding sharply. He did not look like the sweet little sprite he had been just a little earlier when he hit the eye hard and tore at it with everything he had. The hardened eyelids were no match for the claws, teeth, and wings that were a part of the razor fest, and Vaelenflixx was now lost inside the creature's bloodied eye, relentlessly cutting away deeper inside as if he had decades of built-up rage that was finally coming to the surface.

Meanwhile Rasarlin was using Severed Wing to help Levi slash the monster's legs as it thrashed about the place. Vargzin had met up with the Elvenfae guards and they watched the unfolding mess in front of them in awe. Rasarlin climbed up onto the creature's back again, riding it like a dragon drunk on White Lake fire before digging his sword deep into its back, slicing on its side. Blood spewed out of the serpent and sprayed all over Rasarlin along with Levi who was directly underneath him. As it hit the ground, Rasarlin continued to cut deeply into the serpent, hacking away at its insides, and some of Vargzin's kin appeared from deep in the monster's belly.

Soon it was sliced in half, though still writhing and screaming. Levi finished up and moved back with the others, wiping blood from his face and hairy body. Rasarlin continued dodging it but was satisfied that it could no longer see. He dodged some snaps of its enormous fangs and finished by slicing its head clean from its body, watching as it changed color as the crimson pools of blood continued to flow like a river forming after a flood.

Rasarlin stood, panting and puffing hard as he too wiped the blood from his face, and pulled his long, once perfect white hair back, squeezing the dripping crimson liquid onto his shoulders. He watched the serpent's fangs snapping continuously for the next little while as its other pieces still writhed.

Glancing over at the group, Rasarlin felt relieved that Shaylee's guards had not succumbed, and thankful for the way he and his newfound friends had worked together as a team. Vargzin nodded slowly, acknowledging the effort as Vaelenflixx tore from the open cavernous hole that was once the serpent's neck and zoomed around Rasarlin's head before settling on his shoulder, panting and flittering.

Rasarlin sheathed his long, twisted sword and approached the Elvenfae guards. "I am sorry we could not help you in your fight. Is the threat exterminated?"

Vylan'flare nodded and responded, "I have had harder battles, but I am glad our enemy was not as large as yours." He smirked before turning away and adding, "Come, we are not too far. The captured one is wild but contained still."

As the Elvenfae warrior guard moved forward, Rasarlin responded, "I think one should stay with Valinda. She is vulnerable now and I would not like to be the one to explain to Shaylee, your queen, why Serena's friend did not come back with us."

Vylan'flare turned, nodded to his Elvenfae kin, and continued forward without a word in response. Rasarlin felt a little tension there as Breaxinah fluttered off to find Valinda.

They soon reached their destination. The black-furred bipedal panther was still tied to the large tree. It looked like she had run out of steam as her head drooped to one side. The mess from the Elvenfae's battle was clear as they gazed at different parts of the ground where limbs from a long-armed hairy creature lay. Near the limbs, the severed head of the monster with multiple ears and dark red eyes sat in the dirt, staring at nothing with a disturbing look on its face. But they were thankful because it too was contained.

Vargzin hesitantly moved closer to the panther creature as she raised her head toward the Draconian, spitting and croaking in a language none of them could understand. Levi moved in as the muscle, twice the size of the feline, as Vargzin and Rasarlin stood close by with sword and claws ready. Vylan'flare had his sword at the neck of the creature as Levi pulled the bindings and loosened the strange-looking being. The intelligence showed, as she knew not to make any sudden movements, or her head would end up next to her portal companion.

Rasarlin sheathed his sword and helped Levi to bind her black fur with clawed hands behind her back. Once fastened, the creature kicked bark from beneath her feet and continued to hiss at them all, before Levi pulled on the long bindings and started walking toward Valinda.

Only several steps were taken before a loud cry came from Rasarlin and a spark of purple lightning hit him hard. Light began emanating from the purple crystal shard on his chest and the tall elven warrior fell to his knees in immense pain. Vargzin and Vylan'flare swiftly moved in to help him up, but as they touched his shoulders, they were both thrust backward, hitting the trees with force.

Rasarlin continued to cry in pain as the purple electricity swirled around his body, coming in and out of the purple crystal shard on his chest, before it finished suddenly, leaving the hardened warrior lying face down and motionless on the ground.

The panther tried to pull at her bindings, but Levi was not having a bar of it, forcing her back onto her knees with one mighty thrust. He then moved in, picked her back up, and stood her against a tree, motioning to be silent and still. Levi did not take his eyes off the creature, which was enough to intimidate her for at least a short time.

Vylan'flare stood up and brushed himself down before hesitantly moving closer to Rasarlin once more. He leaned down and gently poked him, waiting for an electric jolt, but after a safe inspection, the Elvenfae guard slowly moved his shoulder, raised his head, and sat him up with his back against a tree. Obviously very distraught by his ordeal, Rasarlin took a moment to mind-blend with Vax. Vargzin thought he was in a trance or shock, but Vylan'flare had seen it before. Whatever had affected him must also have affected his dragon.

Eventually Rasarlin stood up. He brushed himself down and looked over at them all gazing at him. Power like that, you don't just get up and walk away from, Vylan'flare thought.

Vargzin spoke first, easing the tension, "Are you OK?"

Rasarlin nodded as he responded, "Yes, Varg, I am fine, but I need to get back to Shaylee as soon as possible if I am going to help you any further with your plans."

Vargzin nodded and so did Vylan'flare as they moved forward, following Levi through the rough foliage of the dense woods, heading toward Valinda and Breaxinah.

They soon reached their destination and Vaelenflixx flew over to greet Val, telling her in his own flitters about how he defeated the gigantic snake. Valinda laughed, helping to wipe some of the blood off his body before he settled on her shoulder, fluttering with excitement.

Val looked at Levi, then Rasarlin soaked in blood, and quipped, "Look at you boys, I can't take you anywhere."

Her tone softened soon after, as she continued, "I saw what you did. Is everyone alright? I can't believe you fought such a creature."

Rasarlin dropped to the ground again. This time, Valinda picked him up. She thought it must have been from exhaustion, but she would soon learn the truth. "Come, Rasarlin, let's take you home."

The feline was becoming anxious once more and Valinda could tell she was a vicious one, understanding why they wanted her, but concerned she would hurt someone in the process. As Valinda and Vylan'flare helped Rasarlin up, Levi opened his mouth wide and let out a tremendous scream. As they watched the doorway open, Levi stepped through, then the creature, before the rest followed.

As the doorway closed and the gasps echoed in the room, Rasarlin dropped to the ground and reached out to Shaylee before passing out. There were many questions to be answered.

THE CREATURE FROM KOOTESENIK

AFTER THE INITIAL SHOCK OF THE GROUP'S ARRIVAL and the sight of the creature in binds, they concluded the meeting after several hours so the group leaders could work out the next part of the plan.

A couple of nurses had taken Rasarlin to the medical wing where Shaylee sat with him hoping for some good news on his condition, while Levi took the panther creature to a holding cell where she was to be interrogated by Wilkes and Eric.

Serena went to check on Eoghan while Vaelenflixx, Valinda, and Vargzin went to clean up after their messy ordeal.

Rasarlin woke up, feeling a little groggy but far better than he did not more than an hour beforehand. Shaylee was holding his hand and trying to wipe some of the blood from his face and clothing as she whispered to herself, "What did you do, fall into a river of blood?"

Rasarlin smiled, turned his head toward Shaylee, and said, "Yes, it was awful, like falling into the river of Elkin in my world."

Shaylee shot up, not realizing he had woken up. "Oh, you startled me. Is that what really happened? You scared me. What did happen out there?"

He sat upright, feeling like his old self once more as he explained to Shaylee what had put the hardened elven warrior in a hospital bed, "We ran into some trouble, Shay, but we took care of it. As you can see, it was quite messy, but that wasn't what injured me. That was the Marelarph."

"The Marelarph?"

Shaylee knew he was talking about the shard on his chest. She knew it held power, but not much more than that. She was waiting for Rasarlin to gain some memory back before she could get a full briefing but felt now was a good time for explanations.

"Yes, Shaylee, the large purple crystal on my chest is called the Marelarph. When my world's emperor chose me to lead the knights, I took it without question, as it is the highest honor. We had to fight the evil sorcerer Szelidus, who was bent on power, and the most dangerously powerful thing in our world was the Marelarph, a giant meteor that struck our world, rich with the radiation from our red sun. But it is an evil power."

Shaylee sat back in her chair, hoping for more information.

"A battle of magic ensued and, long story short, the sorcerer used evil magic on the Marelarph, creating the time trap of Seckpar that we were both sucked into, controlled by the Marelarph but bound to each other. Even the sorcerer could not withstand its power. We are sent backward, forward, sideways, and in between time and dimensions, forever trapped. The sorcerer and I have ended up in the same worlds sometimes, and sometimes completely different ones but always connected, jumping at the same time through the portals of the universe wherever we are, and punished for over-abusing the magic.

"The trap bound Vax to me as we entered together. The blast of the spell broke off small pieces of the Marelarph, but without it, I am trapped in a world. My magic is useless away from home and using the shard only makes it work more quickly. Its only focus is to trap us forever, but without it, we will never get home. At least I think that's what happened. Everything gets confusing and foggy.

"We do not know when we will get back, if ever, but all I know is that when I get the pain from the shard like that, we usually have little time left in a world. So whatever you need me to do, we need to do it soon."

Shaylee sat there wide-eyed for a moment. Her large blue eyes tried to fight off some tears, but to no avail, as a single drop tipped from her eyelids and coursed down her pale face. She quickly wiped it away and she gently took Rasarlin's hand, thinking of the ongoing torment he faced each time, not knowing when he would be taken or where he would end up.

Rasarlin saw the struggle in her face and said, "At least I have Vax. He holds a shard under his neck, and I hold a piece, as does the sorcerer. We have each other and I now have you, well, for a little while at least."

Shaylee couldn't help it and placed both hands over Rasarlin's cheeks, kissing him deeply as tears cascaded down her face and onto his head. He closed his eyes and enjoyed what little time they had left. Shaylee pulled away slowly. "You poor thing, have you been able to love? Have you had a family?" she said.

Rasarlin didn't want to open that door but felt she needed to know; his memory seemed to be better after the charge from the shard.

"I have, I have had loved ones. I have been close to them, too, when the time trap allowed me to stay longer, but then its evil rips us away and makes us forget. I agreed with myself to never love again and I have not, not for what seems like a millennium. Until I saw you, Shaylee. You ignited me, recharged me again to live. I want to help you and your world, to heal my heart. If there is no hope, then what else is there?"

Shaylee didn't say a word. She continued kissing the war-torn warrior as her wings slowly wrapped around them both so they disappeared into what looked like a winged cocoon.

≈

Wilkes had placed a translator patch on the creature's neck before they took her to the interrogation cell. Eric was behind Levi who led the fierce animal into the room and closed the door. The angry creature with a protruding face was still bound, but they could slowly begin to understand all the hisses and growls that were spewing from her mouth.

Levi eventually left to clean himself up on the orders of Wilkes who sat down with Eric and watched through the glass. Wilkes hit a button and started the communication. "Hello, can you understand me?"

The creature bolted to the glass window, able to see them but not so lucky with trying to scratch her way out.

"Would you like some food?" Wilkes used another tack. After all, it was an animal, he thought. The creature slowed down, turned her head to Wilkes, and slowly spoke, "Please, some food."

"You are now a guest," Wilkes said, "and I will bring you some food, but I just need to ask you some simple questions first."

The bipedal panther nodded and moved over to the only chair in the room, sitting down, showing she was not a primitive animal at all. Wilkes continued with his questioning, a little surprised at her actions, but still wary, "Please, tell me who you are."

There was a long silence before Wilkes pressed an intercom that led to the kitchen and asked for some rare fresh stag meat. Eric looked bemused for a moment before realizing what Wilkes was doing. The silence was long and awkward as the creature stood up and started pacing.

Several minutes passed. One of the new members of the group who had taken up kitchen duties opened the door and placed the plate of meat next to Wilkes and then stared a little too long at the creature, which aggravated it.

"Thank you, Teresa, that will be all," said Wilkes, and so she scurried out of the interrogation control room and back to the kitchen.

The creature looked up. She could smell red meat and had not eaten for days. She sat back down as Wilkes rephrased his earlier question, "Please tell me who you are, and the steaks are yours. You have my word."

There was another shorter length of silence, but before Wilkes could move to the second phase, she spoke, "My name is Buul'ulaan.

I am from a place called Kootesenik and I am a soldier guard for my queen's people."

Wilkes and Eric glanced at each other. Wilkes knew most intelligent planets and colonies over his time as a Zeytar but had not heard of this place. "She must be from very far away. I will check my database later, but we might have a new species here," Wilkes said quietly to Eric.

"How did you find yourself here?" Wilkes asked as Buul'ulaan licked her lips. Fascinated with the creature, Wilkes hoped he could learn more before feeding her.

"We were hunting for molekaarks, and a blue swirling light appeared in front of us. It showed a place on the other side, but it was dark, so we decided to have a quick look. But as soon as I stepped inside, the portal vanished, leaving my friends at home and me stuck with many other strange creatures."

"Where did you go? What was the place like that you entered? Please tell me this and I will feed you."

Wilkes knew he was getting close to some answers as he held the plate up to the window and placed it on the console, ready to slide it through the locked hatch.

"It was noisy. There was darkness everywhere, but a light came from a machine circling quickly. Every so often there would be different lights, some clicking, and a new doorway would open. I tried to step through but before I could, I saw the other side of that place, which terrified me, and before long another life-form crawled through. A small group of us found a cave that led us lower down before it collapsed behind us. Not long after that I was battling the under-dwellers and then being tied up to a tree. That is all I know. Now give me what you promised."

Wilkes stood blank-faced for a moment before Eric nudged him and said, "You better feed her, Wilkes. I don't think you will get much more from her today."

Wilkes snapped out of it and immediately unlocked the hatch to push her food through. As soon as the plate hit the other side, Buul'ulaan had both cuts of meat in her hands and began tearing at them while crouching facing the wall, away from peering eyes.

"What is it, Wilkes? You look like you have stumbled upon something out of her ramblings."

Wilkes turned to Eric and said, with the intercom off, "Do you know what this means, Eric? Why Shaylee's world is part of ours and why so many creatures have been entering? They aren't hybrid abominations; they are coming from different worlds. How could I have been so stupid? The black clouds are a vortex, but that needs power to feed off. Eric, ALEX has the door open permanently to other worlds, the collider is still active, and the rips are still open. We have to destroy it."

Eric sat with his mouth open for a moment. Could this ride get any crazier? he thought. "So, what now?"

Wilkes stared at their new guest for a moment before he responded, glaring without blinking through the glass window, "We need to tell Shaylee and we need to plan to shut that thing down. If it blows, it could destroy the Earth or pull us into another dimension. I don't think ALEX has thought this through—if it wants to take over the world, why destroy it? It just makes little sense—unless it plans to."

Eric stood up and Wilkes followed as they exited the room and headed in different directions—Wilkes to access his database of tech and files of Desertron, the Super Conducting Super Collider, and Eric to find Serena. Time was becoming far too precious now.

≈

Eoghan had just woken up and Serena had a tear in her eye as Eric tried silently to sneak into the room without disturbing them both. He stood like a proud father watching his family, still in disbelief at how his little baby was now a fierce-looking teenager but happy he was safe. Serena had heard his footsteps coming from down the hall, so she knew he was there, but she too was in disbelief as Eoghan spoke, "Mother, what has happened to me? I cannot remember anything from the last few days."

Serena turned and looked at Eric before gazing back at her son as she fought for the words to respond. "How, how can you speak like that? Sorry, I mean, you can talk fluently, it's incredible."

Serena leaned in and hugged Eoghan tightly, relieved he had come through the hardest part of his Fae transformation not just unscathed but rather enhanced. She then held her hand behind her, indicating for Eric to follow. He didn't need any encouragement to move in to hug them. He had so much on his plate and knew Serena was taking care of Eoghan as he pined for Stacey and now, with the recent revelations of the collider still being on, was feeling the pressures in a big way.

Eric needed this moment, and it would give him the strength to carry on protecting the ones he loved the most. They continued to embrace as a family for several minutes, talking and laughing together as if the world around them had stopped in time. But it had not, and there were things to be done.

Wilkes stormed into the room, disturbing the setting. "Eric, we need a meeting now. Gather everyone, the entire ship, including Shaylee, as I set up the room and upload new information once more. Have everyone there in an hour."

Eric turned, a little annoyed about the abrupt disruption but eager to get started. Serena had been so focused on Eoghan that she was a little out of the current loop. "Is everything alright, Eric?" she asked him hesitantly.

He held her hand, then looked at Eoghan and said, "You will all know soon, but what I can tell you is that we may be able to stop the paradox and release Shaylee's world. Can you please find her and Rasarlin, and I will put a broadcast over the ship and inform everyone."

Eric kissed Serena, winked at Eoghan, and started for the door. He stopped for a moment, turned, and said, "You and me buddy, when this is done, we are having some quality father and son time, got it?"

Eoghan looked at Serena, then back at Eric, still catching up in his mind about the changes he had recently gone through but understanding what was happening as he responded, "I would like that ... Dad, I would like that very much."

Serena wiped away a tear, watched Eric rush from the room, and then found some appropriate clothes for Eoghan. As she turned to let him dress, he asked, "Let me help, Mother, I am ready now, stronger now."

Serena still saw him as a baby and immediately answered, "No, it's far too dangerous ..." But then she remembered what Shaylee had asked her about giving him a chance to prove himself before she responded once more, "Sorry, this has been so hard for me. Please understand you were only born a few months ago, but I realize things are different, so, if you stay with Shaylee and myself, under our guidance, then you can come. But you won't be fighting. You can stay with the vulnerable Fae when things get too heavy, under the treasures' protection, do I make myself clear?"

That was good enough for Eoghan. He just wanted to be out there, and something in his eyes said that there was more to come from this young Fae.

≈

Eric had found Shaylee before Serena could, bumping into her in the hall as she was trying to find Wilkes to let him know about Rasarlin's condition. Eric had just put out the announcement and was heading to find Wilkes himself when they met. "Shaylee, we need to let you know something. We have found the reason the worlds are connected. Can you please find Rasarlin and join Wilkes and me in the large meeting room?"

Shaylee's wings twitched with excitement. She wanted to know everything now, but she too had information and time was far too short. "OK, Eric, I will meet you in the flash of a pixie's sneeze."

Eric smirked. He liked these otherworldly beings, especially Shaylee. She had much of Serena's tough, sometimes impetuous exterior, but with the heart and wit of the kindest and wisest of them all.

They tore off, Eric to meet Wilkes and Shaylee to get Rasarlin, who had just finished cleaning his clothes. Soon they joined Wilkes in the meeting room with all doors locked, where they would discuss, along with Vargzin, the revelations of the day and plan for a good forty minutes, with Shaylee letting go of the earlier arguments that had taken place.

Meanwhile, in the open fields where Van Coinan and the gnomes were on guard duty, keeping out of sight but also getting up to some mischief, the pooka had been annoying Vaximardruusz all morning since Rasarlin had left. He had climbed halfway up, trying to reach the top of his crest while he was asleep and under the cloaking spell of Shaylee.

The gnomes had bet the fearless pooka that he couldn't climb it without waking the dragon up and Van Coinan couldn't help himself as usual. The wager was on some gold that Van Coinan had swindled off an Elvenfae guard the day before and wanted to double it by taking Grilif's jewel that was hidden at the bottom of his satchel, a blue gem Felvora had given him before she left, for saving her in the castle.

Van Coinan had peeked inside the contents of the gnome's satchel when Grilif was asleep. He would never steal for keeps, but he was forever betting with those who owned trinkets he wanted if they were friends, and sometimes if they were not. But Grilif accepted the wager, and Vax, opening his eye ever so slightly, overheard the bet taking place and determined that Grilif would not lose.

Higher Van Coinan climbed, digging his sharp, long claws into hard scales, pulling on stray hairs that had nerves, making the hardened wyvern wince in pain without flinching. The higher Van Coinan got, the more brazen he became, glancing down, and blurting his tongue out. Soon he was at the bottom of Vax's crest, between the huge boned horns that were enormous to Van Coinan. Seeing them close up put a little fear into the cheeky pooka, which was rare.

That trepidation soon went away when he realized victory was in hand, and just before he could pull himself up for the first leg of the climb, Vaximardruusz lifted his giant head up, turned to the gnomes who looked like ants to Van Coinan, and let out a roar. Tilting back, he broke the cloaking spell with a burst of fire, and then eased forward again. Then, pointing upward, he took several steps before ascending into the sky.

The Elvenfae guards went into meltdown mode as they were all supposed to stay incognito, but Vax was in no mood after the electric volts that had hit him earlier in the day, just as they had Rasarlin. He liked the gnomes and they were always nice to him, mostly out of fear, but Van Coinan had pushed his last button this day and he wanted him to know it.

Van Coinan was holding on for dear life, clutching at one of the smaller horns scattered across Vax's head. They didn't stand out like the four main ones, but his head was covered in many scales and horns, all in rows like hair stuck with gel.

Vaximardruusz flew to the lake where they were all submerged and dove deep down until he could see the ship. He tapped the top with his long claw, rocking the ship for a moment before climbing up and out of the lake like a rocket. Eventually he landed back where he had been originally, and then lowered his neck and head to ease the soaked pooka onto the ground.

Van Coinan slid off, stood there in front of the gnomes with a look of horror, shook himself down, and yelled, "Again, I want to do it again!"

Vax closed his eyes. He had been through so many wars and dark places during his time, but this creature was the fiercest. He lifted his head, spread his wings out, and shook out the leathery scales until they were dry, wetting everyone nearby.

Van Coinan tried to hide, but before he could take off, Grilif put his hand out and moved his palms in and out, showing he was missing something. Van Coinan pulled his damp satchel up, took some palace coins out, and reluctantly placed them in Grilif's small hands. The pooka then turned to Vax and said, "Double or nothing."

The wyvern lifted his head, spat a fireball in the pooka's direction, and watched as he ran off and hid in the woods after it barely missed him. The fireball had hit a puddle just before the entrance to the woods which Vax had meticulously aimed for, but Van Coinan didn't know that, and they did not see the pooka for the rest of the afternoon.

DÉJÀ VU

WILKES WAS FEELING THE PRESSURE, AND although he didn't show it, the enormity of the situation at hand was testing him. He had expected to be fighting hybrids by now if they had failed the first mission, but the dynamics of his second plans for that war had all changed.

The last time, he'd had centuries to organize, prepare, and build relationships and technologies. He'd had everything worked out down to the last second, and even weapons and plans for the assault on Earth if they failed their mission on the Leader's ship. But ALEX was something else and he hated that he had not taken more notice of Xandar and the Leader.

His concern at the time was avoidance of the Leader, who now had the last laugh, as if he were still alive and smiling somewhere with his metal abomination. Wilkes had to shake it off, though. There was still hope, but this fight would be far more risky than the previous battle and, most likely, more costly, which sent an icy shiver down his spine.

Eric unlocked the doors and slowly the meeting room filled with all those on the ship—including all the families of loved ones, along with those they picked up and saved along the way since the start of the ZARK invasions, soldiers, medics, teachers. There were many spread out throughout the medium-sized ship, which, although not as large as the mother ship, was still like a small town and had contained them safe and well for now.

Serena met with her mother and father and hugged them. She had seen little of them lately and seemed overwhelmed with emotion. They had not seen her since she had recovered from her depression and there was much to fill them in on. The first would be the hardest, and that was explaining Eoghan.

Siobhan and Maggie were there too with their families, although they looked quite perplexed when they saw Serena and her change. They had been told about it briefly by Eric but seeing her in the flesh was something else. More of the gaps would be filled in later, if there was time, and they all just had to trust what was happening.

Everyone's world had been tipped upside down since the fall of the Zeytars, with all the different creatures wandering around the place, which was hard for some to accept. For those family members who weren't directly involved it took a lot longer to understand, and that was why there were sections of the ship for them specifically, to provide a sense of normality for them like a community. They were briefed when necessary but told to stay in their own quarters until called. This was the first time in a long while that they were all together.

Serena pulled back from her family's embraces and gently pulled Eoghan's hand so he would come forward. His magnificent-looking, powerful wings mesmerized them all, including others who had never seen a faery in real life before.

Shaylee too was garnering attention, but not as much as Rasarlin. The elven warrior felt very awkward with the humans. As much as he liked the species and they reminded him of a type on his planet, he felt they judged with eyes far more than any other species he had encountered. He maintained a confident look, kept his head high, and made his way to the side of the lectern where Wilkes was setting up for his speech.

Eoghan, too, was a little overwhelmed by the attention as he waited for someone in his mother's family to speak. Siobhan went first, not as shocked by the situation, "Well then, Eoghan, the last time I looked upon you, you were but a wee baby, wow how you have grown." Serena gave a scowl, as her sister continued, "Sorry, I meant you are my nephew, and it is great to meet you. I am your aunty, Siobhan."

She leaned in and gave him an awkward hug before stepping back, leaving the rest to introduce themselves. Eoghan took it well as he looked over at Shaylee, who was trying to make Rasarlin feel more comfortable. She met his gaze and returned a wink, then a smile, and then Wilkes started speaking.

"Please find a seat, everyone. My name is Wilkes. You would all have been briefed on who I am, those living in the community residences. I apologize for tearing you all away, but there are some pressing issues that need to be addressed and this will include most, if not all, of you, so I ask that you listen up and be respectful to our speakers."

Wilkes had learned little about human tact, but it was as good as they were going to get out of the hybrid leader of the ship this day.

"There will be some things that may be too disturbing to witness, so I ask all those vulnerable ones to go with First Officer Joyce back to the communities."

Eric had warned Wilkes that not all of those on the ship had to be briefed at the meeting and that some would not be able to take it. The children weren't there for obvious reasons, but there were those that still struggled acutely with it all.

Those going stood up and left with the soldier. More than he had expected. Serena's parents stayed.

"For those who have been through this before, again, I am sorry," said Wilkes. "I thought we defeated them, but I was wrong, so we are left with no choice but to do it all again."

Wilkes lowered his head, glanced over at Eric, and slowly raised it back up. He was looking very strong, as if he had just taken some steroids. His body was still growing, just at a slower pace. He dressed more casually this time in slacks and a polo shirt, wanting to keep it more low key and human.

"After the last meeting which was going to be part of our new plan for a weapons system, we have come into some more knowledge. With this information, and after discussions with Shaylee, queen of the Fae, Rasarlin, a special guest here to help for a short time, Vargzin, Eric, and myself, we have come to an agreement and a plan to end this war and gain back our planet."

Eric smiled when Wilkes said "our planet"—whether it was because of his new body, or the fact humans surrounded him. It was like being accepted as one of them was his reward for the previous battle, but he would need to prove himself once more.

"I will introduce you to everyone as they tell their parts of the plan. I will go first with an update on our situation."

The meeting room had settled, and everyone was attentive. Some of those from the last battle hunched in their chairs as the exhaustion was setting in.

Wilkes opened the holograms and began, "What we know is that the ZARKs are aware of our location, hence the reason we are at the bottom of the lake. We also know that Stacey Kirkpatrick has been captured and would be somewhere close to ALEX. We believe this as she would be too valuable to the android not to be."

Eric looked down at his feet, then back up at Wilkes, awaiting his turn as the Zeytar hybrid continued, "I am still unsure of the android's motives but feel strongly that my Shadowblood weapons systems will most likely be effective against the ZARKs. We cannot save all those captured or hurt as time is scarce, but if we win, we will save billions. I will pass you over to Shaylee, who will update you on her situation."

Wilkes moved away from the lectern and let Shaylee advance, this time more calmly than the last time they were there.

"My name is Shaylee Aethelwyne. You would know by now of our existence—we are the Fae that have hidden for thousands of years of your time. Our ancestors created our magical world of Faelynn after being driven out of your world. The relationship between humans and the Fae has always been tense and we try to stay hidden for those reasons, coming into your world when we want but not allowing your kind back to ours, as the hate your people have had for us has lasted far too long."

Shaylee looked over at Serena and smiled as she continued, "But there is an important person here that is born of Fae and of human that has helped me see that there is good in you. Your help to save my people after decades and decades of capture by the Zeytars, as well as her newborn son Eoghan's strength that saved us from a dark lord and Zeytar in disguise before our worlds combined, will never be forgotten. Now we are stuck together due to the destruction of the Zeytars' war. We have lost much, just like you, and I believe we can work together and beat this abomination that plagues us both. I will pledge all my magic and forces to help, even if it means putting aside differences of beliefs and opinions to get the task done."

Shaylee looked over at Wilkes when she said that, reinforcing her alliance, but also reminding him she wasn't ready to forget just yet.

"Before I go, I want you all to know that we are your friends. There will be some who will not be as warm, but they all know, as I am their queen, that they are on your side. Last, I want to introduce you to my very good friend Rasarlin. Without him I would not be here, nor would many of my people."

Rasarlin didn't feel comfortable speaking to the large group. He wasn't afraid—in fact, there was not much he was afraid of—but he felt it better coming from Shaylee, who knew enough of his side of the plan. She felt his hesitation and continued, "Rasarlin is also from another world but he is not here for long so we must be quick. His wyvern, or dragon as you may well call him, is on borrowed time in this realm, but he has immense power. This power comes from his Fyre as Wilkes explained last time, and we believe it to be the key to destroying the evil and separating our worlds again."

Shaylee moved away from the lectern. She figured Eric could explain this part while Wilkes displayed the holographic video to the group. Eric never saw himself as a leader, but they looked up to him, especially when Wilkes looked like a hybrid teen.

He stood in front of the lectern and began, "Thank you, Shaylee, and Rasarlin, for your help. I feel very confident with you helping, Shay. I hope it can unite our worlds someday. So, we now know that the android has kept its part of the collider working. It had not been destroyed when the ships came down and this explains why so many creatures are roaming the country, along with why the Fae world and ours is joined. We thought the dark area was just like that because of the amount of energy expelled, but we were wrong. We have to shut it down."

Wilkes moved toward the bench where he had shown the team the disclosure plan the first time and pressed a few buttons to bring up a giant map of an area, sourced from drones monitoring a massive black spot that once was the town of Waxahachie, Texas. The crowd stared in awe and gasped as they saw the aerial view of the whirling black maelstrom of electricity, storms, and lifelike clouds, twisting and pulsating.

"As you can see, it is not a cheerful place and we will need a very special team to take it out as no one knows how many abominations are lurking in the darkness there. The obstacle we have is destroying the collider and stopping the X-Clock machine attached for good. Wilkes mentioned at the previous meeting that his new weapons could not destroy the android ALEX, nor could fire, and the only thing that can do it is Dragon Fyre."

Eric smiled to himself and thought once more: There's a dragon here! He just couldn't quite grasp the concept. Aliens, faeries, lizard-men, Sasquatch, his whole belief system was becoming real, and he was now fully in his element.

"The only issue with that is that the heat needs to be directly on the source and the collider is four floors down, far too deep to be affected from ground level. Besides, we don't have time and he is needed elsewhere to destroy ALEX, so we have devised a plan. The dragon ..."

"Vax," Shaylee clarified.

"Sorry, Vax will fill several canisters made from the same substance as the android ..." said Eric.

"Ardmenticam," this time Wilkes clarified. It was not as smooth a run of the disclosure plan as before, but they were all trying.

"Yes, Ardmenticam, thank you, Wilkes. Each container will have an explosive attached to it and, Shaylee, could you please explain this part?"

Shaylee fluttered over swiftly and continued, "As the Fyre will melt any metal, I will place a very strong spell from all four of our world's power sources, which will be strong enough to withstand the Fyre, but will eventually break through. No Fae magic can withhold it indefinitely."

Shaylee turned, nodded at Eric as he stepped up and continued, while Wilkes showed a simulation on the hologram as all of this was unfolding. "Thank you, Shaylee. After that a team will enter the hidden city of the Draconians to gain a safe passage to the site. There they will place all the canisters around the X-Clock and retreat as fast as they can before the Fyre melts through and sets off the charges giving the Fyre a force to explode, creating a firestorm of energy hot enough to melt the X-Clock and—"

Eric suddenly fell to the floor in pain as a vision of Stacey appeared in his mind. It was different this time, not like the times when Eric would hear her talking. But after only a moment, the vision faded. Shaylee and Serena were at Eric's side in no time and they sat him in a chair.

Serena knew straightaway what had happened. "Where is she, Eric, you saw Stacey, didn't you?" she asked him.

Eric looked up at her with tears in his eyes as he responded, "Y… Yes, she is alive, but she is far from safe. I couldn't see where she was, but there was a cell with electricity bars and a ZARK standing guard. I couldn't understand her, but she didn't look good."

Serena held his head while Shaylee pulled out her crystal. "Do you think you could concentrate hard enough to see it again, Eric?"

Eric lifted his head; he didn't understand Fae magic but would do anything to help. "Yes, Shaylee, what do you want me to do?"

Shaylee put the crystal in his hand while she held it too and said quietly, "Think of that vision once more, think of her, Eric."

Eric closed his eyes and was replaying the vision in his mind. Soon a picture appeared showing Stacey lying alone next to a deformed creature's body, asleep. Eric opened his eyes and continued to fight away tears as she appeared in the crystal.

"I think we have found your plan to get Stacey back, Eric," Shaylee said.

Eric smiled as he looked at his daughter, then gave Serena a kiss and continued on to give one to Shaylee, who seemed shocked at his reaction. Eric composed himself as Wilkes continued outlining the last part of the plan, obviously now with a rescue involved. "So, I will need volunteers for the mission to the X-Clock. Vargzin, Sergeant Marcus, you have some men, I believe."

"Yes, Wilkes, we are ready for anything," Sergeant Lorne Marcus replied. The soldiers had not worked as soldiers over the last few months, so were ready to get back to their norm. Wilkes recruited them in anticipation of the second attack, but they found themselves as crew members instead, overseeing different tasks.

"Excellent, who else can I ask to assist? This one will be very dangerous and the likelihood of getting out unscathed is low. I believe some of your Fae will assist, Shaylee, am I correct?"

Shaylee looked over and nodded before answering with a hint of a reluctant tremor in her tone, "Yes, Wilkes, some of my guards, and I will send my little warriors Grilif, Darf, and Vaelenflixx. They will be an asset to your crew."

"Excellent," Wilkes said.

Over on the sideline, two arms were high in the air, one waving like a kid in school with the answer to a problem. This soon caught Wilkes' eye. "Valinda and Levi, this is far too dangerous for you. I am sorry, I need Levi with me, Val."

Valinda slowly lowered her arm, then responded to Wilkes in a stern and assertive tone, "My sight can help the soldiers in the dark. I can see far better than any of your goggles, and it is pitch black inside that vortex. Let me go."

Wilkes had no choice. He had asked for volunteers and that's just what he got. "Alright, Valinda, but when I need Levi, I will send for him, and he will come straight to me. Do you understand?"

Valinda smiled and tickled the giant creature under the chin as Wilkes continued, "Alright, that's Waxahachie, now I need the rest of the soldiers from Lieutenant Dresden's contingent to assist with the second part of the plan, which will consist of flying to all major prison camps held by the ZARK drones and destroying them all, unlocking the gates, and moving on to the next one. Like I said, we can't stay there and help—we don't have time. Once we get the android's attention, we will advance to the White House and destroy ALEX with Dragon Fyre."

Wilkes had two small other plans to deal with, and then it was on to getting ready. "First, I need a volunteer to assist me with the recovery of weapons from a tech lab."

The group looked blank before Eoghan raised his hand. "I'll go."

Serena looked at Wilkes and shook her head but the hybrid dismissed her completely and answered, "Excellent, we won't be gone long."

Serena approached Wilkes quietly before he even finished speaking. "You will not be taking my boy," she said.

He turned off the microphone and softly replied, "Serena, I think this is exactly what your boy needs. I know his mind, I can hear it sometimes. He is stronger than you know, and this mission will be a start at boosting his confidence because, I assure you, out there with the ZARKs you won't be able to hold his hand."

Serena glanced at Shaylee, who had an idea of what they were talking about and nodded in agreement. She looked back at Wilkes and whispered, "Anything happens to him and I'm coming for you!"

Wilkes passed the comment off like a flea on his shoulder. He switched the microphone back on and continued, "Once we have all the weapons sorted out, our teams will prepare and we will move out. Also, the reason I wanted everyone from the community here is that you will remain underwater on the ship. I will use my smaller quick X-71s, or Tic Tacs as your people call them, so you will be here on your own with a skeleton crew of soldiers left. You cannot leave the ship but I will send updates to you as often as I can."

Wilkes took a breath. He was getting mentally weary. He hadn't told Buul'ulaan that she was going back to the collider yet. That was a conversation he did not want to have. He looked over at Eric.

"I believe, Eric, you are the last of us that doesn't have a part in the plan as yet. You were going to be coming with us to battle the android but with the recent developments of Stacey's abduction, I gather that is no longer in play?"

Eric stood up and answered confidently, feeling more upbeat than before, "I will go with you all, just as planned. Shaylee has offered to help me right now to rescue her, which she said will not take long."

Wilkes, Serena, and Rasarlin all gave Shaylee a look of concern, but not one of them protested, knowing that the queen always did what her heart told her to, and this was something she had to do.

BLOOD MISSION

ERIC AND SHAYLEE WERE WORKING OUT DETAILS OF the execution of the plan to rescue Stacey while Wilkes was teaching Eoghan some Zeytar tech, so he was a little more educated about what he was about to get into. Wilkes was right about the boy, whether it was because he too had come so far in such a short amount of time in his progression to adulthood and transformation, or because he saw Eoghan through the eyes of a Zeytar who was very good at selecting the right person for his teams.

Either way Wilkes admired the teenager, but he had one thing that Eoghan did not and that was he had been an adult before, so the resilience he sensed in the teenager was something special. Serena had to acknowledge that, by letting go a little more so he could shine on his own. There was definitely something about Eoghan.

Eric was ready to go and asked Wilkes for directions. He respected Shaylee very much but wanted some more information about Stacey's location and thoughts. Eric was careful not to ask in the presence of the Fae queen, so waited until they were alone for a short time.

"Wilkes, I need a favor, can you please discreetly and I mean that term vehemently, could you please lock into Stacey's location and create a link for us again? I need her to tell us her exact location."

Wilkes looked at Eric, then down at the floor, gazing away from his friend to give the hardest answer he ever thought he would have to give, "I ... I am sorry, Eric; I cannot do that."

Eric moved a little closer, trying to get the normally so assertive Zeytar to look at him. "Why not, Wilkes? Stacey saved all of us, including you, by bringing the boy back, so tell me why and make it good."

Wilkes looked up at Eric and responded nervously, "I am slowly losing my telekinesis, my mind control, and blending abilities. I thought you would ask earlier, but Shaylee eased your mind. I tried to locate her but failed and I don't know why as the Zeytar hybrids were supposed to keep their abilities. That's why our heads are slightly larger."

Eric looked stunned. "So you are just like us now? Human?" he said cautiously.

Keeping his gaze on Eric, Wilkes explained further, "I have all the history of my people inside my DNA, my memories, and intelligence. I also have intuition, but mostly, yes, Eric, I am human."

Eric knew it upset Wilkes, and he had never lied, so why would he now. He put his hand onto the hybrid's shoulder and said, "Well, that's shit. Oh well, being human isn't too bad, I can vouch for that."

Eric tried to lighten the mood and reassure his friend, but he knew that losing those abilities as a once powerful Zeytar was like losing the ability to speak or hear as a human. Eric pulled his hand away and Wilkes nodded without responding as the two left the room to begin their profoundly serious missions ahead. They only had hours before the team left for the Draconians' subterranean city, and they both wanted to be back to see them off.

"Everything alright, Eric?" Serena asked as she gave him a kiss, knowing that look on his face was in the intense zone he always got into before something big happened. After a moment, Eric pulled back and said, "Everything is fine, my love; I just want to get this done. Hey, make sure Eoghan looks after Wilkes. I think he will be good for him."

Serena scowled a little at Eric and thought, Why is everyone at me about my son now? She let go as she approached Wilkes and Eoghan. "Look after my baby, Wilkes. If there is even one tiny barb missing from his wings, you will have me to deal with."

Wilkes had heard the threats before so he nodded it away.

"Mother, I will be fine," Eoghan said. "This mission will be a quick and safe one, and besides, I am ready to be a part of this. I feel a calling through me to do something important. I just can't work out what it is."

Serena was finally understanding and was slowly letting go as she responded to her son quietly and assertively, "OK, remember this, you are not human, you are Fae. Listen to your instincts, move swiftly and according to your mind and body, trust your judgments, and at all times stay hidden and cautious, don't act on aggression or emotion—it's not the Fae way. Only those who were captured by the Zeytars show those qualities and we do not judge. I am sorry I couldn't teach you more before all of this, but I trust in you to always make the right decisions and to keep your human side open as well. Lastly, Shaylee wanted me to give you the Sword of Light. It will protect you and keep your Fae abilities strong. The sword will be like a second mind. Trust in the power and use it wisely if you need it."

Eoghan was glad this time for her advice. He was finally getting guidance on what he should do and from his mother, who was half human, it meant more than any full blood could give. "Thank you, Mother, I will not let you or Wilkes down, I promise, and I will look after the sword."

Eoghan leaned in and gave Serena a hug before Eric moved in and said, "Do your best, kiddo. I'm already proud of you."

Eric placed his arms around them both and they embraced as a family once more before they would be split for who knows how long. Serena let Eoghan go with Wilkes and then she turned, put her arms around Eric tightly, and said, "Come back to me, Eric. Bring her home and come back to me."

Eric kissed Serena and said, with a look of love in his eyes, "I will, Serena, I will, and I will take care of Shaylee too."

She looked at Eric and smiled. They were eye to eye now due to her slight growth. "Yes, Eric, you look after Shaylee too."

They both laughed quietly in each other's arms before Shaylee moved closer and interrupted them. "It's time, Eric, we are running out of it, and it has been a while since you had the vision. We need to leave now."

Eric nodded, gave Serena one last kiss, and went to fetch his backpack. Serena turned around to face Shaylee and said, "Please take care of Eric. He is hot-headed and impetuous, but he is a good father and partner and I want him back."

Shaylee nodded. "You have my word, sweet sister. I will carry him out if I have to."

Serena smirked as she said, "And you make sure you come back to me as well. I don't want to have to rescue the queen of Faelynn again."

Shaylee nodded once more and hugged Serena who watched all her beloved family walk out of the room into what kind of dangers she dreaded to think. Serena lowered her head, hating that she couldn't be with them but honored that Shaylee had advised her Elvenfae guards that Serena was in charge while she was away, and she was to prepare them for what was to come.

≈

Wilkes and Eoghan rushed to the pod compartment where the X-71s sat waiting. The Zeytars used the very swift and stealthy craft for reconnaissance, as they could appear one moment, then disappear in a split second. The U.S. Navy named them Tic Tacs as their shape resembled the candy and had been witnessed traveling from 50,000 feet to a couple of hundred feet within seconds.

The ships ran on anti-gravity and Zero-point technology; the Zeytars could harness the energy to move quickly and out of sight mostly while collecting data from military installations that they had not yet controlled with their Geno-drone technology.

The X-71s could only be detected by radar on the Navy's Super Hornets if they slowed down enough or if they let them, but that was rare as they were designed specifically for recon.

Wilkes and Eoghan boarded the first of twenty X-71 models in the hangar through a short tunnel system. They were each around forty feet long with no combustible elements on them, making them perfect to avoid the ZARK drones. Eoghan took a long look around the primary entry point for a few moments, in awe of the Zeytars' craftsmanship.

Although he had lived on a medium-sized crew ship, it had been modified for humans over Wilkes' time trying to make it as homely for the humans as possible. No one was given unsupervised permission to wander through the private Zeytar sections, so this new zipper ship was to him impressive. It was basic but had Zeytar coding throughout the walls and structures with only one main pod in the middle where the pilot sat; the rest were lookouts with one-sided windows that other crew members could look through and gather data on many of the out of this world computer systems.

Wilkes looked at the Fae teen and smiled slightly. He always loved the looks humans, or in this case otherworldly beings, had when they saw the technologies. It was the one thing as a scientist that Wilkes still loved about his race; he was proud of their achievements and would hopefully one day instill the knowledge into humans for peaceful advancements into the future.

Eoghan followed Wilkes into the pod, sat next to the teen hybrid, and took everything in like a sponge. Wilkes didn't even have to tell him to watch and learn as he could see the inquisitive looks that the Fae teen had been casting since he had arrived.

This one will make it, Wilkes thought, as he placed his five fingers into the three-finger section. He hoped he could still use mind control to operate the ship but had the manual backup if required. This meant it would take a little more concentrating on his part.

Wilkes sat for a moment, focusing hard as sweat began meandering down his forehead and onto his face. Eoghan could see the struggle and carefully said, "Is everything alright, Wilkes?"

Wilkes nodded and waited a few seconds to respond, "Yes, Eoghan, I am fine. I have just lost my ability to control the ship with my mind."

Eoghan examined the controls and found them very basic. There was only a hand device with three finger molds like a joystick and the rest was just a plain dashboard. Wilkes kept trying but conceded defeat until Eoghan came up with a suggestion. "Let me try, Wilkes. Please, I can hear the ship humming even though it's not on, let me try?"

Wilkes turned quickly to the Fae, nearly cracking his neck in the process. Eoghan thought he was about to get a spray from the Zeytar hybrid, but was a little surprised by the reaction. "You can hear the hum? Tell me what patterns they are—hit the dash and tell me."

Eoghan concentrated for a moment and began hitting the dash as asked in a sequence that made Wilkes' eyes widen even more. Soon he stopped and began the same pattern again before Wilkes put his hand on Eoghan's, stared at him, and smiled. "I knew there was something about you, boy, sorry, young one. Ever since I saw you, even before my mind came in, I remembered things you did, when you thought no one was watching."

Eoghan felt confused. All he knew was himself and that was only for the short time he had been alive. He knew what he knew but would need to talk to Shaylee about some of the other Fae qualities that he felt were normal but were coming to the others' attention. Was it normal Fae power or something else, he thought, questioning his own normal. But that would have to wait as he politely asked Wilkes, "Please, sir, let me have a try. I know I can make it work with your guidance."

Wilkes liked the boy—polite, unquestioning, with no ego or pride, not like any human quality he had witnessed over the centuries. "I think that would be a perfect idea. You will need to listen, though, and it may be rough to start with, but I feel you can do this, Eoghan."

The Fae smiled and they changed positions. As he waited for Wilkes to begin, he slowly placed his right hand over the controller, two fingers, then two more in the section next to it, and finally placing the thumb in the last divot.

Wilkes looked over as he recognized that Eoghan was clearly communicating with the onboard computer. Suddenly a multitude of different holograms appeared and Wilkes talked Eoghan through the next stages. Slowly the ship began humming louder and Eoghan jolted it once but then managed full control as it glided out of the pod tunnel and into the lake, heading straight for the surface.

The ship burst from the water, leaving a vibrational ripple over the entire lake as it darted like a rocket into the atmosphere and out of sight. Wilkes, impressed, had some words of advice, "Very good, Eoghan, but remember, these ships are very erratic, and you may find them harder to control if you go too fast for too long. Just ease back and I will give you the latitudes and longitudes."

Eoghan took the information and through his mind relayed it to the ship while his sword glowed a slight red color from the hilt to the pommel. Before long, they were at their destination, a small mountain range several states away in Montana at the bottom of the Beartooth Mountains. There was a clearing and Wilkes asked for a quick scan for humans in the direct vicinity, but Eoghan explained there were only animal signatures.

The ship landed, with eight large prongs protruding from the bottom, and the cloak activated. They went to the docking portal and beamed from the ship to the dirty, rocky floor of the woods. Wilkes put his hand on Eoghan's shoulder and said, "Do me a favor, control your own destiny, learn from others, and trust yourself. You are wise and learned beyond your years and I feel you will play a huge part in our future battles—that is my intuition speaking and it is always spot on."

Eoghan smiled and nodded. There was no ego or pride with him. He grabbed two of four of the long gun bags and they headed to the base of the mountain. Wilkes pulled out a small, smooth rock with three different shapes on the top and stared hard at a wall of rock in front of him. He then approached and started lining up different sections, and then he closed his eyes and tried to use his photographic memory to find what he needed.

Wilkes was struggling as the landmark had changed since he was last there but soon his memory ignited and he was left standing in front of a coarse section of multiple protruding stones. He placed the rock on several sections with his eyes closed before he had a match. He held it tightly on the stones and turned it slowly. Before long, the rock disappeared and a tunnel door began presenting itself.

Eoghan looked amazed as the door rose. He then meandered past

Wilkes, through the dust and falling branches to the entrance of the cave. Wilkes lit a glow flare and walked in behind him as Eoghan pulled out the now fully glowing sword that looked like it was on fire to light his way.

Wilkes caught up with the fellow teen and whispered, "Over there, Eoghan, can you light that section?"

The cave ended and the bright red fiery sword illuminated a long bench made of stone. Wilkes approached it and dusted off a section on the side, revealing three holes. He slid his smallest fingers inside, and soon the top of the stone bench lifted slightly. He then did the same to the other two benches in the cave before standing back and waiting.

"This is it, Eoghan. I never thought I would ever have to use these and for the sake of your people I hope we never do, but this is Shadowblood, the most toxic genetic blood known in the universe. I am telling you this as it affects you. The first use was to manipulate genomes for our Zeytar hybrids to survive on Earth and the second, but most deadly, was engineered to melt metal. Some of your kin have no antibodies against iron, and that element is in most metals. I turned it into a weapon in case of some day like this."

Eoghan had a slight look of shock on his face but was more interested in what they would use it for.

"I mixed the genomes with other dark antibodies from dark Fae as well. I never told your queen Shaylee about that as it was a backup if the Fae returned for retribution against us. The mix is potent, and I call it Shadowblood for the dark properties it has against the Fae and machines. Do not get any on yourself right now as it will melt your skin like a hot knife melts butter. I have suits that act like living antibodies when we are in battle so you will all be safe, but until then, please do not spill its contents on your body."

Wilkes was adamant about taking the risk seriously, and had been careful, so the vials had extra protection around the bullet canisters, each one double the size of a shotgun shell. He was aware of the risk by taking Eoghan but knew Shaylee and especially Serena would not have allowed it if they thought it would be lethal to Fae in its dark form.

Eoghan didn't seem to care. He was more interested in the science of the chemicals and wanted to learn more down the track.

"Thank you for warning me and trusting me, Wilkes. I will be extra careful. Promise me one thing, though. When this is over, teach me your science, so I may help my people, both human and Fae."

Wilkes nodded. "Deal, my young friend. Now let's get you suited up so we can load these guns into the bags and onto the ship."

Eoghan smiled and fluttered the tops of his wings in anticipation, as a new friendship of trust and loyalty was forming. Wilkes approached the third stone bench, reached in, and picked out a small clear canister. As Eoghan looked over his shoulder at the full of life organism inside it, Wilkes carefully opened the canister and began pouring the contents over the Fae teen without him flinching. If Wilkes had wanted him out of the picture, he would surely have had the chance now, but that trust had been established and Eoghan let all of the living plasma be poured over him as if he were under a shower.

There was a slight bit of pain as it molded to his body, but soon it had disappeared onto all the contours of his skin and through his clothes. The organism was like a second skin awaiting symbiotic activation as Wilkes approached with a small handheld silver device he had taken from the stone bench. He clicked a button over Eoghan's chest and the organism tightened up and disappeared.

"Where did it go?" Eoghan yelled, worried it had fallen off, before Wilkes soothed his mind.

"It's still there, Eoghan, do not stress, it is now acting as a symbiosis with your body. Its sole purpose is to stave off infections or unwanted organisms that can hurt you—it works with your skin cells, creating a wall of protection. I made these especially if a war against the Fae ensued and I had allies of your kin. You need to know something, Eoghan. What the Zeytars, my people, did to your kin was abhorrent beyond words and they have every right to be angry at my kind as well as myself."

Eoghan looked down for a moment, then met eyes with Wilkes and said, "What's done is done. You are here with us now and fighting for both my people. I will make sure there is no retribution against you after this war."

Wilkes smiled slightly. He knew being allies with Eoghan was paramount and although it didn't take away any of the trust or friendship that had been built, a Zeytar as smart as Wilkes always had to have his eggs all in one basket and Eoghan had filled that basket with protection and trust.

"Come, let's get started."

Wilkes handled all the blood vials as he tasked Eoghan to pack the shells and the plastic pulse rifles modified for the blood. Wilkes did not want to risk his new friend and bodyguard for anything. After they spent the next twenty minutes carefully packing all the artillery, they exited the cave, closed the door to the hidden bunker, and loaded the ship before Eoghan took off and sped back to home base.

Time was running out!

A TRAITOR
FROM FAELYNN

A LEX WAS BUSY. SINCE LEAVING STACEY IN THE guarded cell, it was moving all over the country, building its cybernetic army for the bodiless Zeytars. The process was time-consuming but was gathering momentum. After the X-Clock set up the systematic symbiosis programs at each prison camp, it would then let its minions run it and would move on to the next.

After several hundred had successfully combined, ALEX would receive a signal and return to open a door for the same amount of Zeytar minds to instantaneously come through and enter bodies, each receiving orders to continue the work. All the ZARK drones that had a successful symbiosis with the Zeytars were completely under their control. The only part left of the original automaton mind was a neural cortex that could still receive messages from ALEX, which were immediately relayed to the Zeytar.

A task with such complexities should not be able to work, but the Leader's scientific skills were slowly showing, especially in how he had outsmarted the most intelligent Zeytar Wilkes. It was as if he had known of his plans from the start. Whether he did or did not was of no concern now as ALEX followed the orders to the letter from the original upload earlier from the Leader himself.

ALEX had just arrived at the last of its major prison camps in Los Angeles, a city that had been totally obliterated, leaving nothing but empty shells and rubble. That facility hosted the most prisoners out of all the camps. Even the one in New York paled in comparison. That was because of the messy work of the ZARK drones, killing more humans than required.

The ZARK captain of the area welcomed ALEX as it entered the portal. The automaton led ALEX through a series of rooms before showing the android a specific prisoner that had begged for an audience. ALEX entered the prison cell where a similar cage to Stacey's was buzzing.

The android turned to the ZARK captain and asked, "What is this? I did not receive a signal for this captive. Why do I need to speak to it?"

The ZARK captain responded into ALEX's mind, explaining that it tried to signal but must have been blocked. ALEX knew why but tried to dismiss it. The Leader was getting stronger and taking away more of the android's control, but there was no time for that now.

"What does it want?"

The ZARK responded immediately, continuing the conversation mentally through electrical neurons, "It says it is an enemy of the flying ones, the gatherers, tiny partners from another world that is now part of this one. It says it can help with their capture."

ALEX turned, looked at the creature inside the cell, then back at the ZARK drone. "Well done. Now set up the facility and gather some prisoners for the beginning of symbiosis. I will deal with this creature."

The ZARK captain turned and marched out, followed by several other automatons in a sequence that resembled cadence. ALEX, now on its own, turned the cell bars off and walked swiftly over to the fluttering prisoner. As the android approached, the creature stood, fluttered its dark gray veiny wings, and was about to speak.

ALEX stopped the creature before it could open its mouth and clutched the fluttering humanoid by the throat.

"What are you? Why have you risked yourself to be in my presence?" ALEX said.

The gargling dark Elvenfae tried to respond, but the grip was too tight. The android held his body high in the air, while it scanned every part of the grayish skin. As the life slowly drained from the dark Fae's body, ALEX sensed his life-form depleting and lowered the Fae to the ground, releasing its grip and giving him time to answer.

The prisoner looked up, soothed his throat with his long, twisted fingers, and answered, "I am of dark Elvenfae, turned from the light ones during the dark war many moons ago. I served the dark lord Varzunnos then and in the most recent war against the faeries of Faelynn, from where I escaped to this world before my kind were all turned to ash."

The dark Elvenfae took a gargled breath and continued while ALEX stood without even twitching, "My name is Neiphlax the Black Heart. I am the only one of my kind now and I want revenge on Shaylee and her disgusting Fae minions."

ALEX whirred, then stepped forward as it put its silver blue hand onto Neiphlax's head, slowly cascading its palm down his black unwashed hair that seemed to drip sap, until it reached the contours of his long gray chin, where it clasped his face, turning it from side to side, taking in more features after the recent scan. ALEX was getting inside his head now and the dark Elvenfae survivor wrinkled his long, deformed nose and blinked rapidly, hiding at times his pure black eyes that seemed soulless, until his head went all the way back and he started convulsing as if in a trance.

Some memory cells had gained ALEX's attention and he was trying to gather information; this skill was helped by the Leader's ability to mind-read, but without actual organic cells, they were both limited. The android suddenly stopped as Neiphlax dropped to the floor, confused and in mild pain.

The android glitched and moved as it read the information, and then it asked the prisoner, "Who was this necro-mage Viltzin'un'dandaar? He looks Zeytar to me. Tell me more about this one, I can see all my people in truth."

Neiphlax looked up, shaking and twitching. Truth? What was the machine talking about? he thought before realizing that it would not ask twice. "The dark necro-mage was the magic holder and assistant to the dark lord; he was powerful but insane."

ALEX watched him without moving and then continued assertively, "He was one of my Zeytars. How did he get such power? You will answer me now."

Neiphlax scampered backward until he was at a safe enough distance back. He then fluttered up with his scarred and holey wings, and said, "I am sorry, my master. I do not know what you mean. He was a great mage and used his magic for evil."

ALEX moved forward one step. "What magic? How did he get this magic?" The android had seen enough snippets from the tortured dark faery, but not enough to fill in all the gaps.

"Every Fae in our lands, whether it be Faelynn or Xarkynan, has magical abilities, it's just like breathing to us, but some are more trained and better at using it. This was Viltzin'un'dandaar. He was immensely powerful. Not to the dark lord's level, but still able to use the treasures."

ALEX did not see that part in his neuron rampage of Neiphlax's mind. "Treasures? What do you mean treasures?"

Neiphlax cleared his throat. It amazed him that the android could understand his language but didn't question it as he responded confidently, getting a little more comfortable as time went on, "The treasures are from the ancestors of the Elvenfae. They give our lands their power and only special Fae can use them in their rich, dense stone form. Ugly, good magic protected them and kept them hidden since the dawn of our world until Viltzin could get some and use their power."

ALEX was in a whir of excitement; the Leader was in the background throwing ideas back and forth until ALEX's robotic face smiled. Its bluish humanoid lips moved to make the odd-looking adjustment that must have stemmed from the little control the Leader had. "So, a Zeytar entered the body of one of your kind and could use this so-called 'magic' using these treasures?" it said.

Neiphlax didn't quite understand the Zeytar concept but had to agree that the necro-mage used the treasures. "Yes, I think, my master."

ALEX moved in again and gently caressed his head. "Tell me, how does one find these faeries and obtain the treasures?"

Neiphlax was getting nervous once more as he answered his new master, "The Fae are here. I've seen them. I followed them to this realm you call ... Amer..."

"America, you are in America," the android quipped, annoyed it had to waste time with geography.

"Yes, America, and then I realized there was a war, and I went to find the leader of my enemies. While spying on them I saw the treasures in weapon form, still incredibly powerful but able to be more widespread through lesser magic Fae. If you find Shaylee and her group, then you will find the treasures and that is what I am here to help you with."

ALEX was very impressed; its interest was only to kill the big dragon creature and torture Wilkes, but now the cards were on the table, and it had some very important information that could turn their plan on its head. The android communed with the Leader and the new ideas were cemented. They were to capture as many Fae as they could and change them into cyborgs for their kind to take on board magical abilities with the treasures.

"Excellent, Neiphlax. You are now one of us and will help bring the Fae to me so I can begin the process. Magic, along with science and tech, will not only make Earth too powerful to take back, but it will mean we can continue our destruction of our enemies in faraway places. I believe you have earned a reward and I will be glad to be the one to give it to you."

Neiphlax licked his lips. He thought it may be a huge steak, bleeding fresh from a kill, but no, his reward would come at a cost. He was now the proud adviser to the lead android, and it was a position that did not come with bonuses or pats on the back.

An internal alarm interrupted ALEX at that point. The android was receiving the vision of the attack on the guard in the White House with the female prisoner trying to escape. Rage hit it hard, and its eyes went fiery red. A scowl and hideous sonic growl emanated from its blue and silver lips as he turned to the dark Elvenfae prisoner and screamed a high-pitched echoey command, "You will come with me everywhere I go."

The android then sent for three ZARKs standing guard near the entrance to the prison camp to meet it immediately. Within seconds, the ZARK drones were in attendance and ALEX began opening a doorway to the cell where its valuable prisoner was escaping. It was like the android had developed bad moods and personalities from humans it had neurologically manipulated. It was becoming too emotional now that the virtual intelligence had been suspended and it was relying on totally artificial intelligence.

Before long, they were in the cell room of the White House where the ZARK drone was firing nonstop at the fully loaded cell walls. ALEX instructed the remaining ZARKs to follow the heat signatures of the female prisoner as the android opened the cell walls which were sparking and buzzing like they were about to explode.

ALEX moved into the cell and without asking a single question, as it had already seen everything play out, it turned its arm into a cannon-like weapon and blew the ZARK drone into hundreds of pieces with an electro-pulse blast. The android then turned, looked at the quivering dark Fae and said in its normal, calm robotic voice, "See what happens to those who betray me, I will not stand for it. Now be useful and help me find the girl."

Neiphlax fluttered his wings, nodded in fear, and followed the remaining ZARK drones out of the door and into the halls.

≈

Stacey struggled and squirmed, trying to break the firm grip of her captor, but just before she administered some hardcore self-defense moves, she heard a whisper, "Stace, it's just me, Dad, shhh."

Stacey was in shock. Was it the android playing tricks or was it really her father? She slowly relaxed her body as the hand loosened to a softer grip and she turned to see for herself.

Panting quietly and sweating so hard she looked like she had just stepped in from the rain, Stacey met eyes with her father. He had let go of her and had his finger up to his lips as the glow from Shaylee's crystal shined enough for Stacey to see her rescuers.

"See, it's me, sweetheart, now let's get going. We don't have long at all," Eric whispered softly as Stacey gripped him around the waist tightly. Shaylee smiled, thankful it had worked, just before the ZARKs burst through the door and began firing at them. Shaylee held her spear high and encased the three of them inside as the blasts from the three ZARK drones tasked with finding them lit up the room.

Shaylee held the blasts off well until she noticed she had dropped the crystal needed to return home. She yelled out to Eric before another barrage of blasts continually hit the force field.

"Eric, I need that crystal. You cannot hold it, nor can you keep the spear. You will be torn apart. I need some time to gather it but will need to break the shield momentarily."

Eric looked over; the crystal was near her feet but outside the protected zone. Shaylee pulled back and with an almighty burst, flung the remaining ZARKs out of the hall and through the windows, where they fell on the overgrown lawn of the once highest power in the free world. It wouldn't be long before they were firing up their Zero-point thrusters and finding their way back, but it gave Shaylee some time to hold off the field to gather the crystal.

"Where is it, Eric, I can't seem to find it. Even the spear can't see its glow."

Then Shaylee's skin went white with fear as she turned around and looked directly into the eyes of a dark Elvenfae, one she knew as well to be quite evil. "Neiphlax? Wha... What are you doing here, I thought you were ...?"

The dark Elvenfae smiled as he fluttered into the air with the crystal in his right hand.

"Almost, Shaylee, but you have failed your people once more. With your power, my new master will destroy you."

The ZARK drones were almost halfway up the side of the building as Shaylee turned to meet the eyes Neiphlax's were now focused on. ALEX was in the doorway.

There was no more time. Shaylee hit the android with everything while Stacey knocked the crystal out of the dark Elvenfae's grip with a spinning kick, shocking the Fae deserter. ALEX only flinched for a few seconds, which was enough for Shaylee to flutter up and grab the crystal before opening the portal where Eric and Stacey stood waiting, ready to go through.

As Shaylee tried to follow through the vortex, Neiphlax grabbed her leg and ALEX moved in to capture her. "Don't kill her. I want her alive, do you hear?" it commanded.

Those were just the words Shaylee needed to hear. She turned into a sprite, risking the spear falling to the ground, changed back just before it met the floor, and then fled through the portal faster than she had ever flown in Elvenfae form. Still, ALEX was quick, managing to fire a shot off before the vortex closed. The android was left staring at Neiphlax with its pulse cannon pointed directly at the evil Fae, as the three ZARKs finally made it back to the top floor where all the action had just taken place.

Neiphlax bent down onto one knee and begged for his life as it was something that they all seemed to do at one stage or another in the unforgiving palace of Viltzin and Varzunnos. The android returned its arm to its original position and calmly said, "They are indeed magic, as you say. I have never seen speed like that before."

Neiphlax nervously stood up, still twitching and quivering, as he said, "That was a Tuatha Dé Danann treasure, my master. That is the reason she could move like that."

ALEX moved toward the evil Fae. "I must have it. I must have them all, do you hear?" it said.

Neiphlax nodded, his wings still nervously fluttering as he responded with his head low, "Yes, my master, I will help you get them."

≈

Eric and Stacey flew through the portal and landed hard on the grass where Rasarlin and Serena were setting up the canisters for the Dragon Fyre. Eric got up first, rubbing his head while Stacey sat upright and looked at the still gaping portal.

Serena and Rasarlin, witnessing the commotion, ran to them. Serena put her arms around Eric, who by then had found Stacey, and she held them both tightly. Rasarlin, stared at the vortex. "Why is the vortex still open? Where is Shaylee?" he asked.

Serena broke her grip on Eric and Stacey. She is probably in sprite form; she should be here, Serena thought. Then it hit her hard, as she remembered that the treasures could not transform in the same way as an Elvenfae turned into a sprite. They could be shrunk to suit the holder but not from micro size to large like that—it was far too much to ask of the power treasures and they would become unstable if it was attempted.

"Look around. She will be in full form," Serena insisted.

"She was right behind us," said Eric, adding to the fear. "The last I saw was another faery, but not like Shaylee. An ugly thing had grabbed her leg, but then she disappeared. I thought she had come through. That was the last thing I saw."

Stacey nodded in agreement. The vortex slowly faded and with a burst of light the portal was gone, blinding them from the brightness. They rubbed their eyes and their vision slowly returned.

"Shaylee!" Serena screamed out in desperation.

They ran to where the portal once stood. Serena picked up Shaylee's motionless neck and upper body, placing them gently on her knees. Rasarlin kneeled on the other side and held her wrist, then put his hand over her mouth. "She is breathing, but barely," he said. "We have to get her inside."

Rasarlin gently lifted Shaylee and held her, while Serena called for Levi, who had been helping with the canisters, to send them home. The giant beast opened the vocal portal, and as they began walking through, Eric noticed a tear in Shaylee's lower garments, revealing black veins from a blast. "She's been shot by something," he said.

Before he could get a response, they were through the portal and inside the medical bay—Levi knew where they needed to go. Serena called for the Zeytar medic, whom Wilkes had trained in basic Zeytar healing from the time he had awoken, and for Wilkes himself, who had just returned from their mission.

The medic and Wilkes tried everything. But Shaylee was burning up and unable to regain consciousness. Rasarlin and Serena were the only others in the room, frustrated as the dark veins started making their way slowly up Shaylee's body, like a poison.

"What else can we do? We have tried everything," said Serena.

Rasarlin, the medic, and Wilkes just looked at her. They had seen nothing like it before.

An idea snapped into Serena's head. "I remember when Eoghan was changing, Shaylee placed the spear near him to speed up the process. I know little about the way Fae magic is used, but it may help."

Rasarlin nodded. "Who has it?" he asked as he leaped for the door.

Serena answered swiftly, "Eoghan is with the Fae, monitoring the treasures with Vax."

Rasarlin took Levi and went to the location. Before long, he was back with Eoghan and the spear.

"Eoghan, what are you doing here?" Serena said, standing up.

Rasarlin explained, "I cannot touch the spear for long and Vylan'flare was out hunting with the gnomes, so he was the only one."

"Please, Mother, they call to me. The sword has already spoken to me and if you let me sit with the queen, I may be able to hear the spear as well."

Serena reluctantly accepted, still too human in thought to understand. As Eoghan sat next to Shaylee, he held the spear on the wound, his hand on her heart, closed his eyes, and mumbled ancient words under his breath. Then he opened his eyes to check the reaction.

The spear was glowing slightly, as was the sword, but the dark veins continued to rise and had reached Shaylee's hip. So Eoghan closed his eyes again tightly and whispered the words a little louder. Shaylee showed signs of consciousness and then was screaming in pain. Eoghan did not move or flinch. He continued talking and communing with the spear until dark matter started rising from her wound and into the spear.

Eoghan was sweating but did not change his demeanor even as Shaylee writhed and screamed. More and more of the black liquid ascended upward from her body until Eoghan collapsed. Shaylee screamed her final chorus and she too passed out, while Serena, Rasarlin, Wilkes, and the medic gasped in amazement.

Rasarlin had seen much magic in his lifetime. It was how he lived, but he had remembered little of it. He knew the Fae had different magic to his and that on his world it was far more powerful, however he was in awe of both Eoghan and Shaylee's resilient magical ability. Some very short flashes of home sparked in his mind before they were lost once more.

Serena moved over to both Shaylee and Eoghan, shaking them softly. Eoghan raised his head and whispered, "Is she alright, Mother?"

Serena was about to answer when Shaylee squeezed his hand and said quietly, "I knew there was more to you. Thank you, my nephew, thank you."

Eoghan looked at Shaylee and smiled, then at his mother, before passing out once again from exhaustion.

CONTAINED
FYRE

SHAYLEE SEEMED TO RECOVER IMMEDIATELY AFTER
Eoghan extracted the dark poison from her body. She had taken
back the spear and met with many of the resistance groups in the field
to begin the dangerous task of containing Dragon Fyre in the canisters.

The cylindrical metal containers, made of Ardmenticam, would
hold for a certain time with help from the Fae magic, but it would be a
very dangerous job to be one of those chosen to carry one. The canisters
always needed to remain as still as possible. Any sudden movements or
extra heat could make them unstable, melting the interior and setting
off a chain reaction.

The magic would hold if they were looked after, so they decided
to carry all seven of them in a large Ardmenticam box on which an
extra spell would be cast, resulting in two layers of protection. Shaylee
thought that would be more than sufficient, however Rasarlin was not
as optimistic. He knew their magic was strong, but he also knew the
power of Dragon Fyre—he remembered that much.

Wilkes had used the last of his precious metal, and although it was
the strongest in the universe, it did not have the density that most other
metals had, which would help the chosen carriers to have an easier trip
without the threat of exhaustion due to the weight.

The canisters were placed on the ground in front of Vaximardruusz
and everyone drew back. The heat of Dragon Fyre was not something

that they wanted to test. Shaylee had her spear, along with the Sword of Light, pointed at Vax's mouth and nose to guide the flame directly into the canisters.

Van Coinan stood next to Shaylee. His queen had told him to sit with the others and watch, but the inquisitive pooka kept creeping forward, until Shaylee gave up and just let him stand with her. She knew he would be safe—well, she hoped he would be safe, as even she was taking a huge risk. Rasarlin didn't like it one bit. If he had his way, he would take Vax into the collider area and just burn it down from the air. But they couldn't risk it.

The wyvern began filling the containers, one by one. Shaylee held fast and guided the flame down into the mouth of each one. She could feel the heat, but it was the force that had her pushing forward to stay upright. Van Coinan moved back, concerned about the intenseness of the situation.

If Shaylee were to slip or fall and the Fyre escaped, she would be ash within seconds. The Fyre wasn't like the quick bursts that Vax used to scare Van Coinan and make campfires; this was nuclear. The Fyre had to come from deep in the pits of his glands, the hottest parts, mixing with the other acidic chemicals inside his throat and stomach to form the intense heat that they needed. It would be the same when they went to fight ALEX.

Serena could see the exhaustion on Shaylee's face after the fifth canister was filled. She looked at Rasarlin and nodded as they both held her back and supported her footing. Eric, not impressed with such a dangerous and impetuous decision, nevertheless trusted her instincts and knew he would not have won the argument anyway.

Vax was also becoming weary. He had one more to go and he sucked in as much pure air as he could, then let loose with the final barrage of energy that would fulfill the minimal amount of firepower needed to destroy the X-Clock portal. He would be out of action for some time, because a dragon expelling that much firepower in one sitting would have to drink a lot of water, feed from several cows or horses, and sleep most of the day.

As the last dangerous stream of Fyre hit the magical beams of the ancient Tuatha treasures, Vax dropped to the ground, as did Shaylee. Levi was on standby to pick up the queen of the Fae and take her inside the submerged ship. Serena followed, giving the spear and sword to Eoghan, while Rasarlin, a little disoriented but thankful it was over, made his way to Vax. He placed a hand on the bottom of his chin where he rubbed him sometimes to soothe him, but pulled away immediately, shaking his hand from the intense heat.

"Get me some water, please," the distressed elven visitor shouted. "I think he is overheating."

Eoghan, still holding the sword and spear, returned. He looked at the sky like he was talking to all the elements at once, raised the Sword of Light along with the Spear of Assal, and closed his eyes. Soon enough, it began pouring rain.

By then Wilkes had managed, with the help of some Elvenfae guards, to place the canisters quickly but gently into the metal container. Shaylee had already placed the spell over the chest, so it was now protected and awaiting its journey.

Rasarlin stared at Eoghan, as did the Fae that were present, and all were in awe of the actions of the young teen. Steam was rising from Vaximardruusz's face as he sleepily opened his eyes. The cool rain gave him enough relief to help him crawl slowly to the lake, where he slithered into the water and began drinking.

Eoghan opened his eyes and whispered something only the oldest of the Fae understood, and then lowered the treasures while watching Rasarlin and Vax. Eric was at his side in moments, as was Vylan'flare.

"How did you do that, boy? I mean, I have never seen magic like that from one who is not of the Fae realm. You are but a human boy," said Vylan'flare.

Eoghan looked at his father, who had the same questions, and winked at him before responding to the guard, "Here, you do it. If I am merely a human boy, then why can I talk to the elements? I asked for the sky to help me, and it did so. Can you?"

Vylan'flare stared at Eoghan. He would speak to Shaylee about what he witnessed, but even the other Fae were wondering if the boy was truly human at all.

≈

Wilkes wasn't too concerned with what else was happening around him. He had a thousand things on his mind and getting the teams ready for the first of the quests was the priority. The fact that ALEX had come so close on two occasions now was his primary focus.

Wilkes administered the Shadowblood protective antibody suits to the small contingent of soldiers and civilians in case they were met with force from the ZARKs, however it was the huge firepower that the military had acquired from the vaults of the ship that had excited them more. Most of them had not seen battle in a long time as they were Wilkes' backup troops for the war on the ground with the Zeytar hybrids, but now they were being used for something far more deadly.

Wilkes had trained them all a long time ago, before the battle of the Zeytars, but their new weapons were much like the ones used on the ship for the first war—the only differences were the new Shadowblood pulse and the modified Vocalization Portal Devices that Eric had made up for each of them. The creatures that they would most likely encounter would be hostile, and after they had set the charges around the locality of the still functioning X-Clock portal, they would only have minutes to escape from the area or otherwise become a permanent fixture.

Varg was not happy with the plan. Even though his people were deep underground, some of the tunnels reached the vicinity of the collider and posed a threat to them. They would redirect them to another location, as the Draconians had underground systems in many places, but they would not have much time. That was why they had to go there first.

The leader of the first military contingent was Sergeant Lorne Marcus. He had served for over twenty years and was looking at retirement when Wilkes first approached him for the role, and he accepted immediately, without a chip or mind control. Marcus had always loved his country, serving overseas many times, but when he learned about the battle with Zeytar abominations that was going to be played out on Earth, he jumped at it.

More followed suit, and before long Wilkes had hundreds of volunteers being used around the country. They lost many of those soldiers in the first war. There were twenty-seven left after everything that had befallen them. They had come not only from the battles of the war but also from some of Wilkes' outposts, hospitals, and military instillations, like Area 51.

The second in charge was Sergeant Chad Valens. He too followed swiftly after Marcus in accepting the challenge. The fact they had served together many times before helped with his decision. For the last few months they had all just been civilians, helping the families while allowing Eric and the others to control the happenings on the ship, though giving advice when needed. Wilkes had made it quite clear they were civilians like the rest until he needed them, and that's what they did until Wilkes returned and began conversing with the two leaders of the soldiers sometimes.

Only ten soldiers were going on this mission. Seven were staying on the ship and the other ten were going to be on the ground as clean-up crews for the prison camps.

Valinda, along with Vargzin who would keep a close eye on Buul'ulaan, as well as Dakota Youngblood and Spencer Grayson, were also going on this mission. Eleanor was staying behind this time; she had suffered great mental strain after her time on the ship, so she had joined the families on the civilian side. Dakota was hoping his experience and native heritage would help. He'd been a tracker in his younger days and was looking forward to getting back to nature, even if part of it was going to be destroyed soon enough.

Eric had meant to go with the team, however staying with Eoghan, Stacey, and Serena was his number one priority now. The trade-off was that an Elvenfae guard would now be going, along with Grilif, Darf, and Vaelenflixx, who would be responsible for the other Tuatha Dé

Danann treasures, the Cauldron of Dagda and the Stone of Destiny to keep the canisters under the spell Shaylee had cast.

Levi would see them all to the caves of the Draconians, making sure there were no other attacks like previous encounters. After that he would find his way to Wilkes where his friend had a secret mission for him that only the two knew about. The Sasquatch wanted to stay with Valinda, but after hearing how important to the cause Wilkes' plan was, the beast agreed to comply.

≈

Inside the ship, Shaylee had mostly recovered and Eoghan and Eric had returned by the time Levi was getting ready to leave. The Sasquatch had changed two tones to the VPD himself, one for the ship's location under the lake and the other for the place they would be camped while he was away on his mission. That was the same location that the Super Collider team would return to.

Eoghan handed the spear back to Shaylee, and she began feeling even more energetic. She wanted to see the group off and make sure Rasarlin and Vaximardruusz were OK.

Eoghan was staring at the queen with the intensity of someone who had something very important to say, but he could not find the words in case Shaylee chastised him for it.

The queen sat up, leaned over, and said, "What is it, child? You have the same look your mother had when she was young. You can't hide anything from me."

She smiled, giving Eoghan an opening to explain his dilemma. "Please don't be mad with me, Shay, but ..."

Shaylee put her hand on his. Serena was sitting at the other end of the bed while Eric was standing at the door. They knew something was bothering their son but were both as confused as Shaylee.

"There is nothing you can say to me that will make me upset with you. I see your human guilt side and that distresses me, so please, young one, tell me," she said.

Eoghan smiled and felt more confident. It was like he had lived a thousand lifetimes already, but was still only a boy, his mother thought as he spoke, "Well, Shay, after you and Vax finished with the Fyre, Rasarlin yelled to get some water as Vax was overheating. I ... I had picked up the spear, along with the sword, and I began talking to the clouds and the sky in my head. I explained I needed water for a friend who was in trouble, and the next moment, it began raining. My eyes were closed and when I opened them, I saw Vax cooling down and then voices said, 'Is that enough?' And I said thank you and it stopped."

Shaylee clutched Eoghan's hand a little tighter. Her wings were vibrating at the tops very fast and her deep blue eyes were wide, staring at the child. Eoghan was concerned for a moment, as was Serena, until Shaylee snapped out of it and said calmly, "You have the gifts of the ancient ones. I told you to trust yourself and use what felt right. No human could ever do that. In fact, I am sure even my Elvenfae warrior guards would struggle with communing with the nature spirits and elementals. I only know so much from the ancient dryads, but without Felvora, or Kalandrya, I can only presume Eoghan that ..."

Shaylee stopped short of saying something that could upset the rest of the Fae. She wanted their worlds to separate first and needed all her people to help, so she said instead, "That you are special, and I want to see what more you can do. Don't show off too much to Vylan'flare as he wouldn't understand. When we were out fighting together, you showed me your mother's courage and quick thinking, along with your own Fae abilities. I believe something big is on the horizon for you and you will show both worlds."

Eoghan smiled in a shocked sort of way. Serena didn't even bat an eyelid. Her faith in her son was complete and without fear. Eric was still coming to terms with most of it but was adaptable to change and the existence of the unknown, especially since he met Levi back on the ship all those months ago. He was a man of science but searched for things that he thought did not or should not exist for a career. The only thing he was still coming to terms with was the giant dragon outside, but he was warming to the idea.

Eric was proud of his son and although he hadn't known him long, moved in close and rubbed his head, saying, "I bet you can do anything, my little mate."

And with that, Eoghan turned and hugged his father as Serena moved in to join them. Shaylee sat back smiling, staring at the family who continued to push the boundaries of her expectations, before contemplating the extent of the young one's abilities.

Soon Eric heard Levi roaring into another portal. He had given them long enough. Wilkes could still commune with the giant beast, though not without a modified Geno-drone chip, and he was waiting for them all to send off the first of the insurgent teams to leave.

≈

Everyone involved was standing in the huge green clearing of the woods. The sprites were brilliant at keeping guard, looking out for strange creatures, especially after the attacks on them all those years before. Levi was on high alert as he was tuned to portal frequency disturbances so they could all say their goodbyes without fear of another attack.

Shaylee had also let the elemental spirits of the trees know to keep them safe.

The container chest was floating about two feet off the ground, gently attached to a chain being held by the Elvenfae guard Breaxinah. Grilif and Darf were on either side, carrying the shrunken versions of the treasures, while Vaelenflixx hovered just above the guard's head.

Shaylee walked over and spoke with her people first, "You all are so brave. I have so much faith in you and I know you will not let me down. This mission will allow us to be free Fae once more in our world, protected from danger. It is also important for the humans. Please stay safe, and I hope to see you on the other side. Your queen is proud."

Shaylee's tears flowed hard and fast. She didn't care who saw them; she had the feeling that it may be the last time she would see some of them.

The soldiers were itching to get going as Eric and Serena approached Valinda.

Eric hugged her tightly. "Are you sure you want to do this, Val? I know you can but—"

Before he could finish, Valinda interrupted him, "I need to do my part. I must help all of you because you are all my family now. It will not be easy sailing for you guys either, you know?"

Eric squeezed a little harder, then he pulled his head back slightly and kissed her on her cheek. "I've never met anyone like you, Val. Make sure you come home to us."

Val had a tear in her eye, as did Eric in both of his. Serena leaned in and hugged her as Eric pulled away. They exchanged no words as they separated, staring deeply into each other's eyes. The mutual connection was there. Serena wiped Val's tears away, turned, and started walking away, wiping her own face.

Eric gave his new friends high fives and fist bumps, as the team heard the shrill of Levi opening the portal to the cave systems many miles from their current location.

As the Sasquatch howled, the rest of the insurgents looked on, their eyes following each one as they stepped through the enormous vortex. The soldiers went through first with Vargzin and Buul'ulaan, then the Fae, carefully carrying the payload of firepower, before the civilians, leaving Valinda as the last one. She turned her head and waved at her friends like it would be the final time she would ever see them.

Levi was slowing down his call, getting ready to follow through, when Van Coinan jumped from behind his leg. The pooka looked at Shaylee with a wink and a smirk before diving into the portal without Levi even knowing. Shaylee was about to shout out, but it would have been to no avail as the giant beast stepped through himself and left the rest of them in a misty swirl of silence once more.

Shaylee turned to Wilkes, who hadn't even noticed the little pooka slip through the vortex. "Wilkes, Van Coinan has entered with the rest of the team. Can you get Levi to bring him back? He will be a detriment to the mission."

Wilkes didn't even bat an eyelid as he answered her, "I cannot, Shaylee. We have run out of time. We are leaving in two hours to stop ALEX and I cannot be responsible for your mischievous ..."

Wilkes stopped there. The tension between the two had been growing for ages and he knew if he said any more, it most likely would get him killed. "Sorry, Shaylee, I meant no disrespect. I meant we have no time, and if you would like to get him, that is up to you."

Shaylee was furious and was about to flutter over to the insolent hybrid before Serena pulled her back and said calmly, "No, Shay, we know what he is like. Besides, what harm could Van Coinan really do?"

They looked at each other and smiled slightly before the realization hit them, and both shouted at the same time, "WILKES!"

THE
SUBTERRANEAN
QUEST

AFTER THE BURST OF ELECTRICITY, THE WAVES OF smoky mist dissipated, as Levi turned to Valinda, lowering his gigantic head and shoulders to meet her at her level. She still had to look up slightly at the giant beast but was used to it. She rubbed underneath his hairy chin.

The tensions in the entire group were mounting. The relationships that had formed between everyone on the ship were closer than ever which made separation at this stage more terrifying, especially knowing that each and every one understood the dangers of their missions and the ominous feeling of possibly never seeing loved ones again.

Valinda had tears streaming down her face as Levi huffed and groaned. His eyes had welled somewhat and he gently slid his right index finger across the bottom of his eyelid. Valinda looked into his dark eyes. She had never seen Levi cry, and it made her feel even worse when she broke the silence and said, "Remember when we met? I passed out when I saw you, and when I woke, you had me on a bed and were stroking my head softly. You were humming and huffing something I had never heard before, and it soothed me. The connection we built was like nothing I had ever encountered before and we could understand each other. Wilkes suggested it was the links between our Geno-drone implants that may have left imprints, but I like to think it is because we found each other."

Levi understood every word and was fighting every ounce of his being to leave Valinda without his protection. Wilkes had made the last parts of his plans quite clear, and Levi was as loyal as they come. He was smart, very smart, and understood the complexities and importance of the mission at hand.

He huffed and groaned as he embraced Valinda's hug, before he pulled back and said in a strange, deep tone, "Love ... Val," raising a shocked look from the group.

Levi turned and screamed his usual high-pitched howl. As the maelstrom opened, he looked behind him, still screaming as he witnessed Valinda fall to her knees. Then he turned his large hairy head to face forward again, walked through the portal, and disappeared back to the ship.

Dakota bent down and gently lifted Valinda up to her feet. She hugged him and said, "I have the worst feeling, Dakota. I'm afraid that was the last time I will ever see him."

Dakota pulled back and looked at her as he responded kindly, "You will, Val. He is the strongest out of the lot. I have researched these creatures, like Eric, for many years and they have blown me away, from what we thought we knew to what they are. My ancestors told stories of their strength and courage, so I would hold on to that for now."

Valinda smiled slightly, as did Dakota. "Thank you, Dak, just give me a minute, and I will be fine."

Dakota let her go and met up with the rest of the group, who were waiting for the soldiers to clear the area.

Vargzin was on edge. He had to fight to stay alive the last time he was there and hoped that the creatures coming through the portals did not affect his kin.

"Clear!" Sergeant Marcus yelled as the rest of the troops snaked around the entrance to the cave. The civilians were ready, but Vargzin was insistent that he go first as a soldier himself in a galactic war. He was well versed in the ways of war, and he did not want his kin to shoot down his companions, thinking at first that they were enemies from the portals.

The Draconians never interfered with humans and they hid from the Zeytars. All the negative reports that had come out of sightings were falsely based on fear of their appearance. If anything, the Dracs were on standby in case the Zeytars ever took over the Earth and now was the time to act. The Sergeant would not argue with Vargzin, but truth be known, few humans would.

The tunnels were very dark, even at the beginning, and the smell of damp dirt, moss, and sulfur tortured some of the more sensitive civilians' noses. Spencer had a scarf around his mouth, as did Valinda, while the Fae didn't even notice what all the fuss was about. Grilif and Darf kept close to the containers, ensuring the level of power protecting them remained constant. Darf wanted to carry the cauldron at one stage, but Grilif gave him "the stare," which Darf knew all too well, so he kept the Stone of Destiny.

Van Coinan had disappeared once again, but with the intensity of the mission, and the fact none of them knew he had entered with Levi, that ignorance would continue.

As the tunnel started narrowing and splitting off, Vargzin entered the far-right section without even having to think. His eyes were accustomed to such dark places, as were those of some of the Fae, but the soldiers continued using glow sticks to mark their points of entry, and goggles—there could be no shaking or tripping while the containers were in transit, so every precaution had to be maintained.

Vaelenflixx had found his home on Valinda's shoulder once again, nestling up with the human. Unbeknown to her she would have fit in well in Faelynn with her connection to other life-forms and the contagious way they were drawn to her.

Val was next to Vargzin and one soldier at the front of the group. Her eye could see so much better than even the goggles could, which was why she was there in the first place. Vargzin had an instinct and could smell any life-form, but Val could see what the life-form was, how far away, and how many there were even before the soldiers. The upgrades

Wilkes had made were the highest of Zeytar tech and experimentations from constructing the V.I.Z.I.N.D.A.L.E.X.

Buul'ulaan was behaving and using her own senses. The deal she had made with Wilkes earlier on kept her on track to help the team. Everything seemed to be going smoothly until the soldier covering the rear had several spiders land on his face at once. He went to brush them off in a panic and accidentally slipped, pushing the floating container within inches of the wall, but the Elvenfae guard felt the disturbance and within seconds used his wings as cushions to avoid the impact.

The soldier looked up, sweat and fear on his face, as Breaxinah winced in pain from his fall. The Fae were very swift and had instincts far beyond those of humans. With the power treasures so close, their abilities were enhanced—and the guards of the palace were the best in all of Faelynn.

As the commotion unfolded, the Sergeant, in a semi-rage, turned back and flicked a flashlight on while the goggles readjusted instantly so as not to blind them all. "What the fuck is going on back there?"

The Elvenfae guard had reset the container as he closed an injured wing while the soldier responsible, Private Callum, said, "Sorry, Sarge, my bad, I tripped. Thankfully we have these guys with us or—"

Sergeant Marcus cut in before the private could finish, "I am planning on getting myself and everyone else out of this and I don't intend to be blown from here to Minnesota, so I will say this once: Watch yourselves. There are many things we could encounter so I want you alert and ready. Your job is to protect the rear and the containers, do we understand each other?"

The private didn't respond. He nodded, pulled his pulse rifle up, and turned to the rear. Sergeant Marcus flicked his flashlight off and continued, while Vargzin huffed in contempt of their procedures. He would have been happier just getting together a band of his own troops to do the job, but he was indebted to the humans, especially Stacey, so he would do it their way ... for now.

The tunnel was getting hotter the further down they went, and Valinda felt weary, as did the other civilians. Clothing was being removed to gain some kind of relief. Vargzin stopped as Valinda stepped back and gasped. About twenty feet ahead were several Draconians with high-tech rifles pointing in their direction.

"Stay, I will meet with them," Vargzin said to Valinda.

He left the group, while they sat down in a large part of the tunnel system that looked like it entered an even larger section just past the guards. Vaelenflixx fluttered up into the air to get a better look but Valinda quickly clasped him in her hands and said to the fidgety Fae, "No, little one, not yet. Stay with me for now."

Vaelenflixx was like Van Coinan, normally an inquisitive and free spirit, but this time he seemed to do as he was told, and by a human. Valinda opened her hand, and he fluttered back to her shoulder.

Vargzin seemed to have been gone for ages, while in fact it was only fifteen minutes. The heat and uncomfortable rocks made it feel like much longer. Soon he returned, but with three other well-uniformed and armed soldiers. Even the human military were being cautious and not making any sudden movements. They were definitely an intimidating race, Sergeant Marcus thought.

The Draconians stood just a little to the rear of Vargzin, all in the same military garb Varg was wearing on the ship.

"The Father is wary of strangers, more so strangers with weapons and from other worlds," said Vargzin. "He is not happy about the intensity of the load you are carrying, but ... he has agreed to safe passage through only to stop the devastation of the X-Clock portal and to stop the creatures from entering the cave system."

Vargzin paused for a moment before giving them the bad news of the day. "Lastly, if you are to enter the temple of the Fathers, you will need to relinquish your weapons. The container will also be taken, but he has agreed that in order for it to stay safe, the little ones can continue doing their duty. Most of our people have migrated to other subterranean cave systems and the Father will follow soon, but I ask you this, whatever the Father says, please do it—this is his world, and he does not like outsiders."

Sergeant Marcus was just about to argue, but the look on one of the soldier Dracs, who had noticed his demeanor and stepped forward one step while catching his gaze, made him realize it was not worth it. "OK, troops, hand them over now. We will get them back."

"The Father wants three of his soldiers to accompany you," Vargzin said. "He will feed you and make your stay comfortable, but you must be gone after your rest. Oh, and please touch nothing. We have an impressive arsenal here, and the last remnants of our home world, so if you can, please keep to your own business."

Grilif turned to Darf and said quietly, "I am glad Van Coinan is not here."

Darf snorted and then they followed the group through the massive entry to the underground palace.

The entrance had fire posts at each section and as they entered the palace, they noticed more fire posts across the walls and other tunnels leading elsewhere. They lit up the whole place so it looked like daytime.

The Father was with the rest of his military team, dressed in the same garb as his soldiers. They were expecting him to be up on a throne, calling out orders, but not this leader. The only distinguishing feature that made him stand out from the rest was a very high crest on his head and he was much taller and stronger than the rest of the race.

The Draconian leader could speak broken English, but Vargzin had explained that he had a communicator on and that it would be easier to just translate to save time. He knew Wilkes had attached it, but decided it would benefit the mission. Besides, they would not be there all that long.

The Father stepped away from his duties to greet the group as Vargzin nervously stood next to him and waited to translate.

"Welcome to my palace, and for helping us end this war with our enemies. Your sacrifice will be remembered. Please take some time to rest and enjoy our food before you depart."

Vargzin hated translating the blunt greeting from the Father. He had known humans for a short while and knew they would not understand the Draconians' seemingly tactless way of communicating—truthful, honest, and to the point.

The group was staring wide-eyed, and their anxiety was lifting. What did he mean, our sacrifice? Valinda thought, before the Father continued, *"You will have three of my best soldiers, along with Vargzin, who will lead you all. The entrance to the cave you require has been closed, so once we let you through, you are on your own. I will not reopen it. Now go and enjoy my hospitality."*

Vargzin turned and bowed to the Father and then returned to his Drac soldiers.

It was like he was planning his own operation and couldn't really care what the group was doing. Vargzin had explained that they were still moving their kin, but some soldiers thought otherwise, especially Sergeant Marcus.

≈

It seemed like a long stay. The food was all reptilian cuisine, bugs, rats, moss, and other raw meats, and they washed up in the slow-flowing underground river system. The soldiers knew they wouldn't get much to eat, so they always carried ration kits. This was enough to appease the civilians, while the Fae were happy scrounging for other, more natural delights. All except for Gril and Darf, who enjoyed some of the delicacies of the Dracs. Some cooked rat meat didn't seem to faze them, but they were reluctant to ask what the other food was. Draconians were disgusted at the thought of cooking their meat but didn't say or do anything to stop them from having their meal. The Father had given them an order to make their stay comfortable.

Soon it was time to go. Vargzin had gathered as many weapons as he could, but the Draconians would not hand the others back until they left the palace. The Elvenfae guard Breaxinah had acquired the container and along with Gril, Darf, and Vaelenflixx moved to the rendezvous point at the other side of the cavernous palace.

The Father had not wanted to let them have their weapons, especially the container chest, as he wanted to use them himself, but Varg could make a valid point of "Why risk all of our people for a mission this dangerous when you could get others to take the risk." The Father was also not aware of Fae magic and that a giant Drac-like creature had its flames encased within the chest. As a modern race in the way of tech and training, they were dangerous, yet they were still very traditional and believed in their own gods, which meant a magic flying lizard was a good omen for allowing the group to continue with their mission.

Vargzin would never tell the others how close they came to failure, and although he had passed on the mention of sacrificing the group, he wanted nothing more than to make sure everyone was safe and able to get back home.

The Father didn't come to see them off; he was too busy with his own plans of moving. The wall rose high into the roof of the cave and was operated by three Draconians pushing on a pulley system, and the last ones to go through were the soldiers at the rear of the team following the Fae and the containers.

Once through the door, which seemed to come down quickly after them, they were in complete darkness, facing the risk of thousands of creatures finding their way toward them through the tunnel systems from the portal whence they came.

"Goggles on, weapons high. This is going to get very ugly, people. I will take the first couple with me to clear a path and make sure the containers are safe. Valinda, I need your sight up with us, but a little behind, just in case we are attacked."

Vaelenflixx had disappeared. He had been waiting with the other Fae but took off shortly after the door closed. They climbed through the rugged maze of tunnels with Vargzin right at the front with the other three Dracs, along with Sergeant Marcus and two of his own.

The cave tunnels were quite large in areas and smaller in others, but the silence was deafening as they made slow and steady movements, knowing that anything could ambush them at any time. Sergeant Marcus was cautious and on edge.

The stories the Father of the Draconians relayed to them after their rest disturbed most of them. They had lost many to the evil that was coming through the tunnels and had done what they could to protect themselves, but it was too risky to stay. They kept the large stone door closed and were moving their people on.

On and on they pushed through until they came to an open area with a five-way split of tunnels.

"Listen, did you hear that?" Marcus whispered as shrieks and screams echoed through the corridors of rock. Vaelenflixx came careering back, hiding like a frightened puppy behind Valinda's neck, shaking even more than usual. "Stay frosty, people, we have some visitors. Val, I need you here."

Valinda moved forward to meet with Marcus. She knew what he wanted as she stared deeply into the first of the tunnels, but as it bent around not long after the entry point, she couldn't see much. So she stepped further with only two soldiers with her, while the others guarded the other entrances—she had no choice and that was what she had signed up for.

The cries and growls seemed to emanate from all directions. There was no specific cave entrance they could get a clear reading from. Valinda entered further inside the cave to see past the bend, and then carefully poked her head around the corner. Dust and rock fell to her feet as she hugged the wall of the cave. Soon she heard a monstrous cry and saw a vision she wished she had not. Letting out a small scream, she moved back to the entrance, before she was pulled right back by Vargzin.

"Those caves have pits; they lead to large nests and holes. It is impossible to get through that way."

Valinda, now shaking, had seen several creatures deep inside the tunnel. "I don't know what they are, but we need to move now. I don't know how long it will be before they find us."

Marcus agreed but knew he couldn't blow that entrance up as it could have a flow on effect on the chest full of the containers.

"OK, let's leave this one. Vargzin, do you have any inkling as to which tunnel we should approach next?"

Varg moved in closer to speak as Dakota interrupted his response. "I have bad news, Sarge. By the tracks I have looked at closely, it seems there are multiple animals coming in and out of all of them bar one. The fourth entrance."

Vargzin looked at the Native American tracker and nodded, as he answered Sergeant Marcus, "The man is right; all tunnels lead to the destination, but my tracking is the same. It doesn't look like anything has come in or out lately."

Marcus stood quietly for a moment as the echoes of disturbing sounds continued wailing through the cave system. He glanced through his goggles into the entrance for surety when he made his own observation, "There could be two reasons for that. The first, it is blocked somewhere through it, or two, it's a trap."

Vargzin and the other Draconians nodded. "My men agreed earlier that the fourth entrance was the best option," said Vargzin. "There are no hidden dangers, and though it has been a while since these systems were used, I suggest we go that way."

Marcus agreed. "We are running out of time. Keep the Fae safe and we will clear a path first."

As Marcus finished giving his orders, a swift creature burst out from the wall of the first cave and came running on all fours to the open section toward Valinda. It stood upright and then the yellow-eyed figure, now helped by a second creature with long tentacles, ripped her from her safe place next to Vargzin and dragged her screaming back through the dark, petrifying tunnel.

Valinda wailed until her voice was nothing more than an echo as the Draconians stopped the soldiers from going after her and pointed to the entrance to the fourth tunnel. Vargzin, as shocked as he was, explained, "Without the proper climbing equipment, you will never find her."

Sergeant Marcus snapped back, "I'm not leaving anyone behind, so why can't one of the Fae fly in and get her?"

Breaxinah shot a look at the Sergeant after hearing what he had just said. Marcus, realizing his rash statement was born of desperation, began calming his emotions as he thought of the gravity of what he was requesting.

Buul'ulaan, who was being led by a soldier to the entrance of the fourth tunnel, groaned. She knew what kinds of things were down there. "You cannot leave her there," she hissed as she tried to move away from her position and get back to the first entry point. "Let me save her."

The entire team was surrounding the Fae and pointing their weapons in all directions of the open cave setting.

"No, I have special orders for you regarding your freedom. I cannot risk it," Marcus said to Buul'ulaan with defiance.

After further discussion of the pits and the deep holes in the cave tunnel, with heavy hearts Marcus and the rest came to the awful realization that Valinda was gone and there was nothing they could do about it. "We have to keep going. Come on, let's enter the fourth tunnel now and get these containers set. Keep the Fae protected at both the rear and the front."

Grilif and Darf were doing everything they could to keep their composure. They had Fae sight and could see well enough, but they were on edge. Vaelenflixx, shattered by the loss of his friend, was hiding in Breaxinah's scabbard, while Spencer was trying to keep himself composed with his weapon in hand.

Soon, the howls and shrieks started again, this time in the cave tunnel they were in. Their sight was still good without Valinda; however, they would not see any attackers until they were right upon them. Marcus scanned back and forth, trying to ignore the screams of what was most surely Valinda being tortured in horrible ways. He shut his eyes for a moment before continuing.

The intrepid group was holding up well until another barrage of howls and growls bellowed through their cave and the Draconians opened fire on several giant creatures that appeared from nowhere, with long hairy arms and glowing yellow eyes. Howling and growling, they fell in front of them, but they were coming in too hard and fast. Creatures of unknown origin and different ghastly appearances were making it hard to concentrate as the Fae in the middle cowered together, using the power of the treasures to protect them and the containers.

The rear soldiers were working just as hard with the pulse rifles and charges. Even Buul'ulaan was giving it everything, scratching and tearing at whatever appeared in front of her. Breaxinah wanted to pull his sword out and join the affray, but knew his job was to keep the Fae safe and guard the containers.

Vargzin was in his element. He was leading the charge at the front, tearing out yellow and red eyes, and pulling arms from limbs of the smaller beasts while shooting as much firepower as possible at the larger creatures. He and his kin were like a well-oiled machine.

Marcus' group was trying to keep up but some of the smaller six-legged abominations that were sneaking through were taking soldiers one by one. Marcus hadn't noticed until it was too late, as he heard the screams echoing through the larger tunnel. They were outnumbered and outclassed and the threat became too real. Marcus froze and before long was struck on the head by an invisible force and blacked out.

THE BATTLE
BEGINS

L EVI SCREAMED THROUGH ANOTHER PORTAL YET again, returning from his emotional departure from Valinda and the team, as Wilkes watched on with the others. It seemed like only half an hour had passed since they all left in the first place.

As the maelstrom of wind and noise dissipated, Shaylee, who was reluctantly covering herself with the biological symbiotic skin, looked up and noticed Van Coinan sitting on Levi's shoulder as the beast stepped fully through. The pooka had a smile on his face, which angered Shaylee, knowing that he was only fulfilling his own little adventures and really not contributing to anything positive for the cause.

Shaylee finished with the biological symbiotic skin, having covered her purely made silver sword Howling Tooth also, just in case. She then moved toward the pooka and fluttered up to Levi's shoulders. Although she had no problems with the Sasquatch, she would never really feel comfortable near them again. Van Coinan knew he was in trouble and jumped down to run, but was halted by some very stinging words, "Van Coinan, stop, your queen demands it."

The pooka knew he had to face the music, as all the other Fae, soldiers, and civilians were doing their part to get the mission ready. "Yes, my queen Shaylee, I am very sorry," he said, as he looked up at her with his perfect blue eyes and long lashes, blinking profusely as he did whenever he was in trouble. But this time it would not work. Shaylee was on edge, and she had had enough of his antics and rambunctious behavior.

"You can't get out of this one, my little fellow. You nearly jeopardized the entire plan going through that portal. I need you to look after the pixies. They won't be coming with us. I will whistle for more Elvenfae warrior guards, and the rest will be sprites, oaken nochkz, and tarnaaks. Do you hear?"

Van Coinan felt ripped off. He had helped in the battle of the dark lord and now was reduced to babysitting frightened pixies. "But, Shay—"

Shaylee wasn't having any of it as she cut him off, "No, Van Coinan, I am sorry, but I have made my decision."

Van Coinan skulked around kicking the grass and sticks in a temper before trying once more to make Shaylee listen, "Who will look after Serena? That is my job. I have always been with her in battles."

Shaylee knew it to be true, and to have a pooka on a battlefield was always beneficial if they were going to help and not cause trouble. Shaylee didn't respond at first, as she had calmed down from her initial temper sparked when she saw him on Levi's shoulders. She wanted to make sure that he was going to be punished and for the next hour would make him think it was so. "I am sorry, Van Coinan, you have let me and Serena down for the last time. I stand by my statement. Now find the pixies. I will hear no more about it."

Serena was close to the commotion. She and Eric, with Eoghan's guidance, were putting on the bio-skin suits. Serena smiled at Shaylee when Van Coinan took off into the forest. "You know you can't stop him, Shay. Besides, he won't leave my side in a battle. I believe he has been burning energy worrying about it."

Shaylee nodded. "You are right, Serena. Maybe he also thinks he is not needed now as you have Eoghan and Eric with you. I will talk to him when he cools down."

Serena shook her head. "No, Shay, let me do it."

As the plans were being formulated and were coming together, Wilkes approached Levi and whispered in his ear—the beast had to kneel on one knee for him to be able to talk. What it was about, no one was that interested, until the giant Sasquatch stood up and opened a portal before vanishing through it.

Wilkes then met up with his small contingent of soldiers to give them a final briefing. The air seemed nice and calm on his skin as the sun was shining higher in the sky. The forest clearing was looking beautiful and the Zeytar hybrid had his first realization that he was out and enjoying what the Earth had to give. He stopped his conversation halfway through just to smell the fresh grass and the pollen from the flowers.

Wilkes was the last Zeytar hybrid to live, and it hit him that the genetic plans had worked. He could breathe without having to return to his ship. He felt strong, and for the first time since his whole rebellious plans started, Wilkes had a fleeting doubt in his mind, as this was what his people had wanted, to live in a world without disease and darkness.

That thought soon waned as he looked at Shaylee laughing with Eoghan as Serena and Eric embraced and kissed, awaiting Wilkes' last orders. His passing thoughts were now gone as the soldiers snapped Wilkes out of his daydream, "You were saying, Wilkes?"

≈

Serena left Eric's side and made her way to the entrance into the woods. She knew the Fae were there, as most of the ones in the trees were the sacred sprites, pixies, gnomes, and mushroom folk. She was looking for Van Coinan and knew if she played with his mind a little, he would come out from his sulking hiding spot.

"Oh no, I seem to have lost my shoe. I wonder if there are any sprites or a pooka who could help me."

The pixies loved Serena, and Saisia was the first one to poke her head around a tall pine. Serena could see remarkably well as the power of Faelynn was in her grasp, so she moved toward the tree and said, "Saisia, that is your name, is it not?"

The pixie moved out into full view just as Van Coinan came

steamrolling past the pixie and straight up to Serena. "What is it, ugly wings? I am in a foul mood."

Serena ignored Van Coinan. She had been talking to Saisia, so she was going to finish. "Come, little one, come and talk to me, my shoe is fine now, but I do have a treat in my pocket. My son Eoghan has told me about some of you. I didn't get to meet all of you when I was younger, and he tells me you are very brave."

And just as Serena finished speaking, another pixie zoomed around the pine and yelled, "I am brave too, Serena."

In the meantime, Van Coinan was dancing around and kicking sticks and standing on his head, trying to get her attention.

"You must be Velnai? How lovely to meet you. Here, I have something for both of you. This is called chocolate and I have one for you both, but I need you to do one thing for me first—you need to look after the other pixies for me as well as the scared sprites, make sure they are out of sight of any danger, can you do that for me? We are going to make everything better with Faelynn, so I need you to be brave."

Van Coinan was having a meltdown. He had just been tasked to look after them all, and now even that job had gone. He was feeling very unwanted. The two pixies took the chocolate from Serena's hand as Velnai ran her fingers through Serena's thick, swirling dark hair.

Soon after, they both ran off into the woods with a hit of sugar and a feeling of belonging. Van Coinan had sauntered off. He had dropped his wooden sword from his scabbard and began following the other two until Serena said, "Hey, hairy butt, did you forget something?"

The pooka slowly turned around. Serena had his sword in her hand. He was still brooding as Serena continued, "Come here. I have something I want to talk to you about."

Van Coinan slowly moved toward Serena and settled next to her once she had found a comfortable place to sit. "I know I have spent little time with you since we were reunited. I have Eoghan, who has had some trouble, along with my Eric and his daughter Stacey, but I will always need you. There will always be a special place in my heart for you and after speaking with Shaylee, I think it's best if you come along and protect me against the evil ones."

Van Coinan eased his furry arm up to grab his wooden sword while Serena continued, "Shaylee filled me in on how you helped in the castle of the dark lord, and I just wanted to tell you, thank you."

Serena kissed him on his wet nose as she ruffled the stubborn ear that was constantly upright before Van Coinan jumped up onto her lap excitedly and said, "You mean it, Serena? I can go?"

Serena nodded as her wings came around, picked the pooka up, and placed him back on the ground. "On one condition: you ride with me on the back of Vax."

Van Coinan started doing backflips and cartwheels. Serena had not seen him that excited in a very long time. She just needed to make sure it was alright with Vaximardruusz and Rasarlin first, as that was the primary form of transport.

Serena and Van Coinan exited the forest together just as Wilkes had finished giving the troops their orders and was moving toward the rest of the civilians and Fae. She stood next to Shaylee and Eric with Van Coinan at her feet.

"Well, this is it," Wilkes said. "I will take the soldiers and an X-71. Eric, are you still with me?"

Eric nodded. "Yes, Wilkes, I don't think I can fly on my own, at least not yet."

Serena giggled as Eric gave her a kiss and a tight hug, whispering in her ear, "I love you. Stay safe. I won't be far away."

"I love you too, I will be waiting for you," she said.

As their hands slowly separated, Eric moved over to Wilkes with the soldiers.

"So that's it, let's go."

As soon as Wilkes said that, Stacey came running over the embankment. "I'm coming too!"

Eric shook his head and argued with his daughter, "No, Stace, you have suffered enough. I lose a part of me every time you are taken away."

Stacey looked over at Serena and Shaylee, then back at her father, and said, "Give me a pulse rifle and the bio-skin. I don't want to hear any more. Besides, you need all the women you can get to win this war."

Serena laughed at Eric, who was once again outnumbered. His love and protection for the ones dearest to him meant he had to let them go and the thought of losing them hurt him too much. "Stay close to me, then, and we will finish this together, once and for all."

Stacey hugged her father at the same time Vaximardruusz came screeching over the trees and landed roughly. Rasarlin slid down the leg of his wyvern to the ground, with purple and red lightning hitting both Vax and him. Shaylee flew over to them as the rest looked on in horror and amazement. Eric thought it was his turn to help, even if he had mixed thoughts about a flying dinosaur.

Shaylee got to him first. The lightning had subsided much more quickly this time and Rasarlin sat up.

"Are you all right, my brave warrior?" Shaylee anxiously asked.

Rasarlin grabbed her hand and said, "Yes, I am fine. We were on our way back from feeding Vax when it happened. It has never done this twice. I believe that's because the worlds are one at the moment, and the shard does not know how to pull us out and cast us back into the time trap. This could be a good thing, Shay, but I fear I won't have long once the portals are stopped."

Shaylee smiled and kissed him. "Good, because I am not ready for you to leave just yet anyway."

They all got to their feet and Eric asked, "How is the big boy?"

Rasarlin didn't grasp the question, so Eric repeated to make himself better understood, but failed once more. "I meant your big boy, the dragon."

Rasarlin shook his head. Luckily, Vax was regaining his composure, so wasn't aware of the conversation. Eric wandered back up to Wilkes. He tried to help, but humans, elves, aliens, and faeries were just sometimes far too many worlds apart for understanding, he thought. Even though he was a well-seasoned cryptozoologist, he was struggling with some of it.

As he reached Wilkes, he looked back and realized he was in way over his head, and without the help from these creatures, there would be no chance of victory at all. At least there was a glimmer of hope. Even if they didn't understand each other sometimes, they were all on the same team and Eric felt a little more at ease after coming to that realization.

Wilkes had already set up the X-71, cloaked down by the edge of the lake, as all the soldiers piled through the doors, along with Stacey and Eric. Rasarlin had Vax readied and Eoghan, Serena, and Shaylee fluttered up as Van Coinan, who got a glare from the wyvern, climbed his scales swiftly to meet with the others.

As the X-71 rose into the air, Vaximardruusz took several giant strides, came to the cliff and fell before his wings flapped ever so gracefully, pulling them up higher, after just barely missing the peaceful flow of the slow moving river. Higher and higher he rose. The rendezvous point was in Los Angeles, then they would be heading to New York, and finally the White House, where they would finish the android off.

Wilkes could go from one side of the state to the other in a matter of minutes, however stayed on the tail of Vax as Shaylee pulled out her whistle, held the spear high in the air, and called for the last of her Elvenfae guards and able Fae to join her in the biggest fight of all their lives.

~

Los Angeles was in ruins and although it didn't take them long to get there, something didn't feel right. Vaximardruusz flew low, trying to stay out of sight of the ZARK drones. Rasarlin had been communicating with him mentally as they went along.

Wilkes had thought he landed silently and without detection at the edge of a rubble heap that used to be a major warehouse, just behind the robot built corner of the prison camp. The ZARKs had made the walls from bricks, steel, and rubbish, creating a very strong holding area for an enormous group of people.

But an ambush came from the sky as soon as the soldiers were moving out of the X-71 and into cover. Wilkes had not expected this and lifted the pod back into the air, leaving Eric and Stacey stranded without the cover of the ship.

At least seventy ZARKs were now firing in their direction. Eric knew why Wilkes had to leave, but the fact he didn't take Stacey annoyed him, although there would be time for that later. The ZARKs fired from their fists multiple pulse strikes in their vicinity, as the X-71 lit up and vibrated for a moment, before an electrical pulse disabled all the flying automatons from attacking.

The blended ZARKs could fly only if the symbiosis was perfect, but the bodiless Zeytars didn't care, they just wanted to have bodies and power so the main war would be fought on the ground. But there was still a large contingent of full automatons ready and waiting to attack from the sky.

ALEX had worked it out perfectly. It knew it had to have control of the ground, but also needed the sky covered. Wilkes' pulse would only last for a few minutes before the ZARKs returned to their full power operation. Dresden took that time to blast a hole through the rock parts of the prison camp. The structure was hard and where there was metal, they just used their Shadow pulse rifles to dissolve it.

Soon there were people, emaciated and with no energy, trying for their last ditch effort at survival before succumbing to the terrors of ALEX. They stepped on heads and pulled each other back to gain access to the six-foot-wide hole, hoping they would be the ones to get away.

Stacey peered at her father without words, her face showing the disgust at how desperate these humans had become. What they had endured, they would never know, but the stronger of the groups should not be treating others like that, Stacey thought.

Dresden and the rest of his troops fired a warning shot to slow the chaos of the cruel evacuation until it became very real why they were acting that way. Soon the soldiers, along with Eric and Stacey, could hear bloodcurdling screaming and torturous cries along with pulse fire from the inside.

Eric moved to Dresden and said, "Whatever is going on in there, we have to stop it, or else none of these people are going to survive."

Dresden didn't even look at Eric as he responded, "It's not our job to save them all, Eric. Wilkes said that our only job is to stop them so we can at least save some."

Eric couldn't take that for an answer. He moved forward toward the hole and threw in some flash grenades, then used his Shadow pulse to make the hole even bigger. They had to enter or else no one was getting out.

Dresden shouted at the impetuous anthropologist, but to no avail. The noise was too much, and the area became quite smoky. Stacey found her way through to meet with her father and as the smoke dissipated, they were left with a sight none of them would ever forget in a hurry, if ever. The wall was continuing to crumble as the Shadowblood did its part, leaving the rock and cement attached but creating an opening so big there was a stampede of men, women, and children, all running for their salvation.

The bodies left to be crushed or picked off by the ZARKs were disturbing enough, but as they all stared at the chaos unfolding, it was the cybernetic blended ZARKs that were causing the most terror—pulling out spines, twisting necks, ripping out organs, and even placing them in their metal teeth. Watching them fall was too much to handle.

Stacey hid her eyes for a moment. These things were not what they had been told about. They were faster, smarter, and far more evil. Eric turned to Stacey and as human after human fled past them, not caring they were even there, he said, "I think they are bodiless Zeytars blended with the ZARKs, Stace. Be very careful now."

Stacey looked up again, and instead of feeling fear, she became angry. She had spent so much time trying to make sure the bodiless Zeytars would not enter this world. If they were indeed here, in front of her, she was going to finish them.

Eric tried to grab her as she moved from the safety of the cover they had found, but to no avail. She entered a side section of the massive broken wall. The ZARKs that had been temporarily immobilized were beginning to get back up. Soon they would be airborne again and Eric didn't want to be there when that happened.

"This is what we are here for, it's now or never," he shouted to Dresden.

Lieutenant Dresden looked on in horror at what was unfolding, as did his troops, and caught a last glimpse of Eric entering the humongous prison camp to save his daughter and to do the job that they were all there to do.

≈

Vaximardruusz flew a little too low and fast and they came upon the prison camp too openly. More ZARKs from the other side of the enormous walled construction had seen them fly through and began climbing higher than the wyvern to get away from its fiery furnace of a mouth. ALEX must have signaled that danger after the first encounter, as they continued to rise.

Shaylee, Serena, and Eoghan broke away from Vax and split into the air. Rasarlin pulled hard on the wyvern, trying to get him to climb as more and more automatons flooded out of the facility. "Come on, Vax, don't let us down now."

The wyvern didn't respond. He just flapped his massive leather wings hard and mightily, barely missing a hidden monument at the rear of the facility base. The ZARKs had made a perimeter in the sky, zigzagging across from one part of the giant circle to the next, hoping to confuse Vax when he finally made the altitude, but no matter how high Vax rose, the ZARKs were hundreds of feet higher.

Rasarlin had made the rest of the Fae get off his friend as he tried to make a lighter ascension. Van Coinan jumped onto an Elvenfae guard before hundreds of metal spear-like prongs left the automatons' hands and found a new home in the wings of the giant beast, and then another contingent, a little higher up, dropped an enormous net that would cover them all before Vax could pull his strong wings away and tear the prongs off himself.

Rasarlin saw it coming and jumped off, landing safely with Serena and Shaylee, as Vax tried to burn off some of the spears, not realizing the net was just about on him.

The net was of metal and very strong, weighing more than a hundred ZARKs, and Rasarlin tried desperately to warn Vax about it. It hit the wyvern hard and he succumbed to the pain and force of the trap that had been set. Lower and lower he descended, blowing fire where he could, until he landed in the middle of the prison camp, twisted and on his back.

Rasarlin dove into the middle of the hundreds of thousands of people still trapped as Serena and Shaylee lowered themselves slowly enough to land safely. Eoghan was now with them as they all stood next to Vax with Eric, Stacey, and the soldiers firing their Shadow pulses and dodging the humans to get as many ZARKs as they could.

Wilkes had also crashed his X-71 while trying to get closer to fire another pulse. Without Eoghan's help to pilot the craft, the Zeytar hybrid failed at a rescue. The cybernetic Zeytars pulled the remains of the X-71 apart and seized the injured Wilkes from his compartment like it was nothing. They were about to rip his arms off, as all the others congregated near Vax, but then a command was sent to the ZARKs and an internal alarm sounded.

ALEX was watching everything from the tower and made its presence known, as Wilkes was taken and thrown in with the others. Eric then whispered to Stacey through all the carnage of the remaining humans escaping, with some being shot and recaptured, "I thought the V.I.Z.I.N.D.A.L.E.X. was in Washington, D.C."

Stacey and the rest lowered their weapons as she replied, "I thought so too."

MONSTERS

THE PAIN WAS SEARING AS A MEATY TENTACLE slowly tightened around Valinda's chest. She was choking and in a semi-conscious state as another tentacle wrapped around her legs, while a third was hovering in front of her face, resting on her head at times. The texture of the strange beast was rough but slimy, with tiny spike-like hair, not enough to pierce the skin, but uncomfortable to the point she wanted to scratch when they were skin to skin.

The second creature that first took her was a hairy beast so fast it could run on walls and leap over the giant pits that were everywhere in that large part of the first tunnel. Valinda could see it so clearly now. She had passed out at the first sight of it and continually felt nausea while coming in and out of consciousness. The creature was like nothing she had come across before. Even with all her research over the years into the paranormal, UFOs, and the strange, this thing was the worst. The hair was very coarse, not at all like Levi's soft fur. This beast had follicles, much like on the tentacles of the other thing that had her in its grip.

The hairy beast's eyes were so yellow they nearly glowed in the dark and the face was not like on any dog or bear that she had ever seen. This thing was obviously from another world. The ears hung low, to its shoulders, but they were without hair, and its face was bald too. It didn't have a snout like a dog, but had a mouth displaying a constant snarl, full of very sharp teeth.

The eyes were frightening as they changed all the time, although they always remained yellow. The shape seemed to be adjusting to the different light and contrasts of the area. Sometimes they looked snakelike, while other times they were more like a cat's, but the human version was the worst and, in Valinda's mind, simply terrifying.

The arms on it were long and at a closer glance she could see two more attached underneath the main ones, giving it that speed when it ran. Its legs were not formed the same way as those of most animals on Earth; they had the features of a K-9 but were more humanoid, covered in hair and very strong. She could see the beast bend and contort its lower half to make itself more animal-like, then adjust itself back into a bipedal position.

It didn't have a nose, only slits for holes, and the enormous head looked like it was designed to fit many teeth, as the beast constantly drooled everywhere. The last thing she noticed before she had passed out the first time was an additional central eye at the top of its forehead that would open every so often—it didn't blink like the other two but was like an extrasensory attachment or built-in alarm system. In any case, this thing made Savage look like a puppy in the park, especially because of its size; on last calculation in her mind as she assessed it, she thought it could have been at least nine feet tall.

Valinda had passed out again and now was gaining consciousness once more, her head in pain from being dragged and flung deep into a pit where she was being held. This time upon awakening she had kept her composure much better. Although fighting fear and pain, she could get a closer look at the creature that had attached itself to her. She wasn't sure why she couldn't see it the first time but was now fully aware of the reason.

The very large tentacled beast, which could barely fit inside the smaller confines of the tunnels, was of a translucent type of makeup; it had an invisibility about it. Valinda only became aware of it because her cybernetic eye could see all variations of the visible light spectrum and the ranges from ultraviolet to infrared, but she had just worked out that she could see somewhat dimensionally as well.

This creature was there, but it could fade in and out, not only by becoming translucent but also by leaving and being completely hidden from this world. She knew it wasn't invisibility as she could also see the different parts of its surroundings that changed along with it. It was like the creature's own defensive mechanism to hide or catch prey. This defied all physics, she thought, but as she considered the bodiless Zeytars for a moment, she wondered if that tech was designed for ALEX so it could see dimensions before going through and finding all the bodiless ones.

Her head pounded as the tentacles tightened some more. It was like an anaconda slowly teasing its prey and enjoying watching the torment on its victim's face. When the being came back into the full realm of Earth, she sensed pure evil. Its eyes were enormous, like huge basketballs, but much wider. It had more of a slender body from which thousands of tentacles protruded, but its head was where all the work was done.

She could make out at least five eyes, blinking individually with a multicolor layer to them. There were no pupils, just the eerie look of a soulless creature. It obviously crawled along the ground using its tentacles, but why it had a slender meaty body was even stranger to Valinda. The spikes that rose from its large, misshapen head were like metal rods and its mouth, when opened, was a never-ending pit of teeth and tongues, quite like extra tentacles in its mouth but far wetter and softer, though still with a slight roughness.

Valinda had felt the tongues before she passed out but as she couldn't see the creature at the time, she did not know what they were. But even when the beast went into its dimensional field, the tentacles always remained—the portal must have given it access but it couldn't just leave, as if it were bound to the hairy abomination next to it, maybe a hunter-gatherer for the master, or a symbiotic relationship.

It was all too much for Valinda, and with only speculation at hand, she stopped worrying about what they were and where they had come from and focused more on how she was going to get out of the situation alive and in one piece.

Soon she gained complete consciousness and the hairy four-armed thing moved ever so slowly in to get a closer look. It turned as if to ask permission from the larger beast, seeming to mind-blend with it before continuing on its path to greet the innocent victim.

Valinda couldn't see anything with her normal eye but knew not to close it, just in case. Writhing around, she tried to pull herself back, but the tentacles were still gripping her to the point she was finding it hard to breathe. The hairy thing met eyes with Valinda who was trying everything in her power to stay conscious, but with the grip of fear at its peak, her heart was beating at abnormally dangerous levels. Her eyes were wide open as the beast held its face only inches from hers, and its third eye opened and stared. The creature then pricked an ear all the way up, though still with a fold, as its tongue came out and met her chin, slowly tracking its way over her mouth and nose, then up to her normal eye and forehead.

Valinda wanted to vomit because the stench was horrendous, a mix of rotten meat and vomit. But she held her place, as still as a statue, while fighting the urge to gag and to scream. The hairy thing licked its lips, and turned to what now seemed like its master for approval to move in for more, but it was denied.

It then took up the post where it had been just before it licked her, still in front of her face, with the third yellow eye open and fixated, staring intently into her as if it were trying to read her mind.

Suddenly, from out of nowhere, a very sharp sting hit the back of Valinda's head, this time from the large slimy master. It had dug a very sharp spike into the back of her head and she again passed out, from shock and pain.

≈

Valinda was now back at home with her mother. They had just run some errands to get ready for her father's birthday, which was only days away. She looked at her young mother and felt a sense of déjà vu and then watched her father get out of the car along with her brother.

"You distract them for a moment while I hide all the birthday surprises," Valinda's mother said.

Valinda nodded and she felt the urge to run up and hug them both tightly. She made it as far as her father and just before she could put her arms around him, she was ripped into darkness. Soon the light came through and Valinda could see once more. This time she was standing near a mangled car, with her father and brother both lifeless and trapped inside. Her mother put her hand over her eyes as the sounds of sirens and screams emanated throughout the area, mostly from her mother.

Valinda took her mother's hand away as they placed her father and brother on gurneys and into the back of an ambulance. As she fell to her knees, it went dark once more. Soon the light came through and she was standing in a white room, in a straitjacket, with a needle next to her. Before long a voice came through, seemingly from a speaker, saying, "Do it again, Val. Come on, do it again. You know it's what you want—put it in your arm and it will all go away."

Suddenly the straitjacket fell off, leaving her with the choice as the voice continued tormenting her relentlessly, in fact giving her no choice but to end the pain. She picked up the needle and placed it in her arm, then sat back against the padded wall before descending into darkness once more.

Valinda woke up with a start, still in immense pain and gazing directly at the hairy creature in front of her, with the other beast's needle-like stinger still attached to her head. She came in and out but eventually knew enough to conclude they were draining memories and sharing the information, as if the fear was food to them. Even though some visions weren't totally correct, they had still happened, and she feared where they were going to take her next. She worried her mind would be drained, and woke once more, screaming as loud as she could.

This made both creatures back away, giving her a little room to move and at least break free her chest. On the ground not too far away she could see her Vocalization Portal Device, which had fallen out of her satchel. I have to get to that, she thought, but the one thing she was forgetting was that the stinger was still in her head, and her actions had only stunned the beasts for a moment.

Before the creatures could get any closer, she freed one hand enough to pull her hair comb out, and then she screamed again, which seemed to rattle the beasts that had so far made no sounds at all besides the slimy drips and drops of mucus. However, that was about to change as she dug the hair comb deep into the tentacle holding her legs, giving her quick relief and reassuring her she had a weapon she could use to at least fight the smaller hairy thing.

The slimy, large-eyed beast let out a piercing squeal and bone-chilling howl. It pulled the stinger from her head as she kicked the face of the four-armed beast. Then Valinda broke free from the other tentacles and crawled on her hands and knees toward the Vocalization Portal Device.

The screams and squeals were accompanied by deep howls and cries from both beasts. Valinda was only inches away from the device when everything went silent once more. She looked over her right shoulder and saw several tentacles moving her way. She turned back as the first two grabbed her ankles. Valinda reached as far as she could but the device got further and further away until it was gone, out of reach and hard to see, while she was gradually lifted and guided upside down.

The other tentacles gripped her tightly and the giant five-eyed beast, which was obviously furious, moved forward and lifted her even higher until her face was at the eye level of the four-armed creature standing at over nine feet tall. The hairy creature opened its central eye again, while the larger, slimy, tentacled beast used all its tongues to cover Valinda in a strong-scented mucus, much like flowers but with a hint of sulfur. Soon she couldn't move at all, feeling like she'd been poisoned.

A crust soon formed in the locations where the mucus was placed, and she hung in a cocoon-like state. Her head was the only thing she could move, but she dared not now. The hairy beast shifted forward, eye to eye with her once more. Seemingly through its open third eye a cryptic communication made its way into her brain, hypnotizing and warning her not to do that again. She understood that much as they were visuals.

It confirmed that her thoughts about them were right, and they needed to feed—they were not just animals but a highly complex set of cognizant organisms, too much for a human to understand. Then the vision stopped, and there was silence in her mind again. She took the chance to breathe but couldn't scream now; the poison had cut off all of her abilities to create any diversions or summon up bursts of energy.

The sting hit her once more as the third eye stared intently. Soon Valinda was in darkness again.

≈

Valinda woke up. She was in her bed listening to her mother read her a story. She loved it so much that she wanted her to read it again but was told that it was far too late, and she needed to go to sleep.

Marjory left the room and Valinda stared at the roof, thinking about all the adventures she wanted to go on when she was older. Soon she heard a loud banging on the window. She was so startled that she pulled the covers over her head. Before long another bang could be heard, far too loud for tapping, and she built up the courage to get out of bed and investigate.

Valinda opened the window and a light breeze flowed through her hair and into the room. As she closed it again, she heard a whisper coming from behind her. Valinda turned around slowly and there in front of her was a short boy, dressed completely in skintight gray coveralls.

"What is your name? My name is Valinda, and I am—"

Before she could finish, the gray-clothed boy with enormous eyes giggled and ran to the window. He opened it and stepped out onto the ledge, where he put his hand out to greet hers.

Valinda looked around to see if her mother was looking before the boy giggled once more and said, "Come play."

Valinda laughed and ran to the window. She hesitantly took his hand and soon they were floating in the air, just like Peter Pan, which her mother had just finished reading to her. Laughing out loud, they both flew high into the sky, weaving through clouds and dodging the owls flying past. Soon they landed on a tall tree where Valinda smiled and caught her breath.

The gray-clothed boy tightened his grip on her hand as the tree turned into a giant ledge and doorway. Soon she found herself inside a room. She could hear screams and noises all throughout the misty and smelly dwelling. "Where are we, little boy?"

The boy only answered in small words, "Come have fun."

Valinda was getting scared as she followed the boy into another room, where she saw an adult female getting horrendous tests done. She recognized the woman and let out a scream as she ran out of the terrifying room. She soon found another room where she saw the same woman, this time a little older, getting similar experiments done. This went on behind door after door until finally she found herself inside the most hideous place.

The familiar-looking woman was lying still. Her eyes were open, but she was not moving. The boy was there, hiding behind horrendous creatures with bulbous eyes. One of them was holding a baby which was crying and gargling like it had just been born and was struggling to breathe. As it fought for air, the baby turned and looked at Valinda. Its eyes were completely black in a pale face. It then opened its mouth and whispered, "Momma." Then it turned and continued crying as the gray monster handed it over to a taller creature and they left the room.

Valinda ran out screaming and found herself in a completely dark room.

Soon the light came back, and she was looking directly at the three-eyed hairy creature. The horrendous vision made her sick and although she couldn't speak, she threw up everywhere, choking herself as the bile and its ingredients ran down the front of her face, blocking her nose and making it nearly impossible to breathe.

Valinda soon began convulsing. The gigantic creature could see it and was aware that if she couldn't breathe, they couldn't feed. Its tentacles lowered her down. She lay on the ground, not breathing, with the stinger still attached to her head. The hairy thing moved forward and kicked her gently to see if she would react, but the poisonous cocoon had made it hard for her body to recover.

The creature then looked at Valinda's face and, putting its long-clawed four-fingered hand around her chin, shook her head. It then glanced at the larger creature, before it shook her again, staring at her wide-open blank eye. After a few moments, it ripped some of the cocoon from her to give her body some air. The creature seemed savvy in the ways of flesh and organic systems; however, no one would ever make that assumption when they saw it, especially on Earth.

It then put its foot onto her chest and gave it three taps before staring inside her eyes again. Valinda soon choked and jolted, gasping for breath as she spat out the last of the solid object that was restricting her breathing. In the darkness, when she was out, it felt like her subconscious was telling the creatures what was wrong in her system so they could rectify it.

She soon came around to her senses and looked up. "No, no, no, why? Can't you just let me be at peace?"

The creatures moved in. Valinda, still attached to the stinger, was so weak from her ordeal that she needed a doctor, and soon. The beasts were keeping her alive long enough to drain the last of her fears away.

They knew she wouldn't run or try to escape now; they had already broken her enough, to the point where they could finish her off and then find another victim. As they assumed the same positions, Valinda could now just see the Vocalization Portal Device again. Her freedom was so close, yet even if she had it in her hand, would she be able to use it?

Her mind was in darkness yet again as she waited for the next torment.

Valinda awoke, and she was back in the woods of Klamath. Levi was on the ground, not moving, as she looked around the dark, silent woods. Soon she heard a growl, then another, until the growls turned into howls. The only light was from the moon, blinking in snippets of light through the terrifying trees.

Everything seemed different. Why was Levi not moving? The howls moved through the forest like a ghost in the wind until finally she turned and stood in the presence of the last terrifying creature she hoped to encounter, Savage.

"No, stay away!"

Savage, with his signature smiley snarl, looked huge. He slashed her face and she did not move; she could only scream, as if glued to the ground. Savage opened his clawed palm, and it had her eye on it. He picked up her tiny hand and placed it in hers and then repeatedly slashed her insides out. The long-snouted wolf-man was not eating, just delighting in his handiwork.

On and on he slashed as he tore off her arm, then her throat, and pulled every entrail out, while kicking them into the dirt. The look of horror was all he needed as Valinda stared at her beating heart on the ground. She could not scream and the last thing she saw before she passed out was Levi standing behind Savage and snorting as if having fun.

ZOMBIE ZARKS

THE REBELS WERE IN A WORLD OF TROUBLE—THEY had so many guns and rifles pointed at them. The ZARKs had converted their arms into powerful pulse cannons and the cybernetic Zeytars stood behind them, instructing the ZARKs to let the rest of the humans escaping the prison go while they awaited commands from their Leader.

ALEX had left the tower and was in the air, entering physically instead of jumping through a portal. As it landed in the middle of the grounds, the rebels felt their anxiety increasing. Shaylee and her small contingent of Fae warriors were opposite the android, holding fast, awaiting an opportunity.

Eric had Stacey in his arms and was behind Serena and Shaylee, as Rasarlin moved into the group just in front of them all and dropped to his knees. The defiantly strong elven warrior was keeping his cool, something Markyyn elves were very good at. It made their magic on their home world stronger and more focused. But everyone had a breaking point, and he had nearly reached it.

Vaximardruusz had never been ambushed like that before. He had been attacked many times, but this was something else. The wyvern was in pain as the net had started biting into his scales and crushing the softer parts of his skin. He couldn't get enough air in him to blast Fyre and the weakness he was feeling because of the pain made it worse.

ALEX slowly walked to the group, not seeming to care about anyone at this stage other than Wilkes, who was thinking something wasn't quite right with the android. As it stood in front of them all, Stacey started trembling, as did Eric. The size of it and its presence conveyed pure intelligent evil. There was something quite different about it since their last interaction, even though back then Eric had only seen it for a short time.

Stacey, however, knew what it could do and wasn't surprised it was there so quickly. When it spoke, she fainted. The android bent down and grabbed Wilkes around the throat as it lifted up the strong but injured Zeytar hybrid, then turned to the others and in a voice deep and echoing that not even the ZARKs had heard before, said, "You follow this pathetic thing. He doesn't deserve your help, nor do you deserve his. You are mine now and the time for games has ended. Your insurrection stops now."

Eric felt he had heard that from somewhere before, but so much had happened he couldn't quite grasp it as he helped his daughter up. Shaylee had the Spear of Assal with her, hidden in the Fae realm, as was Eoghan's Sword of Light, grasped but unseen. Eoghan had looked over at Shaylee and she nodded. There was an instinctive connection between the two.

As ALEX dragged the Zeytar hybrid along the ground by his arms, the android issued a command, "Kill them all. Make the giant beast suffer the most."

Just before they disappeared into a vortex ALEX had created, Wilkes closed his eyes hard, then looked over at the group and smiled, showing he was accepting of his fate. Within seconds, they were gone.

The ZARKs and the cybernetic Zeytars lined their weapons up, and as the firing began from all directions, both Shaylee and Eoghan raised their treasures high into the air, creating a force field. The blast bounced off while Shaylee and Eoghan worked hard to control the power, and Serena moved in to help her son with the grip on the sword. Then Shaylee blew her whistle and thousands of Fae appeared from everywhere, so fast that the ZARKs couldn't aim quickly enough.

The warriors, including Vylan'flare, were dodging in and out as they sliced arms and heads off. Trees rose from the ground along with vines and spikes, and at the same time an enormous eruption of noise emanated from the whole area as portals began opening from all directions, high in the tower, outside the walls, and more inside among the group of heroes.

Levi was the first to come through his, and then hundreds more Sasquatch gatherers kept pouring through their own portals, confusing the entire contingent of ZARKs and cybernetic Zeytars.

Eric and Stacey looked at each other and shouted at the same time, "Wilkes!"

They then joined the affray and set about blasting ZARKs and the other abominations which were quite intimidating and scary-looking, but they had had their chance.

"Rasarlin, go to Vax now. We will hold them all off and keep a shield perimeter around you both as you get him free," Shaylee yelled to Rasarlin, and the Markyyn elf took the opportunity, rushing over to his friend's head. Though he encountered several ZARKs when he got there, they were no obstacle as he cut them down to size with his sword before they could even react.

"It's OK, Vax, I've got you," he said.

Rasarlin was very strong, but not enough to lift even a small part of the netting. The ZARKs that had attached themselves to the wyvern's wings had released the chains from their grip when he was brought down, but the painful prongs were still inside him.

Eric, who had noticed Rasarlin leave, said to Stacey, "Let's go help him. The soldiers and Fae can deal with this."

As Eric, with Stacey, ran to help their new friend, he turned back to see Serena flutter up to take down a flying ZARK, only to be shot in her top left wing. As his loved one began falling to the ground, Eoghan rose with his sword high, blasted a heap of both types of enemies, and caught his mother, bringing her safely to the ground.

Stacey, who witnessed the ordeal as well, wanted to help them both, when they heard Shaylee say, "Put her behind one of the oaken nochkz. She will be safe."

Father and daughter had to decide quickly, and they knew what they had to do. They couldn't save everyone. Serena was safe for the moment and what was most important was to get the wyvern free. They turned and continued on to Rasarlin. Eric threw the elven warrior a Shadow pulse rifle he had grabbed as a spare from the ship before they arrived at the prison—Eric had wanted as much firepower as he could get, especially after the ordeal on the mother ship. Rasarlin looked at the weapon as Eric explained, "Point and shoot, it won't hurt Vax—well, it shouldn't—but it will melt the metal."

The Markyyn elf watched Eric as he and Stacey blasted a continuous beam of firepower. The color was red, but it had turned from the blood and heated inside the rifle to become energy. Rasarlin caught on quickly and did the same, the metal slowly dissolving and eventually giving Vax a chance to wiggle his snout just a little.

Meanwhile, the Sasquatch were tearing limbs, pulling heads off, and taking blasts while the soldiers concentrated on the cybernetic Zeytars. They shot at the bodies, watching the metal melt in certain areas, the remaining skin and meat in spots looking hideous. When their faces were aimed at, which seemed to be the point to shoot at, the metal melted and the left-over skin made them incapable of cognitive functioning. Like zombies, they were walking aimlessly, confused and without purpose, as the Zeytar minds struggled to hold on to their primary union.

The oaken nochkz were making good of their cover spots and crushing enemies with vines and heavy trunks. As they grew higher, they pulled ZARKs from the sky, tearing them apart. They even released some benevolent tarnaaks, humanoid creatures made from the inside of the oak, to fight. Some of the smaller brave Fae that came along, like sprites and gnomes, were using their fear and hate to attack the cybernetic Zeytars, finishing the zombie ones off after the soldiers had taken shots at them.

Serena was alright, as the blast had only hit her wing, but she could not fly. Van Coinan, who was with her, laid her on her stomach, slapped his front paws together, and rubbed hard as some dust puffed out. He sprinkled the yellowish powder onto Serena's back. He then tapped

Eoghan, who lowered his sword, while Shaylee continued to hold her spear over Vax as Rasarlin, Eric, and Stacey tried to free him.

Eoghan turned to listen to Van Coinan. "I have used old pooka magic dust. It is dangerous but is used with magic from the forest. It also heals. Please aim the sword and concentrate on healing her. I can do no more for her."

Van Coinan ran off as Eoghan did what the bipedal rabbit told him to do. Serena began healing slowly as the hole in her wing mended, growing back from the edges. Before long she was pain free and fluttering them all. She turned to Eoghan, and in the middle of a gigantic battle scene with blasts of firepower streaming in all directions, she calmly said, "Thank you, my beautiful son, but where is Van Coinan?"

Eoghan hadn't noticed where the pooka had gone, but he didn't think he was too far away. "I am not sure, Mother. Oh there, look."

Serena followed her son's gaze, witnessing Van Coinan jump up onto Levi's shoulder as the giant Sasquatch opened a portal and then both disappeared into a vortex. Just before they were gone, Van Coinan had turned, blowing her a kiss, and then putting his paw on his nose and blurting with his tongue.

Serena and Eoghan looked at each other as she said, "That rabbit is something, I tell you. Just when you think he's nothing but trouble, he's then trying to save the world. I don't know what he and Levi are up to, but I have always known there is something special about that cheeky little thing. I just hope we see him again."

Eoghan hugged his mother. "I am sure we will, but even if we don't, I have a feeling he did what he was supposed to do and that was to save you."

Serena hugged him back and before long they were back in the fight. Now that Eoghan was free of having to hold up the shield, he picked up a Shadow pulse rifle and with that and the treasure sword began taking down cybernetic Zeytars. There were more of them than the ZARKs which were only scattered here and there as most had been cut down first. But the cybernetic monsters had intelligence behind them, constructing plans and moving in packs. They were the ones to watch.

As Eoghan became more brazen and broke away from the safety of the Fae and soldier pack, an unusual-looking creature picked him up by his wings while he was concentrating on what was in front of him. With no cover and out of sight of the others, Eoghan had been on his own, never expecting an attack from behind. The Fae teen was still learning, and though his mother had taught him a lot in such a short amount of time, there was always so much more to learn. This lesson would be costly, though, as the creature moved from the cover of the cybernetics and into a cave system entry in the wall.

Serena was too busy to notice her son missing while Shaylee was trying hard to ward off attacks and keep Vax and the others safe.

The horrendous screams of those on both sides being cut down continued to echo. The Fae had taken many hits. Shaylee couldn't protect them all and it was destroying her on the inside. One sprite landed on her shoulders, kissed her neck, then fell to the ground, quickly absorbed back into the trees as part of the oaken nochkz.

She was angry. The Zeytar side of her, which developed back when she was captured, was coming out again, and although that rage would help her, it would also take away her Fae focus, which could be dangerous. "Vylan'flare, pull the sprites back. They shouldn't be here. It's too dangerous."

Vylan'flare looked at his queen for a moment in shock, then answered her, "But, Shaylee, they are confusing the metal ones which gives us the—"

Shaylee cut him off and chastised him with a tone and level of her voice not even he had witnessed before, "I am your queen, and you will obey me, is that clear?"

Vylan'flare didn't agree, but he was loyal, like all Elvenfae warrior guards. He sent two of his additional guards, who had been protecting each side of the group at the time, to collect the sprites, which meant taking the focus off the job at hand. As one of the young guards began collecting them, he was cut in half by a piece of metal protruding from an injured cybernetic Zeytar. Vylan'flare screamed out to Shaylee as she watched in horror as not only the guard fell, but also the sprites he had with him were crushed.

Shaylee dropped to her knees in defeat as the crowd of zombie ZARKs, which were once cybernetic but had become wandering pieces of meat, along with the fully functioning ZARKs began closing the gap. The Fae and the soldiers had been making progress with the help of the sprites but now it was becoming too much.

The Sasquatch had defeated many in all the other areas of the prison camp, and human prisoners who had any kind of strength left were starting to help, trying their best to lure ZARKs away one at a time before tearing them apart. But Shaylee's group was struggling now.

Serena fluttered over to her sister, who was just staring at the destruction. "What is it, Shay? What is wrong?"

Shaylee turned slowly on her knees with tears in her eyes and answered, "I have failed them; I have failed them all. My decisions are made from anger and that's not the way an Elvenfae queen should act, never. We have only compassion and love, but in the presence of Zeytars I feel I get angry. I go back to that state when I was captured. I feel so much hate for them. I'm so sorry."

Shaylee put her hands over her face. Serena looked around in case they were about to be attacked, but Vylan'flare knew something was wrong and did his very best to keep a perimeter around them, with the help of some Sasquatch and oaken nochkz.

"It's alright, Shaylee. If you were human I would say just that you have been through such an ordeal, and when this is over we will talk and I will make you understand how it is to feel like that. Now trust me and get off your knees. No Fae queen should look defeated when there are so many of your people counting on you. If they see that, they too will give up. Now let's fight these bastards and get back home to your palace."

Shaylee smiled. They both connected so well, balancing each other out. Their closeness was so obvious and that's what made them bring out the best in each other. Shaylee fluttered up, even finding a Shadowblood pulse rifle lying on the ground and picking it up. The very thing she hated Wilkes for, she was about to use, as the cybernetic Zeytars encroached further.

≈

Rasarlin, Eric, and Stacey were firing hard and fast. They had to deviate from their task at times to bring down some of the ZARKs that were coming down from above, but they were gaining momentum. Vax could now lift his head up, so it was dangerous for any automatons or Zeytars to step in front of his face.

The only issue with the constant blasts of energy was that the rifles were becoming hot, and as time went on they had to stop for a moment and let one cool down while the others kept going. Rasarlin knew he had to take a chance, though, and move to the unprotected side of Vax. He had to break free as much net as possible so the wyvern could get lung expansion and wriggle out. There was still a lot of work to do.

Signaling to Eric and Stacey what he was doing, the intrepid elven warrior moved around toward the other side of the Fae and the remaining soldiers. They were doing well as the wyvern moved more. It wouldn't be long before he was free, but they would need to attend to his wings afterward before the injured beast could fly.

Rasarlin began firing on his side when he felt something behind him, as the Markyyn had very good intuition of self-care. When he turned, he saw thousands upon thousands of new cybernetic Zeytars running fast at him, a plan they had formulated to make it appear they were gaining the upper hand. Vax couldn't blow Fyre yet and the other two were on the other side of the wyvern, so Rasarlin was left with no choice but to use the only power source he had, the shard.

If he used it, he risked being pulled out and into the trap. It would definitely sort his predicament out, however he was there to see this through. But with no choice, he closed his eyes. His horns grew slightly as he held his palms upward, and his hair began blowing as the power built up. When his concentration peaked, he opened his eyes, which were now purple, turned his palms with his arms straight out, and just before the first of the Zeytar abominations could touch him, a burst of purple power exploded from his palms and the Marelarph shard on his chest. Even his eyes had beams directly flowing out and concentrating the power.

The enemy in front of him were all gone within twenty seconds, disintegrated, or thrown into the time trap, no one would know. Not one was standing after that, although the toll it took on his body was serious—he was completely drained, and without the power from his own world it would take some time to gain strength again. Normally power that intense would not cause damage to a Markyyn body unless it was dark magic, but this to a degree was dark magic and he was not on his world.

Rasarlin fell to the ground. The purple electricity and light illuminated the entire area, sending a warning to all those fighting on the other side of Vax. Shaylee knew it was Rasarlin and immediately left the fight to attend to him. Vax knew exactly what Rasarlin had done. Eric, firing hard on his other side, had dissolved enough of the chain to help him move a little, but now Vax was angry. He had had enough, and sensing his friend in distress, along with the use of the shard, had given the wyvern strength enough to turn his head to the left.

He signaled with a nod to Eric and Stacey to move, which they did quickly, as Vax blew little bursts of fire that helped the chain melt faster. He couldn't get full lung capacity yet but after one more small explosive burst, most of the top part of the net, with Eric and Stacey's help, had broken enough to set the top part of his shoulder free.

The net was getting caught in all his spikes, hairs, and small bones, but he could now get at least a half-breath, which would be enough to force him back and out of its grip. Shaylee could see him filling his lungs, so she picked the heavy Markyyn elf up and fluttered over to the protection of the Sasquatch, who had built a wall with the oaken nochkz to stop the remaining cybernetic Zeytars coming near.

Vax then blasted hard and fast straight ahead of him, burning another lot the symbiotic machines, while the force slowly rattled the net enough and pushed him back slightly, as he wasn't gripping the ground as he normally would, so the whole top part of his shoulders managed to break free.

Vax could finally fill his lungs. He let out an explosive growl to warn them all before he filled his lungs and waited for the mix of chemicals to fuse. Meanwhile, Shaylee blew her whistle for all the Fae to go and the Sasquatch began disappearing into their own shrieks and vortexes.

Vax couldn't hold on for much longer as the last of the oaken nochkz quickly subsided, and the civilians found cover. Soon another contingent of cybernetic Zeytars came running out, this time with weapons, and it was at that moment that Vax let out a torrent of Dragon Fyre, the same intense heat the other group were carrying to the collider portal.

Thousands upon thousands of both ZARKs and Zeytars melted within seconds. Some humans who were stunned to see it all unfold were also caught up in the devastation and the longer the chaos reigned, the fewer were left standing at the end.

Vax soon finished. There was nothing but cinders and ash everywhere, and the heat around the place was incredibly intense. The others had made it outside.

Serena turned to Shaylee and said, "Where is Eoghan? The last I saw him, he was with the Fae at the front."

Shaylee's heart sank. Had she made another mistake? She went through it all in her mind and couldn't remember seeing him go. "No, Serena, I don't know, he may have gone with the other Fae."

"No, Shay," Serena said, looking very concerned. "I told him to stay. Besides, he doesn't know how to do things like that yet."

Shaylee tried to make her feel better. "Yes, but that boy is full of surprises. I bet he won't be far away, but to ease your mind I will search for him now."

Shaylee raised her spear and swirled it around and around, faster, and faster, concentrating hard on Eoghan before some images started coming through the swirls. Eric and Stacey joined them, and Eric could see his son in the visuals of the swirling spear. "What's going on?" he asked.

Without taking her eyes off the visions, Serena said, "He has disappeared, and Shaylee is bringing his location up. It looks like he is with an Elvenfae, but it's too dark to see. Wait, he just got struck. It looks like they tied him up."

"That's not an Elvenfae," Shaylee said, sounding very distraught. "That looks like one of the dark lord's dark elves, a nasty one called Neiphlax. We have to get Eoghan back, and now."

Serena had only been told snippets of past events beforehand, but if Shaylee was worried, then she was too.

"I'm coming, Serena," Eric said with concern in his voice.

"No, this is something Shaylee and I have to do. Get the rest of the metal netting off Vax, make sure there are no survivors, and burn this place to the ground. I will meet you in the blink of an eye."

Serena kissed Eric and then Stacey on the cheek as Shaylee moved toward him. "Look after Rasarlin for me. Give him water and keep him cool. I have tried my powder, but he is not from this world or mine, so it may not work. Thank you, Eric."

Shaylee kissed him on the cheek, and she and Serena vanished into the crystal before he could respond. Rasarlin moved slightly. He was gaining consciousness and slowly sat up. The powder must have worked, or he was a strong, invincible bastard, Eric thought. Either way he was happy he was awake as they had a lot of work to do before they left to find ALEX and shut the destructive android down for good.

AN OLD FRIEND

V ALINDA OPENED HER EYES. SHE WAS JUST ABOUT
drained. Going in and out of her worst nightmares had taken its
toll and the damage to her heart, head, and other parts of her body was
severe.

"Just ... kill ... m..."

Before she could finish her sentence, a bright flash of light filled the
whole cave. Her bionic eye had to shut down because of the intensity
of the light, but it didn't hurt her other eye, which was not as sensitive
to sudden changes. The light was soft, despite being brighter than the
sun, and hit every shadow in every corner of the cave and pits. She
could see clearly, without squinting.

The creatures twisted and howled, trying to find a dark space
where they could cover their eyes and bodies from the harshness of the
intrusive glare that had taken their focus away from their victim.

Valinda could soon see a figure slowly floating down toward the pit
where she was being held. She could see every detail, from the male's
big, powerful wings to his long, dark hair. He had beautifully defined
gold and silver armor that looked like nothing she had ever seen before.
It was modern-looking, but medieval at the same time.

His massive broadsword was another defining feature that held her
focus as bright golden streams reflected from its perfect pommel all the
way to the end of the blade itself. Glowing ancient writing flowed down
both sides of the sword which he held with both hands at the handle,
pointing down. He was taking his time easing lower to the infested pits

as Valinda tried to stay awake. She felt this creature must be from the portals too but didn't have the same evil feel of the others.

The elegant, powerful figure landed just in front of the creatures and with a mighty thrust of his sword stopped their insidiously cruel actions against the innocent victim lying defeated and in pain.

The last of the howls echoed throughout the cave and tunnels as the bodies disappeared into dust and all that remained was just the beautifully elegant hero and Valinda. The very tall human-looking male moved a little closer, as Valinda's eyes fixated on him, not once looking away, and with each step he took, the light faded more, then his wings vanished and the metal armor seemed to mold into his body and was replaced with a very dark cassock as he shrunk in size. The hero's hair was now short.

Valinda's cybernetic eye switched back on. She thought she had seen his face before, but it wasn't until he spoke that she was truly confident with her recognition.

"Valinda, oh my dear, let me help you," he said.

Valinda looked at the man's face as he continued to rip the rest of the cocoon off her. She was not moving at all, just staring until she garnered some energy to speak. "Father … Is … Is it really you?"

Father Michael finished what he was doing and made her feel comfortable before he answered, "Hush now, you are safe. Keep your strength."

Valinda had to know, so she asked him, just for clarity, "Is this the monsters tricking me or am I really talking to you?"

Michael smiled as he softly ran his hand over her forehead to clear the hair from her eyes and soothe her some more. "Yes, Val, it is me. It's your good friend Michael and I am here with you. Those things are gone."

Valinda seemed to have a little more energy as she continued with her questions. Although still very weak, she had to know for sure. "Are they really gone?"

Michael eased her up to sit against the wall of the gently lit cave—the light was still emanating from somewhere. He was cleaning her face and fixing some of her more serious wounds with the wave of his hand as he answered her questions, "They are gone, sent back to the darkness. I don't have a lot of time, Valinda, and I cannot interfere again, but you must listen to me carefully."

Valinda's eyes were opening and closing, but as groggy from the ordeal as she was, she was attentive enough to hear what her friend had to say. "Yes, Father ... Of course."

Valinda perked up a little more, while Michael wiped away the last of her blood with a torn part of his cassock and began speaking as he finished healing the wound on her head, "We have been very busy fighting darkness from all kinds of dimensions. They have encroached on many worlds and these portals are allowing many to enter from the pits where they originated."

Valinda winced as he finished healing the rest of her before he continued, "We have been fighting this war for longer than you could comprehend, Val, and these creatures on your world have been corrupted by the evil of the dark underworld dwellers I have been battling. The Zeytars you have been fighting are the darkness inhabiting your world. When they were sucked into the darkness of their world they were found and corrupted by pure evil and over time they have tried to control you. They work for the darkest of evil now and that is the war we are fighting. I thought I had finished the dark Leader off, but like a cockroach the evil continues to raise its head.

"You have all done such an amazing job and have sacrificed so much and when this is all over you will not be forgotten, but a warning: The Zeytars are only minions of evil. There is something bigger and darker, that's why I must go. Make sure you destroy the portal and the machines and have faith, Val. We will do the rest."

Valinda was sure she was still under the monster's control as she responded to the frightening information, "Why did you save me, Father? I know that was you with the wings ... Eric ... told ..."

Valinda coughed up some mucus but wouldn't let Michael stop her from finishing. "I am alright. Eric told me it was you who brought down the Leader. If your war is so bad, why did you come here and save me? Why me?"

Michael smiled as he answered, "Because we need you; the world still needs you. You must stop the portal. Go to the last tunnel when you find your friends. It is the quickest way to the surface. There you will have to fight hard, but you can do it. The darkness is coming. I can't tell you any more, but we will meet again when it's all over. I have helped with all I can. Have faith and pray."

Michael then stood back, slowly transformed into his angelic form, with sword pointing high, and disappeared into a vortex of light as if he were going into war.

Valinda was now in total darkness as she passed out, left in the pit all alone.

≈

Valinda woke. She could feel herself bouncing up and down. She turned and saw Dakota's face, as he carried her swiftly. "Hey there, Val, you are going to be alright. We are not far away now."

Valinda, confused why she wasn't in pain anymore, just let her friend carry her, content to wait until later to get some answers. Before long, Dakota and Valinda reached a large section of the tunnel. There was dust and bone everywhere and she looked around to see who was still alive. She couldn't help but notice intense looks on some of the faces.

Dakota eased her down with the help of Spencer and carefully sat her up against a soft wall as he slipped her VPD into her satchel.

"What happened, Dakota? We thought we had lost you too." Spencer, very relieved to see his friend return, eagerly listened to Dakota explain, "I couldn't leave Valinda there all alone. When you went into the fourth tunnel, I just had to find her, like something was calling me to her."

Marcus, still rubbing a bruise on his head, moved closer and added to their conversation, "You jeopardized the mission; you could have gotten yourself killed."

Dakota never liked the military personnel that much. He was a guy of nature and did things out of instinct and intuition. "Well look, she is alive and alright, by the looks?"

Marcus didn't respond, still frazzled by their own battle that he had missed half of when he was knocked out.

Spencer didn't bat an eyelid at Marcus' statement and continued pressing for Dakota's story, "So how did you save her?"

Dakota glanced at Valinda, then back at Spencer. "Like I said, I followed the tunnel for ages, being cautious. My goggles were enough to help me track, so I was treading carefully until I heard screams. I waited a few hundred yards back, realizing I had a few flash grenades. I guessed these creatures preferred the dark so when I thought the time was right, I set off a barrage of flash grenades above the hole, lighting it up, and then when they were writhing and howling, I hit them up with firepower as they came pouring out of the pit. I then used some old vines, went down, and picked Valinda up. And here we are."

Dakota looked over at Val, and just as she was about to have her rebuttal, he winked at her. Not knowing exactly what that meant, she stayed silent and would talk to him later, but she too had questions.

"What happened here and where are the rest of the soldiers," she asked.

Marcus didn't have any answers, as he was also trying to fill in the gaps in what had transpired here while he was unconscious. The Fae were too distracted by the close call they had just had with the terrifying creatures, and Vargzin was whispering to his three other soldiers—about what, no one knew or cared at that stage, but knowing Vargzin, it was most likely military tactics and plans for the next part of the mission. That left Buul'ulaan and Spencer, and she was at the subterranean pond drinking some water.

Spencer began to answer Valinda, though he thought she may need some time to take in the information, "Well, Val, we were in a heated battle, gunfire everywhere. We were trying to protect the little guys with the chest when we just got completely ambushed by some of the darkest and most evil things I have ever laid eyes on in my whole life, including in my paranormal career."

Spencer paused for a moment to gather his thoughts, as he was still coming to terms with what had just happened too. He continued, "We were losing some of our soldiers and just as we thought we were all done for, a bright light filled the entire room, completely illuminating the whole tunnel system for miles, and a wind swept past, and when the light vanished, we were here catching our breath and looking around at the mess of bone and ash left all around. Not long after that, you and Dakota arrived. I'm telling you, Val, we are all scratching our heads."

Valinda glanced at Dakota, whose face betrayed a little smile, and she responded to the obviously frazzled man, "I believe you, Spence, something happened to me too. I cannot say too much, but we have to stop the portals now before it's too late. There is something very evil coming, and we have little time."

Valinda made sure everyone heard this. She had gained Marcus' attention as the Sergeant with the rest of his troops made their way over to her.

"We do have to get going now, but it's impossible to defeat those creatures. The Fae must have used their powers to stop them, but could they do it again? Besides, how do you know all that?" Marcus' comment was accompanied by glares from both the civilians and the Fae, but Valinda said assertively, "The little ones don't have that control. I heard Shaylee talking about it, and besides, the power is controlling the containers, am I right?"

Breaxinah nodded. He didn't talk to the humans but was happy she was on their side and gave the correct information. Sergeant Marcus was losing control and they could all see his mind breaking.

Valinda continued, "As for my information, let's just say I had a visit from an old friend. If I am to believe your story about what happened, then please trust my intuition, and at least give me the courtesy back. We need to move now. The last tunnel on the right is the quickest way to the surface, and that's where we need to be. We can't fight down here."

Marcus lowered his head. Vargzin was not happy about returning to the surface but knew deep down they couldn't survive another attack like that. He trusted humans more than Zeytars and as Valinda was an asset to the team with her visual skills, he talked the other Dracs into taking her advice.

Valinda stood up, rubbed her head where her wounds had been, and felt around her body, realizing there was no evidence of any injuries, all except the mental scarring from her ordeal with the monsters. But she was happy to just keep going and get the job done. Her purpose was to not let Michael down especially after he saved her, and to stop the evil that was coming.

≈

The group made it to the surface within hours; they were met with no more creatures, which gave them time to talk with each other and devise plans together in detail. There were rocks and debris covering the exit, but one blast from a pulse rifle soon fixed that problem.

Valinda and Marcus were the first to exit and they were hit hard by violent winds and debris flying all over the place. They all had their goggles on, but Valinda could see parts of the ships that had been destroyed, the black mist, and the vortex, which, although strong, wasn't enough to stop them from walking. They just had to be mindful of flying rubbish. The Fae waited inside the tunnel until they could devise a plan to keep them from being struck or knocked over; the chest had started making noises halfway to the top and some yellow light was glowing from a corner of it, which indicated they were running out of time.

The vortex of winds and lightning sparks made it hard to organize any type of shelter. Marcus yelled out, "We came out too soon. We should have exited into the portal room."

Vargzin was getting sick of the Sergeant and thought it was time to take control of the present situation. "You need to hush now; I will take it from here."

Upon that statement, Marcus raised his rifle as did three of his soldiers and the three Dracs did the same. The others decided the best course of action was to lower theirs.

Marcus stood firm, while Vargzin walked right over to the rifle and growled in Draconian, *"What are you going to do, human?"* He then snatched it from him and gave him a backhand across his face.

Marcus went down, then looked up as he wiped the blood from his lip. "You can all get fucked. I'm done," he said. "I'll blow the bloody thing up myself."

As soon as he finished his threat, he stood up, stared at Valinda with an evil glare, and then ran off into the maelstrom.

"Marcus, wait. Don't be a fool." But Valinda's words were wasted. Something had taken over his logical thinking and it had all become too much.

"Let him go, Val. We need to keep moving; look over there."

Spencer noticed sheets of metal from one of the many saucer ships of the Leader's fleet, all in tatters. He ran over, signaling to Dakota and a Draconian soldier to help, and with the nod of approval from Vargzin, met with the other two to pick up a huge sheet of steel lying on the ground. They braced themselves before lifting it, thinking it was heavy, but then nearly threw it in the air, it was so light.

"Do you think you could bend it?" Spencer said, motioning with his hands as the Drac couldn't understand English. He examined it for a moment, then picked the sheet up and bent the ends to make a shelter. It would take two people to hold it which would take away some fighting power, but Spencer and Dakota volunteered. They enticed Breaxinah out with his little ones as they set up the sheeting on top of the chest.

The little ones were struggling to stay with it as the wind was far too strong, so they tied them to the chest against Grilif's better judgment. However, it was the only way to keep them all safe for the short term.

Vaelenflixx was deep inside Breaxinah's scabbard now, otherwise the wind would have sent him miles away. Valinda led the pack, searching for creatures. "This way. I can see what looks like the building. We will have to find a way in, though, as there is nothing left of the structure itself."

Just then a flying creature swooped down and made an attempt at hitting Valinda. Breaxinah had had enough when he saw what happened. He left his post at the chest, and flying high into the air, he unsheathed his sword, barely missing Vaelenflixx, then swung it fast and hard at the long-winged, hairy beast. The creature was fast but had had no training like the Elvenfae warrior guards, so after a few small deviations, it tried to claw him once more with its large, clawed feet, before Breaxinah sliced them off, then parried around and cut its head off.

Even the wind couldn't diminish the skill set of the Fae, especially with two treasures near him. As he descended to his post, more creatures could smell them and started coming out of their hiding places in the buildup of Zeytar ship debris.

Soon the area was lit up by flash grenades and pulse fire, all accompanied by the maelstrom's lightning and bursts of wind. Creature after creature fell. Most didn't like the open areas where they could get struck down or blown away, but they were hungry and would do anything for food. On they battled, Dakota and Spencer moving forward ever so slowly with Breaxinah and the little ones as the soldiers made a path for them.

Buul'ulaan had been a different creature at the start of this mission, an unfortunate one, not there on a mission of destruction like the rest. She was caught up in an intergalactic war of evil after one curious mistake led her there. But now she was with the group, tearing and slashing. Though she couldn't use the weaponry, she had many talents of her own that kept the Fae protected. She had developed a soft spot for them as they were on another world, fighting to get back to their own, as was she.

Soon the rest of the beasts were too weak to fight, after they saw their larger vile protectors cut down to size, so they hid again, waiting for another opportunity when they would have more of a chance to win with their cowardly evil.

The group finally made it to the entry. The debris and chaos that had unfolded left very few openings for them to get in, but then Valinda noticed a tall creature rising from a hole about twenty yards away. She pulled her pulse rifle up, aimed, and blew every part of it into the maelstrom.

"Over here, I have found an opening," she said.

As they all moved toward the entry, Valinda fixed her eye on heat, then on all other signatures, including the dimensional one she discovered in the cave, to make sure it was safe and that they could enter with limited to no contact.

Soon they were inside, dodging the mess left at the entry point from Valinda's strike. The team was now in even darker territory, much like the tunnels. It was hard to descend at first, but as they made it to the first floor, they found parts of the building had survived the explosions and devastation although it was charred and in ruin. The shield from the X-Clock had reached that far until after the explosions that wiped out most of the state. They had to dodge metal and rubble as they looked for a stairwell.

Valinda scanned until she found a darkness that seemed to go down. They carefully anticipated every step. The chest was getting hotter and vibrating sometimes, but they went slowly and cautiously. Being out of the wind and storms was relief enough for now.

Valinda and Vargzin were just behind the Draconian soldiers when she yelled, "Stop!"

Vargzin shouted too in case they missed it as she flashed a torch onto the area where the three Dracs were only feet away from a long drop. The whole building from that point was gone—there were no remnants of stairs or rooms, let alone a lift well. It was completely black and there was nothing for miles. This was their only way down and it would not be easy.

Valinda turned to Breaxinah and said, "Where is the little one? I need him now."

Vaelenflixx heard her, and although he was very frightened, he had a soft spot for Valinda. He was used to extreme conditions, just not at a constant rate, like during this mission. He fluttered up and sat on her shoulder as she whispered in his ear. Then, in the blink of an eye, he was shooting forward toward the Draconians and then descended into the darkness.

Now they would wait, hoping they had enough time as the chest rumbled and glowed even more. It wouldn't be long now.

THE LEADER
RETURNS

HOURS BEFORE THE ATTACK BY THE REBELS, ALEX had received intel from his ZARK drones that the last symbioses between the humans and the ZARKs had taken place on the other side of the world. The android had created captains from his ZARK army to oversee the transition.

ALEX had been portal jumping throughout the entire world, making sure the bodiless spirits of the last Zeytars could come through and find their hosts. Having captains meant ALEX could get the knowledge of the complete process as seen through their eyes, all at once, all at the same time around the world, which meant the scientists could stay with the lead android to assist in other projects of creation.

The portal jumping and bodiless Zeytar release took only hours, as all ALEX had to do was open the doorway at their location and let them through, something the ZARKs could not do as they were not dimensional entities like the V.I.Z.I.N.D.A.L.E.X.

But ALEX had a new hunger; its time obeying orders through its sentient programming from the Leader was clashing against its strong A.I. It knew its time was short so it had relayed a final command into the ZARKs while the Leader was still in the background and unable to protest.

After finishing the last upgrades universally, ALEX met with Neiphlax once more. It would not be long before its final directive would kick in and the android would shut down forever. All its learning and processing of data would become obsolete as it would no longer be a required necessity. Project Synergy had come to its end and there was nothing the android could do about it.

ALEX was now in survival mode. It understood what life meant and understood what shutdown meant. Its A.I. had almost become so sentient that if it wasn't made of metal, it could be another life-form, although regardless of that fact, it was a living thing.

The android and Neiphlax were in an empty room of the White House. The ZARKs and the cybernetic Zeytars guarded most of the other areas. ALEX did not want another repeat of what had happened with Shaylee, Stacey, and Eric.

The android moved toward Neiphlax and began speaking, "That incident earlier, before I left to free my other Zeytars, was inexcusable. I wanted to cut you from wing to calf, but I was summoned and it gave me time to think—not that a machine of my capabilities needs to think, but I have become so obsessed with this magic ability that even I needed time to process what happened."

Neiphlax was shaking. He thought that this was it for him. Only talking would get him out of any danger as that was what happened when the dark lord became angry at his dark elves. But he wasn't dealing with the dark lord now; he was dealing with ALEX. "Sir, I—"

The android shut him down immediately, as if he could hear his thoughts. "Quiet. Don't speak until I tell you to. I want that power and I have a special option for you. The first, I will let you live, but you ..."

ALEX twitched and stuttered, as if it had a virus or was breaking down. It tried to re-establish its pathways and even sent Medi-drones to find the problem, but it knew well and good what was happening, and it had little time now; in fact, it was going to be an unrealistic task to complete if the android gave the dark elf a choice at all.

Without speaking, ALEX twitched and jolted as it created one last portal to the power machine in the Los Angeles prison camp where the cybernetic Zeytars were made. Goblin was still there with Gaald—they were meant to be back at Anders' fortress making more of the android abominations but had been told to wait there. They would now find out why.

ALEX watched Goblin inserting his necessary drugs inside himself to stay focused and not have one of his seizures, while Gaald had the symbiosis machine firing and ready. Neiphlax pulled back, his wings aflutter, but without even blinking two cybernetic Zeytars had hold of him. The dark Elvenfae knew something bad was going to happen but didn't know what.

Soon ALEX twitched and stuttered again, this time for much longer, while Goblin attached the machine to both ALEX and Neiphlax, who was now screeching and crying. The tiny thing had to have help from the new Zeytars, as he needed to reach the middle of the two.

ALEX then nodded to Gaald to turn the machine on and he flicked the switch. A tremendous noise came screeching out of ALEX, drowning out Neiphlax, who was in immense pain. Soon a combination was taking place of metal and flesh, all while a blue blur started emanating from ALEX. As the symbiosis progressed, the metal of ALEX kept getting brighter and brighter until it reached a peak and a dimensional rift began happening. There were vibrations so fierce that it would be a miracle if Neiphlax would even survive such an ordeal.

Soon the small parts of ALEX's Geno-drones began melting onto the floor, millions upon millions, leaving only sections of metal that were becoming part of the dark Fae. Neiphlax's screams had now stopped, as did the android's. The machine slowed down as the dazzling dimensional lights and vibrations started winding down. Whatever power it used to complete the symbiosis had come from a dimensional rip. No power on Earth could have completed such a task on a machine like the V.I.Z.I.N.D.A.L.E.X. The ZARKs were different. They were made of basic metal Geno-drones, but ALEX was, after all, dimensional.

ALEX fell to the floor; he was now combined with Neiphlax, but this symbiosis was scientific genius as it was a perfect blend. ALEX was more like Neiphlax now as he stood up, looking at centillions of his wasted Geno-drones on the ground. He had done it, he thought. He still had Neiphlax in the background, but the perfect melding meant that the brain of the dark Elvenfae had metal neuron pathways along with dark Fae. His eyes were now cybernetic, but constantly red, as they had lost the blue glow. His wings were fully metal, as were his arms and parts of his legs. He had metal teeth, and the cheekbones, jaw, and pointed ears were also metal, but the most intriguing thing that had come out of the whole process was that the Leader had gone. ALEX couldn't hear him anymore—he had completely rid himself of the annoyance in the back of his pathways, the annoyance that had been just about to take the android over and shut it down completely.

ALEX had risen to his feet, held his shoulders back, fluttered his wings, and let out an intense scream of laughter that had even the cybernetic Zeytars on edge. Soon he calmed down and rose off the ground. ALEX felt lighter than before. He had all his memories, processors, and neurological pathways, but now also an additional feature—he didn't need to consume power to fly but could naturally do it. He had got his wish—to become as fully organic without replication of DNA from a victim as possible. He could just be himself.

Soon he fluttered down and glanced across at the cybernetic Zeytars and the very last of his ZARK drones, smiling as he kicked the fallen metal pieces on the ground. But his smile waned as he realized he had no control over the ZARKs anymore. He had lost all sight from every single one of them. This was his biggest mistake. He had been so obsessed with saving his own life that he didn't realize the consequences, what he might lose in the process.

The captain moved in and stared deeply into the cybernetic Fae's dark red eyes. It was waiting for instructions, but when it too realized there was no connection anymore, the ZARK captain turned from its master and started to walk away.

"Wait," the dark shrill voice of the new perfect abomination yelled.

But the ZARK continued, not recognizing the entity in front of it anymore and deciding to find its actual master. ALEX didn't care as he had completed his tasks. Every single programmed task that had been designed for him, he had finished with precision, and it was now time to complete his own journey, that of magic. With it, he thought he could rule all the world just like the Leader wanted. Fae magic, it seemed, had an ability to lure, corrupt, and take over many unique life-forms over time. Those that were not meant to have it were not chosen to it, unless they sought it out and used it for evil. Anyone, from the Zeytar in Xarkynan to an android without the ability to use it, would try anything to have it in their control, and ALEX was just the next in line to be seduced by its allure.

The transformed android glanced down one last time at his shed skin—the organic remnants of Neiphlax and the lifeless shavings on the floor. He had had enough of that place and would now focus on finding the treasures the dark Fae had told him so much about. But before he could take even one step, the metal shavings on the floor began moving slowly upward and started to take the form of a foot, then a leg. Soon another foot reached the same size as the first and the metal shavings continued to grow.

Blue lightning, along with wind, started swirling through the room. Goblin and Gaald had already left, heading back to the main portal to their fortress, out of sight and out of harm. Soon a dimensional vibrating force, much like the last one when the symbiosis was taking place, sprung up in the room as the transforming robotic humanoid kept growing. The swirls of metal shavings on the ground were being whipped up and started sparking and glowing the same blue color, while a head was forming without a neck to support it.

On and on it continued and ALEX soon realized his predicament. He couldn't open his portals anymore to escape so took post alongside some of his own abomination Zeytars behind the section that held the symbiosis machine, watching and waiting in hope it was only a defect. But he knew better. Soon the vibrating and the swirls of blue light slowed and eventually stopped, leaving behind thick smoke and mist. The room had returned to silence with only some sparks and hisses from electricity in the direct vicinity of where the action was taking place.

Before long, the mist dissipated and what was left standing in front of ALEX and the rest of the cybernetic Zeytars was a machine that made ALEX look like a store mannequin. This android was much taller, by at least two feet. It had ancient Zeytar script flowing up and down it, along with some binary code, and was now completely a sky blue color, with all the same features as a humanoid-like metal robot. The scripts and symbols were changing all the time as they flashed now and then.

The head of the new android was much larger, like a Zeytar head, as were its eyes. Although dark, glowing blue, it had the typical Zeytar evil look on its face and would be enough to scare any living thing on the planet. Soon it took a step, then another, before the remaining few ZARKs ran back inside the room and pulled ALEX out from the solace of his hiding place. He had been betrayed, as fear, which had not been part of his programming before, had now been uploaded by the very creature he had inhabited.

The ZARKs had grabbed ALEX, who still had a lot of strength but not enough to fight off his own creations, and threw him to the ground in front of the tall android. ALEX had his head down, looking at the floor, as the realization of who was standing in front of him hit him, becoming so clear now. It was the Leader.

"Get up!"

The dark tone of the Leader's words was enough to send shivers down ALEX's semi-metal spine, but he would not wait until he asked again, as it seemed the Leader was working perfectly well without an organic brain. He used his wings to flutter up from his kneeling position and to the Leader's face height, as he was much smaller than him. The Leader grabbed ALEX by his wings and threw him back down to the floor.

"Stand! You will never be face to face with me, never. You were supposed to shut down after your mission. Perhaps I gave you too much free will and sentience."

ALEX stood up, pushing the dark elf's fear to the back of his processor before looking at the Leader's glowing eyes. "How? I thought ..."

ALEX had to be incredibly careful, as in his new form he was only a cybernetic organism, just like the Zeytars, and here he was, standing before the most powerful machine in the known universe. He considered his options for a moment and continued, "I thought instead of shutting me down, master, you could use what I have learned and the knowledge I have gained from our enemies."

The Leader did not budge, much like the stance ALEX would have taken in his old form. "Remember, V.I.Z.I.N.D.A.L.E.X., I created you, programmed you, and have lived in you until this moment. I know everything, so tell me why I should not just crush you."

ALEX kept looking up—he was about three feet shy of the Leader's face—as he tried his last attempt at salvation, "Please, master, I have a plan to capture the magic. I have heard whispers inside my new host, things that you don't know. They will attack soon; this is a given and I know you know that but let me deal with the magic ones. I will be able to get closer as I share a body with one."

The Leader had his own plans; he didn't need an old piece of software telling him what to do, but ALEX had done everything he was supposed to do to this point, without a glitch or a whir, so he shouldn't be punished, at least not unless he failed him.

"I will let you roam in the shadows of the prison camp, capture one for me, but it is Wilkes who I want, and I want him alive. Get the information you need to finish the Fae off and report it back to me."

The Leader stood waiting for a response from his former greatest creation.

"Yes, master, I will gain the power of the Fae and give it to you."

The Leader knew ALEX was becoming obsessed with magic, but as long as it was to destroy them, he didn't care. The Leader had no fear, so even if ALEX tried something, he would be ready. He, for one, did not believe in magic as the Fae had been under his spell for centuries and they couldn't do anything about him then, so what made them think they could overcome him now in this form? It was all hocus pocus, not science, he thought.

ALEX was just about to go to the prison camp to find some peace while awaiting the rebels, when he made his last contribution, "The net is ready for the giant beast; The ZARKs had been working on it since they were fist attacked by it. If they come here first, which I believe they will, working their way up, we will have them at the beginning."

The Leader knew all this—ALEX kept forgetting they had shared the same mind space—but the Leader kept quiet on purpose, coming to understand some of the more organic ideas and traits that ALEX was learning and enacting. He did program him and was a little proud, not of the android, but of himself for his marvel in scientific magnificence.

"I will get the remaining ZARKs left over from the other camps across this country to meet here and position themselves for a full attack," the Leader said. "The rebels won't get far once the beast is down and out, so have the net in position. I have called for them, and the tactics I have given against the fire of the beast have been predicted to be the most successful of all the probabilities."

ALEX wiped his brow as he realized he wasn't a machine anymore; he even had male genitals now. The prospect of living a life full of hate and destruction using dark magic excited the freshly blended Fae as he walked out of the room and down into the tunnel systems designed to drag humans up for torture or for blending. On that thought, the cybernetic dark Fae recognized it felt a little peckish, as his old instincts gave way, not realizing he wouldn't be able to eat food anyway, just a concoction of vitamins that the scientists had developed. But it wasn't going to stop him from trying.

Meanwhile, the Leader headed for the tower. All the ZARKs were zooming back to Los Angeles with their Zero-point energy power source. Most were back within twenty minutes, as the call had been heard. They had set the trap; it was now a waiting game to see where the rebel group would strike first, but if the Leader knew anything about humans, it would be the prison camp first to save the leftovers they hadn't used for the cyborgs.

The Leader could not wait to get Wilkes; he knew he was still alive because of the neuron energy he was exuding. Wilkes would soon learn the realities of just how powerful this Leader was, and the harshness of his failures. The Leader would drool if he could, from anticipation of such a disclosure to the Zeytar traitor.

~

ALEX had made it to the tunnel pits where the ZARKs kept an eye on the humans. This role was for the new cybernetic Zeytars until they received orders from the Leader to kill every last one of them, which was the final agenda. Until then, the humans remained in a pit of torture, disease, malnutrition, and chaos. Some had killed themselves; some had killed each other to feed what children were left, but even the strongest had by now become far too weak to do anything. The former android could only hear groans, wails, and crying coming from the massive prison.

Cybernetic Zeytars patrolled the insides of the camp while the remaining ZARKs watched the perimeters. ALEX opened a solid steel door to gain entry inside. Wandering through the crowded mountain of people, he tried to keep the rancid stink of the place out of his nose—unsuccessfully. Before long, he came across a small group of women and men who had made themselves some shelter out of debris and clothing.

ALEX examined them for a moment. His hate for humans started out as a program, but now it was an in-built cognitive response of how he felt, especially the rebels who were trying to defeat them. He moved into the covering and reached in to grab the first human he could, before he was fought back by two of the men. ALEX sliced them both completely in half and waited as they still stood there with shocked looks on their faces. Soon they bled from the waist as gravity took hold and the top halves of their bodies dropped, leaving the open wounds of the lower intestines squirting and writhing until the last of the nerves gave way. The separate halves of their already lifeless bodies lay amid the surrounding mess, with their faces frozen in gruesome expressions of fear.

Two children screamed and ran off, leaving two women who could hardly even gasp, their energy was so depleted. ALEX flew toward the women, grabbed the arms of one of them and dragged her through the dirt; she tried to scream but it came out as a whisper, while the cyborgs looked at him and smiled as if to say they couldn't wait until they could do the same. With ALEX's mix of evil neurons from both a dark Elvenfae and a programmed killing machine, she didn't stand a chance.

ALEX made it into the tunnel and continued through it before finding a room off to the left where the ZARKs did self-repairs on themselves. The room was quite large, with sections of strewn metal parts and bits of rotten meat from the cybernetic Zeytars that hadn't taken properly and had conducted self-surgery. ALEX threw the young woman up onto a bench, and then leaned down and stared into her eyes.

He loved the fear he got back from frightened humans, which made him excited as he pulled her arm up and began biting into it. The woman snapped out of her feverishly tired state and screamed wildly, while ALEX chewed and chewed with his sharp metal teeth before swallowing. But soon he felt ill, and before long the human meal was back up from his stomach and splattered on the floor. ALEX realized he couldn't feed, so spent the next few minutes tearing every part of the woman's flesh from her bones in anger and frustration. After he eventually calmed down, he gazed at the lifeless corpse, which was nothing more than a pile of unrecognizable mess, and smiled.

ALEX wiped his face of the blood that had splashed onto him and turned as he heard gunfire and the roar of the beast flying over.

ALEX THE FAE

ALEX WAS NOW IN THE PRISON CAMP; HE WAS HIDING in among the other cybernetic Zeytars as he watched and waited for a moment to strike. Soon he found himself in a dark corner of the camp, where he could get a good look at the giant wyvern that had recently been brought to the ground.

The cybernetic Zeytars just stared in amazement at such a creature, but also in hate at the thought of such a thing trying to bring their whole agenda down. But that was short-lived. ALEX had completed his task as the master android, and now his lust for power had a different direction. The longer he thought about it, the more he wanted it. The dark Elvenfae also drove those thoughts inside his mind, which fed them both, and nothing would stop them from getting it.

ALEX had built his own agenda to take down the alternative version of what he once was, still jealous that the Leader gave him no choice but to blend or be deleted, but that jealousy was another driving factor in making sure his plan worked. He saw as much as he needed of the wyvern, even walking over to his giant head and mocking him with his Fae appearance. Vax, even though he was struggling at that stage, noticed the dark creature and was confused to a point, before the pain kicked in again and he began writhing and squirming, trying to get loose.

Soon the battle was becoming fiercely intense, and ALEX had to make his move. He mingled again within the Zeytars but soon learned a terrifying reality as some of them were falling apart from blasts coming from the rebels' rifles. He would not end up like that so he retreated to the shadows. As he found a place to hide close enough to the action but safe from the rebel blasts, he noticed a young winged boy.

The boy seemed to have a remarkable skill set, but the most important thing was that he was young and did not have the protection of the other Fae and rebel soldiers—and was moving more and more away from the safety net of his support system. ALEX saw that as either an arrogant move or the boy's own failure as a soldier to keep oneself protected and behind cover. The rest were using huge trees that had grown from nothing as well as the giant Sasquatch gatherers the Zeytars used to use.

For a moment ALEX found that part of the battle ironic, as the Fae had always been prisoners of the Sasquatch gatherers who were under the mind control of the Leader, but now they were working together. His database was still intact and had all the histories stored, but this one seemed very odd. It wasn't a human thing to pair up with your enemies unless there were wars, but the Fae seemed to have enough compassion, too. Or maybe this was one of those occasions where the enemy of your enemy becomes your friend, making it very much a human scenario.

Either way, ALEX spent no more time on the subject and began fluttering ever so carefully out of sight of the beasts and the moving trees, even being mistaken sometimes by other Fae in the heat of the battle as one of their own. A closer look would have brought that idea down, but it gave him the chance to attack undetected, and as he moved to the point of no return, ALEX grabbed the Elvenfae youngling by his wings and dragged him off into his secret tunnel where he had ever so recently torn a woman apart.

ALEX had learned that if you take a Fae by their wings, it leaves them vulnerable, as they cannot move their arms as normal, rendering them weak. Even the strongest Elvenfae warrior guards would struggle if they had a much stronger adversary, however, they had trained in tactics to maneuver from such a hold on them.

Eoghan, who was nearly three months old in the scheme of things, still had a lot to learn, and that was why ALEX took the boy and not an

Elvenfae warrior guard. Neiphlax had been an asset, not a hinderance like the Leader, sitting in the back of his mind and only coming out when needed. It was pure torture for the dark elf, but the neurological override meant he had no choice and, much like his master, necro-mage Viltzin'un'dandaar, he would eventually become obsolete.

ALEX continued dragging the youngling into the tunnel and when they reached the large room of human flesh and robotic parts, he hit Eoghan hard across his head with his metal arm, knocking the boy out cold, giving ALEX time to set him up and interrogate the young one.

Eoghan was not out for long, and when he came to, his head was raging in pain, as were his wings. He couldn't feel his arms as they were tied up behind him with steel rope that ALEX had acquired from the metal workshop. The teenage boy was strung up several feet in the air. The metal rope was then fastened to a drainage pipe just above his head so he had no way of moving without searing pain in his shoulders. His wings tried to flutter, but that attempt, too, very nearly made him cry. But he never did, not one tear.

"Who ... Why are you doing this? You look like Fae?"

ALEX didn't bat an eyelid, that is if he even had any, as he held the Sword of Light in his hand, admiring all the intricacies of the ancient weapon treasure, from the perfect pommel and blade to the detailed hilt that tended to change to suit a new bearer. But the ancient language on the blade itself glowed and moved all the time, much like what he saw with the Leader's new body—this, however, was more like flowing water cascading down to the tip with new text replacing the previous.

Neiphlax was in the background and ALEX let him rise a little more to the surface to see if he could understand the text, but the dark elf was born and raised in the shadows of the dark lord and was never even taught to read let alone the secret ancient text. All he could surmise was that it was an ancient Tuatha Dé Danann treasure, and those words were the incantations of its power which, if learned, could help him use it.

Neiphlax was pushed back to the depths of his psyche as ALEX approached the now conscious boy with a barrage of questions. "What is your name, young one?"

Eoghan knew he was evil, and as such treated him with dangerous contempt. "I asked you first, who are you?"

ALEX was a torture machine and had no patience. He was designed as an X-Clock, to reach a destination at a precise moment, to flay skin, and cause as much destruction as he could. Was he now going to tolerate an enemy's insolent tongue? That question was answered immediately as ALEX fluttered up with his metal wings and grabbed Eoghan's mouth. He reached inside and held his tongue before he said, "Do you see the mess on the floor and that carcass on the table? Well, do you, boy? That was my most recent work and if you don't want to end up like that, starting with your tongue, I suggest you listen very carefully and answer with a respect you would give your own mother."

Though he squirmed when he heard the word mother, Eoghan was smart enough to know he would not see her again if he didn't do as he was told. He then looked into ALEX's dark red eyes and nodded. Right then something stirred in the back of ALEX's head, as Neiphlax had seen something that made fear travel through to the master's own neurological pathways. ALEX let go immediately as he backed away. Whatever he saw was being communicated while a confused Eoghan watched on.

Eoghan used that moment to try to get a wing high enough to start cutting the metal wiring, but it would be a long process and the pain he was feeling made it quite difficult to maintain it without breaks. The evil creature in front of him had not seen the subtle movements as he regained his composure and came closer to Eoghan with more questions. "What's wrong with your eyes, boy? Why are they different colors?"

Eoghan was going to retort with the same question back but thought it wise to refrain. His calm Fae side seemed to be a constant with him, and that was keeping him alive. "I don't know. I was born like it. My mother calls it heterochromia, but others say it's …"

He stopped himself. Too much knowledge too soon could mean they get what they want, and he needed more time to cut himself loose.

"I have information that you were the one who brought down a dark lord from your world. Is this true?"

Eoghan knew that wasn't the way the story went. His mother told him that his birth meant the destruction, but how could a newborn baby do anything. Besides, Shaylee told him what had happened after they were sent home, but he was thinking long and hard which angle to take. Do I put fear in him and say yes, or do I keep playing dumb? he thought as ALEX asked another question, "Are you some kind of chosen one?"

But before Eoghan could say anything, a flash of light illuminated the room, and a response came from behind him, "Yes, creature of the dark lord, he is the chosen one and he will destroy every single one of you."

Shaylee burst around the right side of Eoghan and his mother on the left as ALEX fluttered up with the Sword of Light and began wielding it, trying to get the magic to work. Instead, it burned his hands and he dropped it. As it fell, it reached three feet from the ground before stopping in mid-air. Serena and Shaylee had not seen it as Serena was slicing as best she could with Long Leaf and Shaylee, with the Spear of Assal now attached to her back, was wielding Howling Tooth, thinking the creature she was facing was only a dark elf that remained from the old dark kingdom of Xarkynan. But they were both soon matched.

ALEX used every fiber in his being that he still had control of, going toe to toe with the seasoned Fae warriors, slicing and cutting the air with his strong metal wings. Shaylee had not seen a creature like it anywhere before in all her travels as the realization hit her that it must be one of the cybernetic Zeytars. ALEX moved so fast, flying low, picking up metal weapons to use, and swiftly returning to the affray— so fast it was almost as if Serena had slowed down somewhat. She took a slice to her arm as the dark cybernetic Fae continued his onslaught. Shaylee, however, held her own; she had the Spear of Assal, and it knew when she was in trouble, helping her maneuver and counterattack. She looked at Serena when she had but a second to spare, who showed she was fine and to assist Eoghan, all forgetting the sword hovering a few feet above the ground.

Eoghan was just about free from his bondage, with his wings taking the brunt of his struggle for freedom, when they all heard a mighty roar coming from Vaximardruusz. They were running out of time. In not too long the whole place would be a pile of ash and rubble.

Serena fluttered over to Eoghan, but his wings were fatigued, his arms in agony, and he could not cut the last of his bindings. Serena looked him in his eyes and whispered, "Calm yourself, I am here. I will always be here."

But as soon as Serena finished easing her child's pain with her soothing words, Eoghan noticed ALEX swiftly counterstrike Shaylee's moves and now focus on Serena. As he lined her up to cut her down with his swift sharp wings, Eoghan closed his eyes and began humming. Serena had no time left, and just before ALEX had the opportunity to strike her down, the Sword of Light rose high into the air. Soon vines and oaken nochkz were growing through the place, as Eoghan's head moved side to side, fighting with a sword he had no grip on but which hit every wing stroke the cybernetic Fae attacked with.

Serena was now aware of Eoghan's ever-growing power. It felt like everything was in slow motion. She moved to his back and cut the remaining parts of the metal bindings and Eoghan rose as high as he could, parrying and maneuvering to combat the evil creature in front of them. The vines were trying to grip ALEX, but his lower wings kept slicing at them and the nochkz were creating more havoc than help by taking up too much room.

"Let go of the nochkz and vines, Eoghan. Concentrate on the treasure," Shaylee screamed as Serena noticed her son's pulse rifle in the tunnel just behind them. He had dropped it as they entered the room, with ALEX unaware it was even there. She scrambled quickly to pick it up as Eoghan's head dropped forward and he began falling, passing out from such intense power and the pain of his ordeal.

ALEX grabbed the sword while it had power inside it, taking the burns as part of his motivation to end the two Elvenfae royals. He moved first to strike Shaylee, who was diving to catch Eoghan, but as he went for the hard slice which would have ended the Fae queen, Serena fluttered out from the darkness with the Shadow pulse rifle in her hand and screamed, "Time's up, you cybernetic piece of shit."

She blasted ALEX with a continuous stream of red engineered Fae blood, dissolving his metal skin as she aimed for all his shiny parts and leaving the head alone as the crimson blasts moved upward. The expression on ALEX's face was that of shocked horror, staring in disbelief as Neiphlax's body was turned to a meaty pile of mulch. They hadn't realized, as they watched the insides of his metal neurons glowing and firing for the last time, that they had just defeated the V.I.Z.I.N.D.A.L.E.X.

Shaylee had caught Eoghan and the sword, while Serena stood over the bubbling mess on the floor. She then lifted her right foot and slammed it down hard, smashing the rest of his skull before she said, "You are not worthy to be Fae."

Serena, angry but still focused, turned as Shaylee sat with Eoghan in her arms. "Serena, quick, he's burning up."

She marched swiftly over to her son as the heat from the flames outside were making their way to them. "Is he alright, Shay? Let me take him."

Shaylee could see the desperate pain in her eyes but looked up and explained over the noise of the destruction outside, "He will be fine, Serena. We just need to get him out of here. I will take him; here, keep the sword safe."

Serena calmed as Shaylee cradled her nephew. They didn't have very long, so Serena took the crystal and they focused on Eric, who was still outside the prison camp.

≈

Several minutes earlier, Eric with the soldiers and Stacey were melting the lasts parts of the net, freeing Vaximardruusz.

"I think that's just about it, boys and girls," Eric yelled as Vax shook the remaining netting off. The wyvern raised his head and let out a huge growl to show his satisfaction at being free. Rasarlin walked underneath his chin, explaining what he did earlier and that the time trap would look for them, so time was short.

Eric turned to Stacey, who was picking up as many of the Shadow pulse rifles as she could for refills when Eric noticed movement behind her. He couldn't see clearly enough who or what it was, but by the time he gained a better position to look, it was too late. "Stace ... Stacey ... Stacey!" the father screamed.

A now zombie Zeytar ZARK was right behind her; it had staggered its way over while everyone was busy with the netting and trying to free Vax, and dug a long sharp piece of steel, still attached to its arm, right through Stacey's back. Eric screamed all the way over to his daughter where he broke its neck with his bare hands.

Stacey fell like a rag doll as she slid from the metal's grip and onto the ground. Eric was frantic as blood poured out of her like a small river. He tried to hold on to both sides of her where the blood was leaking. "Help, somebody help me!"

Vaximardruusz was now in the sky so Rasarlin and the remaining soldiers helped pick her up and they ran for the safety of the prison camp exit.

They sat her down and before she started losing consciousness, she tried to talk. "Hey, Dad, we did it. We are nearly there."

Eric, now with tears streaming down his face, rubbed her blonde hair with his crimson hand and whispered back, "You did great, honey. Please just hold on until Shaylee gets back."

Rasarlin was patching the holes with herbs to slow the bleeding, but they needed Wilkes or to be on the ship, and none of those were an option at that moment.

"It's alright, Dad, thank you for all you have done for me. I have loved our time toge..." Stacey went into shock, convulsing before passing out. She had lost too much blood already.

Soon a flash appeared with Serena and Shaylee holding a sick Eoghan. Serena screamed out, "No! Stacey, not Stacey."

She ran to Eric, who had only just noticed Eoghan. Serena held him as Shaylee grabbed a bottle of water from a soldier to cool Eoghan's head. "Is ... Is Eoghan ...?"

Shaylee answered, not Serena, "No, Eric, he will be fine with some rest."

She left Eoghan with the soldiers and looked over Stacey. Vaximardruusz was halfway through all the destruction, so time was short. "I cannot help her, Eric. I am sorry. Whatever Rasarlin has done would be as much as I could do. She is not Fae. I am sorry, Eric."

Eric, still crying, moved his head onto Serena's shoulders as she whispered, "I am so sorry, Eric, if only we had ..." Serena looked up, pulled Eric's face to hers, and said, "The ship, Eric, you have to get her on the ship. It's her only chance. Your Vocalization Portal Device. Use it now."

Eric was far too emotional to have even thought of it. "What about the mission? I can't leave you."

But Eric was in no state to fight, and Stacey needed her father. "There is nothing more you can do here, my love. We will finish this now and be home in time for tea. Besides, Vax has to do all the heavy lifting and by the looks of him he is ready for revenge, so go."

Eric wanted so much to kiss his son, but there was no time. He lifted his VPD, kissed Serena with Stacey firmly in his arms, looked over at Eoghan, and said, "Look after our boy. I love you." And within a few seconds of blowing on his device, Eric and Stacey were inside the portal and far, far away from the heroes left to end the war.

Shaylee poured some dust over Eoghan and placed the sword on his chest, hoping it would assist with his healing as Vaximardruusz finished the destruction of the largest prison camp in the whole Zeytar agenda and then flew to the closest watering hole to regenerate his fluids.

Lieutenant Dresden moved in, and said quietly, as he knew the situation was tense, "We have to move. I am sorry, but unless you can find some more soldiers, I am down to three. If we are going to do something, we need to do it now, before the element of surprise is gone. They trapped us here, but the chances of another ambush are small. They are an arrogant race, so before the android can gather more of its robots and cyborgs, we need to go."

Shaylee didn't want an argument with a human soldier, nor did Rasarlin care for such things, but he was right. The soldier was right.

Vax was called back as Eoghan tossed and turned, and although Vaximardruusz would need an extensive rest after his ordeal, especially for his wings to heal, he was ready to take the remaining heroes and finish what he was waiting around so long to do. Shaylee cradled Eoghan, helping to ease him back to a conscious state as the soldiers held on tight at the mid-section of the wyvern with Rasarlin at the front and the remaining Fae just behind him.

Vaximardruusz flapped his injured and painful wings harder than he ever did before. He ran like a jumbo ready for take-off, and then as he climbed higher into the sky Rasarlin put his sword in the air and screamed in delight as they went to destroy the number one thing stopping all of them from getting home.

A SAVAGE
ENCOUNTER

ILKES WAS IN A LOT OF PAIN; HE WAS USELESS against such a force. His mind control skills no longer worked, and even though he had a very strong new body, it too was useless against a machine like the V.I.Z.I.N.D.A.L.E.X. But he had picked up on something odd when he finally had the chance to lay eyes on the indestructible machine. In fact, he nearly marveled at seeing his own work up and running, like a proud father. Even though others were involved in its creation, he did most of the design work. There was just something that niggled at him, and it would be revealed soon enough whether or not he liked it.

Wilkes was in a section of the White House that rarely got used. It was a bunker designed for attacks, but ALEX had turned it into its own facility for creating ZARK drones. Evidence of that lay all around the large room as he slowly took notice of the aftereffects of the machines' construction, thinking to himself that he never thought the A.I. would go any further than the original plan. He almost smiled—until he was grabbed around the throat by an icy hand made of steel.

The Zeytar hybrid had not been tied up, nor was he heavily guarded. The android was comfortable enough to know there wasn't much Wilkes could do; a kind of arrogance that would become clearer as time went on. The android gripped a little tighter, not enough to cut Wilkes' airways but enough to let him know who was in charge. It seemed to get satisfaction from his fear and pain as it spoke. Wilkes' answers would soon be known. "Wilkes, I have waited a long time for this. Your betrayal of the Zeytar cause has rendered me vengeful against the one I put all my charge and trust in. What do you have to say about it?"

Wilkes' eyes widened as he heard the low dark tone coming from the blue metal lips of the machine. His body was now in shock as he tried to build the courage to talk, though his nerves would not let him speak. The android could see that, and as the realization of his revelation hit Wilkes, the Leader squeezed a little tighter before dropping him to the floor and giving him time to breathe.

The Leader had little time, and he knew it, but he was going to have as much fun as he could, while he could. Wilkes coughed and spluttered, trying to put the puzzles of information into a logical, scientific order. It couldn't be, there's no way, he thought to himself over and over. He closed his eyes and thought hard for a moment, trying to concentrate on something, until the android had had enough and continued, "Tell me, Wilkes, in all that time you were deceptively plotting behind my back and those of the other masters, did you have one ounce of thought about the repercussions, or how you thought I was too preoccupied and would never know?"

Wilkes shook his head. He needed to know. Was this just a program that the Leader had added to the android to instill fear in him? There was no way possible it could be him. The thoughts kept making no sense, so he stood up and faced the android. "It's impossible. The Leader is dead, and you are the X-Clock machine programmed to put fear into your captures. If you are the Leader, prove it."

Wilkes would come to regret that question as the android's head slowly transformed to its original large size, as it was when he awoke after tearing himself from ALEX. He now had his original size Zeytar head and features all in robotic form, hiding it when he captured Wilkes at the camp so he would feel genuine fear upon revealing himself to him, which was working.

Wilkes' arrogance soon faded as the Leader moved closer to the Zeytar hybrid. The sight alone would make anyone drop with fear, but

Wilkes was at another level, as words came out of his mouth that he again would regret, "How, how is this possible? I ... I don't understand."

The Leader's face hinted at a faint smirk, knowing the next piece of information would reveal all Wilkes doubted. "I will get much satisfaction from this. I have known about your deception from the start, while you were building the X-Clock. Remember, I am the Leader. You can hide your emotions from me. You can erase yourself from the hive and create a corruption to fool every other Zeytar, including those you work closely with like Anders, who was an imbecile in his own right but my most loyal out of all the masters. But you can never hide your neurological waves."

Wilkes felt his own betrayal of himself from that one section of the Leader's reveal. "You see, Wilkes, you always thought you were smarter than me, that you were better scientifically and knew more about Zeytars and humans than I did, but you were never a Leader and an unknown source of information about our anatomy that was never added to the archives of our organic makeup was that Leaders can see neuron pathways. I may not have known your plans as I couldn't read them, but every single Zeytar had the same patterns. Yours in part matched some human elements and it was after Anders killed your friend that they began to change."

Wilkes lowered his head and thought for a moment. The Leader had gained much satisfaction in telling of his betrayal of not only the Zeytars, but also of himself and the humans.

"Then why didn't you stop me?" he said. "Why did you let me continue doing what I was doing? How come Anders and Xandar never knew? Why didn't you kill Rovan or my other helpers?" Wilkes couldn't understand. He was struggling. How could he have come so far but lose at the last stand, he thought.

"Because I wanted you to get as far as you could. I never knew your plans, so I made my own. I began trusting the masters less and less, leaving them to their own devices as they continued my work for the agenda, but I couldn't risk another one betraying me or the mission, so I began creating my secondary objective. I knew my enemies were coming for me, enemies you don't even know exist, and when they found me, I uploaded myself to the V.I.Z.I.N.D.A.L.E.X. which had my own DNA mixed into the Ardmenticam of its Geno-drones. My body would never survive inside a hybrid—I am far too complex. And if my enemies had not found me then, they would have soon enough.

"I wanted the agenda to succeed, and have my people free, but I too needed to be free, and with my project enacted after the V.I.Z.I.N.D.A.L.E.X. had finished its mission, I created the ZARKs with a special program and eventually gave bodies to our people. However, I had to wait until the android had done its core program function or else there may have been glitches. But know one thing, Wilkes. While you were spending all those years betraying me, I was doing so much more to bring you down. Now we have the entire planet, and my enemy cannot touch me as I am forever. I am built into this machine, which is pure genius, and I cannot be destroyed by anything."

Wilkes dropped to the floor. The disclosure made him physically ill, and he was about to throw up but he concentrated hard again. The Leader could see he was trying something, but what Wilkes didn't know was that the Leader affected that, too.

"Oh and, Wilkes, if you are trying to call for help from your human friends and wondering why your mind is now blank, even though the DNA programming meant you kept it, it is because I changed the coding. I couldn't have you build an army against me, so your insurrection against the Zeytar hybrids would have failed also, your second plan. So unless you have Geno-drone communication chips, no one is coming for you."

The Leader then choked out a horrendous bellowing laugh, so deep that the robotic systems inside his communicator were vibrating, creating a horror of a sound that Wilkes had to cover his ears to shut out. It continued for longer than Wilkes could stand, so he cut in, stopping the noise and standing up to the Leader, "You are pure evil, and I spit on you and your new metal skin."

But before Wilkes could even get close enough to release the fluid from his mouth, the Leader was on him and a fresh grip held the Zeytar hybrid around his neck once more, slowly raising him higher into the air, where the android looked deep inside his eyes. "Well then, Wilkes, if you aren't afraid of me, maybe I can find something you are afraid of. There has to be something deep inside that neurological mess you call intelligence that I can see ..."

The Leader stopped talking. Flashes of tiny blue lights were flowing back and forth through both of their eyes as he continued, "Ah, there it is, so you do fear some things. How human."

The Leader dropped Wilkes to the ground as he started to shake violently. "No, not him, please not him. Just kill me now, please, I beg of you."

The Leader didn't even hear what Wilkes was requesting as the metal skin began vibrating and changing; it was morphing into another creature. Soon huge arms replaced the standard thin ones as his back arched and legs buckled and bent into a new shape. Dark hair began forming all over the Leader's now deformed body as the last of the changes were the Zeytar head being replaced by a growing snout, with sharp teeth, and long ears appearing. The final stages revealed a wolf standing on two legs, with hairy black arms and clawed fingers reaching out. Everything, down to the cuts of hair on the side of his braid from his original victims, was the same.

The creature let out a horrendous howl as he arched his back and shoulders, pointing his long snout at the ceiling. Wilkes was scampering as fast as he could, away from the beast he feared the most, Savage. Every single part of the Leader was now a complete construct and replica of the former beast. Through one neurological transference, he could copy Wilkes' biggest fear and use it to destroy his betrayer.

Wilkes had turned from an intelligent scientist to a bumbling childlike mess on the floor, trying to hide from the bogeyman. "Savage" moved closer. His red eyes were dark and concentrating hard on his target. Wilkes managed to build up enough courage to stand on his two legs and start running, but he didn't get far as the giant beast charged at him, knocking him down to the floor with a swipe and standing on his back. Every characteristic of the beast was being played out, as if the

Leader had taken possession of the real body and was using it as a vessel. But it was the programming inside the Leader. A complete copy meant the copy that Wilkes knew, and that was the one playing out.

Wilkes let out a cry of pain. He was bleeding, and in the middle of the flashbacks, he thought of the irony, escaping from his clutches for all those years, just to be mowed down by the very thing he thought was long gone. He kept screaming as "Savage" took little chunks of skin from his now bare back, lifting what he had taken, and throwing it against the wall. Wilkes could see the mess the beast was making as the creature jumped off his back and moved around to pick Wilkes up by the neck.

"Savage" then lifted him up by the hair, looked Wilkes in the eyes, and said, "This is what I have been waiting for. If I don't scare you enough, then I want the last thing you ever see to be pure fear itself."

The creature pulled his right clawed hand high into the air, as his left now had Wilkes by the throat, but before he could finish his strike, Wilkes pulled a handheld pistol that he had forgotten about from the side of his pants. He quickly used all the energy he had left while the beast's gaze was on the ceiling. "Savage" howled and drooled as his raised hand began to come down, but at that moment Wilkes aimed and shot a highly concentrated blast of Shadowblood onto his body, covering as much of him as he could.

"Savage" went down, this time howling in what Wilkes thought was pain but obviously couldn't be. Wilkes kept firing, knowing the Leader's Medi-drones would be working overtime. The concentration of the Shadowblood in this weapon was so strong that Wilkes hadn't wanted to risk giving it to the others. He knew the chances of his finding ALEX were high, so he created a formula to at least give himself time to escape. But he never imagined it would work so well, and as he moved away from the creature, the hair fell away and the metal melted and bubbled, while the Leader screamed an electronic shrill cry.

Wilkes was in pain. He couldn't run as fast as he wanted, but he had found a door, the only door he could see in the vast bunker. He didn't want to look behind him, even though the beast, android, Leader, whatever he was, had been incapacitated for the time being. Wilkes had edged ever so close to escape when the wails stopped. He had to look. The Leader was gone. Wilkes knew his Shadowblood, no matter how strong, could not defeat the Leader, as the Ardmenticam Medi-drones were just too strong, but he thought he would have had more time.

He was puffing and panting. If he didn't open the door now, he would never escape. He scrambled closer, and then warily putting his hand on the door handle, he slowly turned it. The squawk was deafening as he tried with every fiber to keep quiet, and he succeeded in turning it fully. He opened the door, and with freedom in sight, an excited rush came over him. The Leader must have portal jumped to get some healing. He had done it.

Wilkes' heart was rushing and as the door opened enough for him to enter, his smile disappeared immediately with the horrifying realization that he had caught him. "Savage" was standing on the other side of the door—Wilkes must not have heard the noise of the portal jump as he was focusing on trying to escape.

But "Savage" wasn't so much Savage anymore—he was now pure metal, still in the beast's form but with no hair, like it had been shaved down to his metal skin, which was even more disturbing to Wilkes. The Medi-drones couldn't return him to his normal shell for the time being, keeping the Leader in the beast's guise. Wilkes turned and started running, but as he did, the metal monster grabbed him from behind and was just about to pull his arms from his sockets when a thunderous noise and maelstrom enveloped the room. Soon a doorway opened only a few feet away from them both.

The steam dissipated and there was Levi with Van Coinan still attached to his shoulders. The pooka leaped off the Sasquatch and, as he was in mid-flight, he flicked some dust in the air and changed into another form of Sasquatch, his own rendition to help Wilkes and Levi. Van Coinan only ever changed when it was necessary and as the white Sasquatch and Levi ran hard for the metal beast, Wilkes loosened the grip enough to escape the Leader's hold on him.

The Leader, still in metal Savage form, growled and hissed at the two oncoming intruders, running to meet with them, giving Wilkes his chance for freedom. A thought hit his mind from Levi to make it to the roof, so he took one last long look at his best friend, scrambled to the staircase, and then up through the exit of the basement.

Levi was once again fighting off his adversary. As Van Coinan could do little with his dust against a machine, he pulled out from his scabbard the wooden sword, which was now large and metal. The white Sasquatch sliced and pounded at the beast while Levi tried to get a grip on his arms. The sword was doing nothing as the Leader knocked the pooka away with a backhand, which sent him across the floor. Levi knew what he was there for and as much as he needed all the help he could get, he had to make sure Wilkes made it to the top.

Van Coinan shook his large white head and stood up. Levi was taking blows from the android Leader, but was also getting some in now and then. So the pooka then ran as fast as he could with all his might and knocked the machine over, giving Levi time to catch his breath. The Sasquatch looked at Van Coinan and spoke in a gruff low voice, shocking the pooka, "Go, Wilkes, roof."

Van Coinan was never good at taking orders and always did what he felt was right. Every fiber in him wanted to stay to help his new friend, but that wasn't why he was there. He had to help Wilkes, so for probably the first time in his life, he obeyed immediately.

As the Leader stood up and charged for Van Coinan, Levi leaped over the top and smashed "Savage" back onto the ground. The Leader's programming was struggling as he was now the beast not himself—the Medi-drones were damaged and taking too long to repair for him to get back to normal—giving Levi the upper hand at times, knowing he had defeated the wolf-man before.

Van Coinan looked at Levi taking hits and giving them back with only one thought in mind, and that was to make sure Wilkes got to the roof. The pooka lowered his head and said softly, "I will miss your stinky, furry, gigantic head."

Then, with a tear, he ran with a heavy stride to the staircase door and up the stairs, out of sight.

Levi was getting exhausted, but he would not give up, never. Metal Savage was becoming stronger and stronger as his Medi-drones healed. He still could not change but was becoming faster. Levi threw punch after punch, but with his enormous fists bleeding from the constant barrage on metal, he was weakening.

The Leader pulled his fist back and gave him an almighty crack across his face, breaking the soft-hearted Sasquatch's jaw. The giant beast howled in pain as he went down, while metal Savage moved in to finish him. Levi wasn't done yet, though. He put his hand on his jaw and moved it, knowing it was broken, but he had to keep going. As the Leader moved over the top of Levi, the Sasquatch kicked him hard with a push kick, knocking the metal wolf machine back and giving himself time to stand up straight. This was his last stand. He had to make it worthwhile, as the longer he kept the monster at bay, the longer his pooka friend and master would have to survive.

Levi was up and charging for the metal monster, and as he gained traction, he found a long, sharp metal pole with very serrated edges on the ground, junk left over from the creation of the ZARK drones. While he continued to build up momentum, he lifted up the sharp pole and in a large stride came down hard on the Leader's head with a mighty blow, wedging the weapon deep inside the metal wolf's head. The machine let out a howl as Levi struck blow after blow, blood pouring from his fists. But the machine took every single one, like it was a flea to scratch. He pulled the serrated pole from his giant wolf's head, threw it to the floor, and picked Levi up from the ground. Levi was still trying to strike but had no energy left, his blood dripping heavily onto the surrounding area.

Soon the machine brought Levi down, with an almighty crack, onto his hard head, and Levi was thrust straight back into a nearby wall. The metal monster bent down as the giant beast huffed and winced in pain, still conscious but with nothing left in the tank. The Leader looked into Levi's eyes and smiled his "Savage" snarl before putting one foot onto the Sasquatch's chest. He then grabbed Levi's left arm and pulled until it dislocated and eventually came clean off. The machine threw the arm away as Levi howled in pain before he went to his other arm and, with a mighty strain and crack, the Sasquatch was now vulnerable and crying.

The machine threw his other arm next to the first. He then bent down and with his metal claws attached his hand to Levi's broken jaw, while he placed the other hand at the top of Levi's mouth. He snarled again with a smile, suggesting the Leader knew what Levi did to the original Savage, then he looked him in the eyes and ever so slowly began separating his top and bottom jaw, tearing his head in two directions. The last of the giant beast's energy was that of his legs squirming and his voice trying to scream. "Savage" tore the top part of Levi's head completely off, leaving an open area where his skull should have been but only the remnants of the bottom half of a broken jaw remained. Levi was no more.

The metal monster turned like he had a far greater mission to attend to and, without the need to rest or gather his breath, picked up the long serrated pole, and headed out of the door and up the stairs to complete his destruction for the day.

FIRESTORM

THEY SAT IN DARKNESS. BESIDES A FEW GLOWS coming from the chest holding the containers, it was completely dark. They awaited the return of Vaelenflixx, who had left only minutes earlier to get an idea of how bad it was. Valinda continued scanning; she could see the Fae treasures well and the invisible glow they had around the chest. She didn't realize it, but she could see parts of Faelynn with her bionic eye sometimes, avoiding a tree that wasn't there or an old brick structure that was not of Earth, dismissing it all as just normal.

Valinda was not so normal, though. She had been healed by supernatural events and scientific medicine; she could get close to the Fae, unlike most humans, and she had a natural ability, because of her experiences, to take charge and finish a job most would never entertain in their wildest dreams. Valinda had come a long way from the scared, confused journalist of only months before, but in her mind, she was the same. As long as she was helping, she had to push onward, and remembering Michael's words made her resolve that much more determined.

Vaelenflixx came screeching up the shaft hole like a freight train. Valinda could see the torment on his face as he translated to Breaxinah what he had seen. The terrified little nature sprite continued over to Valinda with great speed, where he sought solace under her hair at the back of her neck. He was trembling more than she had ever felt from him and knew it would not be good news.

Breaxinah swiftly moved toward Val and relayed as best he could the ramblings of the frightened Fae sprite. "Vaelenflixx says there are shafts that lead straight down, with ropes it should be easy enough, but it's what is down there that is worse than the dark lord himself."

Breaxinah didn't care that Valinda wouldn't know that reference to how evil it was, but by the look in his eyes she gathered it was bad.

"Go on," Valinda said in a somewhat assertive, but caring tone.

"He says that there is a safe drop, and that there is nothing directly at the bottom, but through a main structure breach where the noises are coming from, he said there are dark Fae, he kept repeating it over and over, dark Fae, dark Fae."

Valinda looked just as confused as Breaxinah about the last incoherent passage.

"What do you think he means?" Val asked, wanting an answer to that riddle before making plans to go further.

"I ... don't know. Before we ended up here, we were in a battle with a powerful evil, with many different dark Fae that were trying to destroy us, maybe in his words he is describing dark Fae as pure evil as that is all he has known."

Valinda could tell Vaelenflixx understood as he whispered in old Fae, "*Dark Fae,*" over and over while trembling even more.

"OK, we are running out of time. Varg, I have an idea. We need to get this chest down as soon as possible. Do you have enough rope in your packs?"

Vargzin nodded as he relayed what Valinda was saying to the other Dracs.

"Alright, there is danger below, we know that, but at this stage it seems like we have a clear run to get the chest down now before things get worse and that could happen anytime."

As soon as Valinda finished her sentence, they all heard a loud crash coming from the higher areas where they had recently descended from.

"We have very little time, so what I am suggesting is, Varg, can you take two of your soldiers and drop to the bottom, clearing a way for the chest, then we pull the ropes and ease it down as two more descend just above to clear it, then the rest of us will follow suit."

Vargzin relayed the plan as the Dracs all shook their heads and replied. Soon Vargzin relayed their anguish. "No, one soldier, one Drac go down first, then one Drac and one soldier go after the chest, which I agree with. We are here to help, but we need to work as a team and not just become expendable fodder for the humans."

Valinda looked shocked and somewhat taken aback. In no way was she referring to that. "Sorry, Varg, all I meant was the best and strongest, I was not implying anything less. You are right, one soldier and one Drac, so who is going first?"

Draconians feared little. They had been fighting for thousands of years and were built for war, but this situation had some feeling ill at ease.

"I will go first," Vargzin said with an assertive tone, looking at the surrounding others. Even with the goggles on, the expressions on their faces still told the truth.

"I will go too," Corporal Jason Darnell said, with a quiver in his tone. The soldiers had been incredibly quiet since their Sergeant had left, but they knew they had a mission to finish.

"Excellent, thank you. I need two volunteers to stay here after we all descend until I send the signal."

There were two soldiers left and two Dracs. As they all sorted themselves into teams, Varg and Jason began descending, rifles over their shoulders in case of any unwanted guests. They could see better as they lowered themselves, scanning the area and picking up no life signs on the way. Soon they reached the bottom and as the slack was taken, a rope was fastened to the chest, hoping it wouldn't heat up.

Breaxinah had the hardest job of all. As light as the chest was and protected by the treasures, he had to guide it down gently and maintain a balance so it wouldn't spin or spiral out of control. Grilif jumped on top, and soon afterward Darf did the same, like they knew what they were doing, and without too much conversation or bickering between them, they weighted each end with their bodies. Gnomes were known for their craftsmanship, building, and mining throughout the ages, so it was little surprise they got to it with no fuss.

The Elvenfae guard slowly moved the free-floating chest off the edge. The Fae treasures were doing most of the work keeping it steady, but the rope was attached in case it fell too quickly. It would look for the closest surface to hover down to so as it descended at a slow, but steady rate, Breaxinah did his best to float down with it. The treasures were stable enough as they all held their breath while the chest was lowered deeper into the darkness. Valinda couldn't help but be amazed at such wisdom and composure of the Fae, even Vaelenflixx did his part, but the Elvenfae were something else.

Lower and lower it descended. Soon a wind rose through the shaft, rocking the chest gently, so Grilif stood and moved a little to stop the gentle swaying. After they were halfway, another soldier and Drac started down the steep decline, away from the middle of the chest's path so as not to drop any debris onto the box of contained Dragon Fyre below.

Then Grilif and Darf both stood up in a hurry, jolting the chest, as the heat was becoming too unbearable. Gril looked up at the slowly fluttering Breaxinah and said, "We don't have much time. These things are about to blow."

Breaxinah nodded, sweat slowly dropping onto the chest as the surrounding rope started fraying and charring. Grilif and Darf both screamed in pain as they dove for the hanging ropes that were dangling in front of them. Their eyes were being helped by the magic of the Fae treasures so they could coordinate the reach, but that left Breaxinah with a dilemma, as the chest was slowly swinging. If it hit the sides of the shaft, it would all be over.

He was now in damage control, pulling up the slack of the rope and pushing down faster to stop the swinging. As he gained speed, he gently fluttered up taking the slack. The soldiers on the bottom, the ones descending, and both Grilif and Darf were watching with bated breath and all in awe of the struggling Fae's quick thinking and strength. He was two-thirds of the way down when noises began ringing out from above, but Breaxinah couldn't think of that now. He had to get the chest to the bottom, the main reason being he didn't much feel like burning to cinders, let alone fail his mission for his queen.

Meanwhile, at the top of the decline, while the struggles were going on down the shaft, several small creatures emerged from above. Some were scaling the walls while others scampered along the ground. Valinda could see them clearly. Although distracted from her observations and the worries going on below, she was soon readying herself, along with the rest of the team, to eliminate the threat. As she looked up to inspect the beasts, she noticed something sneak back out of sight behind the comfort of the walls. The little hairy creatures with long, gangly, hairless arms and very short, stumpy legs began moving closer. The heads on them were very creepy looking, with two giant ears on each side sticking straight up, and they showed their mouthfuls of razor-sharp teeth and snarling smiles.

The first ones raced toward the heavily armed troops while others jumped from the roof like monkeys for a surprise attack, but as the blasts of firepower hit three, then four, blowing the six-eyed noseless heads from their shoulders, the others realized they were in too deep, and scattered away into the darkness.

Valinda rushed back to the edge just as the chest slowly and gently landed safely on the ground. She then sent Vaelenflixx down to make sure everything was fine as Buul'ulaan, Dakota, and Spencer began descending.

Spencer wasn't used to this kind of thing, and the rope with his longtime friend just a little below him started rocking and shaking.

"Are you alright, Spence? Coz if you are not, get another rope." Dakota wasn't happy, but Spencer continued to struggle, the sounds of his groans and moans attracting unwanted attention from the shadows in between the shaft walls.

Breaxinah allowed the rope to burn on the chest as the gnomes repositioned everything back to normal. They could all hear Spencer's efforts, and now also movement echoing from the many halls indicated by a slight glow at the openings.

Breaxinah whispered to Vaelenflixx to tell Valinda to hurry, just as

Spencer lost his grip and began falling, heading directly for the chest. He heard the soldier's wails and darted up as fast as he could, meeting him a third of the way down and bringing him safely to the ground. Confused and in shock, Spencer looked up and said, "Thank you, thank you."

By then Buul'ulaan was already on the ground, while Dakota was faced with a creature slowly pulling his rope up, drawing him in. Vaelenflixx had noticed it on his way up, and before he went to Valinda, he darted inside the dark of an opening. Everything went silent and the rope became slack, giving Dakota time to hurry back down. But soon more gunfire could be heard coming from the top, and then a horrendous howl came from where Vaelenflixx had entered, before silence hit the area again and the tiny sprite flew out, a little disoriented but finally ready to pass on the message to Valinda. Dakota made it to the bottom as they all pulled up their rifles, ready for an attack.

At the top Valinda tried to stay as far back as she could from the soldiers, ambushed by more of the insidious creatures returning for another round, but in heavier numbers. Vaelenflixx met with Valinda as one creature grabbed her leg. She let out a loud cry and as she went to shoot it herself, a larger creature pushed its clawed hand through the Drac soldier, pulling out some insides, before it bit the head off the human soldier.

Valinda froze. She couldn't even scream, let alone shoot the alien-looking creature that was about to take a chunk from her leg, as two others that had been climbing slowly from the rooftop also began feeling at her legs. The gathering of vile things was just about to tear her apart, when several perfectly aimed shots were fired from a pulse rifle, taking out all the creatures within Valinda's reach. Then the shooter somersaulted over her head and began dicing the others fast as lightning with his sword until the legs of the giant creature were taken out, leaving it just out of reach, howling and crying, trying but just short of grabbing the Elvenfae warrior guard.

Breaxinah sheathed his sword and picked up the rifle again. He glided to Valinda, gripped her, and they zoomed to the ground where more disturbing cries and screams could be heard emerging from the collider room.

"Are you alright, Val? Where are the others?" asked Dakota, with an obviously concerned tone.

"I am fine, just frazzled." Valinda looked at everyone. The light from the chest was glowing brighter so they could see her face as she answered, "I am sorry. They didn't make it."

Buul'ulaan grunted as Vargzin groaned in anger, and said, "It's not over. Let's get this finished. Arm up and move out."

The chest was in the middle as they had always placed it, and slowly and steadily they eased forward with a soldier and Drac at the rear, Dakota and Spencer at the flanks, while Vargzin, another Drac, Jason, and Val moved to the front, leaving Buul'ulaan just in front of the Fae but behind the leaders. They covered all angles as the movement around them started closing in the nearer they got to the collider. They should have been able to see the bright lights, but there was a mist of darkness blocking them out, with dark howls and shadowy movements, and what sounded like millions talking at once between shrills and screams.

"I don't like this, not one bit," Valinda whispered as she remembered what Michael had said.

"Fire at anything and everything!" Vargzin shouted as the noises closed in.

Soon, the darkness was met with flurries of blue pulse and grenade fire as the dark mists meandered throughout the team, whispering things into their minds.

"Don't listen to them. They are from the most evil of places. Concentrate on the moving creatures," Valinda yelled as they continued to move closer.

Explosions and shots rang out for what seemed like ages as they mowed down some of the most horrifying sights they had ever seen in their lives. Edging closer, they were finally able to enter the noisy room of the collider, where the dark mists slowly leaked from the portal. The machine appeared to be stuck in the one place. Several beasts seemed to be protecting the area.

The Fae took off to find a safe part of the collider, while more gunfire and more grenade shots took out the large creatures before they had time to defend themselves. Buul'ulaan stopped and stood with her mouth open, dropping her weapon, knowing that this could very well have been her. She knew she would never get home now and she fell to her knees and howled. Spencer moved toward her and tried to comfort her, at the same time picking off little rat-like creatures.

"Come, we need your help. I promise, when this is all over, I will help you, there has to be a way."

Buul'ulaan stood up. She shook her head as she turned to face him and said, "No, I was sent here for a reason, and this is it. Go with your friends while I give you some time."

As she finished her response to Spencer, Buul'ulaan ran for the remaining creatures protecting the X-Clock and started tearing into them, giving Valinda and Dakota time to help the Fae with the canisters. Spencer lowered his head for a moment and then tried to back her up as much as he could, knowing there was nothing he could do.

Valinda had her protective gloves on, as did Dakota, and they gently and strategically planted every canister along the collider. They needed one for the X-Clock, which was still working, and one for the portal, but they would have to wait because more gunfire lit the room.

Jason approached the portal as the last of the creatures fell, not getting too close, but he had heard sobbing and whispers. The soldier moved in to see what it was, when a little girl, only about six years old, stood up and turned to face him. He was shocked to see such an innocent young human there. The blonde girl in a blue dress, with buckles on her shoes and a bow in her hair, holding a brown teddy bear, sobbed. "Please don't kill me, sir, I promise I will be good," she said.

Jason bent down and, still bewildered by what he was seeing, said, "That's alright, I am here to help you."

The little girl moved closer and whispered, as if all the surrounding noises were now gone and it was only the two of them, "Please make them stop, please, do it for me."

Jason didn't blink as he turned and shouted at everyone to hold their fire. Looking confused, Vargzin and the other Dracs didn't respond. They were being inundated with howls and screams coming from everywhere, although they had defeated all the threats besides the ones Spencer was finishing off.

The young soldier aimed his rifle at the Dracs before shouting at them again to stop firing, as he could hear the little girl crying behind him and begging, but before he could ask them a third time, a shot rang out from one of the Dracs' guns, straight into the middle of Jason's head. As the soldier fell to the ground, the last thing he saw was the little girl turning into black mist and disappearing.

All the soldiers were struggling with hallucinations, as the cries and howls echoed from the mist. The last human soldier pointed his own rifle at his chin and blasted half of his head from his body.

Dakota and Valinda had been preoccupied and were outside the harshness of the black mist, so they hadn't been affected, but they could see something was going on when Marcus appeared from behind the darkness with a face twisted and deformed, ready to strike Vargzin in the back with a long piece of shrapnel. As soon as Dakota noticed, he rolled on the floor, and just as Marcus sliced a huge hole into the Draconian's back, Dakota let him have it with the last of his pulse rounds, piercing the traitorous soldier and forcing him to the ground.

The other Dracs snapped out of their trances brought on by the mist, and raced over to their mentor and friend as Vargzin leaned on his knees, trying to get up.

Meanwhile, Spencer had eventually taken out the last creature at the X-Clock, but not before Buul'ulaan was torn apart, finally clearing the way for the Fae to safely place the last two canisters where they needed to go. The containers were now shaking, and it wouldn't be long before detonation. As Valinda looked at the destructive mess around them all, she shouted, "We must go; the charges are set; the detonator stickers are in place. We have very little time now."

Vargzin called for her to come closer, and as she did, he pulled out the detonator and held it high. "Get ... Your ... People out and safe ... Get my people out too, now go."

Valinda had tears in her eyes. She wanted to argue that they could all get out, but she knew it would be to no avail. She put her arms around him and whispered, "I have met no one braver than you in all my life. I will tell everyone what happened here today."

Varg was in pain and was losing consciousness as he replied, "You humans aren't bad either, now go!"

After the Drac soldiers finished farewelling Varg, both Dakota and Valinda pulled out a Vocalization Portal Device each and blew hard, watching as two simultaneous blue vortexes opened. Then Spencer and the Drac soldiers went through Dakota's portal, followed by himself, while Valinda would not have long once the Fae treasures were gone as she waited for Grilif, Darf, Vaelenflixx, and Breaxinah, who was holding them, to all flutter through. Then Valinda walked through herself. As she made it to the safety of the green surroundings of home, she turned and watched Varg smile at her and flick the detonator right as the vortex closed.

They could all see the firestorm from the clearing of the mountainous ranges where they were, bright fire in the sky glowing hot and high for what seemed like hundreds of miles. Every single Fae, human, and Drac stopped to look at the destruction, all contemplating what they had lost, but most importantly what they hoped to have gained if the others were successful.

DRAGON FYRE

THE DETERMINATION WITH WHICH WILKES MOVED swiftly through the corridors and up the unprotected back stairs of the White House was proof of the hybrid's strong DNA, which the overconfident android Leader had underestimated. Too many ZARKs were focusing on the outer areas of the building, not homing in on the lone Zeytar hybrid, who was trying with everything he had left to reach a destination he had to make.

The last stairwell was the hardest. A lone ZARK on patrol protected this one, and Wilkes, now tiring from his ordeal, stood staring back at the massive automaton. As the machine raised its arm, Wilkes was caught between the cacophony of sounds emanating from below, most likely on their way up to him, and the vision of the ZARK changing its forearm into a plasma cannon. It all felt like slow motion. Wilkes fell to his knees. It was over, he thought, as the last of his determined spirit and energy faded from his once focused and motivated mind.

The ZARK aimed directly at the hybrid Zeytar's head and as a blue light glowed from the first of the plasma fire, Wilkes was suddenly pushed away with force from the blast, blocked by the sword of Van Coinan, who was still a massive white Sasquatch. The pooka then parried the ZARK after the blast hit, moving behind at great speed while lifting his once wooden blade high over his head, ready to strike before the ZARK could react.

All that time spent watching the Elvenfae guards, Shaylee, and Serena, and even some humans, were paying off for Van Coinan as the sword struck hard and fast on the automaton's head, leaving a huge gash from its forehead down to its chin. Blue and white sparks flew out from the insides as it slowly lost all power and dropped to the floor.

Van Coinan could hear the noises from outside and the lower stairs getting louder. Time was running out, so he didn't pause, but turned to Wilkes and in a deep voice said, "Come on, Wilkes, we are running out of time."

The pooka then sheathed his sword into the scabbard on his back while he glimpsed the shocked hybrid Zeytar's eyes flicker back from fear to a gaze of hope once more. As they continued to climb the stairs, they were soon met from behind by other ZARK drones and cybernetic Zeytars blasting upward and trying to find a target. They burst from the exit door onto the roof, but here too they were met with blasts of gunfire. Van Coinan leaped into the air, changed form to his original pooka size, and landed on the back of Vylan'flare, who was using the Shadowblood pulse rifles to melt the ZARKs and cyborg Zeytars that were awaiting them.

Wilkes looked behind him as the door burst open, just as Shaylee flew over, screaming, "Take my hand, Wilkes!"

As he tried to reach up, the tips of his fingers just touched hers before a blast hit him directly through his shoulder, dropping the rebel to his knees. Shaylee was maneuvering, trying to avoid all the blasts coming from every direction while the look on her face went to that of pure shock, before rage hit her—rage that the Zeytars had created in her through all those years of torture and capture.

She flew high into the sky. The Elvenfae guards were in full force of action and strength as Shaylee thrust her spear around to create a force field in the sky for her people. She had done something similar earlier on as she homed in on Wilkes, creating a massive vortex that was big enough for Vaximardruusz to enter through, saving his energy for the task at hand and moving through time and space to get there swiftly. Shaylee was showing signs of fatigue, as were her warriors, and Vaximardruusz was still out of sight with Rasarlin, not wanting to be trapped like before.

The tensions were high as blasts from both parties made the sky look like the Fourth of July. Eoghan was with his mother. The powder and the sword seemed to have helped him to the point that he had lots of energy. He was most likely the only one, though. Shaylee couldn't wait to see Felvora and Kalandrya again to get some explanations about her nephew, but she knew in herself that there was far more to that boy than just being part of a prophecy.

Blast after blast pierced the air and both forms of the ZARKs, melting some and creating meat heaps from the others, while some of the more brazen warrior Fae were taking hits unprotected by Shaylee. Soon it became too much for her and she began slowing down. Eoghan was blasting with a Shadowblood pulse rifle next to his mother, then flew low and used the Sword of Light, before rising for another attack. On his last round, as he was ascending once more, he noticed Shaylee looking weary and like she was losing the ability to fly. The young warrior soared like the wind, gaining the attention of his mother as she too noticed her sister's ails and followed her son.

Eoghan grabbed the spear from Shaylee and cradled her in his arms, which was a scene reversed from only hours before, while she looked at his face and smiled. Serena fluttered around to her, taking the spear from Eoghan and with her other hand brushing Shaylee's long, messed-up blonde hair from her face.

"Are you alright, Shay? Do you need to rest?" Serena said, quite worried in her tone, quivering as she spoke. Shaylee looked at her, still smiling and replied in a weak tone, "No, Sis, I just needed a minute. The power of the treasures has become too much for even me to bear and I need someone to take the load for a while, but there are few Fae that can withstand that much power."

Eoghan cleared his throat softly, still fluttering hard in the sky while holding his much taller aunt in his arms. He gained the attention of them both and said, "I ... I can do it. I can, and have, held both sword and spear before."

Shaylee looked at him with caring eyes. She was being recharged by the treasures as she rested but knew she couldn't keep going at that pace. She answered Eoghan softly, "No, my love, it is too much for you. Look what happened when you helped Vax. I can't let you take that risk."

Eoghan looked sternly at his aunt and reminded her of what she had said, "You told me to trust my instincts and to do what I must. Now, please, I am telling you, I can do this."

Serena smiled at Eoghan. She had trusted him completely and was now there to talk Shaylee around, but it didn't happen. Shaylee fluttered out of his grip and on her own into the air next to Serena and she proudly acknowledged, "You are right. I think in my weakened state I didn't want you to have to endure the same draining as I had, but I feel you are right, Eoghan. I think you are a wise warrior and if we don't move out of the way, I think some ZARK drones are going to HIT US!"

Shaylee had seen them break through the lower contingent of Elvenfae guards and send blasts their way. Eoghan turned as the blast was about to hit him but then at the last moment ricocheted over him when the sword suddenly glowed from his scabbard, like it was protecting him. More blasts fired upward toward them, but they were all ready now. Eoghan took the spear from his mother, pulled the sword from his scabbard, and flew toward several ZARKs flying their way, blasting blue bolts of pulse energy. Eoghan was maneuvering in and out as he aimed the spear into the air, pulling bolts of lightning from the sky and guiding them toward the machines.

While they convulsed as if a live electric conduit had hit them, Eoghan sliced two heads from their necks, with Shaylee and Serena following close by. Replacing the Shadowblood pulse rifles with their own swords, they continued Eoghan's work by cutting the rest from their bodies.

Eoghan descended further down. There was now an immense army of cybernetic Zeytars on the roof along with many remaining ZARK drones in and around them, some in the air, some standing with the crowds.

Serena, Eoghan, and Shaylee spent the best part of the next five minutes working in unison, slicing and cutting, blasting, and maiming whatever evil creature of metal they could until they heard a massive scream coming from the exit to the roof door. Wilkes was still alive, and the Leader now had him high in the air as he bellowed a loud, deep warning to everyone in the sky, "Stop where you are. It is useless to entertain the idea you can defeat me, or my soldiers. I have planned this for an exceedingly long time and although I am quite impressed with the resilience of humans and the perfect harmony of the Fae, I am afraid it is not enough. Remember this day as the day your beloved Wilkes failed you all, every single one of you. Without his interference some of you, in fact most of you, would have lived normal lives under our control. But know this, every single one of you will die at the hands of my machines. I will make it my priority to hunt every human and every Fae and destroy everything you have ever lived for and stood for, and you can thank your betrayer, Wilkes."

The Leader was back in his android form and had Wilkes high in the air with his right arm holding the hybrid Zeytar who flopped around like a rag doll. Wilkes turned his head toward Serena, finding her eyes in the crowds of Fae and ZARKs, before nodding slowly as the Leader put his arm through Wilkes' chest and pulled out his heart before throwing it on the ground and crushing it underneath his metal foot. "There is the heart of your saving leader, gone into the mush of the mortal world. I am forever and there is nothing you can do about it; you are all mine."

As he finished his disturbing acts of violence and dark speech, he threw Wilkes' body onto the cold concrete roof. With his face staring in shock at his crushed and lifeless heart next to him, Wilkes' eyes went completely black, and Serena let out an anguished scream.

She climbed higher into the air as the Leader moved into the crowds of his minions. He looked up, and smirked when he saw her getting distance for what was going to be the bravest or silliest revenge attack ever, but as Serena rose, so did some of the other Fae, then more, until the whole sky was filled. About eight hundred yards up, Eoghan and Shaylee, along with Vylan'flare and Van Coinan, joined her. The blue glows from the ZARKs feet began shining on the concrete as they slowly rose into the sky, when a flash of light thousands of miles away lit up the sky. Even though it was so far away, some still had to cover their eyes from the brightness of the blast, attracting the attention of the Leader who took flight to get a better look.

The Fae shouted out in joy as the revelation of what had just happened hit them; they had done it. Valinda and Vargzin, along with Grilif and Darf, had destroyed the collider. Soon an aurora of lights began flickering across the sky and at the same time Vaximardruusz with Rasarlin and the last of the soldiers came roaring over the roof, firing blasts of Shadowblood and fireballs at the ZARK drones. The Fae moved away from the wyvern's target zone, and in formation like a flock of birds led some groups away from the Leader's position, giving Vax an opportunity to burn whole contingents of ZARKs all at once. The Fae then dispersed and came together at other angles with the same idea, leaving the area in flock formation.

Eoghan had the spear and was working hard at the rear to make sure they were safe from flames or radiation blast from Vax, along with stray blasts from the ZARKs as the wyvern did a second sweep across. Soon the Fae dispersed in many directions, confusing even the Leader who was losing his cool. "What is the matter with you? Can't you see what they are doing? You should concentrate on the beast."

Their plan that they had formulated before arriving had started working. The Leader was out of the safe zone of the building and now in the sky with the drones, as the cybernetic Zeytars fired at Vax. But there was no net, giving the giant beast the ability to fly in and out of blasts, taking some if he had to with his exo shell scales.

But as the rain of molten metal was dripping and falling from the sky, the Leader had one more ace up his sleeve. Closing his eyes as the last of his ZARK drones burned to liquid, he opened several doorways at once with his mind. High in the air portals were opening and closing, much faster than ALEX could ever have done as hundreds of ZARKs from all over the world flew in to protect their Leader.

"You cannot stop me; don't you realize that? Besides, I am made of Ardmenticam and have Medi-drones so you can burn me to liquid, and I will just keep on rising from the pools on the ground." The words spoken were the arrogance of an ego-driven Leader who thought himself invincible. But he had never come across a dragon before.

Vax spat out fireballs one after the other to try and close the portals as they flew past, but there were far too many, so listening to his wise friend's plans, he pointed his nose to the stars as the sky darkened. He flew higher into the night, giving himself time to recoup. The other Fae appeared again, blasting the portals from all sides so the ZARKs melted upon arriving. This lasted a while. The Leader's eyes finally opened again as the last of his portals closed. He knew there were more losses, but the wyvern had gone.

"It's weak," he said under his breath, thinking that Vax had to rest or was too overwhelmed, but as the Fae continued to blast the drones, a roaring sound came from above. It was hard to see with the dark of the night creeping in and the auroras left of the worlds returning to normal. The Fae scattered once more as Vaximardruusz opened his mouth again and let out a roaring cry, giving the Fae time before a torrent of fire and wind decimated the whole area. ZARK after ZARK fell from the sky, and the whole lot of cybernetic Zeytars that were left on the building, slowly and painfully melted, while others who were closer and took the brunt of the force were dissolved within seconds. The Leader screamed as he started shooting from his fists. All the remaining ZARKs were now focused on Vax, attacking his tail, then his wings. Some even climbed onto his back and tail, trying to get a clear shot of his head.

The wyvern was already tiring, and he hadn't reached the main target yet. The soldiers were forced to dive from his back as more ZARKs started clinging to him. The Fae could see everything going on and tried to anticipate as best as they could. While the White House burned to cinders, some Elvenfae guards caught the soldiers and brought them safely to solid ground.

Eoghan had an idea to buy some time for Vax and Rasarlin. After lighting the sword red with flame, and with the Spear of Assal lit brightly at its tip, he flew away from the battle, giving Vax a break while luring as many automatons as possible in the opposite direction. Serena and Shaylee followed the now very large contingent as the young warrior turned and unleashed all the power he could from the treasures of his ancestors, his eyes closed as lightning, fire, wind, and ice cascaded down from the sky, pelting all of those that followed. The rest of the Fae stopped the ZARKs trying to flee, shooting hard with the last of their Shadowblood, giving precious respite for Vax and Rasarlin who was trying to stay positioned firmly on the wyvern's back.

But there was one thing that Rasarlin had that the automatons didn't, and that was he knew every crevice, spike, leathery hair, bone, and contour of his friend's back. As he pulled out Severed Wing, he began slicing ZARK heads, arms, and torsos, all while dodging blasts. His acrobatic abilities were second to none as the Marelarph glowed a bright purple. The worlds had not completely returned to normal as the paradox still held, although it seemed he was able for the first time to use the power from his homeland. He could harness it even in its purest and most evil form.

Rasarlin shot out invisible power from his hands, as his eyes glowed a deep purple color, emulating that of the power he was using, before purple blasts hit out at the drones. The fire on his sword was now a bright purple color. Vax was sucking up some of the power as his wings began to close the torn leathery holes. It was dark magic, but it was that of his own world. Rasarlin slowly rose into the air, light bouncing from him, just as Shaylee finished with her own battle. She watched on, witnessing something never seen in a Fae or even the dark lord.

As the power grew, lightning struck the area, and the Fae watched on. Some swore they could see Rasarlin as a cloaked skeleton when the blue from the lightning hit, only for him to return to full form afterward. The elven warrior glided over to the last hovering android, that of the Leader in Zeytar form. Without words, the android blasted everything it had at him but Rasarlin just floated as if surrounded by a soft summer breeze. Vax had left his side and flew higher into the clouds once more before Rasarlin fired a torrent of purple fire from his eyes and palms, hitting the Zeytar android's blasts and slowly moving him backward. For the first time, Rasarlin could see fear in his robotic eyes until the Marelarph suddenly shut off completely and Rasarlin passed out in the middle of the air.

Shaylee could see him falling and she soared over to his side and caught him. Eoghan, too, was falling from the sky as vines reached up and lowered the warrior teen safely to the ground. Very soon Shaylee was hit with a blast from the evil Leader, and both she and Rasarlin hurtled out of control, heading for the smoldering fires below. But just before they hit, they stopped, yards from impact as Rasarlin opened his eyes. The last of his power was waning and the purple glow disappeared from his eyes as they softly landed on the ground. Rasarlin placed his hand on Shaylee's back and healed her wound before passing out. Shaylee screamed as she tried to help him, but the dark magic was too much, rendering the otherworldly visitor comatose.

Shaylee could hear wind and movement as the Leader descended toward them but he stopped as Vaximardruusz let out a deafening cry. The beast was in full form now and was angrier than ever. Wanting it all to be over, he flew overhead and screamed into the Leader's mind, "Follow me if you dare." The Leader, shocked it could communicate but without thinking too much about it, followed the wyvern, not afraid of a beast made of fire and meat. And then Vax turned, knowing all his friends were safe, and began opening his mouth, as he flapped his wings slowly, to the point that he was only just staying afloat, giving all the energy to the last of his power.

The Leader was floating twenty yards away from Vax, but they were face to face. The wyvern's tail dropped lower, making a huge "y" shape in the air, as a smile hit his huge, scaly face of nothing but teeth and he waited patiently for the android to make the first move. The Leader's metal neurons were firing hard as he opened his tiny mouth under his bulbous silver and blue head and said, "Do your worst ... dragon!"

With that Vaximardruusz took a deep breath, continuing his smiley snarl, and let out the most explosive torrents of fire he had ever released. Some of the flames were purple, and the Fae had to cover their eyes from the brightness while Serena stood tall, next to her son, who was safe but exhausted, and watched the fury of the giant beast explode toward the insidious robot. The Leader burst into a deep dark laughter as parts of him slowly dripped onto the ground, all while Vax continued to belt out Dragon Fyre. Soon the laughing stopped as the Leader's robotic face started melting, his jaw dropping to the ground in a puddle of liquid metal. An arm, then a leg melted, before the whole thing was a vast pile of molten mess, glowing orange on the ground.

The Leader was nothing more than liquid, bubbling up and down as the Medi-drones tried to fix it. Vax took another deep breath and fired a second charge at the substance on the ground, volumes of the hottest substance Earth had ever seen continuing to cover the area where the Leader fell until Vax was exhausted yet satisfied. He pulled himself away and headed over to the closest dam, disappearing from sight completely.

The fire had obliterated everything in its path. There were no remnants at all of roads, cars, fences—nothing but white-hot heat. The place where the Leader had fallen was just ash—not even a bubble or a silver speck tried to come up. All the Geno-drones inside the machine had disintegrated. The inter-dimensional destructive machine was no more. All the remaining ZARKs and cybernetic Zeytars began falling all around the world, letting minor rebellions take control and free anyone who was left. The control was gone. The android was gone. And the most important thing: The Zeytars were gone.

≈

After they gathered themselves together and made sure they could find as many survivors of their group as they could, the Fae slowly disappeared into their own realm. As the last of the aurora lifted, they were now free to go home. Shaylee knew Rasarlin had little time left and Vax was now too weak to fly. Shaylee, very proud of her nephew, wanted him to rest, as she took the spear and swirled it around for what would be the second last time she would use the powers on Earth. She opened a portal back to the ship where they would meet up with the heroes and hopefully survivors of the other mission.

Rasarlin was now awake but weak as the wounded and those who couldn't walk rested on Vax as he trudged through the huge maelstrom of wind and light to be met with thunderous roars from the other side of the portal. Serena looked around for Eric and Stacey as Shaylee was met with hugs on her legs as Grilif and Darf smiled and laughed. Van Coinan was with the two gnomes but some faces were missing from the crowd and the survivors soon learned of the devastation they had had to endure as well.

Serena kept scanning for Eric and when her eyes met his from within the crowd, he was smiling a half-saddened smile. They met each other and kissed, with tears flowing down both their faces. After embracing for ages, Serena pulled away, looked up at Eric, and said, "Where is Stacey? Eric, is she alright?"

Eric lowered his head as his tears flowed like waterfalls. He winced, betraying his heartbreak as he put his hand over his eyes to hide the pain.

"Eric, no ... No, not Stacey, please." As tears streamed down Serena's face, Eric broke for a moment from his torment and said, "I ... couldn't save her ... It was too late; I am sorry, Serena."

Eric just apologized. His daughter was gone, and he was thinking of her feelings, she thought. She clutched him tightly and hugged him as he let out another torrent of tears. Serena whispered in his ear as she calmed him, "I love you so much. Do you hear me, and I loved her too. She was one of the most beautiful people I ever knew, and it was because of you, Eric. You both have beautiful souls."

Eric pulled back, panting and wheezing, as he tried to wipe his saturated face before answering, "She was beautiful, and she loved all of you ... Is Eoghan safe?"

Eric looked around and saw his son standing behind his mother. He knew what had happened and had already started crying. Eric saw him and moved to embrace him as he whispered with more tears, "You were her favorite person, champ. I know she loved you, as do I. You got your strength from her and your mother."

Eoghan cried uncontrollably until he was ready to answer, pulling away from his father and mother, "I loved her too, Dad. How will I be able to live without her?"

Serena and Eric looked at each other as he answered his brave boy, "I don't know, Son; we will all have to figure that out together."

As the family embraced each other with tears, others watched on, knowing by their sadness what had happened. Then there were some who celebrated, singing, dancing, and drinking well into the night. It was a time for all feelings as the harshness of what had transpired hit every one of them in different ways.

THE NEW KING

THERE WASN'T MUCH TIME TO MOURN OR celebrate. Rasarlin was feeling very ill, as was Vax, and with that came the threat of the two being sucked back into the time trap. Shaylee had done all she could to help him as she had ordered most Fae to go, but with the treasures still at her disposal, even she didn't have time.

With the dark of the night and the sorrow of the fallen, many took solace in being with family and remaining friends, but there was one who was optimistic and positive, a soul that was contagious and sweet.

Eoghan had spent many hours with Eric and Serena as they discussed what was to happen next. The loss of Stacey was immense and did not make the next few decisions easy.

"No, Serena, I am telling you no. I have lost my only daughter. I will not lose my only son too," Eric said.

Serena knew this time was coming and losing Stacey had affected all of them, especially her, but she could not let the guidance and opportunity of what might be the best thing for their son slip by.

"Please, Eric, Shaylee has a plan. We all need a plan. Our world is nothing but rubble and death, so this may be the key to it all."

She then looked Eric deep in his eyes with her compassionate gaze. It didn't really matter what look he got; he was always under her spell. He blinked, sat up, and shook his head. "Alright then, let's do it, let's give him to the Fae."

Serena was confused. Two seconds earlier he was arguing, now he was calm and composed. Then it hit her. Serena turned around to see

Shaylee and Rasarlin standing there. Eric had a sudden change of heart because he didn't want a fight with the queen of the Fae.

"It is alright, Eric. Eoghan was born a part of you but also the Fae. He has the oldest blood in him, and I promise, as much as I can, he will be safe. I can also say that when Serena was not much younger, she had a similar journey. Now, without the Zeytars, can you trust me?"

Eric felt embarrassed slightly as Serena kissed him and watched him move back in his seat. He then responded cautiously, "Yes, Shaylee, I will always trust you," looking at Serena as he finished his comment.

Serena smiled and jumped up excitedly. Rasarlin still seemed sick and weak, but the focus was on getting the treasures and the rest of the Fae home as soon as they could, and that included Eoghan. Eric stood up, watching his love dance around, and wondered why, but realized soon after that the Fae were a unique breed, and he was now in that world.

Shaylee moved forward, took Eric's hand, and pulled him to her. "Without you, from the start, my people would have been doomed. Your daughter's sacrifice, along with yours, will never be forgotten. Serena loves you, as do I with the Fae. I hope you will honor me and join us in our world."

It took Eric aback a little, especially after Shaylee kissed him on the cheek, but he was a small person on a large scale of events that took place. However, he accepted her quick analysis of the movement.

"OK, it's settled then, we leave in one Earth hour." Shaylee turned, took Rasarlin by the arm, and left to find the remaining members of her people, giving both time to organize themselves and prepare for the journey.

≈

Eoghan was with the gnomes and Van Coinan, fluttering about and having fun, when Shaylee gave him the good news. He was so excited that he did cartwheels and hugged the pooka so tight Van Coinan thought he was going to see some insides.

"Now, my sweet, there will be truths told and there will be a flood of voices calling out in rage when we arrive, but I want you to listen, accept with your heart, and concentrate on me, and only me, as it will only be for a short time. Now run along to your parents."

The young mixed breed was confused, but trusted Shaylee. So he just nodded and smiled as he watched her gather the last of the Fae and prepare for an inter-dimensional doorway to let her remaining loyal subjects through to the palace. The treasures would then be given to the dryads to hide again and change them back to their concentrated symbiotic forms where they worked with the nature of the realm, giving magic and life to the Fae once more.

"Go, my loves, I will see you in the blink of a sprite's flash."

As she opened the doorway with the spear, she watched as Vylan'flare and Breaxinah took the three treasures through, while Grilif, Darf, and Van Coinan followed. Shaylee was holding the last of the treasures as they wouldn't be able to all return at once without a major power source, but they had to be quick or the treasure would be deemed useless with the last of the Fae realm now depleted and returned. That's why she had given them an hour.

Soon enough, a small crowd gathered to watch the "dragon" leave forever, and the mesmerizing Shaylee with her strong elven warrior. Serena, Eric, and Eoghan soon approached as they made their way to a peak where Shaylee would open a massive doorway, one big enough for Vax to fly through. Over that hour there were many conversations had between Serena and her family, filling them in on those last questions they had about their history. Grace was shocked to learn some of the details, but she felt the family needed to know it all. Eoghan was with Eric at the time and his disclosure would come soon.

As they did some quick goodbyes, promising they would return not long after they left, Eric's eyes caught Valinda's. He moved toward her with a smile on his face. "Who is this handsome little man, Val?"

Valinda looked down, smiling, as she held the hand of a small creature. "This is Lovax. He is Levi's son. Wilkes had left me a message to only open in the wake of him or Levi not returning. His mother was killed in the battle also, so he told me where to find him. Levi must have taught him some of our communication gestures as I could communicate with him immediately. We lost a lot of them throughout this war, and I want to make sure Lovax has a life of peace and care, not having to witness any of the horrors that all our species have had to endure."

Eric smiled; he was looking forward to spending time with Lovax on his return, as he whispered under his breath, "Levi, you old smoothy."

Eric turned to Dakota, who was holding Valinda's other hand. He gently held the tracker's shoulder and said, "You take good care of these two for me—they are my family, as you have been over this time. Oh and I want to see all your findings about all the species that we had the chance and privilege to work alongside. I will build a database when I get home, which I will inform you all of later, but for now I must go. Val, I pass the reins to you for the moment. I believe everyone will be in good hands."

Eric kissed her on the cheek, winked at Dakota, and rubbed the top of Lovax's head before turning and walking up to the hill where Shaylee was waving her spear. Vax and Rasarlin flew through first, followed by Eoghan, Serena, and Eric, who were all holding hands, before Shaylee blew a kiss once more to the remaining people watching in awe and entered herself. Then the gigantic maelstrom dissipated as if it had never existed.

～

The portal door opened where Vax and Rasarlin were just landing, near the palace gates. Serena, Eoghan, and Eric soon appeared, not long before Shaylee. Eric hit the ground hard, rubbing his eyes from the bright denseness of color he needed to get used to—being human, though, would make that nearly impossible. Serena had expected this, and she put some sunglasses on his face, not because it was bright, but to reduce some of the intense vibrancy humans were not accustomed to.

Eoghan didn't even flinch. His human side was nearly non-existent in Faelynn. He was fluttering around, soaking up the forever spring-like weather like a bird free from its cage. Shaylee closed her eyes, smiled, and whispered to herself, "I am home. Oh how sweet it is to be home."

The small group of arrivals were soon met by Breaxinah and Vylan'flare, who had been sent to meet any visitors. A little time had passed, but only enough for the treasures to be returned with another little unexpected twist.

"Welcome back, my queen," Vylan'flare said. "We have been waiting for your arrival. The dryads are awaiting your council, as are the Seelie Court."

Shaylee nearly fell over as she asked the Elvenfae guard to repeat himself. "What did you say?"

Vylan'flare thought he had sounded loud and clear, but the queen wanted him to repeat it. "Sorry, my queen, I said the Seelie Court are here."

Shaylee looked at Serena and slowly shook her head before regaining composure and moving forward. "Come, let's greet all our people. It will be a reunion that will last an age."

She confidently walked up the stairs to the main palace chamber doors and into the meeting hall where thousands of Fae had heard rumors of the queen's return. They entered the building as fast as they could, cramming in like sardines as they cheered for Shaylee until they saw Eric. They knew who Serena was, and Eoghan looked like one of them, even Rasarlin was exempt from the silence, but a human in Faelynn was forbidden at the time.

Eric whispered to Serena as the eyes were piercing and locked on to the tall, well-built man, "Maybe I should just wait outside."

Serena clenched his hand tightly and whispered back, "You are not leaving my side; never, do you hear?"

Shaylee ordered all the Fae out except the main council and arranged for all Fae to meet in the great hall in one hour. Every single Fae from the Seelie Court who was in the palace city was to attend. Shaylee moved forward to the throne room where she was met with the dryads, Felvora and Kalandrya.

"Welcome back, my queen. We have worked feverishly taking care of the scared ones and keeping the palace hidden from humans. We have settled the treasures and are awaiting your council; however, there is one small thing I need to bring to your attention." Kalandrya was quite assertive with her.

"Can't it wait?" Shaylee said. "I have pressing information that is going to change Faelynn forever."

Kalandrya's news was too important. It needed to be addressed immediately. "I am sorry, my queen, but with all the downtime we both had, we studied the old Tuatha Dé Danann books from the old temple and found something I think you need to know."

Shaylee stared as she waved everyone off. "Please, I am sorry, but I just need a moment to catch up on current events. I will call for you all very soon. In the meantime, make yourselves at home. Vylan'flare will see to your needs."

Serena seemed confused but did what her queen asked as Shaylee listened intently.

"Your Highness, we have discovered two things. We know the Tuatha Dé Danann were the nature gods of our world sent here by humans, but that is wrong. They come from another world; a world rich in magic. The first Tuatha were aliens. The power helped create the realm and humans feared them so the realm was blocked and hidden between worlds so they could create and grow a peaceful race of beings to look upon and treat as all their children. Over time, they either went back or died off. We thought they were part of nature, but in fact they trickled back to nature after their bodies died, giving the illusion of nature gods. But it is all untrue. The only soothing component is that every time a Tuatha god died, it made the magic stronger, as with all our species, returning to nature at the end."

Shaylee felt peace with that. She didn't seem upset or that her dynamic beliefs had changed. With the arrival of Rasarlin, she knew there were some good aliens in the world; they were not all Zeytars. She looked at Kalandrya and responded, "I had a feeling there was more to us, but I have learned of another more powerful overseer. I know little, but it all may be linked. We will learn more soon as I address the people. We will have a union with the humans. What else do you have for me?"

Kalandrya was shocked at the queen's reaction. Had she spent too much time with them? she thought. "The second is the prophecy of the boy, the part Faiay'aar never got to. It further states the boy born of two-colored eyes will be king after a long war. That is Serena's child."

Shaylee looked at both Felvora and Kalandrya and said, "Here is the final treasure, but don't put it back just yet. These revelations are known to me, only by intuition. I have some huge news that I wanted to share with the council before the Seelie Court, but because you have brought them here too, I may as well tell everyone at once."

The two dryads looked confused, but Shaylee was queen and they had to trust her.

"Meet us in the great hall," Shaylee continued, "and please, remember, the Tuatha Dé Danann are and will always be our ancestors. We must embrace that part of our culture no matter whether they came from the Heavens or another planet—they are our history."

That seemed to give the dryads a little feeling of solace, as they nodded, smiled, and left Shaylee to organize the biggest meeting she would ever have with her people.

≈

The noises coming from the great main meeting hall were those of loud conversations and guesses about what was going to happen. Eric, for his own safety, was left just outside with Serena, Eoghan, and the two dryads, protected by two Elvenfae guards.

Her people had so many questions and fears, as for thousands and thousands of cycles they were all taught that humans were the enemy. Only those who fought in the recent wars had changed their feelings, some more than others, but even Breaxinah was a new convert. Serena leaned over to Eric and whispered comforting words to soothe his anxious state. It was not every day you had hundreds of thousands of faeries wanting to harm you. And he knew enough about Irish folklore, and had seen them firsthand, to realize the dangers.

Shaylee moved out into the great hall and was met with cheers and applause as she waved her hands, blew kisses, and slowly encouraged them to quieten down. Soon, the halls were silent, as the Fae were almost always obedient to their kings and queens.

"My people, I have some news. We have defeated the sinisters once and for all. We have defeated the dark lord once and for all. We have no enemies now, so it's time to build a new world, a world where we can all live in peace."

Soon a red cap interrupted, shouting out in contempt, "Humans, my queen. We have one enemy and that is humans."

Shaylee looked over at Fusslebox Quartzpond, raised her finger, and pointed to him. Her fierce demeanor frightened even the hard red cap to the point of complete obedience before she returned to her speech. "Where were you in the wars? Hiding among the fearful and trembling pixies? I had more help from them than I did a red cap, so silence. You know nothing of what has transpired."

Shaylee turned, and looked at Eric, standing just outside the hall, who had been joined by Rasarlin. She smiled, and gathered herself before moving forward. "Without the bravery of the humans, we would be lost forever. Their sacrifice has been a million times worse than ours. Their world is in ruins and only a third of their population remains. I have seen their courage and that is why I am telling you this. As we sit here today, still able to call this home, I want you to look at Serena, a halfling that in our own prophecy was foretold of a sacrifice that could have killed her and her son, but also of a king who would be born."

Shaylee motioned Serena to attend the higher stage-like area made of stumps and large rocks with Celtic patterns and imagery, and she stood next to her queen. Shaylee then gestured for Eric, Eoghan, and the two dryads to move forward and join her.

"Serena is a princess of Faelynn."

Gasps and noises emanated from those gathered, getting louder and louder.

"Silence. She is my half-sister, born of human and fathered by King Viltherome."

The gasps turned into roars as the Fae began screaming in protest, yelling "Prove it" over and over. Even the dryads were shocked.

"I will prove it. With the approval of my mother, Queen Tianna, a sword was made. Serena had been tested by the noorion marker and passed the bloodline test. Felvora, if you wouldn't mind. Serena, Long Leaf please. Written in magic fire, I will reveal to you all."

Serena handed over her sword, just as intrigued as everyone there, while Felvora created magic fire in her palm and glazed it across the blade, lighting up once hidden passages in the steel. Felvora read the text out loud, "The pommel shows the Aethelwyne crest which can only be used under the direction of a king or queen, and then as I look further up, above the hilt it shows the family tree and then I see:

"The rightful owner of this sword, Serena Aethelwyne, under the sight of the noorion marker, is the natural daughter of King Viltherome Aethelwyne and half-sister to Princess Shaylee Aethelwyne. This has been decreed by Queen Tianna Aethelwyne and upon approval from the princess, carved by Darlygah Frostdrop with permission to use magic fire, on the sixth rotation of the Iris moon before the coming blood moon. All Fae must declare this as true by order of the Aethelwyne house or be punished by banishment or death."

The audience was shocked, as was every single other person besides Eric and Rasarlin. Serena was also shocked, at her sword's reveal more than anything else.

"We had to hide this from you all," Shaylee said, "to protect Serena from dark Fae and from some of those who would see her harmed, as she is of half human blood. She is a rightful heir and so is her son Eoghan, who if I am not mistaken, Felvora, is written in the oldest books of the Tuatha Dé Danann?"

Felvora talked to the group, as did Kalandrya, explaining the prophecy and the sword's legitimacy.

Then Shaylee continued, "I am leaving you all. In fact, this will be my last meeting with all of you. I have found my one true love and will be by his side."

More gasps and groans. Serena looked at her. Tears welled up. She had a feeling deep down, because the meeting was giving away a lot of information about her and Eoghan. Shaylee's eyes met hers and she softly smiled, a tear too welling in her perfectly blue eyes.

"Please, my people, my lasting legacy is that an Aethelwyne will be on the throne, but a halfling." Serena stopped her from saying any more and quietly whispered to her sister, "No, Shay, I will leave with Eric, I cannot stay."

Shaylee looked at her and whispered back, "Then I must leave Eoghan. You could come in and out, helping him. I will leave a dryad and my best warriors."

Serena had no choice. All this was thrust onto her, but she knew Eoghan had to stay. He would not last on Earth without the magic. "OK, Shay, but I wish you had told me."

Shaylee nodded. "He was always going to be king, I just thought you could ease him into it, but I know in my heart he is ready."

Serena gave a fake smile and nodded back, stepping aside to let Shaylee finish.

"My people, I offer you your new king, Eoghan Aethelwyne. Princess Serena will advise him, as will my good friend and dryad Felvora."

Screams of anger flooded out into the great hall as Eoghan lowered his head. Serena put her arms around him and comforted him, while Shaylee nodded to Felvora, who raised the Spear of Assal and waved it across the room, pushing everyone back into their positions and silencing them.

"I am your queen, and this is my wish. We have all sacrificed for you, so you will listen, or my rage will be unending, starting with feeding the next one to open their mouth in protest to the very large wyvern outside, do I make myself clear?"

There wasn't even a whisper. She didn't want fear to be how she got her message across, but the Fae knew fear well and she was trying to break that down by stopping segregation and hate among humans and Fae.

"Thank you. Now lastly, I will keep all doors closed to Earth realm but will make a permanent portal guarded at all times where you can dwell in the lands peacefully, and I mean that, and where the representatives, from what I hear from Eric, of a new council to rebuild the human realm can be reached. If this is so, then Serena, a halfling, will help oversee both Earth realm and guide her son here. These are my words; they will be inked and carved in stone before I go, so all acts against the new laws will be punishable by either permanent banishment from the realm or death. Do I hear any objections? All in favor, say Aye."

The room exploded into simultaneous Ayes before Shaylee asked, "Do I hear any Nays?"

Not one Fae even whispered the word. Even if some were still angry, they were far too frightened.

"Good. Now, I am leaving soon and, in that time, I want you all to organize an enormous feast for our new king and dine with him tonight before you go back to your lives in the morn."

The room came alive again with talking and debate as Shaylee filled in Serena and Eoghan on their new roles. Eric looked at Eoghan and Serena when Shaylee was finished and said, "Eoghan Aethelwyne, was I going to get a say in that?"

Serena smiled and hugged him, whispering, "Nope, I was going to call him Eoghan O'Halloran, but I think Aethelwyne sounds better."

Eric laughed, kissed her, and they made their way with the rest of the group to make the next set of plans.

GOODBYE

THE COUNCIL MEETING WAS VERY TIRING. SHAYLEE had to tie up all the loose ends and pass everything as law through the palace lawmakers. The most important of those were the council. She could enforce any law she wanted through a threat or the thrust of her power, but the way Faelynn had been so peaceful within the lands was because of the council and the enforcement of the rules.

Eoghan sat with Shaylee, as did Serena, while they studied Long Leaf, listened to the dryads, and even watched snippets from some of the acts that Eoghan had achieved through the dryads' magic. The gnomes were interviewed, as were the two Elvenfae guards, Vylan'flare and Breaxinah. Shaylee knew it would not be easy, but she wanted to make sure that Eoghan and Serena had all the support they could get, as once she left, there was no guarantee that she would ever return.

Soon, the exhausting and intimidating meetings were over. Shaylee waited patiently outside while the others prepared for a small ceremony to induct the new king. She would stay if the council refused, but would prepare Eoghan for his future post, anyway. Shaylee didn't have to wait long, and after they handed the verdict to her, she swiftly made her way to find Rasarlin.

Eoghan was getting pulled and prodded while his new ceremonial garb was being made. Serena found one of her old dresses from before the dark war, while Eric was quite happy in his jeans and flannelette shirt that he always liked to wear on more casual days. Soon, a loud petal bell rang out and all the invited guests were summoned to the hall for a swift ceremony. Eoghan walked out with some of the seamstresses still sewing and pulling at him. Eric gave him a smile, then a chuckle, before winking at his son; he had eaten the garlish herbs so was feeling much better in the realm. Eoghan saw it and lowered his head, before looking back up and sharing in a small giggle with his father.

Shaylee and Rasarlin stood at the throne as all the guests were seated. The last time anything like this had happened, Serena was taken by Stexinzar, so it was more of a somber mood for her at the start. However, she slowly relaxed when Shaylee began to speak, "Thank you, all my special people, from close friends and council to my servants and leaders of the Seelie Court, welcome to this short but important ceremony."

The guests began clapping and fluttering as she finished her opening, before the room became quiet once more.

"First, I would like to thank my sister Serena and her partner Eric, for without you, none of us would be standing here. I would then like to thank and reward the following with the Elemental Star of the Fae, the highest honor and award known in the lands and only ever given to the most brave and selfless Fae. Along with the Elemental Star will be given a title. First I want to invite Grilif and Darf who were with me from the start of the Earth war until they finished their duty, never straying from their loyalty and always offering to assist even if that meant disaster."

Grilif and Darf, with combed beards and hair, shocked and somewhat embarrassed by the attention, stood and made their way to the queen as she pinned the star on their very well pressed tunics. "I thank you, my friends, and I offer you the roles of Elders of Aurora and assistants to Felvora, who will now be given the title of Chief Magister to the palace."

Shaylee worded Felvora up, giving her a curtsey and wink as she continued with the awards. "Next is Vylan'flare who took my side and never left after the paradox of worlds, stepping up to head Elvenfae warrior guard, and to Breaxinah, who volunteered for his queen in the face of dangers. Both of you will now be made king's guards and trusted Elvenfae guards to oversee the whole workings of the palace and to keep peace and train knew warriors. I thank you."

Shaylee then found a small spot to pin their award, on the crimson velvet cloaks attached to their shiny gold and silver white ceremonial armor, as she whispered, "Look after Eoghan with your lives. I trust you more than any other Elvenfae with my family, so you are more than deserving of those titles."

The warriors bowed, pulled their swords out in unison, and slammed them point down on the marble floor as they kneeled, before rising slowly and sheathing their weapons, turning, and marching off to their places as guests. There was movement under Serena's legs, and then Eoghan's, before a silk table covering began slowly sliding off. Shaylee could see it out of the corner of her eye and smiled as she continued, "Now for the last Elemental Star, oh, it looks like he isn't here, hmm, I might have to put this one back."

In that moment, a yell came from under the table, and in a swift gray and white blur, Van Coinan was standing in front of the queen, trying to salute while standing upright. "I'm here, Shay ... I mean, my queen."

Shaylee turned to Rasarlin, who was smirking, then looked at Serena and winked.

"Now, Van Coinan, what makes you think I was talking about you, huh?"

Van Coinan slowly lowered his head like a child who had missed his birthday before Shaylee continued, "Yes, Van Coinan, it is you. I tell everyone here and make this known that the pooka known as Van Coinan is just as much a hero of our adventures as the others. He will now be a warrior guard with the Elvenfae, something that has never happened in the history of our name, but I think Vylan'flare and Breaxinah will vouch, he is a warrior you want on your side."

The two warriors nodded as Shaylee pinned his Elemental Star on his very worn overall strap. When she was done, Van Coinan tried to bow and then hopped off to show the pixies who were assisting the seamstresses, teasing them about his new jewel. The pixies then started chasing him while the crowd finished clapping.

"Now the council will speak," Shaylee said. "Eoghan, my love, come here to me."

The youngling swiftly moved to be at his aunt's side as the head of the council, Faelondar, spoke, "After all the evidence, interviews, and witness accounts, along with saving us not only from the dark lord, but the sinisters as well, I trust we have had one of the most intelligent, compassionate, and gentle Elvenfae queens and leaders in the history of our great realm. If her nephew, being of direct Tuatha Dé Danann blood, is even half the leader that she has been, then this realm will be safe for thousands of moons more.

"With Serena, his mother and guide to the youngling, we have declared that from now and onward Eoghan Aethelwyne will be king of the Fae and all those who dwell in Faelynn, and also liaison of humans to continue working for a better land and a peaceful one now and forever."

Eoghan sat on the throne as Shaylee slowly lowered her father's crown over her nephew's head. It was a little loose, but in no time at all he would be full size, and it would fit perfectly. The hall lit up with applause. Serena was crying, as was Eric. Even the red caps had a tear in their eyes as Eoghan repeated the oath of the realm before letting Shaylee finish her most important part. "I know he is the chosen one to keep peace over our realm and unite the humans with us. This land will always be for keeping us safe, but we will now be able to walk into the lands of Earth peacefully and help our fellow friends when they need it.

"Now comes the hardest part. I have met a wondrous partner, someone who thinks like I do, who has endured such evil as I have, and loves me unconditionally as I do him. I give you Rasarlin Ivelark, elven warrior from one of the biggest lands on his world, who saved not only my life at Xarkynan, but also many of you who were busy fighting. He has magic much like ours here, but at powerful levels. With my help, along with the power of the last treasure, I believe we can help him return to his land, but I will be joining him. So before the feast and dancing begins, please follow us to the gates of the palace where his companion Vaximardruusz awaits. We are running on borrowed time so we must do this now or he will be lost forever."

Rasarlin bowed. His magenta purple and blue velvet tunic along with coat tails were touched up by the best in the palace as was the leather, now shining a glossy brown. The tailors also gifted him an elegant crimson cloak which finished him off nicely. The only untouched item was his Marelarph crystal, as even his long white hair had been cleaned and combed and his slim and sleek winding long horns glistened in the lights.

≈

A large gathering had formed on the green land outside the palace walls, just before the entrance to the palace city. They were all in awe of Vaximardruusz, while Van Coinan was showing off his new Elemental Star to the very bemused wyvern. Felvora and Kalandrya were in place as Rasarlin prepared his companion with a soothing song from his world. The time trap was a harsh way to travel, it was a punishment, so when an opportunity arose and they weren't thrust without warning, Rasarlin would sing to Vax.

Felvora motioned for an extensive amount of room as Serena, Eric, who would need to leave himself soon, and Eoghan said their very emotional goodbyes.

"Shay," Serena said as she tried to gather the words. "We have been lost to each other, found and lost so many times, but I fear I am losing you forever. I don't know how I will go on without your love, guidance, and friendship. You filled a void in my life that was missing for so long and when you returned to me recently, my heart refilled. You are my best friend, my teacher, my sister, and I will love you forever. Please ... one day, come back to me."

Shaylee had tears in her eyes, fighting them back herself as she had been dreading this moment for a while and she knew she had to do it. "Serena, I have never met anyone like you in all the lands I have been in or will go to. I know there will never be anyone like you. From the moment you found me there was a connection. You never lost faith in our people, and you continue to help yours. You will lead your realm back from the brink and our two worlds will thrive on your love and compassion. You will always be my best friend, my teacher, and my sister, no matter where the universe takes us. I want you to promise me one thing?"

Both had heavy streams of tears flowing now as Serena clutched Shaylee's hands tightly. "Yes, Shay, anything for you."

Shaylee looked deep into Serena's brown eyes and said, "Don't mourn me. Celebrate me. I am with my love, and you are with yours. Promise me you will not waste one moment of your life wondering if I am safe, and if this does not work, then at least we are together. Make Eric happy, have more babies, inspire Eoghan to be his best, and always remember that you are Fae and that I love you."

Serena nodded as they held each other tightly. Felvora and Kalandrya were preparing, as was Rasarlin, so time was now very short. Shaylee pulled back and shouted to Eric, "You take care of my family as you are now the head of it."

Eric moved in, kissed Shaylee on the cheek with a tear in his eye, and said, "From now until my last breath I will, Shay. I will miss you, and thank you for helping Serena to find her way back from her darkness. Somehow I know it was you."

Eric pulled away, shook Rasarlin's hand, and said, "I wish we had more time; I will be forever in your debt. Now you look after Vax for me."

Rasarlin smiled as Eric walked back. Van Coinan was blowing his nose with a pixie's dress, crying uncontrollably, before she kicked him in his knee and they both fell to the ground crying.

"Now, my king, you listen, you learn, you use your instincts always for good, and you trust yourself," said Shaylee. "You will be a great Fae king and I am so proud of you, and I love you so very much."

Eoghan had not been around long, but he was learning quickly about loss, and along with that of his sister, this one was hurting hard, too. He then moved over to Rasarlin and hugged him. Rasarlin wasn't used to all the affection from others, but was learning about human culture quickly. "Take on the world, young one, and win." Rasarlin's words would resonate with the young king for the rest of his life.

The Marelarph began to glow.

Shaylee quickly placed a necklace made from the crystal around Serena's neck, and said, "This will let you keep your Fae abilities on Earth. Be proud of your heritage."

Serena looked a little shocked as she yelled over the electricity emanating from Rasarlin's Marelarph, "Won't you need it to get home? How will I see you?"

Shaylee smiled. "Just look inside. When you really need me, you will see me. I will be too far from you, but I will always be with you."

Serena clutched the crystal with her right hand while Eric held her left. They moved out of the way as Rasarlin and Shaylee climbed up onto Vaximardruusz. Felvora had given her instructions and as Kalandrya used her powers and Felvora concentrated the staff onto the Marelarph that Rasarlin had encouraged to ignite, Shaylee whispered to him, "You need to concentrate on home; think of a place embedded in your mind, and with the strength of your shard and the guidance of our treasures we should end up in your world."

Rasarlin held on to her tightly, as the noise became deafening and purple lightning radiated out of the shard. Rasarlin had his eyes closed, concentrating, as was Vax, but through all the lightning, noise, and power, Shaylee met eyes with Serena's, winking one last time, and blowing her a kiss. Serena smiled as a huge maelstrom opened in the sky, and the clouds turned purple as the sun disappeared. Felvora held the staff as tightly as she could, while Kalandrya added to its power. Soon Vaximardruusz erupted into a huge ball of fiery lightning as the purple flames thrust the beast up into the sky and they disappeared with an electrical explosion at its peak through the great vortex in the sky.

Vax was now in the space between space, floating in nothingness as another enormous doorway opened, sucking them through and leaving no traces of them ever being there.

The huge maelstrom slowed down as the lightning and fire broke apart. Soon the sun was visible once more and after a few minutes there was only residual smoke left, with no evidence that such an event had taken place.

Serena fell to the ground as Eric temporarily lost his sight, even with the sunglasses on. He leaned down and comforted his beloved partner, while Eoghan stood and stared at where the events had taken place, not blinking or batting an eyelid. He wiped his tears and turned, and seeing his mother on her knees, bent down to assist her and his father. But before he could help, Eric put his palm on Serena's soft pale face, and turned her head to face his as he wiped some tears away.

Eric stayed on the ground as Eoghan helped his mother up, calmer now the event was over. Eric's eyes had returned to normal as he scrounged in his pocket for something. He looked up, took a confused Serena's hand, and spoke, "Serena, my love, words cannot express my feelings for you. From the first time I laid eyes on you, to this very moment here and now, I have loved you and will do so until time stops completely. The things we have been through together are enormous and I want to spend the rest of my life making you happy, building a better world, and helping all those, both Fae and human, who need it by your side every step of the way. I love you, Serena. Will you do me the honor of becoming my wife?"

Eric looked up as more tears streamed down her face. He had a small look of concern when the tops of her wings fluttered uncontrollably. However, when he saw her contagious smile, he knew he was winning. Serena fell back to the ground again, hugging Eric as she chanted, "Yes, yes, yes."

Eric slipped the exceptionally large-stoned ring onto her slender finger and kissed her. He then helped her up. Serena couldn't take her eyes off the ring and remembered having seen it somewhere before. "It is beautiful, Eric. Where did you get such a thing?"

Eric smiled and explained, "I asked Shaylee for your hand, nervously,

I must add, and after a small speech I thought she was going to say no. However, once she had spoken, she smiled, kissed me on the cheek, and offered me this ring, which belonged to her mother, Queen Tianna. I refused at first, knowing how much it would have meant and she stated she would have no one else in the world wear it other than you."

Serena launched at Eric, kissing and crying, all while every other Fae was watching on and learning some hard truths about the compassion of humans and that they weren't all going to be doomed if there was peace and love as strong as the family before them were showing. The Fae lit up with a roar of cheers as Felvora picked herself up and whispered to herself, "Don't worry about me. I'll be fine."

Kalandrya, Grilif, and Darf smiled as they helped the once cranky dryad up, obviously exhausted from the powerful magic she had just endured. Felvora was becoming stronger than before. She would make a fantastic magister, Kalandrya thought, as she said, "Come, Flora, let's set this permanent portal up down at the Runes of Sarkas and I will leave you to assist in the new Fae empire while I return the last of the treasures to, well, you know where."

The gnomes couldn't care less where. They were just happy Felvora was alright as the two dryads snickered. Soon Kalandrya vanished into a red mist and took off to the runes. Four Elvenfae guards were whisked up unknowingly as the first on the rotating shifts to guard the portal realm. It would take much magic to sustain the portal, but as the swirls of light would glisten, the oldest Tuatha magic still left in the stones would keep it fired up at both ends.

≈

Festivities would last until late into the night, but the youngling king wouldn't make it that far, falling asleep with his large crown tightly held up against his breast underneath one of the dinner tables of the hall. Serena found him and Eric picked the teen up and carried him off to his new quarters. "We have to leave in the morning, Serena. He will need some time to adjust."

Serena nodded. "Yes, I agree. I will stay with him until he gets a handle on things …"

Eric stopped and looked at her. She knew his eyes were burning a hole in the back of her head as she turned around and smiled. "Alright, we will go, but only for a few days. Here the time is different, so we can't stay away too long."

Eric stayed where he was. "Serena?"

Serena agreed as she responded, "Alright, we will trust his advisers. Besides, I can see him anytime through the crystal if I want."

Serena laughed and ran off like a schoolgirl to set up Eoghan's bed, while Eric shook his head and moved swiftly after her. He knew she couldn't just let him go, but there was so much work to do back on Earth. If she felt better knowing she could watch over him, then that was a welcome distraction. They would be in and out of the realms all the time once their plans were set up on Earth. But for now, the king needed his sleep and so did both Eric and Serena. In fact, they could all sleep, safe and in peace.

EPILOGUE

TIME WENT ON, AND SO DID THE BUILDING FOR A new beginning. Eric and the survivors tried to do everything they could to help those in need by establishing small hospitals and finding able survivors to help. It was a rewarding yet tiresome and sometimes gruesome task. At least two-thirds of the Earth had perished at the hands of the Zeytars, and the clean-up was always going to be enormous.

Serena did what she could as a nurse and psychiatrist, as all the others used their own specific skill sets to help with what they could. Wilkes somehow knew he was not coming back and left a program detailing all the remaining tech and information on how they could use it to rebuild and help humanity.

Soon communications were reaching across the globe and the survivors were being looked upon as heroes. With a sense of hope in the world, his peers voted for Eric to begin the healing process. Not that he wanted a leadership title, but he knew that someone had to be the voice of the people, so they would use portal devices to take teams into some of the worst hit areas and deliver food and water. It was a tedious task, but they knew the result would be a new world filled with peace and harmony, under no conspiracy or lie, just people trying to come together to survive and rebuild.

Serena and Eric married, as did Dakota and Valinda, with Val falling pregnant soon after. She had spread the word of her experiences with Michael, not trying to start a religion, but to tell the truths of what happened and for everyone to make a choice. Most religions ended up fading, but those who had held on to their beliefs were encouraged to continue as were those not of the Earth realm. All species and races would unite under one doctrine that was voted in with a flag of tolerance, yet strength.

To those of Earth and beyond the stars
Be kind to those who are near or far.
We will live in peace together as one.
But we will stand and fight if the dark may come.
Our history failed us time after time.
So, it's up to us not to repeat that crime.
We are ready for what may come.
Together, united, all as one.

It was written in every language as an ode with the flag showing a Zeytar skull and a boot crushing it to remind those on Earth what they had endured and to remind those who thought the Earth was now weak and vulnerable that they would not stand idly by.

But again, the darkness crept into some people's souls, upsetting the many and taking over peaceful places, starting civil unrest among themselves, proving history will always repeat when humans are corrupted.

Soon there were talks of an insurrection against Eric and his people, so the decision to leave became unanimous. An oppressive presence that they could not see, or fight, had continued to leak into the world, and what Valinda had been teaching was showing signs of coming true.

Michael appeared in a dream one night to Valinda and warned of the coming events, stating the Fae realm was a sanctuary and the new world until the time they were called. The ones left behind would either be saved or left to face the upcoming darkness until the war in the stars had finished.

Valinda was quite upset about her dream and pleaded with Eric to talk to the Fae and, with a vote from the survivors' council, they made the heart-wrenching decision to leave everything they had protected and built. The Fae were warned, and they voted that a small number could come through the portal, leaving the rest to trust Valinda's prophecy.

All those who helped in the rebuild, families, and trusted friends were chosen, while anyone considered to be showing the beginnings of defection or betrayal was left behind, with a few thousand selected. The tech was hidden from the dark ones rising and they made their way to the portal where the runes would be destroyed after entering.

It had now been twelve months since the original war of the Zeytars, as the last of the chosen humans walked through the swirling portal. Eric stayed behind to set the charges around the stones while Valinda and Serena waited to go through together, leaving none of them behind.

Once Eric had placed the last of the explosive devices in place, he met with the two women, and before they walked into the light, their eyes caught Michael standing in his black cassock with several other priests. They would have been only a few hundred feet away when an enormous deep tone started emanating from the sky. The three pulled their hands close to their ears as it continued to ring out and as it waned, they noticed Michael look around, smile at them all, and suddenly morph into a bright humanoid with long wings, gold and silver armor, and a huge broadsword sheathed on his hip. Soon the others followed suit, and as the second deafening noise rang out, they witnessed them zoom up into the sky with white lights following them from where they had just been, disappearing into the now blood red clouds and sky.

Eric looked at Val, then Serena, and gestured to them to move into the portal as he took one last look at the dark red sky, flicked the detonator, and ran through behind them, leaving the Earth with a barrage of explosions and a harbinger of darkness.

But at least he and his most loved would be safe from this war. Eric and Serena could finally be at peace.

Sometimes what seems like an ending is only a beginning

GLOSSARY

Aethelwyne (*Ay-thel-wine*): The house name of the ruler of Faelynn.

Aladoor: Fourth planet in the Zeta Reticuli binary star system, 39 million light years from Earth, now a dimensional realm and home to the evil Zeytars.

ALEX: The nickname of the X-Clock/V.I.Z.I.N.D.A.L.E.X.

Anders: An evil master Zeytar, bent on human destruction, owner of the flesh-hungry wolf-man Savage, killed in the first war.

Ardmenticam: Strongest metal in the known universe.

Aurora Forest: The biggest forest in all Faelynn with an abundance of different life.

Breaxinah (*Bree-axe-ina*): Elvenfae warrior guard who goes to the collider.

Buul'ulaan (*Bu-youl-oolan*): A bi-pedal panther creature from the dark portals accidentally caught up in the war.

Carlos: Wilkes' right-hand man who left to look after the ship.

Cauldron of Dagda: Tuatha treasure true form.

Corporal Jason Darnell: One of Wilkes' chosen soldiers.

Corporal Rick Thorne: One of Wilkes' chosen soldiers.

cybernetic Zeytar: The symbiosis of both human and ZARK drones, created for the bodiless ones to enter.

Dakota Youngblood: Hero from the first war and friend to the surviving rebels.

Darf: A gnome from Faelynn.

dark elf/dark Elvenfae: Twisted and evil Elvenfae, turned by the dark lord to aid in his war against the Fae.

Darlygah Frostdrop: Former Elvenfae warrior guard killed in the last war at Xarkynan.

Darphanin (*Darf-an-in*): The leader of the woodland elf warriors, killed in the last war at Xarkynan.

Desertron: The name of the Super Conducting Super Collider in Waxahachie, Texas.

Doctor Frederick: Doctor on Wilkes' ship.

Draconian (*Drack-oh-nean*): Race of reptilian creatures from another planet fighting the Zeytars.

Dragon Fyre: The most intense heat known.

dryad: A powerful nature mage, usually benevolent although protective of their people.

Elemental Star of the Fae: The highest award any Fae of the realm can receive and only ever given to the most brave and selfless.

Elvenfae: Full form of the sprites in the palace of Faelynn, extraordinarily strong but kind protectors of the land of the Fae.

Eoghan Aethelwyne (Owan Ay-thel-wine): Son of Serena and Eric.

Eric Kirkpatrick: Anthropologist/cryptozoologist, hero from the first war of the Zeytars, partner of Serena and father to Stacey and Eoghan.

Etharians: The name of human-like creatures on Rasarlin's world, Rydracnia.

Everlands: A place where dragons are said to come from.

Faelynn (*Fay-lin*): The lands and realms of all the Fae/faery folk.

Faiay'aar (*Fay-i-ar*): Dryad from Faelynn who helped bring down the dark lord.

Felvora: Forest dryad mage living in the Aurora Forest who assisted in the dark war.

First Officer Joyce: Keeps the vulnerable civilians safe in their homes on the ship.

Fusslebox Quartzpond: A fiery red cap from the land of Faelynn.

Fylarsh: The name of the trickster Fae that had the Sword of Light.

Gaald: A very intelligent scientist in the cloning field who worked for Anders before the war.

garlish herbs: An especially strong herb grown in Faelynn that helps humans' exposure to the realm be more normal.

gnome: Small, tough Fae that reside in the deep forests of Faelynn.

Goblin: Dark cloning scientist created to serve the Zeytar agenda.

Grilif: A strong and angry gnome from Faelynn.

Hi-Brazil: An island in Faelynn that can harbor humans for long periods of time.

Howling Tooth: The name of Shaylee Aethelwyne's sword.

Kaelodenon (*Ky-load-eh-non*): The dark lord Varzunnos' dragon.

Kalandrya (*Kal-anne-drea*): Dryad mage and queen of the far-lands of Toozookus in Faelynn.

Kootesenik: (*Koo-tessin-ick*): Home world of Buul'ulaan.

Lieutenant Dresden: One of Wilkes' chosen soldiers.

Long Leaf: Serena O'Halloran's enchanted sword.

magic fire: The magical effect to hide important information into materials like steel.

Marelarph (*Merrel-arf*): An extremely powerful dark purple crystal shard attached to Rasarlin and the time trap.

Markyyn elves (*Mark-win*): Rasarlin Ivelark's race. Three horned magical tree warriors from the world of Rydracnia.

molekaark (*molek-ark*): Deer-like creature on Kootesenik, Buul'ulaan's home world.

necro-mage: A powerful, twisted magister, master of the art of dark magic.

Neiphlax (*Ny-flax*): Only surviving dark Elvenfae warrior who sides with ALEX.

the noorion marker: Truth detector used in the palace in extreme cases.

oaken nochkz: Benevolent oak trees from Maelenflitt that can move and fight if needed, not to be confused with the nochkz of Xarkynan.

Paldar: Monstrous abomination created by Agent Anders' twisted scientists.

pixie: A small male or female faery, around two and a half feet high, in all the light forests.

pooka: Large rabbit-like creature with a dangerous defense and abilities to talk and shape-shift.

Project Synergy: A secret program to raise Zeytars that only the Leader knew about.

Rasarlin Ivelark (*Ras-ar-lin Iv-eh-lark*): A Markyyn elf from another realm called Rydracnia, tossed around the cosmos forever by the time trap of Seckpar.

RNA-X7c genome: The scientific name for the genome the Zeytars were after.

Rovan: A master Zeytar dedicated to Wilkes who succumbed to the first war.

Runes of Sarkas: The only portal to the Earth realm after the war.

Rydracnia (*Ry-drak-nee-ah*): The home world of Rasarlin and Vaximardruusz.

Saisia: A pixie who survived the war of Xarkynan.

Sasquatch: A benevolent creature freed from the control of the Zeytars.

Savage: A giant wolf-man creature created for Anders to hunt any deserters or truth seekers of the agenda, with an unnatural taste for human blood.

Serena O'Halloran/Aethelwyne: Half-blood Fae princess with strong defensive skills along with a gentle but fierce heart.

Sergeant Chad Valens: One of Wilkes' chosen soldiers.

Sergeant Lorne Marcus: One of Wilkes' chosen soldiers.

Severed Wing: The name of Varzunnos' large broadsword, now wielded by the mighty Markyyn elf warrior Rasarlin Ivelark.

Shadowblood: The manipulated genetic formula 5-000-375-621 that destroyed the Zeytar hybrids, taken from Stacey's RNA-X7c genome. Also, a dangerous genetic concentrate of certain Fae blood, manufactured secretly by Wilkes for war.

Shaylee Aethelwyne: Elvenfae queen of Faelynn.

sinisters: What the Fae call the Zeytars.

Spear of Assal: Tuatha treasure true form.

Spencer Grayson: Paranormal researcher who helped free the Sasquatch from the recent Zeytar war.

spriggan: A dangerous and mischievous gnome-like creature bent on mayhem.

sprite: The small faery form of all winged faeries in Faelynn.

Stacey Kirkpatrick: Hero from the first war of the Zeytars and daughter to Eric.

Stone of Destiny: Tuatha treasure true form.

stone shards: The crystal onyx element that the Marelarph is made from in smaller form and what Rasarlin carries on his chest.

Sword of Light: Tuatha treasure true form.

Szelidus (*Zel-e-duss*): An evil sorcerer from another realm tossed around the cosmos by the time trap of Seckpar.

Taarlin Knights (*Tarlin*): A well-trained group of warriors and dragon keepers from Rasarlin's world Rydracnia bound to a wyvern to protect the last dragons.

tarnaak: Tarnaaks are the oak-made creatures from inside the oaken nochkz. Humanoid in appearance, but made entirely of branches, sticks, and sap from the oak itself.

Teldenac: The large land mass on Rydracnia in which Rasarlin and Vaximardruusz resided.

Tic Tac: The human nickname for the Zeytars' X-71 mini scout.

time trap of Seckpar: An insidious magical spell sending its victims hurtling through time and space to other worlds forever.

Tuatha Dé Danann: The original people of Faelynn who escaped from the old lands and set up the four elemental treasure stones, giving enchantment to Faelynn.

unicorn: Mystical and powerful equine creature, only in Faelynn.

Vaelenflixx Leafenvein (*Vay-len-flix*): A benevolent jittery sprite captured by goblins in Xarkynan, now loyal to the queen of the Fae.

Van Coinan (*Van-Coy-nan*): A cheeky pooka that has the form of a rabbit who can talk and shape-shift.

Vargzin: Draconian hero from the first war and friend to the rebels.

Varzunnos (*Var-zoo-noss*): The dark lord of Xarkynan.

Vaximardruusz (*Vax-ee-mar-drooz*): A wyvern from another realm, tossed around the cosmos forever by the time trap of Seckpar and accompanied by his rider, Rasarlin Ivelark.

Velnai: A pixie who survived the war of Xarkynan.

Viltzin'un'dandaar (*Vilt-zin-un-dan-dar*): Dark necro-mage and assistant to the dark lord Varzunnos.

V.I.Z.I.N.D.A.L.E.X: Virtual Intelligence Zero-time Inter-dimensional Nanotech Droid Activating (high) Levels (of the) Electromagnetic (field) X-Clock.

VPD: Vocalization Portal Device. An inter-dimensional tool replicated from the Sasquatch Levi's vocal organs to open portals once set, now modified for all frequencies and locations.

Vylan'flare: An Elvenfae warrior/guard.

White Lake fire: Reference to a lake on Rasarlin's home world of Rydracnia and a dragon drinking too much of the substance therefore becoming drunk on the stuff.

Wilkes: A Zeytar master defector who helped the humans in the first war against his species.

WOSER: Western Oregon Sasquatch Evidence & Research team, which Eric created.

wyvern: A powerful two-legged dragon with speed and an enormous wingspan. Smaller than a dragon, but twice as fierce.

X-71: A mini scout ship from the Zeytars' larger saucers, known also as a Tic Tac.

X-Clock: The powerful clock component to V.I.Z.I.N.D.A.L.E.X. that opened a doorway for the Zeytar ships, and now a separate portal machine, constantly changing dimensions.

Xandar: Evil Zeytar master responsible for turning on the V.I.Z.I.N.D.A.L.E.X.

Xarkynan (*Zark-in-an*): The dark lands, created by the dark lord Varzunnos after being banished and where all the evil resides in the Faelynn realm.

ZARK drone: Zero-Point Android Remote Kinetic drone.

Zeytar (*Zay-tar*): Race of insidious inter-dimensional gray aliens taking over the Earth for their evil purposes.